MARS MISSION I

SURVIVING THE KESSLER EFFECT
SECOND EDITION

CHRISTOPHER LEE JONES

MARS MISSION I:
Surviving the Kessler Effect Second Edition
by Christopher Lee Jones.

Published by:

On the Hook Publishing, LLC

ISBN 978-1-7342246-3-4 [Paper Back]
ISBN # [Hard Cover]

Library of Congress Number: Applied for.

For Permission requests, write to:

On the Hook Publishing
P.O. Box 12852
Ft. Pierce, FL 34979

—

Dedication

This, the second edition to the first book of like title is dedicated to my Mother and Father without whom it would have never been written and Gabriela Kilianski who dedicated unknown hours to aid in the development of the first edition upon which this book is based.

I also want to give my deepest gratitude and appreciation to Rafael Santoni (@TesLatino) for helping in important key aspects of formatting and editing support.

I owe a debt of gratitude to Donald Kessler for his feedback and endless support as I dipped into a new world of what our mutual futures may be if we do not preserve what we have and make space a sustainable environment for today, tomorrow, our children's futures as well as their children's and the children that follow.

My upbringing included a few years in the Boy Scouts which, I think applies here. The scout motto of "Always be prepared." seems to appropriately apply to this book and my life. Thank you Boy Scouts of America.

A Letter from Donald Kessler

Mars Mission I is a fictional story of humans' first landing and walk on Mars, an event that would be celebrated even more than our first landing on the Moon—but only if the world was aware of this success and didn't face other issues arising from what is sometimes called The Kessler Effect, first predicted in 1978.

The Kessler Effect (also referred to as the Kessler Syndrome) is a phenomenon where objects in Earth's orbit eventually collide with one another, where each collision produces a cascade of orbital debris, causing more collisions and debris. The rate of these collisions increases exponentially with the number of collisions and the collective mass in Earth orbit, with many contributors having a history of continually increasing. The increase continues despite the adoption of international guidelines enacted to prevent it. Earth's orbital space is used by the military, civilian, scientific and commercial communities, with each having different objectives. It has been known for some time that if a major war were to occur, military satellites would be the first subject of aggressive action. In 1985, the US military planned an anti-satellite (ASAT) test and, against NASA's recommendation, launched a rocket on a trajectory to collide with a satellite at the orbital speed of 17,000 miles per hour. The military did not believe NASA's predictions. In 2017, the Chinese conducted an ASAT test without consulting their own scientific community, which would have advised against it.

—

And what did each nation learn from these tests? They learned that they should find a different method of neutralizing enemy military satellites because of the devastating consequences to the space environment.

This book accurately reflects our current understanding of orbital debris issues and introduces another debris issue that has not been fully developed by the scientific community. These facts are combined into a cliff-hanging detective story of what a country might do to gain an advantage over a perceived enemy and becomes a story of survival that humanity may face if we are unable to do what we already know needs to be done.

Donald Kessler

Retired NASA Senior Scientist for Orbital Debris Research

Table of Contents

This is a book of fiction. Names, characters, places, historical events, and incidents are the products of the author's imagination. Every effort has been made to adhere to scientifically verified data and facts. It is still, at least at the moment, a work of fiction.

Chapter 1
Miss Trial

Dong-Hyun went by the name "Don". He had been studying to get his 100-ton Captain's License after working on different vessels used to service the drilling rigs off the Louisiana coast. After paying cash for his taxi, Don entered the boat yard next to the marina at 2:00 a.m. Central time. He had been instructed to meet his accomplice in the boatyard adjacent to the marina wearing a red and blue neckerchief for identification and to look for the same worn by his soon-to-be first mate.

Day workers commonly congregated just outside the boatyard in a small bus stop style lean-to made of roughhewn used dock wood. Typically, they would use the structure for protection from the elements while waiting for either a ride home or work for the day. It was a hot humid night with not even a puff of wind or sea breeze. He was right where he had been instructed to meet.

A man wearing the matching neckerchief approached, looks were exchanged and a simple nod established the relationship. Both men tucked away the neckerchiefs and made their way to the marina. Upon arrival at the sixty-foot tug, Don knocked on the hull fully prepared to present himself as an engineer with Seagate Marine Services, International.

A scruffy round face with dark brown eyes, a two-day beard, and a receding red hairline, popped over the side gunnel and signaled for the two to board with a jerk of his head. The man was short and stocky with an armed forces haircut, and he was covered in blood.

The entire wheelhouse wreaked of the heavy copper odor of blood. It was apparent he had just finished the cleanup operation. "I took care of the issues," was all he said as he stripped off what used to be a white Seagate Marine Services jumpsuit, revealing what used to be a white T-shirt now also spotted with blood. His back, arms, and shoulders were covered in aging tattoos and scars, possibly reflecting previous special forces involvement.

He wrapped up the jumpsuit in used rags and stuffed the blood covered shirt in one of two heavy canvas toolboxes on the deck. Donning a fresh T-shirt and a spare jumpsuit, he made his way off the tug, toolboxes in tow. It took Don nearly an hour to cast off and get underway.

Now sitting at the helm of the ocean fairing tug Miss Trial, he was carefully pushing four barges full of diesel fuel out the mouth of the Mississippi River. Rigid with focus and concentration, he was relieved to be exiting the Western Rivers Regulations area and the mouth of the Mississippi as he entered the less busy and much less complicated traffic pattern for the Gulf of Mexico.

Dong-Hyun was both frightened and excited to fulfill his end of the deal, and better yet, he had been prepaid. Their money was in two backpacks which the engineer showed him and his new first mate. They didn't take the time to count it, but Chuck and Don rummaged through the numerous bundles of $100 dollar bills and made sure they were solid $100s all the way through, not just fake bundles of perfectly cut paper.

It was past 3:00 a.m. Central time, and even in the middle

---

of the night the massive amount of boat traffic coming and going around New Orleans required vigilant attentive navigation. Miss Trial had been staging for the trip to the Bahamas in Poor Boy's Marina on the Atchafalaya River when he boarded her with his First Mate Chin-Hae, who went by the name Chuck. They had never met before that night and were never to see each other again once the job was completed.

The original captain and first mate had been silently dispatched as they were readying the tug for the 1500-mile journey to New Providence Bahamas. Both bodies were in the cargo hold with their throats slit from ear to ear. Don's loving mother raised him on her own doing laundry for the Americans in San Antonio. Apparently, his father had been an American serviceman who was no longer interested once his young Korean girlfriend became pregnant.

The slow simmering of hate began for Don once he understood the pain and frustration that a good-looking Asian lady must constantly endure from the comments, rude remarks, lude gestures and sometimes worse. Don's mother had a hard time controlling her young son when men stared, gestured and sometimes even approached and attempted to grope the beautiful young mother.

Once, at eight years of age, Dong-Hyun had his nose broken and two teeth knocked out before losing consciousness after trying to defend his mother's dignity. They had been carrying a heavy load of clean laundry one Friday night hoping to get paid so they could eat dinner. His mother had been carrying on about noodles with real chicken and some kind of sauce she had been dreaming about for weeks now, when two drunken white guys wouldn't leave her alone.

Dong-Hyun dropped the clean laundry and lurched at the

two guys to pull them off his mother. That's all he remembered until waking up the next day with a pounding headache and his mother's beautiful face puffed up and bloodied. Blood also covered different pieces of the laundry which now probably had to be replaced. Of course, there was no dinner.

Growing up on the rough side of San Antonio taught Dong-Hyun that he preferred to be called Don. The first few teachers that struggled over his real name taught him what a dong is in the American slang. He learned to keep his mouth shut unless they tried to pronounce his name at morning attendance. At which point he anxiously waited to see the teacher struggling with a strangely spelled name.

He would quickly offer up "Don". Usually however, one of the tougher boys would yell out, "Dong, his name is Dong," followed by a classroom of raucous laughter from most of his classmates while others looked on in confusion. By the fourth grade Dong-Hyun had been transferred twice to different elementary schools and was being threatened to be sent to a third or possibly to a reformatory school on the other side of town.

The teachers constantly referred him to the principal for fighting. His mother didn't know what to do, she didn't have a car and couldn't get a bus to come all the way across town to pick up one student, a troublemaker at that. Somehow, he made it through to high school but by then he had learned to take the fight off school property.

Don wasn't big, five foot ten, one hundred sixty pounds, but he was in good physical condition. His mom had enrolled him in Taekwondo when he was ten years old after she realized she could not keep him from fighting. If her son was going to fight, he might as well learn how to handle himself. He had also learned how to use his fast reflexes and superb balance to put an end to an issue before his adversary knew what was coming.

By his sophomore year the word had gotten out not to mess with Don and most of the troublemakers steered clear.

Due to his excellent balance and nimble fingers, he was a natural deckhand. Don worked on some of the different vessels which transported food, supplies and crew to the oil rigs off the Louisiana coast.

He could tie knots faster than you could spell them and lasso a cleat from 30 feet. The hard physical work on board as well as his workouts at home kept him in excellent condition. He had no social life. He didn't trust anyone. Work was his social life and even then, he stayed to himself as much as possible. *People learn things about you, then they can take advantage of you,* he always reminded himself.

On occasion he had a girlfriend, but they took too much of his time and were always asking prying questions, and they expected things. Don didn't trust anyone but his mother. She was the one thing he lived for. He missed her loving eyes, soft touch and the tone of her loving voice. She had suffered long and hard to keep food on the table and to keep Don out of trouble.

He was never able to tell her how grateful he was for taking care of him while he was growing up. He was going to tell her one day soon, maybe on her next birthday. He always took a long weekend around her birthday to spend some time with her. He really needed to let her know how much he appreciated her dedication. One evening on the return trip from delivering a new crew to one of the off-shore drill rigs the captain of the shuttle-tender he was working on pulled him aside.

"Don, I got some bad news."

It turned out that his mother had been run over by a hit and run driver in the same area of town that the two white guys had accosted him and his mother years earlier. She had been toting another load of laundry and ended up in intensive care in the hospital. The captain said he was free to go, but he may not have a job when he came back.

Don made it the five-hundred-some-odd miles by bus to San Antonio, then walked the three miles to the hospital only to find his mother was not there. After diligent searching and numerous interviews and having to spell his mother's name over and over to three different hospital staff members in the admitting department, they kept telling him she wasn't there and maybe she had been checked out.

Finally, a nurse by the name of Mary seemed to be more understanding and finally figured out what the problem was. She looked up from her computer screen at Don, "I am very sorry to have to tell you this, but your mother died from her injuries. There was nothing we could do. That's why we couldn't find her. She was transported to the county undertaker yesterday morning.

Oh, my, she is listed here as homeless. She must not have had her driver's license in her belongings. She may have already been incinerated. I am so sorry, but that's what the coroner does with the homeless. They are closed today. They will be open tomorrow morning at nine. We didn't know she had any living relatives. I'll give you a few moments alone. Oh, my."

Don was lost in his emotions. She was dead! The next thing Don knew, a guy wearing an employee badge walked in pushing a computer on a wheeled stand and looked at him up and down with some kind of expression Don didn't understand. Don was trying to figure out what exactly the look was on his face. His badge said his name was Joey and said he worked in the finance department. Joey sighed with feigned empathy.

"Hello, sir, my name is Joey. May I see your driver's license or other government I.D., please?"

Don stared at him for a long three seconds, gave a confused look and muttered, "Naneun yeong-eoleul moshaeyo," which meant, "I don't speak English" in Korean.

"Sir, I need to see your I.D. so we can release her personal belongings and records to your custody… Sir?"

Don continued staring at Joey and finally shook his head.

"Sir, we cannot turn over her records or personal belongings unless you show me some form of I.D. Sir, our doctors and nurses spent hundreds of hours and a lot of hospital materials and expenses were devoted to saving your mother's life."

Don continued looking at Joey and repeated, "Naneun yeong-eoleul moshaeyo."

"Ok, I think we have some Chinese interpreters on staff today. I will be right back." Joey said with a distrusting look in his eyes as he rushed out pushing the weird looking computer stand thingy in front of him.

Don immediately rushed out of the hospital, trying to make it look like he wasn't in a big hurry. He was afraid they might call the

---

police to detain him if he didn't set up some kind of financing or payment program. For all Don knew the hospital may have put his mother in some unknown corner and let her die of her wounds. Don was crushed. His mother was the only other person in his life.

He had walled himself off any relationships and stayed to himself most of the time. He understood that most people were mean liars and would turn on you at the first opportunity if it could benefit them in any way. Most of his paycheck went immediately to help his mother with rent and food after he took care of his own expenses. Now, he was all alone, and he never even got to say goodbye.

His eyes filled with tears as he remembered his mother's soft touch and loving eyes, her gentle words of encouragement and all the ways she suffered and sacrificed so much of her life to keep him in school, clothes on his back, food in his belly, a relatively safe place to live, and how to fight to protect himself. She sacrificed her life to make sure he was taken care of.

She was the only person in the world he trusted and loved and now she was gone. An overwhelming feeling of loneliness collapsed in on him and enveloped him. Don found a vacant lot two blocks behind the hospital, sat next to a tree to let out his pain and sorrow. But all he could feel was that slow burn in his belly with which he had become very familiar.

But now it was more intense. It surrounded his soul and took what was left of him away. His eyes were crying but he didn't know it. After some time, Don slowly made it toward his old home. The dirty trash ridden streets of his neighborhood still looked the same as it had when he left. The only good thing about this neighborhood was

---

his mother.

This was not going to be an easy night alone in his mother's old apartment filled with memories and his mother's personal items and pictures of him and her. At least he would be alone to let out his pain and mourn in private. Maybe he would be able to feel his mother's presence and apologize to her for not being a better son. Images were whirling around in his head of past birthdays when his mom had gone out of her way to decorate the apartment, take him out to the zoo, anything to make him feel special.

Once she even figured out how to swing the extravagant cost of going horseback riding on his 10th birthday. As he walked into his old neighborhood, he passed the corner where he had been knocked out trying to protect her. His thoughts turned to whoever it was that hit her and left her to die alone. He could still see the faces of the two drunks who had attacked his mother. His pain slowly turned to anger again as he trudged on. He had tears streaming down his face, but he didn't know it. All he could feel was anger, hot lava burning hot in his belly.

When the county undertaker opened at nine a.m. Don was waiting silently to claim his mother's remains. He was seated on an uncomfortable wooden chair probably made 50 years earlier, in the small dingy waiting room with some certificates on the walls in cheap plastic frames covered in dust.

The creaky wooden entrance door opened, spilling bright sunlight into the poorly lit room.

An older Asian looking well-dressed gentleman stepped in and took off a gray hat that looked like ones worn in the 1950s. He wore a brown suit with a matching tie and nice polished tan leather dress shoes.

He looked around and saw Don, who was still dressed in his maritime work jumpsuit and work boots which he had been wearing for three days now. He nodded and smiled kindly. Don just nodded back. The gentleman walked up to the desk and inquired about Don's mother. The desk clerk said surprisedly, "Well that gentleman is here for her as well." Don stood. "I don't know who this guy is, and why is he asking about my mother? Maybe he's from the hospital and wants money."

The older gentleman slowly turned around and looked Don up and down, bowed his head slightly and said in a quiet reserved tone, "You must be Dong-Hyun."

Chapter 2
That's not a piling!

Bob and Brian grew up in North Miami. Born in the 1960s, they saw a lot of changes to South Florida over the years. They had even gone to elementary school together, immediately becoming best friends. They started fishing off the pier back when it was free. Brian and Bob had different jobs for a few years after high school but neither of them seemed to find their niche.

They stayed busy enough and made it along for a few years but when they got together, they both knew there was something better they could be doing. Brian remembered lamenting to Bob that it just feels like there is something more I could be doing. You know, something more important. Then Bob suggested they take an EMT course on a bet just to see if they could stick it out. "What could it hurt?" he asked, shrugging his shoulders. "Worse comes to worst we learn some medical skills and keep doing what we're doing or maybe something will come of it. The first one to back out or quit owed the other a case of beer."

It turned out they could handle it just fine. It ended up being a lot easier than they thought it would be. Next thing they knew they were toughing it out in the Fire Academy. The Fire Academy was hard physical labor with lots of yelling from the instructors for no reason, it seemed to either Brian or Bob. Unfortunately, they started their three-month academy class in June.

Donning bunker gear for a three-hour drill when the

temperature was over one hundred degrees in the sun didn't seem like a sensible thing to do, but it had to be done. They graduated together from the academy in late August and received their State of Florida Firefighter Certificates. Within 2 months they were both hired at the same time by the same fire department and started the year long probationary requirement side by side.

They couldn't have been happier! Imagine the luck of being hired by the same Department and even in the same hire class. They always bid on the same shift and station. So even in the fire department they were always together and watching each other's back. If Brian was having a bad day or feeling a little sluggish, he would let Bob know and vice versa.

Not that anything needed to be said, they could read each other from 100 feet away. It worked and they were inseparable. They knew all the intimacies about each other. They were at each other's weddings, gave each other swaps on one or the other's day off if they needed it. They even took their wives on vacations together, traveling to many of the fantastic state and national parks, the Kennedy Space Center, and many areas of interest across the country.

And now that they were both retired from the fire department, they had even more time for fishing. How time flew!

Brian retired first after picking up a patient in an awkward position, causing him back strain that continued to fester and then turned into neck and back issues over time. The neck pain slowly started causing sleep disruption, then brain fog caused him memory and mood issues.

It began to negatively affect his quality of life, so it was time to call it a day before it became worse and depression set in. Being

---

forced into retirement can be devastating. But Brian knew it was time, so he left after eighteen years. The only thing he and Bob did together besides fish was watch the rockets launch out of Cape Canaveral.

They had been to Kennedy Space Center to watch the launch of all ten of the humongous Starships, including the beautiful *Starship X* that had launched six months earlier with its crew of twenty-one courageous astronauts. This was still exciting for them because *Starship X* was now staging to land on Mars.
Bob set up his home entertainment system to record the Mars landing if they happened to miss anything.

Bob retired after twenty-four years in the Firefighting business. He'd been working for a paycheck for nearly sixty years. Though he liked staying active, he resented the time and effort spent at work. It wasn't like the early days when they eagerly looked forward to every call. It was time to move on. Now the two of them were free to fish as much as they wanted, and they enjoyed it immensely.

They were known by the local fisherman as the B&B twins, and at every opportunity they were out fishing, even if the wind, weather, and seas were not in their favor.

On this day in early August, the summer trade winds had let up enough to give them a gorgeous day 20 miles off Fort Lauderdale in the Gulf Stream.

The flat sea was a beautiful sterling blue, with a slight breeze out of the southeast with tiny wind-driven waves walking their way from who knew where. The Dolphins were missing more than hitting, but it was such a beautiful day that didn't really matter.

———

Things aboard the sturdy little craft were wonderfully quiet when Brian thought he saw something rather unusual. He adjusted his polarized sunglasses and climbed on the bow to get a better look.

It appeared to be a big channel marker that had no reason to be so far out to sea. But even more than that, something was wrong with it. It was bobbing up and down and it looked too big. A broken piling wouldn't bounce up and down like a child in a bounce house or on a trampoline, it would lay flat and be even harder to see. No, this was something else altogether.

Brian was now precariously perched on the bow with his fishing pole in hand and no hand holds to stabilize himself. But he wanted to get a better look at the thing bobbing in the water maybe about half a mile away.

"Hey, what's that, bro?" he said as he pulled his hat down to shield eyes from the sun.

"What's what?" Bob turned to look.

He was just about to go to the helm and start up the engines to get a closer look when suddenly, a huge spray of steam that sounded like a jet taking off, accompanied by billowing smoke, sea spray, and total chaos erupted off the port side bow. It was so loud Brian lost his balance backward as if a bomb had gone off right in front of them. A geyser of water, steam, and fire rocketed upward with a deafening, thunderous roar.

They immediately dropped their poles. At first, Bob thought it was a plane crash. He saw Brian fall back and smack his head on the helm. Blood flowed from the back of Brian's head as he writhed around, holding it with his hands and screaming, but he could not be heard over the incredible noise of a flaming rocket disappearing into the sun. Bob watched it as long as he could using his sunglasses and hat to shield his eyes from the intense light, but he needed his hands to cover his ears and he couldn't do both at the same time.

It was so ear-shattering he couldn't think at all or even imagine what could possibly produce such a horrendous volume of sound. Then the blast wave hit him, and he also fell to the deck of the small boat covering his ears.

The "anomaly", as it was first immediately identified, came up almost simultaneously on both the Fort Lauderdale and Miami Airport radars.

A few seconds later, the anomaly was being tracked on the Homestead Air Force Base radar. Seconds after that, it was spotted on the joint Naval Air Force radar out of Key West. Alarms were immediately triggered, and two F-16 interdiction fighters were dispatched from Homestead Air Force Base with four more dispatched from Key West. Calls immediately went out to NASA to see if they had an unscheduled launch.

The strange thing was, whatever this anomaly was, it was not inbound, so it didn't appear to be a threat—at least not to the U.S. mainland. The response was rapid, and tracking confirmed that whatever it was, it was going straight up.

Chapter 3

Starship X

It was 5:55 a.m., February 14th, and the world was getting a gigantic Valentine. *Starship X* was vertical on Launch Pad 39A, all 387 feet gleaming in the xenon lights as the horizon was turning pink with the first rays of the morning sun. The stainless- steel-clad, nine-million-pound rocket was breathtakingly beautiful and could be seen from as far as 10 miles away. The twenty-one astronauts comfortably strapped inside in their custom high-back chairs were quietly listening to the countdown's progress. The Command deck, lit only from the light of the touchscreen monitors, provided a dark, cool cocoon for the astronauts to focus on the work at hand. The only noise was the ticking sound of the fuel topping up the groaning tanks, as the supercooled propellants caused the metal tanks to contract.

Mission Specialist Andrea Tripp from Houston, Texas, thought the starship sounded like a giant waking from a deep sleep. Commander Peter Carrigan and Chief Pilot Mary Pfeiffer were finishing up their pre-launch checklists. Communications Specialist Steven Henderson was confirming the checklists were complete as the countdown progressed to under twenty seconds. Slowly, the monitor lighting grew in intensity as the general cabin lighting dimmed, as if the stage was being set for the show to begin. The orchestra was all seated. The maestro picked up the baton. The audience went silent as the astronauts heard in their headsets, ". . . nine, eight, seven . . . main engines, start!" The groaning disappeared into a roaring thunderclap that could not be stopped. ". . . six, five, four, three, two, one . . . liftoff!"

Nine million pounds of thrust slammed the 34-story rocket upwards, using 40 tons of supercooled methalox fuel per second. *Starship X* was shaking and banging worse than anyone on board had imagined or in any of their training simulators. As the acceleration increased, the increasing g-forces took control. All twenty-one astronauts were forced deep into their seats and headrests. The touch screen monitors were now virtually unreadable due to the increasing vibrations. A voice in their headsets sounded. *"Starship X, go for roll."*

Commander Carrigan responded with a barely audible yell, "Roger, roll."

The roll program gimbaled the giant engines and set thrust to the correct trajectory for low Earth orbit, the gleaming ship changing course and heading. *Starship* X was no longer talking to Cape Canaveral; they were now talking with CAPCOM in Houston—if they could hear them over the roar of the engines. *"Starship X,* go with throttle up," was the command from CAPCOM.

"Roger, throttle up," replied Commander Carrigan.

Andrea looked at her hands on the armrests. They had trained for this, but experiencing it was out of this world. She tried to raise her left hand. It took all the energy she had to pick it up six inches, battling the ever-increasing g-forces. This is crazy, she thought. Other Astronauts told them what to expect, but…

They were now twenty-one rag dolls being violently shaken in a vertical hurricane of uncontrollable proportions. Was this

---

"normal?" They were thrown left, then right, then forward. Thank God for the five-point harnesses and the custom-made high-impact seating.

They were vulnerable to this gigantic metal tube having its way with their bodies. Did the engineers get everything right? How could this enormous structure that was to be their taxi and their home for the next two years possibly hold together under this stress? Andrea was sure *Starship X* was going to break apart. Then it happened.

Nothing.

Over the comm she heard, "Starship, Houston. We show you MECO (Main Engine Cut Off)."

Andrea's eyes told her she wasn't in heaven, but she was close. Either nothing is noisy, or we all just died, she thought.

They had achieved weightlessness. The blue Florida sky was now the impossible infinite black of space.

Commander Carrigan replied, "Houston, confirm Main Engine Cut Off.

Chapter 4
Starships

Two years previously Starships I and II launched without a hitch, giving everyone involved and all space fans high hopes that the Mars Mission I was going forward without a hitch. Two years went by while Starship III was made ready. During countdown, a glitch kept reappearing, showing that a sensor was faulty. After investigation, it was launched without further incident. *Starship IV*, like I and II, went off without any issues, as did starships V, VI, and VII. *Starship VIII* prelaunch progress continued smoothly until the final twenty-two seconds to launch, when a pressure switch on one of the huge fuel tanks faulted and had to be replaced.

To fix the problem, the engineers spent two days removing all 6 million pounds of fuel before fixing the switch and refueling. Starship IX also launched as expected with no anomalies. These starships left launch pad 39A at Cape Canaveral, Florida, approximately three months before *Starship X*'s launch with its precious human cargo and support supplies. The eyes of the world watched as *Starship X* launched flawlessly and climbed into space on its six-month journey to Mars.

Each of the previous Starships were designed to be grocery stores, hardware stores and supply depots for the human crew that would become the first astronauts on the baren dusty red planet for a year after landing. The Starships were pre-programmed to take themselves to a specific location, all within an approximate half mile perimeter. They were spaced out just enough to land safely without affecting any other starship. They were then to begin autonomously preparing for the arrival of humankind. Their success was mission critical with little room for error or mishap.

Chapter 5

Mars Mission I

As soon as the Starships entered low Earth orbit, they were scheduled to rendezvous with a tanker to refuel. This was completely automated. A tanker was waiting for them intentionally in the shadow of Earth to keep the fuel cool. Cold fuel means more fuel at a higher density. Aboard *Starship X*, Commander Carrigan and Chief Pilot Mary Pfeiffer monitored the approach and operation. Immediately after docking, the fuel transfer began. Before long, *Starship X* had a half million pounds of methane and almost two million pounds of liquid oxygen back in her tanks as the fuel transfer continued.

CAPCOM issued the command for Mars Injection Orbit upon completion of the refueling procedure, and the twenty-one astronauts felt gravity return as *Starship X* throttled up for the thirty-five-million-mile, six-month journey to Mars. As soon as *Starship X* was en route on the correct trajectory, the crew spontaneously began referring to their massive ship as "*Staten*, in conversations amongst themselves in place of *Starship X*.

No one seemed to know who came up with the new reference or pet name; it just seemed to fit. Mission Specialist Andrea had commented to someone, "It's just easier to say," so it stuck. The sleeping rotation, food preparation and exercise regimen were initiated as planned. They were now under way. Next stop, Mars. The crew consisted of men and women from seven different countries. This was intentionally an international effort. Every astronaut candidate had been thoroughly vetted and drilled to the point of exhaustion. It was so ingrained into the consciousness that it was common for many of them to dream about the upcoming trip. Personality and character testing had been conducted by psychologists, psychiatrists, and human behaviorists, with the intention of finding the slightest expression of simple frustration, personality flaw or prejudice, and if expressed, the candidate was quickly dismissed. Even the most patient people had a hard time with the redundancy and monotony of the testing regimen.

By the end of testing, the final candidates were picked because they simply didn't show frustration or boredom. In the end, the successful astronauts understood this as if it were a deep, personal secret, and of course, it was never discussed because each one of them wanted the best character and personality traits to be on the mission. There were no inside secrets or shortcuts. After all, this was going to be the longest mission in history. A couple of key factors to many of the winning personalities of the astronaut candidates (also known as "ascans") was that they could always find something positive to say and, of course, knew they would be the first to land on Mars—or at least among the first, and anything would be worth that. They were not automatons, however. Each had careers, families, and friends which would have to be mentally and emotionally relegated to second priority for the entirety of their mission and most of their training. A healthy recognition of their attachments at home and with friends was not a cause for concern amongst the trainers. It was, in fact, promoted. Healthy relationships supported healthy personality and character.

"Hey, who cares if I'm on the first or the fifth starship to go? How many people can say they went to Mars?" said Flight Engineer Pedro Lopez to the Miami Herald during an interview.

Pedro was tasked with assisting Commander Carrigan and Chief Pilot Mary Pfeiffer, as well as relating data based on position verification, instrumentation, authentication, and accuracy (nothing was left to chance) with CAPCOM (originally meaning Capsule Communication) from Houston Ground Control.

Everyone on board was thoroughly cross-trained and routinely sat in different seats, performing many different duties. That was all except Commander Carrigan, whose job description was basically God Junior on *Staten*—a position few people could ever imagine, let alone handle.

Once the final engine burn achieved its flight heading and speed objective, zero gravity returned, and the astronaut shift rotation began. The three shifts began, referred to as A, B, C, or Alpha, Bravo, and Charlie. Commander Carrigan broke the twenty-one crew members into two shifts of seven astronauts. The first crew took the 06:00 (6 a.m.) to 14:00 (2 p.m.) hours shift, the second from 14:00 to 20:00 (8 p.m.) hours and the overnight shift with six astronauts was the 20:00 to 06:00 hours shift. Usually, the on-coming crew sat in alongside the off-going shift just to get caught up with any changes. Within a couple of days, the shifts were all functioning as expected, and each person was doing his or her part. In less than a week, the ship and crew were functioning so smoothly and cohesively that Commander Carrigan had nothing to do other than verify that the ship's log entries were correct and timely and see to his Command log entries.

Commander Carrigan often found himself working out in

the gym on the circular treadmill, specifically designed for zero Gs, or on the weight training equipment. It was one of the best places for him to allow himself to recall memories of his home in the mountains of Colorado, his golden retriever, and hiking all over the Western United States. While working out he allowed his mind to drift wherever it wanted. He found these opportunities to be invigorating and recharging allowing him to concentrate and focus better after the workouts. He had to stay sharp for what potentially could happen. However, every time he checked on the big ship's technical operations; course, heading, fuel, oxidizer, radiation exposure, engine performance, tanks, or even galley and head cleanliness or the more monotonous duties, they were being taken care of correctly. He even checked in with the flight surgeon Tammy Spencer to make sure everyone was still checking out correctly with their weekly health check-up. It was as if they had been there before, and well, they had. That's what the years of drilling and training had been about. He often smiled thinking how lucky he was to have such a crew to fly with. What was not expected was that after the first three of the six months of travel, everyone was genuinely enjoying the journey and having a good time and the view was completely breathtaking.

At the end of one of his workouts Mission Specialist Haratu Suzuki popped in for a quick workout. He could suddenly pop in when you didn't even know he was there. Quick, silent, intelligent, always in good humor and always friendly with a welcoming smile.

"Oh, hey, Haratu, I didn't know you were here," Commander Carrigan said, smiling as he floated off the circular jogging track.

"Hey, commander," Haratu replied with his usual smile.

"Yeah, I get that a lot."

"I know you do. You're very quiet, unassuming and a pure pleasure to be around."

"Aw, thank you commander. You guys make it easy. Everyone on the crew is awesome!"

"Did you always know that you wanted to be an astronaut? Even before attending the University of Tokyo?"

"Yes, as far as I can remember, ever since I was very young. I would always watch anything I could on NASA, JAXA, Japan's National Space Agency, cosmonauts from Russia, the ESA (European Space Agency) or anything space related. My father worked a lot of hours. He was usually gone when I woke up in the morning and didn't come home from work until I was already in bed. My mom pretty much raised me. When she realized my love of space, she started enrolling me in anything space-related. She even sent me to Space Camp at the United States Space and Rocket Center, on my own, when I was only eight years old. I flew from Tokyo to Nashville, where a Rocket Center van picked me up. I guess they couldn't afford to come with me. That trip locked me in for the rest of my life! I will never forget it and I am so grateful to both of my parents for sending me there. As far as I'm concerned, they launched my career at age eight."

"You were already on the path, my friend. Your parents just helped you along."

"Commander, I'm still in awe that I've been so blessed and privileged to be here. I'm overwhelmed with gratitude for you, the crew, NASA, all of our trainers, the support staff, all of the engineers that made this possible, the list goes on and on. I pinch myself every

---

day.

"I know what you mean, Huratu. It's definitely a dream come true for all of us. I'm sure your parents are both incredibly impressed with you making it through the selection process. Do you know how many people were initially invited to try out?"
"I think it was over six thousand?"

"Yeah, that's what I heard as well. The first cut was over fifty percent. What do you think you'll do when all of this is over, and we're back on Earth?"

"Well, I've been thinking of becoming a psychiatrist and a teacher. I was thinking about helping kids with learning disabilities, at risk teens, orphans and possibly with inmates about to be released. Many inmates have never been out of the prison system their entire lives. They have no idea how to live on their own. It is a big challenge."

"Wow, Huratu! I had no idea. You certainly have a huge heart!"

"I just want to help, Commander." "Have a great workout, Huratu."

The crew was made up of a unique blend of professionals, each with different outlooks on their lives, with personal pursuits as almost as varied as the world they were now leaving. Pilot Mary Pfeiffer grew up in Schenectady, a small town in upstate New York where she gravitated toward her school and Public Libraries wherever she was. She never stopped reading about space, the Apollo and early Mercury Missions and all the Shuttle Missions. In her teens she joined the Civil Air Patrol with her father's help and support. But he was gone a lot, for extended periods of time. Her father told her that he was in the military. That was all he would say. He never talked about his job or why he was gone, other than saying he was needed. Even today she could feel the tears well up as she thought of her father and the day he hugged her and her Mother and stepped out with his duffle bag. He never came back. There was a military funeral, but that only left her with more questions and a flag. Years later her mother finally explained to her that he was in Special Forces. That's all her mom would say with tear-filled eyes.

Mary decided to pursue a master's degree in both Astrophysics and Aerospace Technologies. She knew from early on that she would be involved in space exploration in some manner. Mary's soft smile and easy wit disguised a leader with an unstoppable drive capable of whatever it took to complete the mission.

Flight Engineer and backup Communications Specialist Pedro Lopez came from the desert southwest. As soon as he was able to hold a screwdriver, he was forever taking mechanical things apart to see how they worked. Radio communications became a special hobby of his by age 8. When he visited the campus of the SETI program in California and the VRA (Very Large Array) in New Mexico his imagination exploded. He was more interested in how the system worked than the messages they might hear, but of course, that was exciting as well. Stanford begged him to stay on after graduation because his curiosity was contagious, and he was talented. Students loved him. He was a great educator with a ton of patience and empathy, often staying in the lab after hours to assist students having difficulty. He was frequently heard saying something like, "You know students always teach me something I didn't know or even think about. They open up my imagination and my world." Pedro and

---

Communications Specialist Steven Henderson on their "downtime" could generally be found in front of a data screen filled with technical manuals or elbows deep in a piece of equipment that required no intervention other than a curious check-up. From time to time the pair would find themselves in fascinating discussions with Mission Specialist Barbara Black.

Barbara Black held one of the rare positions that was a real specialty. Each crew member spent some time with her in the tiny microbiology lab which she ran, but they were usually overwhelmed. Just the variety of bacteria, viruses, fungi and more which she constantly tested for was mind boggling. Many microbiota require different testing procedures, incubation and growth mediums specific to the species. Barbara held a PhD in Astrobiology and an MS in Biology and Chemistry, and never stopped making observations of space from a point of view no one on board had even considered. She claimed that her curiosity came from growing up on the farm in Iowa and in the bakery the family owned and ran as an extension of the farm. They used the milk their two dairy cows, "Maryland" and "Patrice", produced, in the baked goods after milking them at 4:00 every morning. She helped before going to school to mix the different doughs and batters for donuts, cookies, or cakes, and she would imagine what the different yeasts and leavenings or emulsifiers were doing in the mixer or at different temperatures and in the ovens or fryers as they did their job fermenting or rising. Baking was chemistry and microbiology, and it gave Barbara an intense interest in their behaviors as she imagined in her mind what each of the concoctions was doing at the microbiological scale.

The large open sky of Iowa helped her to fall in love with

the stars and dream big. She was just as fascinated by a passing star or constellation or shooting star as by the tiniest of objects in her microscope. Her curiosity was insatiable for knowledge and discovery. Frequently she enjoyed conversation and visits with Steven and Pedro. They shared a contagious curiosity and often would play "what-if scenarios" with each other about possible life on the planets of our solar system. The three of them would discuss what different microbes might exist in different geologies, how and what they might use for energy, how they might survive in different possible microclimates, how those microclimates could maintain homeostasis, the presence of water in the atmospheres of different planets including temperature variations, the presence of methane in the Martian atmosphere, and more. It just went on and on, all the different possibilities seemed endless. They each seemed to learn something new in these interesting conversations and it made them feel like high school friends bantering back and forth presenting different possible scenarios.

As expected, the three shifts were rotated bi-weekly so everyone on board had an opportunity to work with everyone else, and no one fulfilled the same duties for weeks on end. This rotation ensured that everyone stayed familiar with different duties, reducing the likelihood of boredom and the tendency of tribalism and territory or kingdom creation.

This human phenomenon of territory claiming could easily be witnessed in many businesses and government offices today. When people clutter their desks and workspaces with multitudes of personal pictures and paraphernalia, they are effectively saying, "This is my territory. Do not touch." No one person "owned" any of the generous public spaces aboard *Staten*, and everyone knew it. The helm and communications level had an out of this world observatory at the bow and was frequently visited by the astronauts taking in the incredible view. Directly below the helm was the astronaut safety seating for launches and landings. The seats could be folded into the floor, creating a large space for yoga, stretching or training. The "day room", primarily used for the dining room, was also used for reading, conversing or game playing. Immediately adjacent to the dining room or "day room" was the galley, and the level below that was the gym with its thirty-foot diameter circular treadmill for use in zero gravity. Hydraulic weight machines, core machines, and bungee cords rounded out the gym. The showers were below the workout room, which could be accessed through a hatch straight from the gym. To conserve water, and since much of the trip would be zero gravity, a shower consisted of wrapping the showerhead or spicket with a towel, wetting it thoroughly, and wiping themselves down with the wet towel. They would then follow with an organic soap infused "soap towel", the size of a washcloth. This was finally followed with the wet towel again to get the soap off. The vacuum sealed shower room had a slightly negative air pressure which kept any moisture or water droplets from escaping to the rest of *Starship X* and it had a special water separator in the air handler which led directly to the reverse osmosis equipment for recycling. This room and its ventilation system were frequently tested for fungi and more by Barbara Black.

Towels were a huge asset and were to be used sparingly. They had six of their own towels stowed in their bunk rooms. These six towels were to last until arrival on Mars, then they would be issued three new towels. The objective was to use the fewest towels possible. Storage space and weight were a premium, and the longer they could make things last, the more room they had for fuel and food. Most used one towel at a time until they couldn't bear to use it any longer. Many of the crew would rinse out a towel after several uses in the shower room and suspend it in their quarters to dry. One of the benefits of *Starship X* was the atmosphere on board was very low in humidity, very much like a desert, so things like towels and laundry dried very quickly and even that moisture was recovered by the air handler.

The medical room was right below the showers and consisted of everything found in an emergency medical clinic: an x-ray machine, cardiac equipment, tools for minor and some major surgeries, as well as trauma supplies.

The computer room was below the clinic and provided a quiet space for work, research and personal email. The surround sound entertainment room sat in a small alcove and was virtually soundproof when the double doors were closed. It had over ten thousand of the most recent and golden oldie movies and music. The digital library contained hundreds of thousands of copies of just about everything ever printed in electronic version and could print or transfer to personal tablets whole volumes if needed. Below the entertainment room was storage space, and below that began the personal bunk rooms.

Each crew member had a personal space, or bunk, as it was identified in the Policies and Procedures manual of Mars Mission I (MMI). Each personal space or bunk room was 8 feet long by 6 feet wide, with a 7-foot ceiling. In zero gravity, this was very spacious

———

and luxurious. Each bunk room had a privacy door and places to put clothing and personal belongings.

Further below were the mechanical work rooms with every tool required for the maintenance of *Starship X* and more. They included welding equipment and gases, saws, hammers, wrenches, sockets, prying tools, drills and bits, soldering, plumbing, electrical, wiring, fastener storage of every kind and more; basically, everything one could find in a hardware store. With one major exception, everything was fastened down preventing unexpected re-organization of everything during zero g or the craziness of launch. Everything in the mechanical rooms specifically fit the nuts and bolts and all fasteners of every kind on *Starship X*. The mechanical genius responsible for all this inventory, equipment and daily on-going maintenance as well as emergency mechanical services was Engineer Specialist Carl White. Carl's dad owned a tool and die shop conveniently next door to the house. Out of curiosity he started to hang out at the shop watching the tool makers run the machines in the afternoons after he got out of school. He made sure to stay out of the way; but after a few months he was helping out from time to time, moving crates and tools around. By the time he was in high school he was filling in on some of the simpler machines and helping with supplies. His dad was impressed enough to start paying him a small hourly rate. By his senior year in high school, he was qualified to run any machine in the shop and often worked on Saturdays while taking some night school classes at Sinclair Community College in nearby Dayton. Carl already had enough credits, between high school and his night classes, to qualify for an associate degree in mechanical engineering upon graduation. So, he set off to Ohio State University.

———

He slowly started to get more and more curious about exotic metals and found himself migrating toward aerospace as well as mechanical engineering, ending up with an undergrad degree in ME and a PhD in Aerospace Engineering. As he progressed, he kept looking at NASA as a possible way to satisfy his curiosity. Next thing he knew he was applying for the astronaut candidate program. Much to his surprise he was accepted. "He is just so easy going and intuitive he just fits right in," his primary instructor commented. "It was almost like he expected what we were going to test him on in advance."

Beneath the mechanical rooms was the huge water tank for crew consumption right next to the oxygen tank for crew and atmospheric controls, a small storage area, which included battery storage, followed by the methane, liquid oxygen, and of course, the engines for propulsion.

There were several smaller lab spaces dedicated to a variety of specific scientific studies such as testing of potential food crops in the lower Martian gravity, studies of the effects of extended microgravity on circulatory and cardiac changes and so on which would be utilized as soon as they arrived on Mars. Some tomatoes were planted soon after departure. They already had 12 tomato plants growing while underway.

Mission Specialist Haratu was from Kobe and had spent some time with the Japanese Exploration Agency (also known as JAXA). He often used his private bunk room to meditate and gather his thoughts. On occasion some crew members sought him out for solace. He was easy to talk to and found to be a dependable upbeat friend for virtually everyone on the ship.

Mission Specialists Ashanti Sumbika and Adnan Ashari

were the deep three-dimensional thinkers on the crew. Both were pilots. Ashanti was from Mumbai, India and flew helicopters for the Indian Airforce and Adnan piloted hovercraft for the Egyptian Air Defense Forces. Both brought a perspective with different dimensions than most would consider. The crew quickly realized that these two quiet astronauts rarely spoke, but when they did it was worth listening. Flight Surgeon Tammy Spencer learned that Ashanti had also been a midwife with her mother in her early days and had actually helped deliver a few babies.

It was outlined in the Policy and Procedures (P&P) that the ship would be returned in "as new condition" as possible upon arrival back at Cape Canaveral. It was entirely possible the ship would be ready immediately for another mission, and any "unusual cleaning services" would be charged to the astronaut's paycheck. So, the manual suggested using discretion in adorning personal spaces. It, of course, worked under the assumption that they were expected to return to Earth.

Mars was rapidly growing in the windows, and it was to no one's surprise when Pedro announced what everyone already knew: that *Staten*'s trajectory was "dead on" and projected perfectly for an inbound landing on Mars's massive canyon— Valles Marineras. Still, the announcement brought a round of applause and smiles.

As expected, the shift rotation was immediately canceled for the landing. All crew members followed protocol by stowing or securing everything not essential for landing and a final inspection crew verified everything secure from bottom to top of the giant ship. Commander Carrigan went over the sequence of events and reviewed the quick reference guide with the crew. This gave them another overview of the landing procedures and emergency procedures for unexpected events such as fire, unusually hard landing, incorrect computer navigation which could mean inappropriate angle of attack, reserve fuel, the ship falling over upon landing and more. If their angle of attack was too shallow, they could skip off the atmosphere. If the angle of attack was too severe, they could burn up in the Martian atmosphere.

With less than an hour until transition to Mars approach, all astronauts took their personal seats, which were conformed specifically to each of their bodies while wearing their Mars suits. They tightened the five-point harnesses that held them firmly in place. Though their personal helmets were on and locked, *Staten* would remain pressurized, so they didn't have to go "on air" unless the atmospheric controls alarm sounded, they were instructed to do so, or if the situation required.

It was dead quiet on board as *Staten* slowly rotated and adjusted its heading, Pedro kept a riveted eye on the navigation and flight parameters as did Commander Carrigan and Mary Pfeiffer. The attitude thrusters kicked in and a slight rushing of Martian atmosphere could be heard increasing the much-needed resistance to slow the giant ship, followed by growing vibrations and turbulence. Soon the vibrations and turbulence combined into a bronco busting ride. The retro boosters fired, and gravity increased significantly as the craft slowed. On approach to Mars, depending on the angle of attack, gravity could approach as much as five gs, or five times a human's weight on Earth. An astronaut of 150 pounds (68 kg) could experience as much as 750 pounds (240 Kg) of gravity like what they experienced when they left Earth so many months earlier.

The landing on Mars was designed to be completely automated and choreographed by the navigational computer, with inputs from two-hundred-seventy-four sensors all working in unison, the onboard radar, as well as active, real-time cameras and Lidar sensors. All thrusters were operational and continued to control the gigantic, 387-foot-tall by 33-foot-wide spacecraft. Chief Pilot Mary Pfeiffer sat at the controls monitoring every aspect of the approach. No talking was required. They were simply observers, observers ready to respond, as the auto-pilot system brought them in. As expected, the noise and bucking decreased rapidly when the descent engines powered down, a confirmation of imminent landing, the crew felt a slight bump as the engines cut out. Anxious eyes looked around from one astronaut to another, grins on every face. Other than the ticking of cooling metal, it was silent as the Martian dust blew out in every direction completely obscuring the view from navigation.

The distance from Earth to Mars is 34 million miles at its closest and 140 million miles at its farthest, depending on the positions of their orbits. Once a year, Mars and Earth were on different sides of the sun, making communication with Earth difficult if not impossible. Fortunately, different satellites help to "deflect" or bend the transmissions around the curvature of the sun. It takes between three and twenty-two minutes for radio transmissions to travel those distances, one way. They were completely dependent on the automated landing system and, of course, Chief Pilot Pfeiffer's supervision. It was a six-month trip to arrive at Mars with a required one-year stay, and another six months back home. As one flight attendant watching the launch was quoted in the Washington Post,

"That's a long layover!" The astronauts were completely relying on the fact that hopefully the Mars Mission I planning engineers and multiple committees had thought of every contingency and possibility. But, of course, they couldn't. It was a very big universe with unlimited possibilities.

An obviously excited Commander Carrigan announced over the PA. "Valles Marineras, everybody!" There was thirty seconds of clapping and cheers heard around the ship, if clapping with flight gloves on counted.

The tenth Starship had landed safely, and this one had humans on board. For the first time in history, humans were on another planet: Mars! A moment of quiet followed by excited cheering as the crew began to realize their new reality. Commander Carrigan and everyone else suddenly felt the new onset of physical effects from the six-month journey in zero gravity. The approximate one-third g, or thirty-six percent of Mother Earth's gravity, felt like two or three times that of Earth's by the crew immediately upon landing.

"It's in our training to expect this situation," Mary said. "But reality still sometimes sucks."

"You're not kidding," Commander Carrigan replied. "I feel like I was either out drinking all night or we landed on Jupiter."

A huge collective sigh of relief was heard as seatbelts were unbuckled and the highly-trained astronauts started adjusting to the new gravity. Some had a little nausea because of the sudden onset of gravity, and one or two were afraid to stand. Some were dizzy as well. Flight Surgeon Tammy Spencer was actually crawling around on all fours evaluating blood pressures asking crew members how did they feel? And telling some to stay seated for a bit. The crew had been trained to expect this. They had extensively hydrated in advance prior to arrival per the protocols. Some recovery time upon landing had been written into the arrival protocols and they were given time to acclimate. A little at a time, they were returning to some kind of homeostasis and a growing feeling of normalcy, as if the first humans on Mars were going to feel normal for some time. Mars Mission I planning committee had estimated that a few days would be required to completely adjust.

The final chief landing briefing from CAPCOM arrived. It described the status of the other nine starships. Everything needed for the two-year round trip that they weren't already carrying on *Staten* was sent in advance on the other nine starships. CAPCOM informed Commander Carrigan, who then informed the crew, that *Starship IV* had fallen over after landing, according to NASA. Since every starship had duplications and redundancies, the mission was still a go, not that they could have turned around and gone back to Earth, Mars was already beyond their return window further heightening the risk of this voyage.

One of their first assignments after assessing the stability of *Starship X* would be to assess the situation with *Starship IV*. The other eight starships were performing nominally.

Starships I and II were sent two years in advance. They were actively producing water from the atmosphere, as well as methane for fuel, utilizing hydrogen fuel cells and solar cells for power. A special, remotely operated piece of equipment had been autonomously off-loaded onto the Martian surface as well. For the past two years, it had been making methane utilizing the "Sabatier

---

method" and safely storing it in one of the onboard tanks, which was about half full by the time *Starship X* launched from the now- world-famous Launch Pad 39A. This guaranteed that enough fuel would be immediately available for their return trip since none of the starships carried enough fuel on their own for the 35-million- mile return trip back to Earth.

After it appeared that the crew was adjusting slowly to the new gravity, Captain Carrigan assembled the team for a quick situational briefing. He knew this wasn't really required for the crew, but he understood too well that if he didn't assemble the troops for a quick in situ overview, he could be second-guessed on his decision-making and communication skills. Everything goes into the log.

"Congratulations on your diligence, attention to detail, and hard work to get us here. I recognize and appreciate all of you for making this six-month trip virtually trouble-free. We had no anomalies on our portion of the trip, so let's keep it that way. You are the most highly trained astronauts in history. My primary objective is to see every one of you return safely with me back to Earth and have the time of your life while you're here! Having said that, let me be the first to welcome you to Mars!"

Applause followed, with hoots and yelling.

"I suggest if you haven't already, take a look at the scenery out of the helm window. It is breathtaking now that the dust has settled. You all know your jobs, and you understand the risks. Of course, any deviation from protocol must be approved by me. I must reiterate that any unapproved deviation from protocol may lead to disciplinary action up to, and possibly including, confinement to quarters. But of course, you already understand this. It's my job to

---

interpret deviation, so if you have any questions or suggestions, it must go through me. If I don't know the answer, we will seek input from CAPCOM. We're all depending on the individual as much as we are the whole. As in the spokes of a wheel, we all need each other. All of our lives are at stake here. Please continue to be professional and friendly as you all have been so far. I'm already extremely proud of each and every one of you. Stay safe, stay smart, stay alert, and enjoy every incredible minute of this journey. We are the few privileged to have this extraordinary experience. Let's make the most of it."

Commander Carrigan noticed Mary rubbing her forehead. "Does everyone feel okay after our exposure to the Martian gravity? Can you all perform your jobs?"

Mary nodded. "Yes, Commander."

"Yes, Commander," more crew members replied as well.

"If anybody needs more time or would like some down time, you let me know. We don't want anyone getting sick in their Mars suit." Commander Carrigan looked around for a response. "Okay, Alpha Shift, we have work to do! Suit up for immediate recon. B Shift, you're on readiness standby. Time is 09:30 Zulu." There was a lot of commotion as the different shifts readied themselves for the first Mars EVA (extravehicular activity) in human history. Since everyone was already in their Mars suits for the landing, preparation for the EVA was greatly simplified.

Deep space can have temperature variations from 1400°F in the sun to a low of around minus 300°F. Due to storage constraints, a minimum number of deep spacesuits were brought on *Staten*, but there were more on Starships VI and VIII. Mars, with its small

---

atmosphere composed mostly of carbon dioxide, was still better than the moon, which has no appreciable atmosphere. As a result of this atmosphere, the temperature range on Mars is a bit more moderate, with a high as much as ~70°F to a low of about -120°F.

This meant the Mars suits were lighter and more flexible than the bulky deep spacesuits. Still, any small tear, rip, crack, or penetration would immediately cancel any EVA activity, and emergency procedures would be implemented. Any perforation would mean the immediate application of a special type of reinforced duct tape they all carried in their emergency packs. Each astronaut had drilled extensively in a multitude of scenarios, but the universe was a big place, and no one could predict all possible scenarios or eventualities.

Before *Staten*'s arrival, CAPCOM was, of course, aware that an EVA would be conducted as soon as the crew felt strong enough to set foot on the surface of Mars. Stephen Henderson, the Communications Specialist, was currently running all telemetry from the helm and communications station. He radioed the safe landing confirmation back to CAPCOM and informed them that the first-ever EVA on Mars was going ahead as planned. Due to the time lag, all EVA communication and coordination was done with *Staten* functioning as the command center coordinating all surface activities. The relay of all communications including video from the surface was already set up. Commander Carrigan chose to personally observe Communications Specialist Steven Henderson, who was coordinating the activity.

Steven grew up in Cuba, Missouri, a small town outside St. Louis. When people found out he grew up in Cuba, they would always jokingly say, "How's your Spanish?" He knew it was coming, so he'd always respond with, "No mucho entiendo, pero tratar." If they understood this, they would get a bit of a laugh out of it because it very much destroys any semblance of proper Spanish. If they didn't understand it and thought he spoke Spanish, the last laugh was his, since he knew it was in very poor form. It somewhat meant, "I don't understand much, but I try."

Commander Carrigan had worked with Steven for around three years. He liked Steven's midwestern attitude and had a deep respect for his work ethic and intelligent insight. He rarely noticed any work incomplete or overlooked, and if he did, Steven always was ahead of him with answers to his questions or reasons why he was delaying the work. He was starting to think Steven would make a fine commander one day.

Chapter 6
First EVA on Mars

The first EVA on Mars began one hour after Commander Carrigan announced its commencement. All comm checks were completed for each of the seven astronauts, and all equipment verification and functionality testing had been completed. The equalization room door was locked, and the atmospheric pressure was slowly reduced to match the surface of Mars. Slowly the hatch door was opened. *Staten*'s crane was initiated and powered up by engineering, and soon they were standing on the crane crew basket being lowered to the Martian surface.

At 10:47 Zulu—or international time—cameras were operating, which meant that the entire world was watching. Even though they had a time delay of nine minutes, it was still considered "live" back on Earth. As the deck of the crane bumped to the Martian surface, all eyes were on Andrea Tripp. Mission Specialist James (Jim) Galway unlocked the safety bar and looked at Andrea, who couldn't have been more nervous. Andrea had been elected by her fellow astronauts to take the first step on the

Martian surface, and the whole world knew how important this moment was forever going to be in history. Many people and all space nuts remembered Neil Armstrong's quote, "That's one small step for (a) man, one giant leap for mankind." Buzz Aldrin gazed down from the top of the ladder knowing all too well that few people would remember who the second man on the moon was.

———

Andrea began to take her forever memorialized step. As Andrea's toe caught the edge of the deck, she gasped, "Oh, God!" Her heart leaped into her throat as she realized the lip of the deck was slightly higher than she remembered from training. Her recovery was phenomenal, however, as she turned to face the main camera.

She took a deep breath, and in a steady voice, calmly began. "We come as one people, as one race, the human race, for the advancement of all, to be better than we were, to advance imagination and understanding, to make this fantastic universe a better place!"

Representing a truly multinational crew of twenty-one, mission specialists Ashanti Sumbika, James Galway, Adnan Ashari, Pedro Lopez, Carl White, and Haratu Suzuki stepped onto Valles Marineras to start the first EVA in the history of Mars, while over 900 million people back on Earth watched in disbelief as the five different nationalities represented one planet.

MS Andrea Tripp's astounding recovery from "possibly tripping" left people wondering if she had actually tripped because she was so composed with the delivery of her first words on the Martian planet. "Did Andrea Tripp trip?" The video was reviewed on national television and talk shows around the world. It just so turns out they had not turned on anyone's mic yet because it picked up too much of their breathing. Everyone was mic'd up so the engineers were waiting until she turned to face the camera before turning on the mics. It was not very evident because the cameraman was behind her, and he was walking and shaking the camera, too. So, Andrea's trip became the subject of the news and daytime talk shows for weeks. It didn't really matter in the end because the moment was historic. And no-one from NASA or the *Starship X* crew was talking.

—

Chapter 7
Pick Up, Drop Off

The captain had filed a float plan with the marina and U.S. Coast Guard scheduling the 3:00 a.m. departure for Miss Trial the day before and at about the same time Don and Chuck cast off, so no one noticed anything amiss. Dong-Hyun (Don) and Chin-Hae (Chuck) had made it out to the Gulf of Mexico surprisingly easily after boarding the vessel and allowing the "engineer" to debrief them on the current status. Before the full explanation and description of the assignment both Don and Chuck were briefed individually on the general idea of what the task was and how much they would be compensated. It had been carefully laid out that if they accepted the assignment there was no going back. A GPS tracker had been hidden somewhere on the vessel. If at any time they veered from the plan or if the tracker was tampered with in any way, they would be tracked down or the munitions they were told were on board could be detonated from anywhere. They both thoroughly believed this to be true. The tough looking engineer who was covered in blood had been on board before them. He could have done anything. Don and Chuck didn't have time to do a bow to stern search and still head out on time, and who knew, maybe the engineer / murderer dude was still watching them. Both Don and Chuck were looking forward to new lives and financial freedom as was promised and neither one of them wanted to mess with the people who were paying them. The engineer had shown them both two backpacks stuffed with bundles of hundreds and Chuck even dumped it out to make sure it was full of real money, then he repacked it in front of the engineer.

"Satisfied?" he asked, before jumping on the gangplank and shoving it back aboard. The motors were running. Don was at the helm and the "engineer" untied the tug, throwing the bitter ends back aboard. He turned and walked away without another word or even a glancing look back.

They were paid cash in advance in good faith and that was part of the plan. Once the mission was complete, they could travel or live comfortably for a very long time as long as they did not attract attention to themselves. Don and Chuck had been meticulously mentored on how to slowly put money in one or more banks a little at a time. No one bought a house with cash. Do not buy a plane ticket with cash. Almost no one buys a new or expensive car with cash. This could be a very good deal for both if they were smart, listened, followed the instructions, and kept their mouths shut.

Now they just had to follow the pre-programmed GPS to the abandoned oil rig where they were to pick up their "equipment". They were in luck. The temperature was a warm 90°, winds were out of the southeast blowing a gentle 7 knots and kicking up only two to four-foot seas, at least at the moment. Things could change. Don just wanted to get this over with.

There were so many abandoned oil rigs in the Gulf of Mexico, it was an environmental and ecological disaster just waiting to happen. Not even the government could keep track of all the abandoned oil wells and derricks after the wells ran dry. The owners claiming bankruptcy would disappear over the horizon, leaving who knew what kind of mess for future generations to deal with. Many of the rigs had continued to leak for years.

Don and Chuck had been advised not to discuss personal business with each other. The less they knew about each other's personal interests the less they could inform the authorities if one of them did something stupid like not listening to their advisors and got caught. So, it appeared their advisors had their best interest at heart, at least in the long term. They just had to complete the job which entailed stopping at this specific abandoned rig and tie off three of the four barges. They were to do this to keep the barges from floating away, being run over by some passing vessel, or floating onshore, giving away any aspect of their mission. They had to keep one barge for refueling the tug, to increase their potential range, take in tow two items of unknown origin or purpose, then drop these two items off at two different predetermined positions, all identified by GPS locations. It seemed like a simple operation. Don couldn't imagine why they were being paid so well and what all the secrecy and murder was all about. When in sight of Florida, they were to put the dive gear in the unnamed and unregistered dinghy, with plenty of extra weight and lobster diving equipment. Then they were to scuttle the vessel at night, after turning off the navigation lights, and motor the unlit dingy toward shore. They were to put on the dive gear then sink the dinghy within sight of shore and swim. Scuttling both vessels was easy, just pull the plugs. The huge twin Detroit Diesel motors in the tug were sure to take it down quickly. Same thing for the inflatable dinghy. Just pull the plugs and stab the inflatable hulls with a knife, the weight of the motor would take it right down. Fortunately, they were both scuba divers, but it was always a little spooky to jump into the black ocean at night, even with a handheld submersible light. Even if the inflatable should somehow wash ashore, the Coasties would think it was Cubans. The VIN (Vessel Identification Numbers) had been carefully removed and recoated with gelcoat to hide the origination and ownership.

"What a beautiful night," Chuck exclaimed as he lit a cigarette and looked up at the stars.

"Yeah," Don agreed. "With any luck and favorable weather, we should be in Florida looking for a nice hotel room, a shower, a bed and a bank in about 3 days." he smiled. "So far the weather looks fantastic for the next three days."

"Sounds good," Chuck remarked as he glanced around observing the empty seas.

"Ok, let's do the night watch together until midnight, we should be far enough offshore by then so you can get some shut eye. I'll man the helm until eleven a.m. You can take the helm from eleven to four unless there is work to be done topside. That way you can get some sleep before the long night shift. Maybe we take the occasional nap in the cockpit, weather and sea conditions providing. We only need to keep this up for about three days." Don suggested.

"Well, that means you'll work fourteen hours from four to six every day?" Chuck said inquisitively, taking off his Cincinnati Reds Baseball cap to scratch his head.

"Yeah, we'll take it as it goes. If we need to adjust it, we can. Maybe I'll extend my 11 a.m. shift to 6 p.m., and you can chill out from six to ten before the long night shift?"

"That sounds a little fairer," Chuck responded. "Sounds

good," Don agreed.

I think I'm going to like this guy, Chuck thought to himself.

Just after sun-up their targeted abandoned oil platform appeared on the horizon. It continued to grow over the next hour until it loomed like a giant prehistoric dinosaur rising out of the gulf. The platform still had the drilling rig mounted on one side soaring over two hundred feet, with the main platform and crew housing beneath giving it a lopsided look, like a gigantic bird trying to turn around to look at itself.

Both Don and Chuck were very glad they did not arrive during the night. The sea conditions were calm and made their approach to the humongous platform easy. They just needed to keep an eye out for whatever it was they were to pick up.

Suddenly Chuck yelled out, "Buoy two hundred meters off Starboard!"

"Got it," Don yelled back.

The design of the sixty-foot tug and the constant guttural noise of the massive Detroit Diesels were loud enough to make communication in the slightest of winds difficult even at idle. Headsets would have been beneficial; however, they were unavailable for this trip, so yelling was required to be heard over the wind, seas, and the drone of the twin Diesels. While underway only hand signals could be used to communicate from the helm to the bow.

Don navigated around two of the giant legs of the platform. Chuck tied off three of the massive barges to the giant platform. Slowly pulling up to the two bouncing buoys Don slipped the tug out of gear and into neutral. He certainly didn't want the props to get tangled in the line attached to the buoys or potentially destroy whatever it was they were picking up. He could not imagine what the repercussions would be, but he didn't want to find out.

Chuck used a boat hook to grab the buoys and hauled them onto the deck. He slid the boat hook down the deck back toward the cockpit and slowly walked the buoys to the stern, attaching them to a stern cleat. Don gave him a hand untying the buoys and dropping their respective anchors. They securely attached both connecting lines through both port and starboard stern hawseholes then each separate line to an internal cleat. Each hawsehole was oval, two feet wide and about a foot high, usually used to run tow lines through and occasionally for secure mooring dockside. After finishing this they watched the tips of what appeared to be some kind of missiles or torpedoes bob up and down like two orcas begging for food. They looked at each other both wondering what the hell they had gotten themselves into?

Chuck started to look pale and said in a shaky voice, "This is some kinda crazy out of control international bullshit! I don't know about this. What did we get ourselves into?"

"I'm not sure, this is definitely bizarre," Don agreed.

Chuck kept staring at the two odd items now securely tied to the tow cleats. "I say we just dump this shit, pretend we're following the suggested route and forget about it."

As he leaned over the stern, Don pretended to look down at the newly acquired tow. He made sure he had Chuck next to him on his left side. Don was right-handed. He deftly pulled his nine-inch dive knife from its hidden sheath in the middle of his back. He turned around as if to face the cockpit. With a quick thrust he shoved the

———

very sharp blade into Chuck's abdomen just above the pubic bone and thrust it up to his sternum. ripping him open like a fish being cleaned. He wanted to make sure that he separated the descending coronary artery where it bifurcates into the femoral arteries. This would cause rapid blood loss and loss of consciousness within seconds. Chuck gasped and looked with confusion first at his stomach, thinking Don had just punched him in the stomach or was playing some kind of joke, then into Don's eyes as he realized what had just happened. He tried to breathe. "What, why?" His legs went first as he slumped against the stern, then slid down the transom, still with confusion on his face. He went pale as he started to hyperventilate and passed out staring at some unknown point in the distance. Chuck let him finish the muscular contractions and convulsions that were expected when the brain can no longer obtain the oxygen required and the muscles and nerves react to hypoxia. He then attended to the dead bodies in the cargo hold, hauling them up onto the deck and cutting them into chunks for the fish that are known to congregate underneath the oil rigs. Before he had half of the captain's body tossed overboard the water was churning with a feeding frenzy. This was disgusting work, but it had to be done. The captain and first mate had gone into rigor mortis, so it was easier to haul them onto the deck, and the blood had coagulated making clean up easier. By the time he started dismembering the first mate there were jacks, white tip sharks, black tip sharks, lemon sharks, grouper, barracuda and many fish he had never seen before, even moray eels were coming up for the feast. He finished with Chuck, removing any identifying tags from his clothing and shredded them before leaving.

Too bad he thought, *I was beginning to like him.* Using some hydrogen peroxide, he found in the chemicals locker he washed the blood from the deck thoroughly with a stiff deck brush. Changing out of his jumpsuit, now completely saturated in blood, he realized the blood had even soaked through to his underwear. He shredded everything with his dive knife and tossed the pieces overboard. He then grabbed some soap from the cleaning locker, turned on the saltwater wash down and took a full head to toe saltwater shower on deck, toweled off and pulled on a clean T-shirt and jeans. The tug's fuel gauge read under half full so he decided he should transfer some diesel from the barge. The seas were calm and now he was alone…again. After mom died, I guess I will be alone for the rest of my life. He thought. He figured the tug could do 300 miles with a full tank and he had around 800 miles or so to achieve his destination. He would need at least one, but probably two more refueling stops, also called "bunkering". He figured he could maybe do his final fuel transfer just off Cay Sal, Bahamas.

No one seemed to know geologically why Cay Sal Bank was a circular ring of islands or what caused them to form. They had been uninhabited since the lighthouse keeper left Elbow Cay in the 1960's. But they formed a wonderful sea break for refueling in calmer seas. The downside is the Coast Guard flies over Cay Sal frequently and takes pictures of any vessels, constantly on the lookout for drug runners, something he would like to avoid. However, a tug transporting fuel to the Bahamas would be considered a normal activity.

Don programmed the autopilot to target the first drop off point. As he pulled away, he admired the incredible feeding frenzy behind him. I wish I had a fishing pole; I could handle some sushi!

—

Then he thought about what he had just done, and the thought of eating left him completely.

With the tug in auto pilot, he scanned the horizon for any other vessels. Fortunately, he was alone. He then went below and found Chuck's backpack and rummaged through it, slowly, throwing his personal belongings out one piece at a time over the miles allowing them to disperse naturally in the wind driven seas. Don had never killed before and was mildly surprised that he wasn't upset about doing away with Chuck. He figured Chuck knew he was getting into some hairy shit that could end up badly. Don had been advised that if his partner were to show any sign of non-compliance, excess anxiety or disillusionment with the mission, he was to end it immediately. As soon as he saw Chuck's ashen face and fear-filled eyes, he knew immediately he was going to be finishing the mission alone. He wondered if Chuck had been given the same instructions. This was going to be a very long night checking course and speed against the autopilot and keeping an eye on his very strange tow and their attached lines. He certainly didn't want one breaking loose and drifting off. Seven knots was the best he could do. Plugging away at it all night Don kept catching himself nodding off from time to time and almost falling out of the captain's chair on one occasion. At sunrise he squinted at the rising sun as the GPS indicated his first drop off point was approaching. Slowing to idle, Don untied the first of his two tows and let it bob up and down seemingly harmless in the middle of the Gulf of Mexico. He then attached a sea anchor as instructed with a thin nylon line which would keep it from drifting off too rapidly in the current. What a strange mission, he thought. What the hell is this thing going to do so far from shore, out in the middle of nowhere? He thought, this line will not last very long. Not my call. Whatever, just following instructions. As he engaged the props, he let his mind wander off to all the ways he could enjoy his newly acquired cash, and now Chuck's as well. He would have preferred to keep Chuck on board but obviously he couldn't handle the mission.

His mother's loving eyes kept popping into his imaginary vision. He couldn't get her out of his mind. Even his exorbitant compensation didn't make him feel any better. The only love he ever felt was from his mother…and now she was gone. He was all alone again.

Don rounded Key West and made sure to stay offshore to the South. The wind had kicked up toward fifteen knots and was producing some six-foot seas. That's ok, he thought, they will be on my stern soon, as he slowly changed his heading more northerly. Key West has the Boca Chica Army/Airforce Base. Who knew what kind of top tech shit they had there. Fifty miles later he was 60 miles to the east of Marathon, Florida and just to the West of Cay Sal Bank.

He grabbed the fuel lines and had to carry them forward to the fuel barge, carefully jump off the bow pulling the lines after him and attach them to the discharge pickups. There was a decent chance of losing his balance and ending up in the drink, while jumping four feet or so down to the moving barge. If that happened, he would have to swim to the transom and climb back aboard, assuming he didn't hurt himself or get knocked out on his way down. Of course, if that happened his fuel lines would end up in the ocean and he would have seawater contamination to deal with in his fuel. This would be a difficult task even with a decent night's sleep. With the thought. *Don't*

Fall foremost in his mind, he was able to carefully accomplish the task and turn on the fuel pump, all while drifting around just to the West of Cay Sal Bank and making sure the tug didn't drift into shallow waters, or onto the rocks, or into the path of a passing cargo ship. This was the perfect place to refuel and get rid of his last barge. It will be so nice not to have to look over that one-hundred-foot piece of crap in front of me anymore, he thought.

After refilling the tug's fuel tanks successfully, he dropped an anchor and tied it off to the barge. It only had about a thousand gallons of fuel left in it and he was sure some Bahamian would be super happy to find it unattended. He now had all the fuel he would need for his next drop point and the subsequent disposal of the tug. The winds had changed to the southeast, but they had calmed to a pleasant 10 to 15 knots with some higher gusts on occasion. The trade winds, he thought, these are the winds Spanish treasure galleons relied on to get them back and forth, to and from Spain. Fort Lauderdale was only 120 miles pretty much due North. He pulled up his last GPS drop point and plugged it into the autopilot navigation system. Fortunately, there didn't appear to be any Coast Guard boats or planes in sight.

One hundred long miles and twelve miserable hours later, constantly having to fight sleep, he was approximately twenty miles to the East of Fort Lauderdale. It was just after three a.m. All he could think about was sleep. Sleep was badly needed but he didn't want to stop until he was done. His thinking was badly fogged and focusing on the job at hand had become very difficult. His back hurt. His neck hurt, his balance and coordination were starting to be affected, he was dizzy and if he closed his eyes for a second or two, he would fall asleep. His heart was pounding away, he guessed just from exhaustion. He had to pay extra attention to always keeping one hand on the vessel to avoid being tossed overboard or thrown down hard on the deck from a passing wave. He was in the Gulf Stream now which was known for confused seas and the occasional strange wave.

Finally, Don slowed the tug, disconnecting his last tow, and watched it gyrate with the seas bouncing back and forth, up and down no longer attached to the tug. Free at last! For some reason they didn't tell him to attach a sea anchor to this one. Which struck him as very peculiar because, well, he was after all in the middle of the Gulf Stream with a good seven knot northbound current. A sea anchor would make more sense here than anywhere. What a weird assignment this is. Throttling up the twin Detroit Diesels toward Lighthouse Point, which should be pretty much quiet this early in the morning, was such a blessing. He also knew that just offshore, maybe only a mile out, there was a nice deep drop off more than two hundred feet deep that should keep the tug unrecognized for a long time. He plugged in the last coordinates and began to make way. Only about an hour left of this crazy trip, he thought as he powered up. He could run at fifteen knots now that he didn't have any barges or tow attached to the sea-going tug. Maybe he would sleep on the beach. Oh, that sounded so good, but he also knew that without a beach towel he would attract attention.

He was about to ready the dinghy for the short trip toward shore when a strange, unfamiliar sound generated from down below caught his attention. Immediately he cut out the engines and listened. He dropped down into the cabin searching for the source of the odd noises, pulling up the floorboards, checking the bilge. Yeah, he could

---

hear some kind of grinding noise or noises, then a pop, then more pops. Don had never heard anything like that on any vessel and he could hear water under the floorboards rushing in. Water began filling the cabin and sloshing around. Don couldn't understand where all the water was coming from or why. Why weren't the bilge pumps handling the water? Then he could hear the automatic bilge pumps kick on. Not just one or two but all four were whirring away. Then more pops and the sound of more gushing water. Through-hull devices were automatically popping open, allowing the sea water to rush in. They had fucked him! The boat was half filled with water before he could even get to the dinghy on the bow, and it had to be unleashed and topped up with air. Maybe he could get it unleashed, but at the rate the boat was going down he was already out of time! It didn't look good. The tug's stern began to dip severely. He wondered if he could swim for twenty miles to the beach if he didn't get this dinghy launched in time. Both five hundred horsepower Detroit Engines died as water choked them out. Suddenly it was calm and serene. What an eerie feeling! It was as if the world were slowly being shut down and taken away. Panic set in. He urgently threw two life preservers overboard hoping he could find them floating on the sea if he needed them later. He also threw a white fender overboard for the same reason, plus it was white and shiny. Then the boat's batteries shorted out. Everything went pitch black. The moon had disappeared over the horizon three hours ago. and the flashlights were back at the helm or in the galley. He couldn't remember. It was then he realized that his backpack with all his money was below in his cabin. Adrenaline began to pump through his veins. He was out of time. Feeling his way back down below he had to be very careful

———

not to trip and fall overboard. He made his way carefully back to the helm. The cabin was now almost completely underwater. He had to dive under the water below his bunk to feel where he had stowed his backpack in a secured cabinet. He was hoping he could grab Chuck's backpack as well. It was right next to his. Diving into the black oblivion of the cabin he was hoping he didn't smash his head on the way down or on the way back up on anything in the process. Don had to move fast and keep his wits about him if he was going to make it out of here alive and with any compensation. How was he going to explain the money to the Coasties if they plucked him out of the drink? They were sure to think he was a drug runner. Free of the cabin, he grabbed a hands-free headlight, pulled it over his head and bounded onto the bow while throwing both backpacks on each shoulder, and began to release the small boat. Time was of the essence! Untying the final stern lashing on the dinghy, Don was sure there would be no time to use the manual winch to off-load it. He was hoping he could just float it off as the tug went down, but first he had to turn it upright. It should float even if it is somewhat inflated or even mostly deflated, he thought…Would it float? He had second thoughts. Suddenly, an explosion went off in his face! A sensor-related trigger must have been placed under the dinghy initiating the explosion, singing the hair from his face and much of his upper body, throwing him over the starboard side into the water and effectively blinding him. Don smashed into the side rail of the rapidly sinking tug, bruising some ribs and knocking the air out of him, but he didn't feel it, he had been knocked unconscious from the explosion. The tug went down with no hands on deck. As a result of the explosion, when he regained consciousness, he couldn't see or hear and had no idea

---

where he was or why or which way was up. He thought, this must be a dream or a nightmare. His arms and his face were numb. Don didn't know it, but he was on the surface, the backpacks were keeping him face down in the water. Panic set in. His lungs kept filling with saltwater, and he had a weird metallic taste in his mouth. Don thrashed in the water trying to get his bearings. Coughing convulsively, he continued inhaling water. He could feel himself drifting down as the backpacks slowly pulled off his shoulders. He kept trying to lift his head to breathe and cough. He didn't know he was already five feet under All he could think was this must be a terrible nightmare, then… nothing.

Chapter 8
Valles Marineris

Valles Marineras was one of the largest canyon systems in the known solar system, at more than twenty-five hundred miles in length from east to west, over one hundred miles wide in places, and over six miles deep. It was chosen as a landing location for many different reasons: it offered many primary areas of interest, and study, its low altitude and proximity to the equator offered the warmest year-round climate with the densest atmosphere. The fact that it was a canyon system offered wonderful geologic opportunities. The winter would be harsh on this desolate planet so much further away from the sun, so preparations were required and scheduled into the work roster. There was a lot of work to be done.

Priority number one was to secure the foundation of the three hundred eighty-foot-tall *Staten*. The six landing legs of *Staten* were flat on what looked like a dry lakebed. There seemed to be no pitch to the ground, which was the best news they could get at the moment.

On further inspection, all aspects of the immediate vicinity matched the mission specifications. There were no soft spots, no holes, no evidence of subsidence or subsurface anomalies such as caves, caverns, or any evidence whatsoever that *Staten* might move. The soundings reflected compacted soil and rock six feet down, followed by what appeared to be solid rock around the vicinity. There were no large rocks in the immediate area, either. Temperature

---

readings and humidity levels were noted, atmospheric samples were taken for later evaluation, soil samples were collected to evaluate toxicity and organic materials and compatibility for humans and plants. There was no apparent wind, no clouds in the reddish sky and radiation levels were within expected parameters.

Astrobiologist and chemist Barbara Black was responsible for *Staten*'s tiny chemistry laboratory, and she was biting at the bit to get some Martian samples to evaluate.

Many of NASA's robotic missions sent to Mars in the past found perchlorates to be a component in the soil. Perchlorates, often a component of rocket fuel, are toxic to humans and most earthbound plants and animals. Therefore, the soil on Mars had to be treated to remove the perchlorates prior to using the soil as a growth medium, or they must find soil that didn't contain these toxins. Once *Staten*'s crew stepped on the surface of Mars, their Martian suits would never be taken back inside beyond the equalization room. They would do a "gross decontamination" cleaning using high-pressure air to blow off their suits, and special attention was paid to the boots, prior to entry. The equalization room was vacuumed out after every EVA. Perchlorates were why hydroponic growing systems were identified as a priority for Mars Mission I.

Two six-foot satellite dishes were laid out as a communication redundancy. The temperature was a balmy sixty-four degrees F and the humidity at forty percent, which MS Suzuki thought seemed a little high. The sun was high in the cloudless sky. It really was a beautiful day. The visibility was remarkable. They could easily see all nine of their starships off to the north, and it was obvious which was *Starship IV*. Even though *Starship IV* was lying

---

on its side, from their point of view, it looked surprisingly intact, as if a giant child had gently knocked over his toy.

Having secured the immediate surroundings and determined the landing zone for *Staten* was safe, it was decided to remove *Staten*'s rover, or Mars car, and carefully make way for *Starship IV*. The Mars car was somewhat like the Lunar Rover used by the astronauts on the surface of the moon, but with many new toys.

The Mars cars have a maximum range of a hundred miles with a solar panel roof and it required some assembly after arrival. The roof offered protection from solar and deep space cosmic radiation. The Mars car also had clear, flexible vinyl sides that offered further UV protection, and they could be unrolled and zipped into place in case of a dust storm or for protection from severe, cold weather. At the end of each day, the cars were zipped up for protection from the Martian dust and plugged in to recharge.

The oversized tires of the Mars car provided a two-foot ground clearance and were sixteen inches wide, allowing traction on the multitude of sand dunes on the surface. They were made of a special rubber polymer to survive the brutal cold and were also UV protected so the sun wouldn't destroy them. The tires arrived empty on Mars and had to be filled with a small compressor that was built into the body of the car, along with a portable atmospheric measuring device, (PAM) and a rechargeable flashlight, which recharged using the vehicle's batteries.

The cars also contained an emergency O2 tank, and of course, spare duct tape. On the front driver's side, just below the windshield, was a power outlet for portable power tools, charging, or auxiliary lighting. *Staten* could track each car up to forty miles away

---

on a flat surface. Each car also had LED lighting with cameras on all sides and in the rear-view mirror which showed all riders on board. *Staten* could access these cameras, and if an astronaut was unable to respond or had fallen unconscious, the Mars car could be recalled remotely. An astronaut could instruct it to return "home", and it would drive back to *Staten* on autopilot.

It was time to do some recon for the salvage job they had ahead of them. As soon as *Staten*'s rover was lowered and assembled for the quick trip, they were off. It took less than ten minutes to get to where *Starship IV* had toppled over. After securing the perimeter and considering hazards such as leaking fuel, potential hyperbolic explosions, or the possibility that the fallen craft could move or roll, some nearby rocks were used to help stabilize and secure the vessel. Upon declaring it safe and stable, the crew was free to start the assessment.

As a result of her tipping over, *Starship IV* had a crack in her hull, right between the two main fuel tanks which held pressurized methane and liquid oxygen. Her payload appeared to be intact, although a more thorough evaluation would be needed. MS James Galway took pictures on all sides and included some from a distance to show the entire craft and her position. To off- load her payload would be a lot of work. They would need to spend some time on this one.

The EVA had gone on for almost six hours. It was time to return to *Staten* with the results and pictures from their investigation, which were actively being uploaded to *Staten*'s computer while they made their way back across the beautiful valley-Valles Marineras. Commander Carrigan's voice came up on their helmet headsets.

"EVA canceled. Return to *Staten*, immediately!"

Lead MS Andrea Tripp responded. "Roger that. Returning to *Staten*." She stole a glance at Pedro, who looked back at her and shrugged.

75

Chapter 9
Sol 1 - No Comms

Once safely inside *Staten*, all the crew was assembled on the day room deck.

Commander Peter Carrigan, stern-faced and obviously upset, faced the crew.

Andrea nervously leaned over to Pedro. "So, what's this all about?"

Pedro looked at Andrea. He was shocked to see her beautiful hazel eyes staring back into his. His admiration for Andrea's beauty was not new. Over the months of travel Pedro found himself enjoying working beside her on just about any task or just chatting about everything. She didn't hide her growing pleasure in his company. He stammered, "Uh, the commander is about to tell us."

Commander Carrigan cleared his voice. "Crew, listen up. I have some serious details here to go over with you. Before I forget, I want to give a big thumbs-up to Mission Specialist Tripp for her thoughtful, appropriate and historic statement. Andrea, good job, and excellent delivery. For the rest of you, I didn't know what she was going to say, but I couldn't have said it better myself."

A nice round of applause followed, and Andrea turned beet red as she nodded to everyone.

As the noise died down, Commander Carrigan's steel- blue eyes took on a look that said pay attention now. "Okay. This is serious." You could've heard a pin drop as he looked around the room. "During the EVA, we seemed to be having communication issues with CAPCOM–Houston. We suddenly had significant static and interference breaking up reception. It was apparent that they were having a hard time hearing us, and we were having a hard time getting clear reception from them. We went from virtually perfect reception to more and more static until we lost them to complete static. We went to the Beam Wave transmitter, which, as you know, is mostly used for data and video, and that isn't working either. I have Communications Specialist Steven Henderson working on it as we speak. We're keeping the working frequency open and checking alternative and emergency frequencies as well. Thank you for being diligent about getting the back-up satellite dishes in place, but they don't seem to be helping. With all of the different frequencies and platforms, even the Deep Space Network seems to be offline. Of course, we will continue working the problem. This was not in any of our playbooks. No policy, no procedure foresaw a complete, extended loss of communication with CAPCOM. We have been offline for well over an hour now, and Steven would have informed me if we had any changes. We cannot foresee all possible outcomes. So, there you have it—an unexpected variable. As far as I see, this doesn't change our mission. We've been operating as an autonomous unit due to the length of time it takes for communications to transmit at this distance. It does not change our mission, but it takes on quite a different perspective. I will notify the entire crew should the situation change. Until then, carry on in the professional manner with which you've been conducting yourself. Bravo shift will carry on at this time, since Alpha shift has concluded."

Andrea looked at Pedro. "So, that's it. We're very much alone, thirty-five-million miles from Earth."

Pedro looked into her hazel eyes again and felt a familiar pain tug at his heart. "Yeah, I guess you heard the commander." Pedro was starting to have more feelings for Andrea than ever before. He liked her as a friend, he thought, then he thought no, it's more than that and she obviously liked him, too. They worked together in training like best of friends, often interpreting a look or an intonation before anyone else in the crew.

Andrea started mumbling. "No email, no communication with our families. That's going to be hard on them."

"Yeah, I guess so, but let's hope they get whatever the problem is, fixed, because it doesn't appear to be on our end. We are getting active responses from the reconnaissance orbiter and our communications satellites, so it's not us. The problem is with Earth."

"How could Earth be the problem?" Andrea looked away. "That doesn't make any sense."

Chapter 10
A... What?

According to the Fort Lauderdale Airport radar, the anti- satellite weapon known as an ASAT exited the water about a mile off Bob and Brian's twenty-seven-foot World Cat's port bow at approximately seventy mph. By the time the Miami International Airport radar picked it up, it was approximating a hundred-sixty mph. Thirty seconds later, Homestead Air Force Base spotted the anomaly exceeding two-hundred-fifty mph and climbing.

Key West Naval Air Station radar, having been alerted by Homestead Air Force Base, visualized it on radar as it broke the horizon approaching five-hundred mph and penetrated the ADIZ (Aircraft Detection and Identification Zone). First Lieutenant Raymond Juarez was a new radar technician fresh out of radar school. He was on his first assignment, and one of the few radar technicians on the base qualified to operate the new HP interferometer and infrared-equipped radar. Raymond watched as his system visualized the anomaly and split it into two images. The returns indicated heat, speed, and altitude all increasing. He was beginning to doubt his equipment until he heard Homestead copying his observations.

Colonel Barry Diggs (otherwise known as "Digger" by his friends of similar or higher rank) was notified that some kind of bird was flying at breakneck speed in his territory without documented or otherwise known authorization. And he wasn't happy. Heads were going to roll, and someone was going to lose their new rocket. He commanded that an all-ships-all-aircraft alert be sent out immediately to anything within three-hundred miles with corresponding latitude and longitude. Imaging was badly needed. Could he get a satellite on this thing? He ordered his support personnel to contact NORAD. This was not going to be an easy day, and after his previous night, he didn't need this BS.

Colonel Diggs arrived in the radar center just as Lt. Juarez was calling out the numbers, calmly registering the target's speed. "Approaching six-hundred miles per hour."

Colonel Barry Diggs demanded, "What is the location?" Everyone in the room turned toward the red-faced colonel, including Raymond, who quietly said, "Up. It's going straight up like a frickin' moon launch . . . uh . . . sir."

Both F-16s standing by in preflight readiness mode staged for immediate deployment were launched before Colonel Diggs had been notified. This was done just in case this was a valid target. They could always be recalled. They were removed from preflight readiness mode to active status within ten seconds of notification, airborne after sixty seconds, and achieved five- hundred mph with afterburner engaged less than four minutes after the alarm sounded. They had the "bogey" on both of their radars, but it looked weird. It was going straight up.

"Miami Command, Zulu. This is an unauthorized missile launch of unknown origin, you are tasked to take it out as soon as you obtain range. What is your range to target?"

Captain Robert Roberts, call sign "Zulu" (because he was always the last one to roll call), responded, "We are approximately ninety miles and closing."

Both F-16s broke Mach 1 at seven hundred forty mph. Miami Command replied, "I show you at angels thirty and climbing."

"Confirm angels thirty and climbing," Major Tobias, call sign "Jumper", verified.

"What is your range?"

"Not good. Bogey is exceeding Mach 2 and continuing to accelerate. Will pursue, Zulu."

Both F-16s were virtually completely vertical, trying to chase what looked like a rocket launched out of Cape Canaveral, but they weren't going to catch it. Apparently, it was heading into space. Miami Command hailed Captain Roberts again. "Zulu, Miami Command."

"Miami Command. This is Zulu," Captain Robert Roberts reported. "Approaching angels fifty. Return to base required prior to loss of apparatus."

They were out of gas. They had burned ten-thousand pounds of jet fuel in fifteen minutes and never even saw their target or came close enough to fire their missiles.

"Loss of apparatus is not an option. RTB (return to base) immediately," was the response from Miami Control.

They weren't allowed and had no desire to ditch their F- 16s in the Gulf Stream; they had to return before running out of fuel.

Colonel Barry Diggs couldn't believe what he'd seen in the radar room. As he headed back to his office, he also couldn't believe what he had to do. Oh, this is going to create a ton of paperwork, he thought. He had to make a phone call to Southern Command.

———

Admiral Thomas Fanning, Commander of Southern Command, was sitting in his office in Doral, Florida, clearing emails and trying to get caught up on his generous list of responsibilities. He came in early before the start of another hectic day. At 08:30 his phone rang, and he doubted his secretary was at her desk since it was café-con-leche time.

On the fourth ring, he picked up, sorry to give up the headway he was making with his emails. "Admiral Thomas Fanning here," he said gruffly, revealing a little more of his frustration than he would've liked.

"Admiral Fanning, this is Colonel Barry Diggs, Key West. We have a situation here . . ."

As soon as Admiral Fanning hung up the phone, he punched up the secure line for the Pentagon. His day had just taken on a whole new meaning.

"Joint Chiefs, this is General Taylor."

Admiral Fanning spoke without his usual greetings and chitchat. "Eugene, this is Tommy at Southern Command."

General Taylor knew by the tone of Tommy's voice that this was a serious call. He drew in a deep breath as he got ready for the bad news. "Yes, Tommy."

"Key West and Homestead scrambled a total of six F-16s less than thirty minutes ago to investigate an anomaly launched twenty miles off Fort Lauderdale. It appears to have been directed straight up into space. We've been in touch with NASA and Cape Canaveral, they knew nothing about it. NORAD has been alerted. It was faster than our F-16s and went off our radar in excess of Mach 2. I'm routing the electronic surveillance data, including

———

corresponding radar images to you immediately. We have a Coast Guard Cutter heading into the launch vicinity, ETA ten minutes. I will copy you as soon as we have more."

"I'm convening the Joint Chiefs immediately. Who knows about this?"

"Only me at South Com, probably most of Key West Joint Base by now, most of Homestead Air Force Base, and as far as I know, Miami and Fort Lauderdale radar operators tracked the target."

"Okay," General Taylor said, "send investigators to Fort Lauderdale and MIA radar operations under strict orders to investigate but not talk about the incident. Repeat, they are to reveal nothing. And make sure Key West and Homestead keep a lid on it until we know more. Update me the minute you know something. Anything further?"

"No, sir."

Chapter 11

Now You See Them – Now You...

KH-11 Kennan, one of the largest satellites ever put into orbit, run by the United States Department of Defense–NRO (National Reconnaissance Office), weighing in at forty-three thousand pounds, was no longer in existence after 12:12 Zulu. It experienced a rapid, unexpected disassembly due to a high-speed collision with what could only be described as a missile that had just left Bob and Brian's location approximately twenty miles East of Ft. Lauderdale. Now two scared, confused, retired firefighters, one with a bandage wrapped around his head, were on-board a United States Coast Guard Cutter Medium, giving their statements, their fishing boat in tow. Fishing was canceled for the rest of the day.

At 12:18 Zulu, TerreStar 1, one of the largest private communication satellites ever sent into orbit, experienced the same fate as KH-11 Kennan, totally taking everyone by surprise. This launch went completely undetected by Homeland Security or United States Coast Guard, the Department of Defense, the United States Air Force or any foreign defense systems of any kind. It was thought to have launched out of the middle of the Gulf of Mexico which could only be approximately triangulated to five hundred miles West of Key West, five hundred miles East of Tampico Mexico and about four hundred miles South of Port Fourchon, Louisiana via reverse trajectory modeling. It was never picked up on any radar due to the curvature of the Earth. Both water-to-air ASAT (Anti Satellite Weapon) missiles triggered similar responses from authorities, but virtually nothing could be done about either one. Neither rocket seemed to pose a threat to any territory of the United States. NORAD, Southern Command, the Joint Chiefs, nor Colonel Barry Diggs understood the implications of the rocket launch—not that there was anything they could do about it. The only thing the tracking stations could do was watch. No one understood what they were seeing or what was to follow.

Satellites are made of many different materials such as aluminum, titanium, plastics, silicone, glass, different epoxies, and exotic metals. TerreStar 1 had its own propulsion system and fuel which led to a significantly larger explosive event. Debris was sent in every direction in three-dimensional space at thousands of miles per hour. The International Space Station (ISS) had been damaged from debris smaller than a millimeter in diameter. Paint chips damaged the shuttle windows due to a collision at estimated speeds exceeding twelve thousand mph. Collision impact forces exponentially increased with speed. So, in effect, size didn't matter as much as speed of impact to do significant damage. The minimum speed required to maintain orbit and not fall back to Earth was seventeen thousand five hundred miles per hour, which was much faster than a bullet fired from a gun. Usually, the higher the orbit, the higher the speed required, especially if it was a geostationary orbit, such as the KH-11 Kennan.

The United States Space Force tracked all space debris over four inches via the United States Space Surveillance Network

(USSSN). There are over one million pieces of debris smaller than one centimeter, over 900,000 pieces of debris between one and ten centimeters, and 34,000 pieces of debris over ten centimeters, all thought to be space junk in low Earth orbit and growing daily. That was before the two satellites experienced their destruction, along with the speeding missiles that hit them. The resulting impacts created millions of new pieces of debris heading off in incalculable directions. The domino like knock-on effect was insult to injury: more collisions with more satellites creating more debris, which caused more collisions with more satellites. A real chain reaction was taking place. One satellite after another was being destroyed as the debris cloud slowly made its way around low Earth orbit.

This exact situation was postulated by NASA scientist Donald Kessler in 1978 and has since been labeled the Kessler syndrome— or Kessler Effect.

Within three minutes of the destruction of KH-11 Kennan, the alarms began sounding on the International Space Station (ISS), which had happened before. However, this time they were informed by Houston's Flight Control to batten down the hatches and immediately prepare for emergency evacuation.

This has never happened before! There was no time for the usual fully planned, organized, and coordinated orbital boost conducted by Houston. They had to get out of Dodge now!

As Commander Amhurst did his best to coordinate the emergency move to a higher predetermined orbit, the rest of the crew began emergency evacuation procedures. Since the largest pre-existing debris fields were in low earth orbit, it was thought that the best way to avoid collisions was to move to a higher orbit. The astronauts in the ISS knew exactly what this meant; it was one of their worst nightmares come to life. They would immediately secure and evacuate the ISS one compartment at a time and seal the hatch of each compartment as it was evacuated. Then, as fast as they could, they would get into their spacesuits, hunker down in the Dragon capsule, and hope for the best.

Typically, the ISS was in orbit around two hundred fifty miles above the Earth and weighed more than 100,000 pounds. Today, they were going to try to move that mass another two hundred fifty miles in a virtually uncontrolled ascent. Who knew where they would end up, but five hundred miles in low earth orbit was the goal, and they didn't have much time. Little did anyone know the new orbit would be of little help with what was heading their direction.

—

Chapter 12

United States Space Surveillance Network

Only one hour to go, and First Lieutenant Natasha Brent, USAF, was looking forward to going home and getting some sleep. She was new to this shift work stuff, and so far, it wasn't sitting with her too well. C shift was slowly starting to drift in for the 06:00 shift change, and she couldn't wait.

She had been in the Air Force for six years now, and just a couple of months ago, she eagerly accepted a position at the United States Space Surveillance Network. She had been in training for her new position for six weeks and had only been at the computer console for just six days. As far as she could tell, the job was boring, but fighting sleep during the night shift was tough, especially with the lights turned down to better help monitor the computer screens.

Natasha glanced up at Amanda, who was coming in to replace Todd. "Hi, Amanda. Good morning."

"Morning, Natasha. How was your shift?"

"You know—same old, same old. Wait…what was that? Something odd is happening. One of my satellites just like…where did it go? It just disappeared. Oh, my God. It's all over my screen! It's in pieces!" Natasha did something she never thought she would do in the quiet, peaceful, air-conditioned computer monitoring

---

surveillance room. She screamed.

The USSSN was quickly overwhelmed. The destruction of KH-11 Kennan alone was more new data than they could handle. When TerreStar 1 was destroyed, it was impossible to track everything. So instead of tracking individual pieces, they began tracking the debris fields as they spread out over thousands of miles at first, then millions of miles in three hundred sixty- degree space. The USSSN saw more debris as additional satellites collided with the remains from previous collisions. Some of the satellites were GPS navigation satellites, some were government defense satellites. There were communication satellites, some were private, some were British, French, Japanese, Chinese, Italian, Brazilian, and Russian, and they all suffered the same fate, and they all created more debris. As the debris fields grew, something started happening to the radar screens, worrying the technicians. Each of their screens became fuzzy and started to show less debris until all their screens slowly went snowy white.

Engineering was called to fix the problem. After they went through everything, listened to the story of what had happened, they reported back. The engineers and technicians learned it wasn't their equipment. Different radars were getting the same thing. The other radar sites reported back on their secure landlines, and, yes, they, too, were getting white-out screens with the worst interference they had ever seen, and there was nothing they could do about it. Worse yet, not even the engineers knew why.

"The radar screens are going white with some kind of massive return," one of the engineers quietly said to his partner.

What they didn't know or couldn't possibly know was that

the debris fields were creating a giant static charge on their own. They began interviewing the radar operators and monitors about the last thing they had seen. The engineers listened quietly as the technicians described the disappearance of the satellites, the creation of the debris fields, and how their screens slowly went white. One by one, the engineering teams filed out of the satellite surveillance room and into the adjoining conference room, then shut the door behind them.

The engineers knew what it was. The aluminum, silicone, plastic, rubber, titanium, exotic metals, and everything else satellites are made of, were mixing, and blending and rubbing and bumping each other at thousands of miles per hour, causing a static charge with multiple strengths and intensities, sometimes massive intensities. The debris and its static charge were acting like a curtain, quickly wrapping around the Earth and absorbing any radio waves that tried to penetrate it, thereby cutting Earth off from any incoming electronic communication or signal trying to leave Earth.

"It's not that we aren't seeing anything," one of the senior radar engineer technicians noted, "It's that we're seeing everything. It's like the Earth is enclosed in a giant Faraday cage from all that debris."

No satellite communication would be possible until it was cleared, if any survived. All space operations were effectively on their own, with no ability to communicate with anyone on the ground, and no one knew how to stop it or clean it up.

The President of the United States made an emergency address to all Americans on all television and radio stations and

---

social media.

A somber President looked into the television camera. "I just left the Joint Chiefs. We were meeting regarding what I am reporting to you now. We are in a de facto state of war. We just don't know with whom, as yet. Two major American satellites, one belonging to the United States Department of Defense—which served untold American interests far and wide—and an American communications satellite were both just d—" All television screens went white with static.

All commercial airborne aircraft were contacted via their VHF radios to make it to the nearest appropriate airport and land immediately. All private and commercial aircraft were grounded for the unforeseen future. Pilots following their GPS guidance systems suddenly started receiving gibberish. They were useless. The GPS system was failing. Until further notice, air travel would be "Emergency Use Only".

Fortunately, the low angle local radar still worked just fine. Hundreds of thousands of people were marooned at airports across the world, many of them with no way to get home. Rental cars sold out quickly then the credit card systems began to fail. Rental cars were no longer an option to get home. Cell phones wouldn't maintain connections and eventually became unusable. And this was only the beginning.

The United States Coast Guard began emergency radio transmissions to all ships at sea. They were told via their VHF radios to change to paper charts if they were within radio range. The fax machines on these behemoths of the sea went quiet, and communications with their headquarters were lost. Radio was the only way to communicate since cell phones were down, satellite phones weren't working, and VHF radios are only good for "line of sight".

All shipping ports prohibited new berthing of ships that weren't already docked, since GPS navigation was unusable, and most ports filled up immediately once the trouble started. The vessels in port were not allowed to leave port until further notice. The internet crashed, and banking transactions started to slow to a crawl as the cell phone network continued to fail. Stock trading of any kind stopped overnight. Most purchase orders were sent and received via the internet, so no trading of any kind was able to continue. The stock market went into an immediate headlong dive with panic selling, and then it went quiet without the internet. The few trading companies that were hard-wired were not allowed by the SEC to continue trading as all trading slowed to a crawl, then stopped completely. Retail prices started to skyrocket when people started panic buying. The grocery stores in all major US cities and most of Europe emptied out as if a worldwide hurricane was imminent.

The ATM machines stopped working, and credit cards were worthless, making cash the only means for making purchases for food and gasoline. All trains across the country were forced to a crawl, their computer-operated control systems crashing due to dependency on the internet and their GPS systems. All train conductors were forced to reduce their speed to ten miles per hour, and once they reached the nearest terminal, they were forced by safety officials to stay there. No planes and no trains.

Chapter 13

This is going to get interesting

While everyone was focused on the communication issue, Commander Carrigan was busy doing his rounds, checking in with each of his officers, and making sure no other changes had occurred. He explained that their logs needed to be complete and more detailed than ever since CAPCOM–Houston wasn't getting daily updates, and their automated systems were no longer communicating.

What the devil is going on with Earth? he thought. Now we really are alone, this is going to get interesting.

He considered how his crew, no longer able to communicate with family or friends, would be affected. This was the most professional crew he had ever seen assembled in one place, but still, the loss of all comms hadn't been considered any further than the loss of an individual radio or some system failure. He knew the problem was back on Earth.

Twenty-seven-year-old Andrea Tripp was having a sudden surge in popularity amongst her peers. Some people would look at her funny and walk away giggling. Some people wanted to know what it was like to be the first to walk on the surface of Mars. She would just laugh and say, "I'm glad it's over." Others who hadn't been on the first EVA wanted to know what the Martian surface was like. "Crunchy" was the most common answer given.

Everybody's stride on *Staten* was a little strange or weird due to the new low gravity, which would take time to get used to. Since the gravity on Mars was approximately one-third that of the Earth, astronauts tended to hop a little. The whole crew was trying to adjust in different ways. Some did a kind of shuffle, some did a scoot, and it was rather humorous. It made the three hundred sixty- degree jogging path designed for use in zero gravity very difficult and interesting and maybe a little dangerous—if they were courageous enough to try it.

Even though communications with Earth were down, everyone on *Staten* was in a good mood now that they had made it safely to Mars. And they were all sure that the communication thing was going to get sorted out sooner or later. Even CAPCOM couldn't do anything to help them if they needed it immediately, so what difference was it in the short run?

Day Two on Mars was a full-blown schedule. Commander Carrigan had reorganized the shifts a bit, rotating some people around and reducing C shift in personnel since more crew were needed during the EVAs. And there were fewer positions requiring attention at night now that they had safely landed on Mars. Eight astronauts were staged for ready deployment, while eight astronauts were sent out on an EVA to verify the effectiveness and productivity of Starship I and Starship II.

They needed to off-load another Mars rover and its trailer from *Staten* for moving equipment around. They then needed to revisit *Starship IV* to see if they could get the hatch open on the far side and get some pictures of the condition of the supplies inside.

———

They also needed to set up the solar voltaic cells with the stands to start charging the battery-powered equipment, including *Staten*.

Commander Carrigan was always around doing something or checking on something. He could be found moving about *Staten* even in the wee hours of the morning, then disappearing in some hatch, checking inventories, fuel pressure, water, food, life support, or atmospheric measurements. It was amazing how he seemed to be omnipresent at all hours of the day, some crew members thought it to be a little creepy. Or he might be found sitting in comms with Steven or working with Carl, the engineer of all engineers. Carl knew everything about hardware, metals, components, welding, tools, and forces.

Commander Carrigan continued to consider their situation from every angle, constantly apprising himself with the situation. He never wanted to be surprised by a situation such as the loss of all communication with Earth. Occasionally things simply could not be predicted.

Never in history had men and women ever been so far from the place they called home, literally at work twenty-four hours a day. Perhaps the early seagoing vessels were away from home for years at a time, the conditions back then were close to slave labor. That was a different time.

No one in his crew was married—at least not legally. It had been decided that two years separated from a spouse would be devastating to the emotional bonds of a permanent relationship and could cause undue mental hardship and crew moral issues. They may have a long-term partner, but that was up to them. NASA always had a no-comment status on sex. If it was brought up, all they would say was that all astronauts are professionals and adults. That's it. It was also an aspect of their training that humans have a strange tendency to subgroup within the team, which can cause division. That's why there were no permanent A, B, or C shifts. That's also why Commander Carrigan constantly rotated people through different positions, to limit people creating territories, or assuming command of public spaces and defining a workspace as theirs. All crew members were taught during the psychological training aspect to stay aware of the potential for personal relationships which could turn from cordial and supportive to protective and exclusive. It was reiterated constantly that every crew member needed every other crew member to make the mission a success and to stay alive. Every member of the crew had strong points and every member had weak points. A semblance of humility was imperative.

Being on Mars made the shift rotation a little easier, but it also made it a little harder. Only Carl and the comms team were rarely rotated, and that was a problem he had to consider.

I think I need to talk to Carl and Steven, he thought. It's time to send them out on an EVA as well. And I guess I should schedule myself into the EVA roster.

Starships I and II were a mile off to the northeast where the current EVA team was reporting that water, O2, hydrogen, and methane were, in fact, being produced as NASA had reported prior to their departure. This was great news. The methane rate of production was within the parameters of expectation, also excellent news.

That was one big worry off Commander Carrigan's mind.

———

The autonomous systems producing the O2 and hydrogen obtained water from the atmosphere. When the sun warmed Mars over 32°F, the ice in the soil began to melt and convert almost immediately to humidity or gas, which the systems on Starships I and II condensed into drinkable water. When the temperature- controlled water tanks were close to full, they start to break it down, via electrolysis, into hydrogen and oxygen. They're triggered to do this by a water-activated switch near the top of the tank, so the tank always stays nearly full. This would act as a primary water source for *Starship X*'s water supply system when it runs low. However, this would only work during the Martian summer, when the atmospheric temperature usually rose above 32°F during the day in Valles Marineras.

During the Martian winter, the temperature never rose above 32°F, even in Valles Marineras on the warmest of winter days. Even the autonomously heated water in the water tanks would freeze in the water lines before reaching *Staten*. *Staten*'s water tanks held enough water to maintain twenty-one astronauts for about six months. It was understood that for at least three months of the year, they would be completely cut off from their water source. But first, they needed to find and install the water lines. They were listed on the inventory schematic. But they were about a mile away from Starships I and II. NASA had packed the water lines in different starships. The assumption was if one of the starships didn't make the trip the other starships would have redundant inventory of life supporting supplies such as the water lines. They were completely reliant on the fact that starships I and II were manufacturing water

---

and their return fuel.

Each starship was normally in communication with a computer at MM1 command center inside Johnson Space Center, but they were also designed to work autonomously, for a period, in case of a communication disruption like what they were experiencing now.

Commander Carrigan was in his office reviewing the operations procedures for Starships I and II. How long would they stay active on their own before requiring a signal or command? He was hoping indefinitely, but he didn't want to find out after they shut down. Could they be started back up if they shut down? He was pretty sure Carl could do it with some help. Still, he had thousands of pages of data to search through just on Starship I. He wasn't going to leave the lives of his crew open to chance.

Chapter 14

Mars Sol 3 – Starship IV

Every Starship from I to X had parts, tools, and redundancies on board to protect MM1 from failure, including multiple redundancies for communications. Commander Carrigan instructed Communication Specialist Steven Henderson to evaluate the other remaining starships to see if they were communicating with Earth or each other—or anything. The answer was no. They were actively pinging, but receiving no response.

"If they are actively pinging, are they asking for something? Some direction? Or are they just saying I'm here?" Commander Carrigan queried.

Steven replied, "The latter. That's what they do when they don't receive any guidance twenty-four hours after landing. It's like Big Ben, but instead of every hour, it's every twenty-four. It doesn't take much battery to send out a ping once a day, and if someone is listening, it'll help them focus their dishes or modulate the frequency if needed. It's also pretty convenient to know when they're going to ping, so you know exactly when to listen for it instead of listening for twenty-four hours a day to pick it up."

Commander Carrigan thought to himself then looked at Steven. "Will they ever shut down if they don't eventually get a response?"

Steven frowned a little. "Hmmm . . . let's see. My initial answer to your question would've been no, they won't ever shut

---

down. Then, you know, that word 'ever' is a very long time. Let's change the time frame and think about what the computer programmers were thinking with the design. The starships were designed to always be in communication with MM1 Houston. If I were designing the computers for the starships, what logic would I follow if the starships cannot or do not get a reply from MM1 Command? You know what I would do, Commander? I would program the starships to continue with their daily duties and actively ping as scheduled unless the batteries go below twenty percent."

Commander Carrigan looked up at the ceiling, as if trying to see something that wasn't there, rubbing his five o'clock beard. "Why twenty percent? Why not ten?"

"If the batteries get too low," Steven said, "you could threaten some of the life-support systems needed to keep the computers and other equipment alive and functioning. If they power all the way down and completely discharge, then some of the more sophisticated and sensitive systems that need to be kept warm, including the batteries themselves, would be subject to the ambient temperature. Normally, that isn't a problem, but during the winter months or during a dust storm, the deep cold of, let's say a hundred degrees below zero Fahrenheit, may crack or break anything that has even the smallest moisture, condensation, or liquid cooling systems. And it would never work again. Also, some of the systems require a bit of power to restart. If the power gets too low, booting them back up may be a bit tricky, if not impossible."

Commander Carrigan stood and paced slowly behind his desk. "How long do you think it would take for the batteries to drain to twenty percent?"

———

Steven had to think about that one. "I guess that would depend on what functions they're programmed to perform autonomously, and the weather."

"Okay, so different starships will drop to twenty percent at different times depending on the power drain?"

"Yes, I would think so, but I'm pretty sure we're talking years here, not months."

Commander Carrigan considered this as he slowly stood and began pacing behind his chair. "Are you sure about that?"

"Well, no, I didn't program them, and I wasn't involved in any aspect of systems designs, nor were any of us trained on what to do if we or any of the starships lost long-term communication with MM1 Command. It was never considered. But that's how I would've done it."

"Is there any way to know which starships will lose power first?"

"Well, we could send Carl out to evaluate battery strength on one of the next EVAs, but in all honesty, it's really too early for that, at least at the moment."

Commander Carrigan continued his slow pacing for a few seconds, then took his chair again, leaning forward on his elbows. "Could we answer their ping? You know, figure out what frequency they're listening to, and tell them..."

"No, we can't," Steven said. "Well, yes, we could, but they'll be looking for the correct authorization to start responding, and who knows what they might do without the correct authentication sequence. Probably nothing but, I'm pretty sure each one has a separate authorization code or administrative access code and frequency."

"You were reading my mind."

Steven smiled quizzically. "Of course, they would be protected from some random remote access code, but perhaps we could do something manually. The computer programmers wouldn't expect anyone to just walk up to them on Mars, open the door, and start trying to fire up the operational systems."

"Access code?"

Steven shrugged. "Probably. Every computer guy locks his stuff up."

With a heavy sigh, Commander Carrigan admitted, "Yes, I'm sure you're right."

Chapter 15

Mars Sol 4 – *Starship IV*

The Mars Reconnaissance Orbiter (MRO) is still an operational satellite circling Mars, launched in 2005. Built by Lockheed Martin in coordination with NASA's Jet Propulsion Laboratory, it was truly a testament of durability and the dedication and hard work of the engineers of both operations.

The MRO constantly circled Mars, taking pictures with different high-resolution cameras, spectrometers, and radar, providing excellent detail for weather data, mapping, and potential landing locations. The MRO produced beautiful pictures of *Staten* and all nine of the other starships, which Commander Carrigan and his teams used as a detailed map to plan their EVAs.

The landings were remarkably close to the planned layout by NASA. The third EVA was planned and organized. B shift suited up while C shift prepared as ready backup with two personnel from A shift. C shift had been reduced to a crew of only four personnel since they had previously been the midnight shift until this morning. The Mars car and its accompanying trailer were used to haul equipment to the fallen *Starship IV*. It had been determined that *Starship IV* had fallen over after safely landing with two of its six legs in a slight depression. If one leg had landed in the depression, it wouldn't have fallen over, but two were enough to start the movement. The momentum took the one hundred eighty- foot rocket ship the rest of the way over as it settled and slowly rolled onto its side.

The onboard radar-lidar system should have recognized the variance before it authorized the final landing sequence. It was easy to see while standing next to its final resting position that from a visual perspective, the ground looked flat. It wasn't until they walked around the landing zone that they saw a gradual hill consisting mostly of sand and dust.

MS Ashanti Sumbika realized that the landing engines might have created the depression *Starship IV* fell into. As the thrusters blew away the lighter sand on one side, it probably created the uneven surface, which explained why the landing sensors didn't pick it up before landing; they couldn't "see" through all of the dust and debris that the thrusters created upon landing.

Ashanti explained this to Steven over her helmet mic, and she took pictures from her helmet cam, so they could be entered into the log along with a report of the incident for MM1 Command. This situation probably hadn't been considered while designing the starships.

There were three primary designs for the starships on this mission. *Staten* was the only crewed starship. Starships I and II were the tanker starships that produced in-situ vital resources and carried a small amount of cargo. The supply starships III through IX carried the bulk of the vital supplies and equipment, which rounded out the four main design platforms.

Carl White, acting lead for today's EVA, reevaluated the safety of attempting to make entry into *Starship IV*, and after a few minutes, decided that the enormous starship was stable, secure, and would not shift or roll. All the high-pressure fuel and propulsion tanks appeared to be intact, and their integrity was not at risk. At least not at risk right now. Things change.

The EVA crew set up the ladder they brought with them from *Staten*. After making sure the ladder was safe, Carl climbed up and attempted to open the hatch thirty feet off the ground as two crew members held the ladder to stabilize it. Carl rotated the manual hatch with a tool that he brought with him from *Staten* and popped it open. It looked pretty good inside since everything was shrink-wrapped and thoroughly strapped in using nylon netting attached to aluminum framing for the violent launch and subsequent landing. All the stored items would have to be manually carried off. There were a lot of supplies.

Thank God for the lower gravity here on Mars, Carl thought. I don't see anything permanently damaged, other than the ship itself. How the hell are we going to get into the other starships? Starships I and II were activated two years before, so they're up and running. But the others have not been activated from MM1 Command? It is not like we can click on a manual switch or access panel at ground level, and I've never heard of any kind of remote access or alternative means of initiating startup. MM1 was supposed to activate them all upon *Staten*'s arrival, but apparently, they didn't have time to do this before communication was lost. Oh, this could get bad.

He off-loaded another set of solar panels and passed them down the ladder to Haratu.

The more Carl thought about it, the more he didn't like it. Was it possible that they had everything they needed but couldn't gain access? The access hatches were one hundred fifty feet in the air. They didn't have any ladders that would go that high, and a fall from that height would probably be fatal, even in Mars's reduced gravity.

I have to talk to Commander Carrigan, he thought. Sure, he's aware of this situation, but he hasn't spoken about it with me or the crew yet. There's probably a good reason why he hasn't.

Carl calculated how long they could last on Mars without any more supplies than were on *Staten* and starships I and II and whatever they could carry off *Starship IV*. He knew that starships I and II didn't carry much in the way of supplies since they were tankers and had on-board water and methane making equipment and storage. As he calculated, he started to get nervous.

Meanwhile, Commander Carrigan was in his study with Steven, who had been relieved by Chief Pilot Mary Pfeiffer.

After listening to the telemetry replay off the automated recording on the *Staten*'s computer, he said, "So far, all we know is CAPCOM seemed a little preoccupied in the last three minutes, by my estimation, prior to loss of signal. This is unusual for them. When we received the final transmission that said, 'Communications may be compromised.'"

Steven nodded in agreement. "Yes, that is unusual, I agree. But then again, there is nothing 'usual' about this situation. And there's nothing further to indicate any issues after that. No explanation, nothing."

"No, I've been over them at least ten times, but that's all we have to go on. Frustrating!"

"So, what do you think happened?"

Steven sat back in his chair, absently scratching his head.

"What do I think?"

"Yes. What do you think?" Commander Carrigan asked. "Your best guess."

Steven had been a little nervous during this chat in Commander Carrigan's study, but now he was confused. "You want me to guess?"

Commander Carrigan had never guessed on anything related to the mission, and he was pretty sure Carl hadn't either. They always dealt with facts, not fiction. Commander Carrigan let out a sigh. "I've been thinking about it, and since we don't have any details, I need your best guess. I very much value your insight at times like this, Steven." It's always good to get a different perspective, a different view or angle.

Commander Carrigan took on a sober look. "Look, it's going on three days since we lost communication. I know you and the crew have been thinking about this, too. What on earth could've happened to lose communication for almost three days? You know it couldn't have been a power outage or some strange power surge. Besides that, the Beam Wave system is down, too. You know as well as I do that it isn't just CAPCOM–Houston or one of the three Deep Space Network systems in three different countries all around the Earth. All have automated back-up- power-generating abilities and nine different transmission and receiving dishes on multiple frequencies. So, this situation simply should not, theoretically could not, happen. Yet here we are. So, what do you imagine is going on—

or could have happened back on Earth?"

"Well, you're right. I have been thinking about it, and of course I'm not the only one on the crew wondering about it. Everyone has their thoughts or ideas—a nuclear attack or a particularly strong solar flare. I think those ideas are both wrong. We would've been told via at least one of the Deep Space Network dishes that something like that was happening, and the Space Weather Network would've had plenty of time to warn us of a strong solar flare. So, I was wondering about an electromagnetic pulse attack. But again, that wouldn't take out all of the communication systems around the world."

"So, where does that leave us?"

"We're sticking to protocol," Steven said. "Attempt to make contact with CAPCOM on all frequencies, every hour on the hour, twenty-four seven. Maybe they can hear us, and we just can't hear them."

Steven sat through the silence as he watched Commander Carrigan think it through.

"Obviously," he continued, "the other starships aren't receiving any data or signal, either, or they would've been taken out of hibernation mode. We've put up three more dishes for improved signal strength, and we're able to communicate, no problem with the MRO. No, CAPCOM knew something was up on Earth, or they wouldn't have reported possibly compromised communications. Even they knew it wasn't us. They could see something was happening—they just didn't have time to explain it. How is this even possible?"

"If you come up with any more ideas on the communication issues or concerning the other starships' situation, please let me

<hr>

know. I need to bring up these issues with the crew soon. It seems ludicrous that all the supplies we need are in the immediate vicinity, yet we have no way of getting to them," Commander Carrigan regretted having to admit.

"Yes, sir. I'll start going over the MM1 procedures and see if I can find a back door or alternative means of entry into the starships. A good 'ol combo lock or a simple keypad would sure have been handy right about now. We need those supplies pretty soon."

"Yes, we do," Commander Carrigan said. "Thank you, Steven. I don't think you realize how much I value your feedback." Steven was surprised to hear the commander say this in person. He usually gave feedback in group settings, and this felt personal and gratifying. It also spoke volumes about their predicament. Previously, he hadn't really considered how dire their situation may be.

"You're welcome," was all Steven could say, which sounded a little shallow to him, but now he felt even more motivated to search the voluminous procedures manual, which could take days, even with the computer's help.

Chapter 16

Bob and Brian

After Bob saw the missile take off, and even before they fully realized what had happened, they were being hailed by a very aggressive, fully dressed-out Coast Guard crew. The machine gun on the bow of the response boat was fully loaded, and it was aimed at them. It was manned by a guy who looked like he was going to war. The Coast Guard landing party of four enlisted men and one officer covered head to foot in blue camo, bullet proof vests and helmets, despite the ninety-degree heat, pulled up along-side their boat, shouting orders at them from a rigid hull inflatable boat. Bob had been attending to the cut on his incapacitated partner's head and didn't realize the Coast Guard was shouting orders at him. His ears were still ringing from the overwhelming noise of the launch and his focus was on Brian.

Coast Guard Station Fort Lauderdale crew members weren't happy with them. Bob hadn't returned the calls on the radio or acknowledged the loud hailer mounted on the front of the response boat. They could see he was on the deck of his boat, but they didn't know what he was doing. This made the small fishing boat and its two occupants extremely suspicious, and potentially dangerous.

The two men were below the freeboard and the railings on the deck of their boat, effectively, but not intentionally, hidden out of sight, and not responding to multiple hails or to repeated attempts at communication. The Coasties simply didn't know what to expect, so they were prepared for anything. It was a good thing Bob didn't stand up unexpectedly with his fishing pole in his hand or anything else for that matter. The Coast Guard crew had their hands on their sidearms as they rapidly boarded the twenty-seven-foot catamaran and surrounded the two men.

As he was being handcuffed with zip ties and taken into custody, Bob yelled, "What do you guys want? My buddy needs help!"

The Coast Guard officers began to realize that Bob was basically deaf, and Brian was borderline conscious, if that. They were able to get Bob to quiet down as they started asking an endless line of questions, using a whiteboard once they were on the larger, forty-five-foot vessel. Background checks were performed, and their stories matched what was known about them. The fishing vessel's registration was current, and it was inspected from bow to stern and put in tow behind the Coast Guard Response Boat-Medium. Fishing was canceled for the day.

Because they had both been firefighters, their fingerprints had been entered into the federal databases when they had gotten their State of Florida Fire Certifications and they seemed to be exactly who they said they were and doing exactly what they said they were doing. The zip ties were released.

Brian wasn't much help to the interrogating officers. He appeared to have a concussion, and the Coast Guard officer in charge called for Fire Rescue to meet them at the dock. A much more empathetic Coast Guard EMT applied a new bandage to Brian's head after inspecting the injury. She used an ace bandage to hold a bag of ice on his injury which was swelling up like a hard-boiled egg on the side of his head.

Bob and Brian were delivered to Fifteenth Street Marina, where a federal Marshal accompanied them to Broward Health Medical Center in the back of a Fort Lauderdale Rescue unit. They would stay in custody for at least another two hours. After repeating their story to some fifty people, seemingly from a dozen different federal agencies. They were finally cleared as witnesses and were reminded numerous times that the federal officers may be back if they felt like it.

Their boat was tied up to the dock outside the Fort Lauderdale police station and marina, where it would be inspected again by more federal employees, some with cameras on the end of long rigid expandable extensions they shoved up into the hulls, some with heavy duty magnets, some with rubber hammers and some with stethoscopes. They even paid the local marina to pick the boat up in the air, so it could be inspected again even after the divers had inspected the entire bottom in the murky water at the dock.

The doctors wanted to keep Brian overnight, but he insisted that he was okay and would check in with his personal physician in the next few days. The doctors were not convinced but when they heard both of their stories and watched the stream of Federal employees coming and going into the ER, they were rather happy to let them both go home, as was the hospital staff, after all his baseline vitals were stable. Besides, they were getting concerned about what just came over the news. Apparently, these guys were witnesses.

Brian ended up spending the rest of the day resting with his wife at home who had to endure the endless repetitive questions a concussed patient asks. "What happened? Why does my head hurt?

———

Where is Bob? Who were those guys? Why am I here? Shouldn't I be at work? What happened? Where is Bob? What happened? Why does my head hurt? Who were those guys?"

Chapter 17

Day One

After making sure Brian was as comfortable as possible at home. Bob was watching the television in his living room, thoroughly exhausted from the day's events. The President was about to make a national presentation or announcement, or something. He thought, it must be important. What could it be about? The speech didn't last long. He suddenly faded out as did every other channel. His Wi-Fi went offline. He had an old television antenna in the attic; after hooking it up he was able to pick up two of the local stations. At first the tv commentators and news crews seemed to be as confused as everyone else but slowly a broad picture began to develop.

At first, the news crews reported and repeated the entirety of the president's speech, which was that the United States had been attacked and one or more of our satellites had been destroyed against international agreements. Then they started covering something they had never done before: their own news services that the news station subscribed to for national and international coverage were going offline one at a time. They were losing connection with their affiliates, and now it seems that GPS services were becoming unreliable, the internet was very slow and seemed to stutter and pause periodically. People were complaining that cell phone connections seemed to be failing or wouldn't connect at all. The news commentators began pulling out their cell phones, staring at them and poking at the screens. Then looking at the camera blank faced. "No, our phones are no longer working," they reported. Not just one service provider, it seemed that everyone's phones in the news studio were not maintaining a connection and they had a variety of service providers on different phones. The manager of the station piped in offscreen and reported that the only station satellite phone used for extremely remote reporting wasn't working, either.

Bob didn't need to hear anymore. He immediately ran out to the grocery store to get supplies. Bread, cold cuts, peanut butter, beer, 2-12 packs of sodas, some batteries, water, corn chips, potato chips, beef jerky, 6 bottles of nuts, some candy bars, a few different kinds of crackers, breakfast bars, a selection of soups, chili and some miscellaneous items. He bought enough for a few weeks to a month's supply. Then he thought of Brian and Lisa and tried to call them. His phone wasn't working. He looked around the store and saw other people and their children looking at their cell phones. Some were talking for a moment or two then they were staring at their phones. Bob didn't know what Brian and Lisa might need so he grabbed some of the same stuff that he had already in his cart, just more of it and added some jelly and honey and more beer. He suddenly got an idea and put his cart in line to check out and quickly stepped outside to look around the parking lot. People were standing in the parking lot and on the sidewalks staring at their phones as if they couldn't walk without their phone. While checking out, the grocery clerk said that their credit card and ATM machines had just stopped working but they were hurrying out the old impression-style credit card machines, he just had to show his driver's license. Bob paid and pushed his cart out against a steady flow of people coming into the store, more than usual. Boy, am I glad I got here when I did, he thought. He filled up his tank with gas, having to pay cash, then ran over to Brian's house. Traffic was heavier than the usual crazy Ft. Lauderdale traffic. He decided to take the back roads as much as possible.

Brian's wife had already gone to the store asking an elderly neighbor, Mrs. Sandoval, to sit with Brian. She had asked Mrs. Sandoval if she needed anything from the grocery store as she ran off. Neither one seemed to know what was going on. Bob threw his perishable items in the freezer and the refrigerator and stayed to see if Brian had an old antennae or old tv wire he could jury-rig to the tv to try to get some kind of signal. Bob didn't mind hanging out, his wife had died a few years back and he only had to look after his kitty, Tiger, who seemed pretty content on his own. When he checked on Brian, he was watching an old NASA video. Brian's face clouded over, and he said in obvious confusion, "Where you been, ol' buddy?"

Well, Bob thought, *at least he recognizes me.*

Three hours later, Bob had taken the elderly Mrs. Sandoval back to her house and he was watching a very grainy news broadcast with a beer in his hand when a disheveled Lisa poured into the kitchen through the garage door out of breath and carrying grocery bags. "It's crazy out there!" she yelled." "I was almost in three accidents; the grocery stores are mobbed. They are about to close. There is nothing left on the shelves. Even the convenience stores are crazy!" Right then the lights blinked and came back on. Bob looked up, then at the tv, and said, "Look, uh, we don't know what we may be in for here. I am going to check on Tiger and make sure he has food and water for a few days. I'll be back."

Bob ran home and looked in on Tiger, who just looked at

him like he thought Bob might possibly be crazy, which was normal for Tiger. He plugged the tub in the bathroom and put a piece of saran under the plug to make sure it didn't leak, then started to fill it with cold water. It's starting to look like we're in for another hurricane, he thought. He emptied the fridge into a few grocery bags and tossed them in the cab of the truck. He hauled the portable 7kw generator, which was about as much as he could possibly lift and jerked it with a grunt into the back of his Silverado. The two five-gallon containers of gasoline and all the groceries he had bought earlier went in next. From his gun cabinet he grabbed his 9mm with two full clips and the pistol grip twelve-gauge with a box of shells. Remembering to grab the two high intensity flashlights, a pillow and a few bed sheets, he turned off the tub and headed out the door. At the last minute he thought to grab the two empty five-gallon water bottles that were in the pantry. As he turned to leave, he caught a glimpse of a picture of his wife just as he was about to close the door.

Marcie, the love of his life, had been on her way home on I-95 when she was hit in the right rear quarter panel. Her Jeep rolled over multiple times and impacted the barrier on the driver's side. At least it was quick, he thought to himself for the thousandth time. He regretted not spending more time with her. You never know when your loved ones are going to be taken away from you, he thought. He had heard that hundreds of times. But you don't know it until you live it, he realized. Brian took Marcie's picture and sat on the couch wondering what she would do in this situation or what she would say. He suddenly remembered Marcie's mother. She was in an assisted living facility not too far away. He would visit her every two weeks to check on how she was doing. It was time to visit her again.

Bob only lived two miles away from Brian and Lisa, but it took him 20 minutes to get back. The sun had gone down and some of the traffic lights were blinking four-way red. The larger intersections were a matter of guessing who was going to let you through. Some of the cars just throttled through the blacked-out traffic lights as if they weren't even there and they had some kind of emergency. As Bob backed into Brian's driveway, the lights blinked off, then back on again. I had better turn off the air conditioner, at least until the generator is set up, he thought; then he realized that he hadn't turned off his own air conditioner. He hid the two guns in the bottom of Brian's toolbox, locked it, pocketed the key and carried the groceries in with his pillow.

Lisa looked at his pillow, smiled and said, "Well, I guess you're staying the night."

"Yeah, if that's ok. I am afraid things might get a little crazy. I brought food, a generator and some supplies that might help. You know, just in case. Will you take me in for the night?"
"Of course, anytime. You know you're welcome anytime. You know where the spare bedroom is. Make yourself at home."

They filled the fridge and put away the food that he brought and put the generator in the garage, making sure to shut the garage door and latch it. "Generators are worth their weight in gold in a storm," he'd heard someone say. While filling up Brian and Lisa's tub and securing the plug, Lisa yelled out that the bath towels were in the hallway closet. He came back into the living room and sat down.

Lisa scowled, saying, "Thought you were going to take a

bath," as she made an attempt to adjust the tv antenna to get a better picture.

Brian had joined her on the couch.

Bob, looking confused, said, "No, why?" Then he started to smirk a little and said, "You know. Hurricane precautions."

She looked at Bob, then at Brian, and said, "You firefighters," with a knowledgeable grin.

The news was reporting that the power companies were having rolling blackouts right when the power went out and everything went black.

"I am going to turn off the air conditioner. It is hard on the compressor to keep starting and stopping like this," he said. He unplugged the refrigerator as well.

Brian said in frustration as he scratched his head, "Hey who keeps fucking with the lights?"

Lisa groaned, "Ok, I'll get the flashlights."

Bob put one of the high intensity flashlights by the front door and one by the back door while commenting that he thought it best to leave the generator securely in the garage and off for the night and start it tomorrow after the sun comes up. "We only have a few days of gasoline, and it is sure to get hot tomorrow."

As Lisa put different battery powered lights around the living room, it somewhat reminded Bob of candlelight, but it was just enough to see. She said in a weirdly quiet way with one raised eyebrow, "Why do you think this is so serious? I mean, yeah, people are acting like a category four hurricane is about to hit, but how bad can it get?"

"Ok. People are probably just frightened because of the

president's speech and the rolling blackouts so far, which was pretty serious on its own. The president said, 'We are at war, we just don't know with whom.'"

"We have not been at war for a very long time. Of course, that is enough to frighten John Q. Public on its own. Nobody likes it when they don't know what is going on. Then what happened?" "He just faded out and the screen went white with static.

That can happen anytime."

"Yeah, but what else happened?"

"We lost the cable and internet, and the power keeps going out. That happens all the time, especially in Florida."
"Yeah, but what did the news say also happened? I think this is the key."

"That cell phone service seems to be interrupted and that some satellite stopped working?"

"There was more to it than that. The president said that a satellite was shot down. That was the act of war he was talking about. Then we lost our cable and internet. And it is not just here at your house. I don't have cable or internet at my house, either, and the last thing I knew, the cell phones were losing service. Not just my phone or yours but the news said that 'cell phone service in general—all cell phones are losing service.' That started to make me think while you were getting groceries. The cell phone companies can no longer stay in service, the internet is offline, national news feeds are down, at the grocery store the credit card reader was down. I am sure it was not working when you were there, either. The cashier said that the customers trying to get money out of the ATMs were complaining to her that the ATMs aren't working, and they couldn't get cash, and now the power is off. What does that tell you? All these services are crashing, what does that mean, Lisa?"

Lisa thought for a few minutes, putting it all together. "Wow, I didn't put everything together like that. I was just getting groceries because we needed some things, and it seemed like a good time to get them. Now that you put it that way in one big picture…you're saying these things are all related?"

"Think about it, Lisa. It is way too much of a coincidence to have all of this happen at once. Maybe losing power or internet or even cable at the same time could be coincidental but first the missile, then a satellite is shot down, then the president declaring war on who knows, then the cable, then the internet, then the news feeds, the phones, the ATM's, the power flickering on and off. What does a satellite being shot down and the U.S. declaring war have to do with all of this other stuff? I don't know, but it all has to be related somehow. It seems like some kind of electronic warfare to me. You know as firefighters we train constantly to try to limit or at least become familiar with some of the variables or hiccups that might occur or get in the way while we are doing our jobs. I have a feeling that no one has trained for whatever we are experiencing or about to experience. So far only a very small percentage of our neighbors understand this. Those were the ones buying out all of the inventory of the grocery stores this afternoon, so what do you think it will be like when the average Joe citizen realizes he can't use his ATM card or get cash anywhere or even buy food? They may think it is all some kind or a mean trick, or worse, an organized conspiracy against the little guy. All we can do is try to prepare for whatever comes next. Whatever that means. All I know is that our standard of living is threatened. Goods and services are sure to be unavailable for the immediate future. People don't like it when they are uncomfortable or in pain or worse. They tend to act irrationally." Bob spent the night on the couch.

Chapter 18

Day Two

Bob was up most of the night. He could hear shooting off in the distance but nothing too close. Vandals, thieves, gangs, looters, undisciplined kids, joy riders, and just stupid people were taking advantage of both the power outage and loss of the phone system.

The rising sun had awakened him right after he had finally drifted off to sleep. He spent the night on the couch not wanting to leave the doors unmanned. He had finally stripped down to his undies and a T-shirt. "It must be 90° in here," he muttered to himself. His T-shirt was stuck to his back. He could feel sweat running down his neck. He finally went to the linen closet, grabbed a full-size towel and put it on the couch so he wouldn't soak it with his sweat. He thought of the spare clothes in the cab of his truck, but he didn't want to wake everyone. Even now it must be… then he looked at his phone. It said it was 06:09 even though it didn't have a connection. Then it hit him. Phone system. Maybe the landlines still work, he thought. Then he wondered, How the hell does my phone know what time it is if it isn't getting cell service? He and Brian had moved into this neighborhood a long time ago and all the houses had landlines originally. He knew Brian still had one, not sure why, he thought. He went into the kitchen and sure enough it was still hanging there on the wall. He grabbed the receiver and put it to his ear. There was a dial tone! *How the hell can the phone company still have the landlines working with no power? Must be they have generators and probably some big ones with huge fuel tanks.* Come to think of it. *During and after hurricanes one of the only things that usually worked, unless the trees took out the wires, was the old landline phone system.* Huh, good to know. *At least now we can call the cops if we need to, he thought. Or the fire department,* he chuckled to himself. Then he thought, *Well, I guess I should see if it works.* He dialed 911 and it started to ring, then an operator said, "911 do you need Police, Fire or Ambulance?" It suddenly hit him that he didn't know what to say. "Uhm…oh sorry, disregard." He hung up and felt like an idiot. *Oh, well, they work. Good to know. I guess I had better check outside and make sure the vehicles are still in one piece,* he thought. Outside everything looked fine and peaceful. Some of the neighbors had set up generators outside which were busily humming or banging away, depending on the make and the size. Some of the neighbors were smart enough to chain them around a tree or a fence pole. He decided that he should move his generator into the back yard and set it up. It will be in the 90's today again with probably 95% humidity. After checking the oil and topping up the gas he plugged in the extension cords. He heard some voices inside and went in to see Brian trying to turn on the air conditioner.

"Morning, Brian," he said, smiling, trying to get an idea as to Brian's current mental state.

"Morning." he said. "Why isn't the air conditioner working? It is 89° in…Wait, why are you here? Why does my head hurt so much? Where is the boat?"

"What's the last thing you remember?" Bob asked.

"Packing up the boat to go fishing, I guess. But it seems like something… I don't remember." he answered, trying to remember why he kept thinking something unusual had happened.

"Ok, well there is a lot we are going to have to go over, one thing at a time. There has been some kind of a huge power outage. I brought my generator over and just finished setting it up in back."

Brian turned around and looked at him oddly and said, "Why didn't you just use mine?"

Bob froze in his tracks. "Really? I didn't know you had one or I forgot. Of course, you have one. How silly of me. Do you have any gas?"

"Sure, ten gallons or so in the shed. I make sure to replace it every year so it's fairly fresh. And the tank on the generator should be full as well."

"Oh, that's awesome!"

"Yeah, we use it for hurricanes, you know. I usually use it to run the window air conditioner that's in the shed, we stick it in that window by the back door. At least it keeps the living room comfortable. Now fill me in on what's been going on. I guess I have been out of it for a while."

Bob was all smiles. An extra generator, more gasoline and a small air conditioner he didn't know about…wonderful!

Brian made breakfast while Bob took a quick hand bath and changed into fresh clothes from the truck. Bob never thought a cold ham and cheese sandwich for breakfast could taste so good. He filled Brian in on what had taken place over the past few days, what had happened to them twenty miles off Ft. Lauderdale, why his head hurt, where their boat is, what the president said, what the news commentators said, all the different failures. Brian was in utter disbelief. They pulled the air conditioner out of the shed and the old generator and started her up. She ran perfectly.

"Now let's get some news," Brian said as he plugged the extension cord into the tv. The air conditioner worked great after blowing out dust, tiny lizard eggs, dead ants and who knew what else for the first minute or so. But it's cool dust and lizard eggs!

Bob thought to himself. He opened the front door and the back door to let the dust somewhat blow out and cleaned up the dead lizard eggs and dead ants as best he could with a broom while thinking, this is what the dinosaur eggs must have looked like…just bigger. He had to laugh to himself at the same time taking a closer look at the potentially prehistoric dino relatives' eggs.

For the next hour they watched the Army National Guard and reservists distributing food and water rations to people in Miami on the tv. Some of the people that were getting the free supplies behaved more like animals than human beings. They grabbed the supplies away from the Guardsman off the back of the trucks as if the supplies somehow had been stolen from them or the Guardsmen were teasing them with the supplies and not really going to give it to them. *Unbelievable,* Bob thought.

There were pictures of Walmart, Targets, Home Depots, Best Buy and more with the front doors smashed in, glass strewn everywhere. Videos of thieves running down the street with a microwave or a tv or some other appliance, some still in the grocery cart.

There were reports of fights at gas stations, a few of which were running on generators. They interviewed one gas station owner who reported he would stay open as long as they have gas for their generators and gas to sell. He promised the price would stay the same as it was yesterday before all of this started. But they were due for another tanker which was late with his delivery. They showed pictures of gas stations that were closed with signs that said, "No power to pump gas." Cars and trucks had run out of fuel. Sometimes they were by the side of the road. Sometimes they were still sitting in the traffic lane blocking traffic. Police were towing and pushing them off the road in some cases. Pretty much all grocery stores were closed, locked and covered with plywood, just as if a level 4 hurricane was due to arrive. Food trucks trying to make deliveries were being mobbed when they stopped at traffic lights or stop signs, the drivers running away in fear for their lives. Almost all but the heartiest of the restaurants were closed. Some had charcoal grills running in back. All the local hospitals and fire departments were running on generators, as were all the assisted living facilities, at least the ones that had generators. All fire and police were required to report in and help contain the situation. They were showing pictures of police manning the doors of different hospitals. Brian wasn't sure why.

The helicopter flyovers were showing the major thoroughfares and highways blocked by stalled cars. They also took the opportunity to fly over the Port Everglades Terminal where the cargo ships carrying most of South Florida's gasoline and diesel was shipped in and off-loaded to the gigantic tank farm by the airport. The helicopter crew reported numerous tankers at anchor off Port Everglades but there didn't seem to be any activity. They then reported that the news helicopter flyovers were going to come to an end. Apparently, there wasn't much gas left for them, either. Then the governor of the State of Florida gave a speech on how to behave during the crisis, and that "everything" will be returned to working order as soon as possible.

In the meantime, the Emergency Operations Centers were being activated, and shelters were being set up for those who needed assistance. He also clarified what the president said in his speech to the nation, adding nothing more than what had previously been mentioned. The only new information was that he had been in touch with their congressmen and the different power companies and "they were working on a plan". It seemed that the satellite that was destroyed in orbit had something to do with coordinating power production between the different facilities. They were diligently working on the problem, and they had a plan in place.

He went on to say that travel of any kind was severely restricted. Gasoline was not widely available; trains and planes had ceased all operations. There was no bus system or any public transportation of any kind. If one was stuck out of town, he suggested staying put until services were restored. The governor would be the first to let the public know of any further developments and on a timeline as fast as possible. After a bit of a pause he explained, "This is not just a state crisis or a national crisis. North America, South America and much of the world is undergoing these same issues. Virtually all developed countries were experiencing the same circumstances."

His primary point seemed to be that everyone had to relax and stay calm. "The National Guard and other authorities are doing the best they can to restore peace and public services under the current circumstances. In the meantime, there would be a curfew from sundown to sunup. Anyone found to be out and about without reasonable cause will be subject to immediate arrest." With that he stepped off camera. Brian turned off the TV.

"He didn't stick around for any questions, I see."

"Probably too many to handle and not enough answers. I mean one little missile and the whole United States, and the world seems to be in a state of confusion, not to mention war," Bob said, shaking his head. "Yeah, I wonder what kind of a mess it must be at the station. Oh, by the way, your landline works. I didn't know who to call so I dialed 911. I felt like an idiot when dispatch answered. Oh, and I should tell you that my 9mm and the pistol grip shotgun are locked up in the bottom of your toolbox and the key is in my pocket.

Brian thought for a minute then nodded, "Probably a good idea. I suppose we should bring them in at night. We don't want to be messing around if we need a gun. I'll let Lisa know. Let's put them on top of the fridge. Ok, bud?"

"Good idea. I assume they would be mostly for persuasion. I mean, just cocking that twelve gauge should be enough to get anyone's attention if not completely scare them off. Speaking of preparing, I suppose we need to take stock of the situation, like I don't think we want to cook inside the house. Thank God for your little air conditioner. It already feels so much better.

"Yes, it does," Brian agreed. "I may not be able to remember everything, but I do remember sweating profusely last night."

"I forgot to empty my freezer. I know I have some steaks in there. We should definitely grab them. Hey, is it ok if I bring Tiger over here?"

———

129

"Of course, he will be good company for us. I will check with Lisa, but I'm sure it's fine. Just put the litter in your bathroom, ok?" Brian looked at Bob with a sheepish grin. "You know Lisa has a very sensitive nose," he added, pinching his nose and making a disgusted face as if he could smell cat poop already, chuckling to himself. "Ok, bud I'm going to fire up the propane grill in the back. I could use some coffee."

Bob was so glad to see Brian returning to his good old self. I was getting a little concerned there, he thought.

"Absolutely, sounds great to me," Bob agreed. "After last night I could definitely use a cup o' joe. You know, I've been a large consumer of the black stuff. Also, I don't think we should travel alone for a while and when we do go out probably should put the 9mm in the glove compartment. I know it's only a couple of miles to my place, but after what we saw on the tv... Do you think we should bring Lisa with us… or…?"

"Good question. I am sure she'll be fine here. But let me ask her if she wants to come along. First, I think we should make some lists, you know matches, propane, if you have any, firewood…stuff."

Brian scratched his head as he looked absently at the tv. "I know you don't remember but we saw a missile take off and apparently it took out a satellite. That is a violation of international treaty and I guess now we're at war. World War II lasted for four years or so for the U.S., longer for our allies. I don't think we're going to be at war for four years, but who knows? We need more information. So far all we know is a satellite was destroyed. The internet crashed, the power went out and the cell phone system collapsed. They have to be related."

Bob's face suddenly lit up. "I used to have stock in our deferred compensation plan and one or two of the power companies, I don't remember which ones, but they sent out a bunch of data on how they were 'strengthening the reliability of the system', some kind of federal law endorsed linking all of the power plants together to back each other up. Do you think this could have anything to do with what the governor said about all of North America being in the same bucket?" he asked as he looked at Brian questioningly?

Brian ran his hand through his hair, "But how could one satellite knock out the entire power grid, man? I mean, it has to be a lot more redundant or residual than that, right? There has to be more to it."

"Ok, so let's say for shits and giggles there is more to it, we just don't know how much more. Remember seeing those power plants up close when we did our safety tours with Station 8? They explained that starting one up from a dead cold stop can take some time depending on what kind of a power plant. A nuclear or coal power plant takes a lot longer than a natural gas plant, this is not a case of a few power lines going down in a storm. It must take a full day to power up some of those giant plants. It seems to me, if I remember correctly, even the peaker power plants used to supplement power during heavy use periods take hours to fire up. So, let's say they're out of communication with the other power plants in the power grid. What would they do?"

"Well, I guess if they cannot communicate with each other through their normal secure internet or intranet systems, they would have to call each and every one of them on landlines, which could be impossible to manage, or completely disconnect from each other. Otherwise, how would they know what the other plants are doing?" Bob asked questioningly. "Kinda like hooking my generator up to too much of a draw. It would bog down, knock it out, and maybe even damage it."

"Exactly," Brian agreed. "I think it could take as much as a day for the power companies just to find out what the hell is going on. It'll probably take another day or so to decide to disconnect from the grid, or whatever they have to do. So that's two days. Because, well, you know, nothing happens fast in big corporations, and this is political, too, which of course will complicate the process. And there are federal laws involved, so that means lawyers and legal issues, questions and debate. Probably around the third or fourth day they disconnect from the grid and begin the startup procedures. I have no idea how long that could take, a day or so? Is it like just pulling a breaker? Then they could start to come back online one at a time. So, four or five days maybe? Hopefully sooner."

Bob suddenly realized the potential gravity of the situation. "Holy shit! How long can the hospitals, assisted living facilities, water plants, police and other critical infrastructure stay on generator power without more fuel? Do you remember how long we could stay on generator power alone at the station?"

"That is a good question. I think the diesel generator tank at our station was like three thousand gallons, but that also had to supply every engine and rescue in the battalion, but I don't know." Brian said solemnly. "Maybe three or four days, I'm guessing? I was thinking when I was at my house that I need to visit Marcie's mom at Golden Acres. It has been a couple of weeks since I have been there. She doesn't recognize me anymore, but it's a responsibility. I told Marcie if anything should happen to her that I would keep an eye on mom. Can you go with me, bud? I mean, I would really appreciate it if you went with me?"

"Of course I'll go with you! We just said that we shouldn't go anywhere alone. I think that's a good idea and something we need to do. Lisa is going to stay here. We decided that someone should keep an eye on things, like the generator and the house."

"Probably a good idea. I am sure that we won't have any problems during the day as long as someone is here." Bob thought about the twelve gauge, then decided not to bring it up. "Too bad we don't have any handheld radios. Sure would be nice to, you know, stay in touch with her while we are out."

"Yeah, well let's put together a list so we can minimize the number of trips we have to make. I am sure we can forget about going to any stores, so let's just get what we can from your house.

After the list was finished, they reviewed it together.

"Wow," Bob said, "I didn't think it would be so comprehensive."

"Yeah, well we don't know how bad it's going to get, but on the other hand we can always go back if we don't want to grab everything today. It's a lot of stuff."

The list ended up being a full page of stuff like bleach, five-gallon buckets, bait from Bob's freezer, fishing poles, tackle box, battery powered tools and their chargers, cat food and kitty litter, plus the entire contents of Bob's freezer, charcoal, firewood, toilet paper, clothes (including extra T-shirts), towels, a propane tank, miscellaneous batteries, and a couple extension cords. They were going to eat like kings for a few days. Bob had steaks, Mahi Mahi, lobster, shrimp, scallops, bags of ice, pork chops and more in his chest freezer. The frozen stuff alone should last for four dinners or more, if they could keep it cold. Then there was the canned stuff and peanut butter (as long as the bread lasted). They were hoping this thing might conclude in about four, maybe five days. They figured things probably would not return to "normal" for who knew, two weeks, maybe more? This was not their first storm, but this was no ordinary storm.

On the way to Bob's house, they decided to stick to the back roads and get a perspective on the situation before hitting any main streets. It was a beautiful day, showing signs that it would also be a hot one, and not a cloud in the sky. It seemed quiet, but it was still early. They spotted a few of the typical handmade signs spray painted on plywood sheets in front of some of the houses like "We shoot first and ask questions later" and "Forget the dog- beware of the owner", "Looters will be shot on sight" and so forth. They picked up most of the stuff at Bob's house, put Tiger in his kitty transporter (much to his chagrin), grabbed a cooler they hadn't thought of adding to the list, put all the ice Bob had in it, and headed back. This time they decided to take State Road 84 and University Drive. Two grocery stores had signs out front which read, "Closed until further notice". Many cars, too many to count, were waiting in line for gasoline. They were empty and so was the gas station. Miscellaneous cars and trucks were parked alongside the road and in some cases in the middle of the road, obviously out of gas.

"Looks like they're going to have a wait," Bob said.

Then they saw two Sheriff's cars parked in front of the bank with their lights running. They slowed down to get a look.

"Did you see that?" Brian asked.

"No, I had to watch that intersection. It's the wild west out here without traffic lights," Bob responded.

"Looked to me like someone shot up that ATM, or at least there was glass all over the place back there. They were taking pictures and had yellow tape all over."

"Huh, I wonder if that bank has a battery backup system. If they do, whoever shot that thing up probably got picked up by the cameras. But how would they playback the video without their computers?"

The mall was on the left and obviously closed. Before arriving, they could see cars lined up out onto the road and army trucks parked side by side in the parking lot. Barricades were set up and there was a hand painted sign that said, "MRE's, FOOD & WATER." Bob pulled into the parking lot but didn't get in line. It looked like people were behaving themselves in large part. There were two cop cars at the entrance, apparently staging the cars in line. The National Guard troops had side arms in their holsters and there were two standing back-to-back on the back of a flatbed tractor trailer about one hundred feet away.

"I wonder why they're passing out water," Brian asked as he looked around the huge parking lot.

Bob had to think about it for a minute, "Wells—people who are on wells can't pump without power. Wow, think about that for a second, no water for drinking or showers or laundry or even cooking. Holy shit, you couldn't even flush the toilets! Unless you're on a

____

canal or a lake."

"Wow," Brian said, shaking his head. "Guess I would be going to the beach every morning to rinse off."

"What if you don't have gas to get to the beach? Bob said in shock. "How can they live like that? Do their business in a bucket?"

"I bet you most people wouldn't even think of that," Brian said. "Gives a whole new meaning to 'Don't even have a bucket to piss in', doesn't it? Holy crap!"

As they pulled out onto University Drive two cars appeared to be racing. They were flying down the road at well over seventy mph; it was a thirty-five-mph zone. The lead car had its windows down. A young kid, maybe sixteen, was leaning out of the passenger window with a gun in his hand targeting the trailing car. The lead car was swerving back and forth as they veered through traffic. The kid with the gun in his hand almost fell out as the driver veered left. They disappeared in the distance, engines roaring, not even slowing down for the intersection. "Holy crap, did you see that? They know the cops are tied up and no one can report them. Unless someone has a CB radio or a ham radio in their car, but who does that anymore?"

"Can we stop by Golden Acres to look in on Marcie's mom for a minute bro?" Bob asked after the two cars sped by. He was already heading in that direction.

"Of course! You have a responsibility. You told Marcie you would keep an eye on her."

Golden Acres was not golden, nor was it much in the way of acres. Maybe one, possibly two acres, Brian thought to himself. It was a ranch style or single level facility shaped like an "E" if viewed from a satellite.

It had apartments to the left and to the right of the entrance with the cafeteria jutting out from the reception area in the middle. The eight-foot ceiling always gave Bob a feeling of smallness and with the lights all off it gave him a new sensation of entering a cave. It was mostly carpet over linoleum tile squares, both originally installed probably thirty years ago or more. The carpet was some kind of dark tan on the sides with an obvious traffic path of an unknown color worn in the middle. Brian always wondered how or when they cleaned it, if ever. It should have been replaced ten years ago by his estimate. It was always difficult for Brian not to show how he felt when the smell of the place hit his olfactory nerves. Still, the staff was always friendly, and Marcie's mom was usually dressed and appeared to be taken care of. Her hair was brushed, and she appeared to be relatively clean.

Bob put Tiger in the shade by the front door. After checking in at the front desk, and obtaining their name badges, they were informed they were lucky Mrs. Fernandez was celebrating her hundredth birthday that afternoon. If they wanted to join in the celebration, they were welcome. Bob and Brian smiled and nodded and made their way to the group living room right next to reception. The staff said she was watching a movie in the tv room, and they had someone coming in to play the piano for everyone later. Bob explained they would only be a few minutes. The place seemed rather warm to him. As Bob looked around there didn't seem to be many staff. Not surprising considering the situation, Bob surmised.

"She doesn't remember me. She always thinks I am the plumber and tells me that 'everything is just fine right now, but 'thank you for coming,'" Bob said with a laugh.

Brian looked at him out of the corner of his eye to see if he was kidding.

"Hi, Betty!" Bob shouted out. The octogenarians and more seated around the tv in a giant circle in wheelchairs and some in lazy boys frowned and put their fingers to their mouths telling him to shush up. Bob was used to this, so he just smiled, waved and ducked like he was trying to sneak in. Betty apparently had nodded off to sleep. Bob touched her on the shoulder and gently shook her while whispering her name closer to her ear.

"What? We don't need any," she said, suddenly trying to focus on Bob's face. "Oh, hah, it's you. We got the leak fixed. It's fine. Thank you for coming." Bob smiled and looked back at Brian who grinned and nodded.

After about ten minutes or so of meaningless conversation, Brian looked at Bob and nodded toward the cafeteria.

"Where are we going?" Brian asked as he trudged along behind Bob's longer and quicker pace.

"I always look around a bit to check the place out a little and make sure the cafeteria area appears to be clean, the countertops have been wiped off, the garbage was taken out…you know, just a quick assessment of the situation. I also want to check the generator outback and see how much fuel they have."

The cafeteria area looked "normal". Thirty or so dark brown fake wood Formica square tables were spaced evenly around, some with four matching wooden chairs, some with no chairs, all of which probably could be considered antiques, but they were clean, and the brown carpet appeared to be vacuumed. Bob didn't want to take the liberty of going into the prep area of the kitchen. If there were any more staff around, they usually hid in the kitchen eating snacks and talking. Bob left by the back kitchen door, Brian trailing behind with a quizzical look on his face. The door had an alarm system which sensed if a monitoring bracelet was passing through.

There was parking in the back for employees and overflow parking for guests on extra busy days. Immediately they could hear a generator humming away behind the cafeteria where the power lines came into the building. It appeared to be a heavy- duty Cummins portable diesel unit pumping out 240 volts at 60 hertz. It sounded to Bob like it was straining under the load. The generator was plugged into the main switch on the building and the switch from the utility service was turned off, just as it should be. When he touched the main power cables, he noticed they were hot, but not too hot. They walked behind the portable generator and found five plastic barrels of diesel covered with plastic to keep the water out with a portable hand pump sitting on one of the barrels. One was empty. Bob checked the fuel level in the generator. It had less than a quarter tank of diesel remaining. Bob quickly walked over to the dumpster by the service building at the end of the parking lot.

Brian sighed, "Now what are you doing?" doing double time trying to keep up.

Bob turned to look at his friend, realized that he was moving too fast, slowed and said, "Sorry, buddy. I didn't want anyone to see us checking out the generator system. I'm sure they would get suspicious or worse if they saw us. We can slow down now. I don't think anyone is going to be upset if we look into the dumpster."

"Why do you want to look in the dumpster?"

"It will tell us what they have been feeding them." Brian replied as they opened the gate to the dumpster and walked in.

He closed the gate behind them. It was almost completely full of black plastic garbage bags, but they weren't tied. As they fought off the flies, Bob emptied the top two bags into the dumpster and dropped the bags back in. Styrofoam plates and bowls, plastic bread bags, a five-gallon white bucket of what used to be peanut butter, oversized grape and strawberry jelly jars, plastic forks, spoons and knives, two two-gallon milk jugs, a two- gallon container of orange juice, number ten cans of chicken noodle soup, some miscellaneous plastic and foam containers labeled ham, a box labeled "American Cheese", some orange peels and apple cores and some unidentifiable miscellaneous garbage all came dumping out. The dumpster was almost full. It was time to go.

They gathered up Tiger, who didn't seem to have missed them, and headed back to Bob and Lisa's house. Brian had been quiet for most of the visit. He sat back in the comfortable seat of the Silverado and looked out the window, taking in the quickly changing residential neighborhoods and enjoying the air conditioning. Some houses had generators chained to trees out front, some had garbage cans overflowing waiting to be picked up, some had people sitting on the front porch, some had no cars, others had four or five cars filling the driveways and spilling out into the street. Still others had mean looking dogs tied up to the front porch on long chains.

"So, what is your assessment of the situation back there?" he asked. Bob, was driving much slower than normal and had been quiet so far on the trip home, audibly sighed and said, "Well, it looks to me that they had cold cereal and orange juice for breakfast, peanut butter and jelly and maybe a few ham and cheese sandwiches and some fruit for lunch. It made me wonder about the foodservice deliveries. Do the foodservice distributors store diesel for their trucks? Probably not, or at least not too much. Maybe they can keep a skeleton service operational for a couple of days. Most restaurants are closed so maybe the distributors can prioritize assisted living facilities and hospitals. Can the food service distributors keep the refrigerated and frozen foods cold or frozen?"

Brian just shook his head, questioningly.

"How long can they keep their generators running for their freezers without diesel deliveries—two days, maybe three? And will anyone show up for work? Not if they can't get to work in the first place without gasoline. This situation is worse than a hurricane. We didn't get the usual warnings that we get when a storm is on the horizon so no one could prepare in advance. And with a hurricane, usually only a small area is affected, you know, like Miami or Ft. Lauderdale or Tampa so power companies and work crews from out of state show up to repair the damage quickly. The whole infrastructure is threatening to collapse. That generator appeared to be stressed, the power lines were hot, and it should have been locked up or secured somehow. I didn't see any cameras pointed toward it either. I guess they're doing the best they can with minimum staff. They're lucky anyone is coming to work, period. I wonder if some of the staff are sleeping there to minimize gasoline usage and to cover all shifts."

"Wow, this could be life threatening for those old folks at Golden Acres!" Brian exclaimed.

"It sure could and it may. Not only that, but these old people at least have someone looking out for them. How many calls did we go on that had an old person or couple living alone? Do they know what to do? Is someone, anyone looking in on them? Do they have a generator in their garage or shed, with fuel available? What's going to happen to them? Golden Acres is a fairly decent assisted living facility. Did you notice the five diesel barrels? One was empty and another was partially used. It has only been twenty-four hours since we lost power. They're using over a barrel a day, they have four and a half barrels left, and the generator's fuel tank needs to be refilled soon. That gives them about three days from today before they run out. What will that place be like on day five if they don't get power? How hot is it going to get in that flat roofed building sitting on a slab in Florida in August with no ventilation? What will they do? Open all of the doors and windows? It will be over one hundred degrees inside within an hour of losing their generator with ninety-five percent humidity, even with all of the doors and windows open. Then they have to somehow monitor the doors, so people don't just walk out and disappear. I hope they have a large tent or tarps available so people can sit outside in the shade. If the power isn't back on inside the next four days people will start dying from heat exhaustion and dehydration. At least they have a generator and some fuel. What about the assisted living facilities that don't have the required fuel for three or four days? Or the places that are multiple levels with no backyard, only blacktop driveway? Like that seven-story place in Miami Lakes? Remember that place?

"Yeah, I remember. I don't even want to think about it.

Scary," Brian said, shaking his head.

A few seconds passed in silence.

———

"People are going to die. They can't take that kind of heat," Brian said, still shaking his head.

"I hadn't thought about it, but what about all of the high-rises all over Miami, Hollywood, Ft. Lauderdale or West Palm Beach, or anywhere for that matter, Ft. Myers, Tampa, Orlando… hell, Houston. Do they have backup generators? This could be a lot worse than we thought or ever considered."

Bob nodded and kept staring straight ahead as he drove, lost in his thoughts. Upon arriving at Brian's house Lisa was glued to the tv. "Hey, guys, I just got off the phone er… the landline with my mother in the Upper Peninsula of Michigan. You probably remember, Bob, I visit her a couple times a year, just not in the winter. They have power outages all of the time after heavy snowstorms. She and her neighbors pooled together and purchased a huge generator some time ago to provide power for the five houses in her neighborhood. Heavy snow can bring down the power lines fairly frequently. Anyway, one of the guys in the neighborhood does the yearly maintenance and keeps it in service. They have a spring just down the road which she could use for water if she needs it, but she's on a well anyway. Mom does her own canning. I used to help her as a kid. She cans everything; venison, pickled beef, carrots, apples, pears, beets, pickles, onions, potatoes, beans, tomatoes, tomato paste, sauerkraut, jams and jellies, preserves, you name it. Her fruit cellar looks like a 4H competition at the fair. She's in her eighties and is virtually totally self-reliant and in good health. What a woman," she added, smiling.

"Oh, hey, look, you guys. They have more information on what's going on and they have been reporting on you two!"

———

"What?" They both said in unison.

The news was on the tv.

"They are reporting two, so far unnamed, firefighters, who were fishing off Ft. Lauderdale witnessed a missile launch which destroyed a satellite and created so much debris that the other satellites aren't working and that's why everything is all messed up!" Bob and Brian looked at each other in surprise. "We didn't expect other satellites to be affected. How did that happen?" Bob said as they surrounded the tv.

Brian shook his head with a smile and said, "What else are they saying, Lisa? What did we miss?"

"Everything is all messed up. The entire economy has come to a screeching halt, the financial markets were frozen by the government, the stock market has been completely shut down. The governor is supposed to give another speech shortly. The rest is drone footage of local police issues, crowds at the food and water distribution sights and where they are located. Then they explained how the launch of a missile ended up destroying a government satellite, like I said, and the debris from the destruction is causing disruption of the signal or destruction of other satellites, or something they weren't sure which. They also are reporting that NASA lost all communication with the International Space Station and with the Mission on Mars."

Brian gasped with his mouth hanging open as he looked at Bob. "What? NASA has lost communication with Mars Mission I and the ISS? Why?"

Bob's eyes widened as he looked back at Brian, "What, how is that possible? Why would they lose communication with both of the crews on Mars and on the ISS? I mean, the ISS is only two hundred fifty miles or so above the Earth. If I remember correctly from some of the NASA videos, they circle every ninety minutes, so every hour and a half they should literally have line of sight."

Brian cut him off, "Actually, it takes ninety minutes to completely circle the earth, so depending on the height of the antennae or dish, they should have line of sight closer to every forty-five minutes or so, because it takes that long to go from horizon to horizon. It may take a little longer if there are mountains in the way, I think," he added, his eyes darting from Bob to Lisa looking for confirmation. "Anyway, there are ham radio operators who can pick up stations and transmit a lot further than two hundred-fifty miles. What the hell?"

Bob nodded in agreement as he observed, "Looks like our brain damage boy has made a full recovery," as he gave Brian an arm around the shoulders hug and rubbed his hair. They all needed the unexpected humor and Brian straightened what was remaining of his high hairline.

Lisa shrugged her shoulders and smiled at Brian.

"Fortunately, I think he has made a full recovery." "What's for dinner?"

Bob's previously frozen food was now thawed because the freezer and fridge were completely packed so some of it had been left in the sink since they got home. Lisa had been occasionally disconnecting the tv and air conditioner from the generator for 20 minutes or so and plugging in the refrigerator to allow it to cool back down again. Steak and Florida Lobster cooked on the grill along with some previously frozen corn, drawn butter, and beer for the guys comprised a fantastic dinner for the three. Lisa had red wine and water.

"It is amazing how good food and friendship can improve the mood," Lisa said as she attempted to wipe the butter from her chin and smiled. "I'm glad you're hanging out here, Bob."

"Thanks," Bob replied as he smiled back. "Good to be here. I hope Tiger isn't too much of a bother. Speaking of Tiger, where is he?"

"Probably under the guest bed. He went straight in there as soon as you put him down." Lisa commented. "Haven't seen him since."

At bedtime Bob was so grateful to get the couch in the living room with the wonderfully cooled air from the tiny air conditioner. Sleep for me tonight, he thought. As he settled into the sheets on the couch, his mind wandered back to the day's events. Today was day two without power, he thought as he closed his eyes. He projected in his mind what each of the power companies were doing now—either getting ready to or are engaged in disconnecting from the grid. As soon as that was done, they could begin to power up each of the power plants one at a time and confirm they were safely working correctly. Then they would go back on-line and start to provide power to their customers. He was pretty sure that they could accomplish that in the next day or two. They had better. People were going to die otherwise.

His thoughts returned to Golden Acres; he could imagine the staff moving all the old people into the backyard under a tarp. The oldest having breathing difficulty did not have enough energy to stay seated upright. They were starting to slide down the wooden chairs.

Pale white faces with their hearts pounding away, mouths wide open trying to get air. Too weak to speak. The staff was sprinkling them with water and fanning them. There was nothing else they could do. Then they started to fall off the chairs one at a time to the ground unconscious, heaving for air. Bob jerked his eyes awake. This is no way to get to sleep, he thought to himself. I've got to stop thinking like this! But he knew this was no nightmare. This would be reality if they don't get the power very soon.

Chapter 19

Day 3

Lisa was up before anyone else. She had coffee brewing on the propane grill using the same camping coffee pot in which Brian had made coffee yesterday. It was made for use on campfires, but it worked great on the propane grill. Bob had gotten up and pulled the sheets off the couch.

While the coffee was brewing Lisa came in. "Do you want to catch up on the news this morning, Bob?"

"I do!" Brian yelled from the bedroom. They had put a small fan in the hallway to get some of the cool air from the living room into the bedroom.

The next news day started with more coverage about who might be suspected or even be capable of performing this terrible act of destroying a satellite and why. But it all appeared to be conjecture. The newscasters were following up with local power companies whose spokesman reported no comment other than, "We are doing the best we can as fast as we can. This is an unforeseeable and unprecedented series of events, which has taken us all by surprise." They also reported on local hospitals, fire departments, police, prison systems, shelters, people with no air conditioning, condominium residents, and general living conditions. Some of the people in high rises on or near the beaches were sleeping on the beach at night soaking in the cooler sea breeze. This was causing issues of who possessed what part of the beach along with privacy, decency, petty theft and garbage issues. The different fire departments were circling the neighborhoods at first to help anyone that may need assistance but were then instructed to stay in the station to conserve fuel, unless responding to a call, of course. Then the news ran a short segment on the different kinds of power facilities in South Florida. It covered the Turkey Point Nuclear Power plant, different peaker plants in the area, the natural gas plant in Ft. Lauderdale, and more. Bob noticed that it didn't say anything about how all the power companies were inter-connected or disconnected from each other before starting up, or how long it would take to start them up after they went offline. The news continued with what people were doing to combat the different situations and on and on. They recommended that everyone check on their elderly neighbors or anyone they know that may require assistance. They were also reporting on what people were doing who had no way to cook food, how the national guard was having a hard time controlling the increasingly aggressive and foul tempered crowds. One guy was shot in Miami when he went berserk at a food and water distribution site. He had pulled a knife for no known reason. The National Guard now had rifles out and loaded for self-defense as they handed out MREs and water. Apparently, there were rumors concerning gangs trying to commandeer the food and water supplies. Most hospitals were forced to minimum staffing when their doctors, nurses, administrators and so forth couldn't make it into work. Some were sleeping in spare hospital beds and not even going home. However, the hospital representatives all gave the standard "No comment" when it came to how long they could last without fuel deliveries and the staffing situation along with, "We are doing everything we can to continue our unending dedication to serve the community." In the background a white tractor trailer refrigerated truck was staging next to the E.R. It was so loud they could barely carry on the conversation. But the reporter didn't seem to understand the significance or even wonder aloud who had access to diesel fuel and why a refrigerated trailer was being staged next to the ER. There were fewer and fewer vehicles on the road every day. Then the news reported a shooting in Coral Gables where a homeowner with solar power was shot when an argument developed after he refused to share power with his neighbors.

"Wow!" Lisa exclaimed, "It's starting to get really crazy out there, and this is what, the third day without power?"

"Yeah, we need to check on your neighbor, Mrs. Sandoval who was babysitting Brian the other day. I don't think she has a generator or air-conditioning," Bob said with a concerned look.

"You're right." Lisa responded. "I'll go check on her."

Bob looked up from the TV, stared at the wall, then he looked at Brian. "Did you see that refrigerated truck?" "Yeah," Brian responded. "It was running."

"I bet if we drive over to the hospital and park by the road but within sight of the ER, that refrigerated trailer will still be running. Keeping it cold."

Lisa asked hesitantly while she put her shoes on, "What are you getting at, Bob?"

Brian looked at Bob's apprehensive face and said, "Are you thinking what I think you're thinking?"

The house went silent except for the drone of the tv and the quiet hum of the air conditioner with the generator humming in the

———

background.

Lisa scowled, "What?"

Brian responded, "I bet, if we run by the county undertaker, it would be either cordoned off by the police department or surrounded by white tractor trailers just like that one. All running."

Lisa stared at Brian, then at Bob. "What is he saying?"

Bob ran his hand over his face. "He's saying that the trailer is being staged to load with bodies, probably late at night to avoid observation by the press and the public, to keep hysteria to a minimum. I am pretty sure the county undertaker is too overwhelmed to handle the load. Most probably."

Lisa gasped. "But it has only been three days!"

Bob looked at Brian as if to ask, should I get into it? "There are people at home and in condos who depend on power for oxygen machines. I'm sure if they can't get the staff, the hospitals have canceled or delayed lifesaving surgeries. People who rely on dialysis machines simply can't receive their treatments. Diabetics need to keep their insulin refrigerated and even though there is less traffic, we witnessed the craziest driving I have ever seen. Drivers are supposed to treat dead traffic lights as a four way stop and many just scream through them. I can't imagine how people are driving on I-95 or the turnpike. The police are probably tied up, with understaffing and maintaining civility. I'm sure gang activity has increased. Break-ins have to be at an all-time high, as we witnessed on tv. We didn't tell you, but we witnessed a high-speed car chase on University Drive with a guy shooting at the car behind."

After that Bob just shook his head in frustration and said,

"I need to go for a walk. Wanna come, Brian? Lisa?'
Brian nodded.

Lisa said, "Why don't we check on Mrs. Sandoval first, you First Responders."

"Good idea," Brian said. "I am sorry, we should have offered."

Mrs. Sandoval's house was surrounded by giant Florida oak trees which cast a continuous shadow over her house, offering a nice break from the baking Florida sun. The good news was that it was substantially cooler. The downside was twice a year she had to have her roof and house pressure cleaned to keep the mold and mildew off. Still, pressure cleaning was much cheaper than power. Her front door was open with the screen door shut to keep the bugs out. She recognized Lisa's voice and came to the door in shorts and a T-shirt. She reported that she was hot, but she had always kept blocks of ice in her chest freezer, which kept everything frozen and provided her with ice for her water. All her curtains were tightly closed to keep the sun out, but the front and back door were open to allow a little air movement. She had a battery powered radio for entertainment and news, and she was knitting a scarf for her daughter-in-law.

Otherwise, she said she was, "Fine, just a bit warm, dear. Thank you for checking on me. I'll let you know if I need anything."

"Damn," Lisa said, "We didn't ask her what she's eating. I am going to go back and invite her to dinner."

"You're right," Brian said. We'll see you back home in a few minutes. Be insistent that she come over and let her know we have plenty of food. It's almost time to start dinner."

They walked around the block not saying a word, just taking in the views, the sounds and unfortunately the smells of the neighborhood. It was very evident that many of their neighbors had to throw out much of the food from their refrigerators and obviously no one was picking up the garbage. The sound of generators filled the air. It was obvious which houses were not inhabited.

Lisa met them at their door. "Mrs. Sandoval politely declined for tonight. She said she was very tired and wanted to lay down. I insisted that she come over for dinner tomorrow night. She was getting ready to take a nice cold shower," Lisa commented as she was preparing the night's feast of pork chops, applesauce, and what used to be frozen corn.

"OMG!" Lisa blurted. "Thank God we don't have any kids to worry about."

"Yeah, I guess," Bob replied, leaning against the kitchen counter with a pained look on his face. He was staring out the kitchen window by the sink. "Marcie and I wanted kids, but I guess, as you know, it was just not in the cards. Bad eggs. The doctor said she had immature eggs or something. She got pregnant once but lost it in the first trimester. I guess you guys remember that."

Brian and Lisa were quiet for a moment, then Brian replied, "Yeah, I remember that day. That was a rough one for you two. I knew you guys really wanted a few kids. We really felt bad for you guys." Lisa nodded and had a concerned look on her face. She walked over and gave Bob a hug. Bob hugged her back and fought back the tears that were forming in the corners of his eyes. Bob surprised himself as he wiped the corners of his eyes with his dirty t-shirt. "I didn't know you guys were bothered by it as well. I guess we were kinda stuck in our own emotions. Marcie was crushed for a few weeks. I took a week off to be with her." They sat in quiet unison remembering the moment, each in their own way.

After a bit, Brian went out to check on the gas in the generator. They were on the third five-gallon tank with only two remaining. "Two tanks left. Probably tomorrow night or the next morning and we'll be out," he observed. Bob had joined him.

"Well, I guess we need to consider how much gas we have in the vehicles and which ones we want to use for transportation." Then Bob suddenly blurted out, "The boat!"

Brian looked at Bob with a confused look on his face, then the realization that the boat had a one hundred twenty-gallon fuel tank! Last he remembered it was over half full, closer to three quarters of a tank or maybe even up to ninety gallons! "If we're going to be out of fuel by tomorrow night, we need to get our boat back! I wonder if they'll let us?" Then he looked at Bob as his excited look ran away from his eyes. "Awe, it's part of an on- going Federal Investigation. We'd be lucky to get it back in six months and they most probably have it completely locked down. I'm sure they won't let us near it. I guess we can swing by the marina and ask though," he said remorsefully. "Or at least ask if we can siphon some gas out for our generator." They both looked at their feet. They knew that wasn't going to happen.

Lisa suddenly yelled from the living room, "Guys! Hey guys, come here!"

The newscaster on the tv was reporting that the Miami-Dade Water Department had just announced a boil water notice for all of Dade County. She then went on to project that the other water companies and municipalities around the country were probably about to announce the same thing, if they hadn't already. After all, they all need fuel to run the generators. She added that even though the government considered municipal water companies to be the highest priority to get fuel deliveries for their generators during a power outage, it seems they are having a hard time getting it distributed... if they even have it. The different newscasters and commentators bounced the issue around the set. She then posed the question, "If the pumps can't keep running, how long before we'll be completely out of water? What about the sewage system? Can it function without backup generators to run the pumps?" They panned the newsroom, and every face was blank. For once it was quiet in the newsroom.

Brian stood up in shock. "Why can't the government even get diesel out to the water companies?" He looked blank-faced at Bob.

Bob stared back at him for a moment, obviously thinking. "Oil refineries?" Maybe the oil refineries can't make gasoline or diesel without power?" Brian started thinking. "If that's the case then there is no fuel in the system other than stored fuel, and you know as well as I do that gasoline goes bad in about 6 months. I'm sure no manufacturer wants to get a reputation for selling old gasoline. So, they probably don't store it. We've become so dependent on our infrastructure that we don't know how to live without it!"

"Do we have any more containers for water?" he asked, looking at Bob.

"I brought the two I had at my house. But you know what

we could do is wash out the garbage cans and recycle bins to flush the toilets. That would give us quite a bit of water, not to mention the water in the tub."

"I have one five-gallon bucket I use for washing the car so it should be pretty clean, and of course we have the same garbage and recycling bin as you. Let's get Lisa to start filling the five-gallon buckets and wash out the garbage containers while we go get yours. It would be nice if it rained!"

Soon they had the four garbage and recycling containers and the five-gallon buckets all relatively clean and they were filling them with the garden hose. Bob, Brian, and Lisa were watching the garbage and recycling bins slowly being filled from the garden hose.

Brian asked if they had any big garbage bags.

Lisa thought for a few minutes then just shook head and added, "Nothing this big."

They ended up being very unhappy with the results. A blueish, greenish and yellowish film was floating on top.

"I don't think I want to use that water for bathing or washing clothes. These garbage and recycling bins still didn't get as clean as I would like. I washed out those bins as best I could, using soap and bleach. I even crawled inside with a hand brush." Lisa said as she walked back to the house shaking her head.

"Well, I think we have enough drinking water for a few days."

Brian shrugged, "Well, we tried. We can still use this water for flushing the toilets. Let's get these covered up to keep the mosquitos out.

They made dinner on the grill, the last of Bob's previously

frozen chicken wings, barbecued chicken breasts, string beans and some salad that Lisa prepared.

After dinner was finished and the dishes were done, they sat down to watch a little more news. The guys each had a few beers and Lisa was still drinking the red wine from last night. The news was doing a human-interest story of sorts of a family that had moved into their boat in Coconut Grove Marina. The marina's backup generator had run out of diesel after three days, but life on the sailboat was still better than their house back in Coral Gables. It was cooler on the water, and they had a little bit of power from the on-board solar panels and the wind turbine. They would take the dinghy out on Key Biscayne occasionally to fish as long as the gas held up, which was only going to be for a few more days.

The least popular guy on the news was the weatherman, since the August weather outlook in South Florida was always hot and sticky with occasional hurricanes. But now the only way to get tropical storm notifications was by contacting the different Caribbean islands by phone or Coast Guard since there were no satellites to offer predictions. NOAA had canceled all weather- related flights to save jet fuel for the armed forces.

The weather guy said, "The fact of the matter is, if the landlines were not functioning, we would be completely blind. We placed a call to AT&T to see how long the phones would continue working and they could not give us an answer."

"Wow," Lisa exclaimed. "What will happen when or if the landlines go down also? No 911 for anybody, no way to contact emergency responders of any kind. Will we have to set up some kind of neighborhood alert system, maybe?" She looked back and forth between Bob and Brian who both just shook their heads.

Just then the good-looking lady newscaster spoke up. "Hang on a second, Jerry. We just received an old-fashioned fax report, actually two reports from Richard Sanders, a reporter with one of our affiliates in Baton Rouge, Louisiana. In the first report he interviewed a manager from one of the oil refineries in the area. It turns out, according to the manager, the refineries cannot make any fuel whatsoever without power. They are reporting that the huge towers that break down the oil cannot stay hot, which is required for refining, and it will take a day or two to fire the system back up. Also, the huge pumps that move gasoline and diesel through the system cannot run without power. So, any gasoline in the system will stay in the system until the power comes back on. According to Richard and the unnamed manager, we can't expect gasoline to start flowing again for at least a day or two after the refineries get power. The second report was forwarded from an affiliate in Kansas City. It seems that the largest farms cannot pump water for their livestock or irrigate their fields without power! Millions of chickens and cows are dying daily without water!"

Bob grimaced as he looked at Brian. "I think we need to do something."

Brian sat back and ran his hands through his thinning hair.

"I agree."

Chapter 20

Johnson Space Center - Hell Breaks Loose

Brad Brown had seen a lot in his twenty-four years at NASA and over the past four years at Johnson Space Center. But the past three days had been beyond belief. As he faced his fourth twenty-four-hour shift in a row, he decided if he ever survived this, he would write a book.

He had taken three three-hour sleep shifts in the breakroom over the past three days, but he never left the building. Even though he needed the three-hour breaks, on the first two, he didn't get any sleep at all. The third night, he was pretty sure he slept out of sheer exhaustion.

He was still trying to get his head around the last three days. Brad had been interrogated, briefed, addressed, re-briefed and debriefed. He had been in meetings upon meetings with his boss, Gerald Adams, the current director of NASA, all kinds of directors, assistant directors, and hundreds of engineers from all aspects of the NASA engineering and aerospace team, and the MMI advisory and planning team. All Brad understood was that some rocket blew up two satellites, neither of which belonged to NASA. This was no accident. No one told him, but these kinds of things just don't happen twice in the same day, at almost the same time.

Someone, he thought, or probably some country... Is it

possible that a single individual would or even could do this? The more he thought about it, the more he realized the technology had definitely been dribbling down to surprisingly pedestrian levels. Or are we just doing a better job at education?

Brad wasn't an investigator, but the net result was the full Kessler Effect—something he had dreaded since he heard about it in college at MIT. At first, everybody pooh-poohed it as totally fictional. Unfortunately, it was real, and it did happen. He was hoping that it wouldn't occur until after he retired, if ever, but no such luck. The theory or hypothesis was that if this ever occurred, space would be closed for business for years to come: No NASA, no ESA, no JAXA, no satellites. Nothing for years, unless someone could figure out how to clean it up.

There were twenty-one astronauts on Mars and six on the ISS if it was still in one piece. What would that mean for them? No one knew. No one had ever given the Kessler Effect that much consideration. Whistling in the wind, hoping it would just always be a theory. Now what?

Brad had worked his way up from a simple entry-level technician position in NASA to his present-day position at CAPCOM and one of the Mission Directors for Mars Mission I. The final starship had landed safely on Mars, right on target. They had had one major anomaly when one of the support starships had fallen over, but at least it didn't explode. Of course, the atmosphere on Mars is mostly carbon dioxide, which substantially reduces the possibility of an explosion occurring. From the pictures he had seen from the MRO, it looked to be salvageable. With all the redundancies built in, they were easily still a go for the mission, not that they could return any day soon. There was one big exception: they couldn't get to their supplies. The design team had considered programming starships III through IX to autonomously off load upon landing and if NASA had lost direct communication with the starships there was always the Mars Reconnaissance Orbiter which could relay the command. Of course, they couldn't turn around and go home now. Not today. Not for another year. Then they had a six-month return journey back to Earth.

The first EVA on Mars was a total success. As the whole world watched, NASA was once again experiencing a huge popularity revival. Shortly thereafter, CAPCOM and all space-related communications began experiencing static interference. It slowly worsened until all their telemetries became worthless. All radio comms were down, and even the Beam Wave technology and the Deep Space Network were useless. They were effectively cut off from the twenty-one astronauts involved in the first manned mission to Mars.

The timing of the communication disruption occurred just as the procedural sequence was being initiated to instruct the remaining six starships to awaken from hibernation and begin their startup process—an order that could only be given from MM1 Command.

What a design flaw this is, Brad thought. We lost communication just before we were able to give the command via the Deep Space Network. Soon after loss of communication, they were informed of what had happened. After all the briefings and meetings, there was nothing MM I Command, CAPCOM, or any of the mission directors could do about it.

Brad was deeply worried about his crew. It was as though they'd sent them on a camping trip and locked up all their supplies. Some kind of mean trick. This was no trick. This was turning into a human survival trip—not a Mars exploration mission. We need to send that command! Brad felt sick, as though they had abandoned the whole crew on Mars, and he had a deep foreboding for them.

Outside the walls of the Johnson Space Center in Houston, the situation was beyond desperate. Almost all the developed countries had become so dependent on satellites for day-to-day activities, no one stopped to think what would happen if they lost them. It wasn't only the satellites for use at NASA, and not only in the United States, but all of Europe, China and much of Asia, Canada, Mexico, and most countries in South America. Even Russia was dependent upon satellites.

After what he had seen and heard what was going on outside of the walls at Johnson Space Center, it looked to him like a third-world nation was a pretty good place to live right then. His wife and kids reported to him on the landline that conditions around Houston were as bad as he had feared and were probably going to get worse soon. Fortunately, Brad was at his desk when his wife found a landline after the cell phone system went down. He told his wife to take their two kids, all the cash and canned food and water at the house, and head to her dad's farm forty miles outside of Houston. He hoped that was far enough out of town before the real craziness set in. Her father had been a military policeman in the Army in the early 2000s and had done a few tours in Afghanistan. He would be able to take care of them.

Brad heard that other than emergency flights, all domestic and international flights had been grounded. The national defenses were on high alert. F-16s and other military aircraft could be seen and heard flying overhead. The National Guard had been called in to help reduce hysteria and limit the looting. Any kind of banking was impossible since banks relied on either the internet or wireless computer systems. The federal government had imposed a national price freeze after there had been runs on grocery stores and gas stations, and pretty much everything else. Not that a price freeze was going to do any good; grocery stores could only take cash, and most of them had closed anyway since their shelves were already empty. Anyone without an old-fashioned television-style antenna or rabbit ears wasn't picking up TV channels. Fortunately, the radio worked for the stations that were still operating their systems in the traditional sense, but there was no national broadcasting of any kind. Some of the larger stations could cover a handful of states, and they were doing their best to inform the public as best they could.

After a severe power surge in the 1980s, the federal government required all power companies to connect their systems together to make the power grid more flexible and resilient. If one power station went down, the surrounding stations could compensate for the reduction in power fairly easily.

In recent years, the power companies figured it would be much simpler if they just monitored each other's power production on secure lines via the internet. When the internet went down due to the satellite loss, the power companies could no longer monitor each other or even many of their own power systems. All power companies went to emergency power production but were having trouble evaluating what the demand was and what their neighboring power company was producing. They could see the demand rising on the system, so they would feed more power into the network, which took time to spool up.

This was exactly what the adjacent power companies down the line fifty or a hundred miles away would do at the same time. This would spike too much power into the system, which they could all "see" after they had powered up the generators now feeding too much power into the system.

It didn't take long before they were just having to guess how much they should produce to keep the system running. After a few hours, it was like watching a badly out-of-balance tire trying to keep up with a speeding car as the tire tore itself apart. Breakers were blowing all over the national grid, putting more variability into the system, which meant more guessing by the power producers, leading to more blown breakers and more variability, and eventually they all had to power off to save the massive power plants and distribution systems from being destroyed.

In New York City, Boston, Atlanta, Miami, Philadelphia, Chicago, Detroit, Los Angeles, San Francisco, and Houston, traffic lights flickered, then went to blinking four-way red, then they just died. Car accidents were common, adding to the already stressed-out police, fire departments and hospitals. No one could use their cell phones to call 911, greatly increasing response times. Within hours, the continental United States, Canada and parts of Mexico (which had both tied into the US power grid) went black. And it was August. The same fate occurred all over Europe. Traffic crawled to a standstill. Generators kicked in at fire stations, police stations, and hospitals, but most facilities only had enough generator fuel for two or three days. The president declared martial law and a seven p.m. to sunrise curfew over the radio. The continental United States was in chaos, as was much of the world. Brad was able to get a call through to his father-in-law.

His wife had arrived safely, thank God. The forty-mile trip had taken her six hours, and that was before the power went down. Brad heard NASA's generators kick in just as his phone line went dead. At least he knew she had gotten herself and the kids there safely. People couldn't get gasoline now that the power was off, and the few stations that had generators—mostly in the states affected by hurricanes—were overwhelmed and only took cash. Fights broke out. People turned to abandoning their cars where they ran out of gas. Trucks couldn't get through to make deliveries, and in some of the larger cities some truck drivers were held up at gunpoint before arriving at their destination abandoning their rigs and fleeing. No one could call the police as payphones have not been serviced for years, falling victim to assumed obsolescence and vandalism.

Brad's phone rang, making him jump. He realized that it had been unusually quiet. As he turned on his headset, the display showed that it was the director. Brad sat up, unconsciously looking around Mission Control and at the blank oversized monitors that were supposed to be showing the ISS.

"Brad Brown. Yes, sir. Conference room G. Right now."

Chapter 21

International Space Station

At 12:25 Zulu, the alarms started sounding and didn't go off. As Commander Amhurst turned his head mic back on, he was met with an unusually serious Andrew Boynton, acting CAPCOM at the moment.

"CAPCOM–ISS," Andrew said.

"This is ISS, CAPCOM," reported Commander Amhurst. "ISS, this is not a drill. Repeat, this is not a drill. How do you copy?"

"Five by five, CAPCOM," Commander Amhurst replied, "Not a drill."

"Roger, five by five," Andrew said. "There have been two satellites destroyed in orbit. We're tracking debris heading in your direction. There's no time for a coordinated evolution to a higher orbit for ISS. We will be initiating PDAM in four minutes. We expect debris arriving at your location in approximately twenty minutes and counting. We'll monitor both the debris fields and your status, with updates every thirty seconds, starting at T-minus three minutes."

Astronaut Giulia DeSantis from Cosenza, Italy, happened to be in the cupola enjoying the beautiful 180-degree view out of the largest windows in space. She had been enjoying the fantastic scenery of Earth and trying to spot her home country as the alarm sounded.

She thought it ironic as she looked around. Here I am sitting in the Tranquility node, with an alarm destroying any sense of tranquility I may have had.

As she quickly rolled the shutters over the windows, Commander Amhurst came over the all-stations PA. "This is not a drill. Repeat, this is not a drill!"

According to the Policies and Procedures Manual, securing each of the different compartments and closing the hatches takes about seven minutes. Cutting some corners could reduce it to four minutes, and that is exactly what Giulia was doing. Speed was of the essence, and she was going as fast as she could. All the shutters had to be closed first to protect the windows of the cupola.

Commander Amhurst turned the radio selector to "all stations, speakers on" so everyone could hear CAPCOM progress with the updates and countdown.

Three minutes after the alarms began sounding, CAPCOM came back over the PA. "ISS, you are 'go' for higher orbit boost. Immediately go for PDAM."

Everyone heard Commander Amhurst repeat, "We are 'go' for PDAM. Roger."

CAPCOM–Houston came back. "Initiating now."

Giulia closed the final hatch on her end of the ISS and was about to head to the Dragon capsule assigned to them by NASA. As she saw Henry Wilson, the other American astronaut aboard, buttoning up his side of the station, she thought of the Russian cosmonauts who were probably heading to their Soyuz as well by now.

Suddenly, her face hit the newly thrust created "floor" rather abruptly, and all of the unsecured miscellaneous tools also found the floor, making clanging metal sounds all over the station while she protected her head from being slammed into the bottom lip of a bulkhead. The station was groaning and making popping noises with the sudden rapid acceleration. It was as if the station were complaining in great metallic groans and whines. Giulia didn't like it at all. It was impossible to stay on her feet with the station moving, so she crawled to the Dragon capsule.

Commander Amhurst continued monitoring the station's vitals. He had secured himself to the floor with a Velcro belt over his socks allowing him some stability.

"Come on!" she yelled at him as she crawled over a laptop bouncing around the recently created floor.

CAPCOM came back over all stations, PA. "CAPCOM–Houston. Debris field tracking reports show a high probability of an impact. Tracking toward your location. Impact probability, ninety percent. ETA of debris field within thirteen minutes."

We are never going to get our spacesuits on in time, Giulia thought as she stripped off her uniform and put on the diapers and undergarments required under a spacesuit. And I just finished my second cup of coffee. That thought suddenly seemed unimportant and rather strange, considering all their lives were now in jeopardy.

Because of the time constraint, she left off the inner gloves and pulled out Commander Amhurst's spacesuit trousers, then set them by the hatch before donning her own trousers while trying to hang on to the bulkhead for balance.

"There's not enough time!" she shouted in frustration, anxiety mounting.

"CAPCOM–Houston," the PA sounded loudly. "Ten minutes to impact threshold."

Commander Amhurst appeared at the door, pulling on the bottoms of his spacesuit, only too aware of the time constraints. He was cutting every corner he could, and even then, he knew he was out of time. "Where's Henry?"

"He's already inside the Dragon capsule, getting it ready."

It usually took forty-five minutes to put on a spacesuit, and that was in a zero-g scenario with one or two other people helping. The spacesuit weighs about three hundred pounds on Earth, but virtually nothing on the orbiting ISS where they normally experience microgravity. They were experiencing about a half-g now due to the PDAM thrusters, which also meant his spacesuit now weighed about one hundred- fifty pounds.

Commander Amhurst heard the thrusters still running, and he could tell the ISS was still accelerating, which meant this was an emergency of unprecedented proportions. NASA was pushing the ISS as far and fast as she could go. In other words, they were in deep shit.

He wondered how Henry already got his suit on so quickly. The thrusters on the Space Station are meant for small orbital changes or attitude adjustments, and Commander Amhurst was pretty sure they had been running nonstop for seven or eight minutes now. He wondered how much longer they could run before completely running out of fuel. As if on command, the thrusters kicked off, and zero g's once again returned to the Space Station as it moaned and complained once more.

CAPCOM came back over the PA once again. "Five minutes to impact threshold."

Commander Amhurst tried to wriggle into the top half of his spacesuit. "Thank God the gravity has let up."

He saw Giulia struggling with the bottom half of her suit and stopped to help her. After listening to her complaints, they heard her suit snap together, and he returned to his own.

"Three minutes to impact threshold. You should be in your spacesuits at this time."

As Commander Amhurst struggled with the top half of his spacesuit, Giulia attempted to help him.

"Don't," he pleaded. "Just get in."

"What about Henry?"

Confused, Commander Amhurst looked inside the crew capsule. Henry was busy getting it fired up and not wearing his spacesuit.

"Two minutes, thirty seconds," announced CAPCOM. Commander Amhurst froze and stared at Henry, realizing nothing could be done now. Henry had made his decision. "Let's hope we can all survive this."

"Two minutes," announced CAPCOM.

Giulia finished with her helmet and gloves and needed to get in her seat next to the window. The commander's seat was in the middle, but he was still putting his helmet on. She began helping him when they heard what sounded like hundreds of pieces of buckshot strafing across the station.

"Get in!" Commander Amhurst shouted. "Get in!"

Giulia shook her head. "You're the commander! Take your seat!" Giulia felt she wasn't really being brave as much as practical. There is no way the commander could crawl over her to his seat fully suited out.

Commander Amhurst grabbed his helmet and gloves and climbed into his personally designed and molded seat next to the unsuited Henry.

A low, hissing noise grew in intensity as CAPCOM came back over all stations, PA. "Sixty seconds."

Commander Amhurst shouted, "The debris must have arrived ahead of schedule. Shut the hatch!"

Giulia did as commanded. As soon as the hatch door was sealed, they heard another round of strafing, along with loud bumps and crashing noises from something skipping off their Dragon capsule and taking the radio antenna with it. A loud hissing came from somewhere inside the ISS, then it dissipated.

From the speakers inside the Station, they heard CAPCOM continue with the countdown and debris track during and after the onslaught. Then they heard CAPCOM's repeated attempts at hailing them.

Commander Amhurst attempted to hail CAPCOM, with no response. "We can hear them, but they can't hear us.

Henry agreed, adding, "Yeah, our radio is not working. We're hearing the ISS radio. That last round must've taken our antenna."

More debris pelted the station and sounded like handfuls of rocks being thrown at a passing car on a highway, louder and heavier this time. The Policy and Procedure for Emergency Evacuation of the ISS states that when an astronaut makes it into the Dragon crew capsule with their spacesuit on, they should lock the hatch and change their call sign. Disembark from the ISS when they feel it's safe, or when they feel they have no other choice.

The Russians decided their best option was to disengage after the second round of strafing began.

The NASA astronauts violated the policy for emergency evacuation on a few different fronts: they didn't all get into their spacesuits, they didn't change their call sign, and they didn't detach from the ISS. As a result, no one knew exactly where they were or what condition they were in. Many were too afraid to guess.

———

Chapter 22

Conference Room G

Conference Room G was where joyful events and announcements usually took place. Brad was sure today would be different, but he was hopeful that at least someone might explain what the hell was going on and help them find a way out of this mess.

The conference room was like an amphitheater, set up with a large table at the front and a small lectern in front of that. There were too many uniforms to keep track of everyone, but he recognized his boss and many of the faces at the large table. The man at the lectern was the President of the United States, POTUS himself, with no formal introduction, just standing there getting the meeting underway.

"Ladies and gentlemen, take a seat. I have a few things to say before General Latimore of the United States Air Force brings us up to speed on a few items. First, let me preempt what I am going to say by telling you that this is an unexpected stop. I do not have a formally prepared statement for you, but what I can say is this: the destruction of our satellites was an act of war. Our generals, commanders, and armed forces around the world are diligently sniffing out the individual who did this. General Lattimore is riding with me on Air Force One as we review our options and coordinate our positions with the Joint Chiefs and the leaders of other governments. As you know, this situation has led to more deaths than can be counted, and unspeakable pain, suffering, and total disruption around the world. It is the act of a despicable coward, and we are diligently pursuing the guilty party. We will make sure they are found, and they will be brought to justice. Trust me when I tell you, they will be found. With that, I give you General Latimore."

As the President stepped away from the dais, General Latimore took his place at the podium. "Thank you, Mr. President. Ladies and gentlemen, I am going to start with some information you probably already know. Just bear with me as I work through this so we're all on the same page. Four days ago, two satellites were taken out by what appears to have been anti-satellite weapons referred to as ASATS. We do not know who or what country is responsible for this aggressive hostility, but their action in destroying these two satellites, and in the specific manner or design of their action, appears to have been aimed at intentionally creating enough debris to start a chain reaction—or domino effect—destroying even more satellites. This reaction, multiplied by the previously existing space debris, continued until the full Kessler Effect took place. It appears whoever is responsible for this situation packed some unusual material into these rockets. They were carrying a payload of something akin to steel ball bearings, or iron or graphite filings mixed with other materials like shredded aluminum foil, to intentionally cause a huge static charge. We don't know all of the different types of materials used, but the debris field was definitely intentional, and at this moment, it is surrounding the globe. The debris is moving through space at orbital speeds, bumping, rubbing, and gyrating in and around all of the now-thousands of debris fields, each containing millions of pieces of debris and creating its own static charge. These static charges are strong enough to absorb any electromagnetic signal, either outgoing or incoming, thereby effectively cutting us off from radio communication or any kind of telemetry. As you know, that means no communication with ISS, MM1—with its twenty- one astronauts and any ongoing space operations—or satellite communications. Each rocket packed an extensively enhanced explosive warhead, creating a larger explosion than you would normally expect from a high-velocity impact with a satellite. The satellites they chose to attack were equipped with thrusters for mobility and propulsion with their own sources of fuel which amplified the explosive effect and distribution of debris."

Whispers were heard as others looked around, and darting eyes were met with concerned looks.

"Some of our satellites that are . . . uh . . . were designed to measure certain kinds of explosions alarmed right before we lost track. Again, now with all of the satellite unavailability, we are having a heck of a time gathering information or even communicating with ourselves. The domestic land lines are overloaded, and the international deep sea or buried cables don't have the capacity for communications beyond the current emergency transmission loads we are burdening them with at the moment. These lines are filled to capacity. The investigation is still ongoing. The results of which will eventually lead us to the guilty parties involved. The last contact with the ISS was that they were engaging Pre-determined Debris Avoidance Maneuver to a higher orbit and hunkering down for possible debris collision. We also know the Russians were able to scramble into their Soyuz. We know they attempted reentry, but we lost radar and radio communications with them shortly thereafter. Nothing further is known about them at this time, and Russia has been quiet on the subject. May God be with them. We do not know how long this static charge will remain as a barrier to communications. We do not know the extent of damage that has occurred to the ISS or the condition of the NASA astronauts aboard. We can only assume that they have taken refuge in their Dragon capsule and are riding it out per protocol. However, this is conjecture, as we did not receive a transfer of command. May God be with them and their families. According to Director Adams, MM1 can function autonomously for an extended time until communications are restored. The United States Air Force and NASA are continuing to evaluate the situation, which is a fluid and ongoing dynamic. To fly a manned rescue mission to the ISS right now would be suicide. If you get a chance to go outside at night, you will see that the aurora borealis is significantly larger and more colorful than it has been in recorded history. I doubt anyone in Houston has ever seen the northern lights this far south before. With the loss of power, you see it easily now. You will also witness hundreds of 'shooting stars', which are pieces of the debris descending through our atmosphere. This is evidence that the debris field is being dragged down into Earth's atmosphere by gravity and burning up upon reentry. So, the debris field is being cleaned up slowly through natural means. Unfortunately, our initial estimate is this 'natural' cleanup will take years before we'll be able to use satellites again. This is a classified meeting, so you are not to repeat any of what I am going to tell you now.

"The fact is that there is no man-made way to clean this up. We continue trying to evaluate the altitude, longitude, and latitude of the debris fields and the different directions of their travel. However, at the moment, the amount of static charge being produced is defeating most of our efforts. Currently, the United States Air Force, NASA, and some different private contractors are cooperating to coordinate a rescue capsule. This is an Air Force mission due to our current state of war. This capsule is not like any capsule ever used or even considered before. We are covering the crew capsule with case-hardened steel designed for high-speed impacts. It also has what is referred to as a Whipple shield incorporated into the design to help absorb impacts. Normally, this type of material would be armor on a tank or battleship. The extra mass or weight adds dimensions to this mission, which are incredibly challenging, as I know you are familiar. It will launch from Cape Canaveral on a fully autonomous rescue mission to the ISS, using one of the starship boosters that had already been produced as a backup for MM1. Unfortunately, this will take a couple of weeks to assemble, even working twenty-four-hour shifts, seven days a week. We will get it done correctly and as quickly as possible. Unfortunately, with sincere honesty, I do not expect it to survive the journey. The statistical odds and dynamics of a piece of debris traveling at twenty thousand miles per hour or more, encountering our rescue vehicle, are, at the moment, very high. You all understand the types of physics, momentum, thrust requirements, and speeds involved here, and you know the situation. We are taking a roll of the dice.

"But as far as we know, we have three stranded astronauts on what is left of the ISS. We will not let them down. We have commissioned different telescopes to get eyes on the ISS. They have been able to visualize it and report that it 'appears' to still be in one piece. Altered, but in one piece. There is one capsule docked at the

ISS. And we trust this is where the NASA astronauts reside. The current orbit and attitude of the ISS appears to be undefined and irregular.

"We are definitely in the middle of this, but I don't expect it to get any worse. What we can do, and must do, is carry on. Carry on doing our jobs. You, me, your staff, and my staff are required to get us out of this mess. We didn't make this mess, but we're the only ones who can get us out of it. We know the situation will change, which is why I, the President, and the whole world needs you to carry on. This is a dynamic and evolving situation, and the world needs you to be at your best and be sharp and attentive. We are all depending on each other right now more than ever. We all have families and loved ones we'd rather be with at this moment. Do what you can from here to be of assistance to them, but it's best if family members shelter in place. I am directing a small contingency from the Air Force Reserves to set up tents and cots and provide some provisional meals for you during this national emergency. Unfortunately, food is very hard to come by now that food production, distribution, refrigeration, and freezers are pretty much all shut down. We will do the best we can. The tents will most likely not be air- conditioned. This is a place for staff to get some rest, if needed, and have a bite to eat. We don't know how long this situation is going to persist, so prepare yourselves for an extended period of time before we get this sorted out. I will take any calls through my office via landline. I will be checking in for messages throughout the day 24-7. The nation needs you. Stay sharp, carry on, and may God be with us and the crew of the ISS."

As soon as the meeting concluded, Brad approached the

———

front table.

"Excuse me, General. I'm Brad Brown, CAPCOM, MM1."

The general extended his hand. "Yes, Brad, I believe we've met before."

"Yes, sir, we have."

"What can I do for you?"

"I was just wondering about the crew capsule rescue mission," Brad said. "We have twenty-one people on Mars unable to get to the supplies we sent up for them in advance."

"I didn't know that. Why can't *Starship X* get to their supplies?"

"Because we never expected to not be in communication with them throughout the entire mission. There would be the expected communication lag times or delay due to distance, but no mission in history has not been in constant, uninterrupted communication with CAPCOM or Flight Control that wasn't previously planned. This mission, as you probably know, is much more dependent than we have ever been on automated systems. As soon as *Starship X* landed, we were scheduled to send a code to each supply starship, which would bring them out of hibernation. It was merely a battery-saving function, placing them in hibernation. We really didn't need to implement the hibernation function at all. We were in the middle of sending the code that would initiate their systems and bring them out of hibernation, right when we lost our ability to communicate with them, effectively isolating *Starship X* from their own supplies. Who could foresee a long-term communication disruption such as this, with all of the redundancies we have in place? We surround the entire world with antenna, nine-meter, and thirty-meter dishes with ten different bands and frequencies, all with their own power back-up and supplies to ensure redundancies. We even have the mars reconnaissance rover to relay our signal directly down from mars orbit if we needed it. You can't say we were unprepared. However, I am afraid that *Starship X* and her crew can survive for only about ten more days without those badly needed supplies. Without them, they may not have access to basic needs such as food and water."

General Latimore went silent while he digested what he'd been told. "Do you mean to tell me that the brightest minds and most experienced design teams NASA has to offer sent some of the most sophisticated spacecraft we could build to support the first ever colonists on Mars and we didn't put a ladder or a ground level latch on the fricking door... or a key code or even a fob? And why put locks on them anyway? Who or what would open them on Mars?"

Brad allowed the General to cool down for a second. "Sir, I don't know if there's anything we can do, but if we come up with something—anything—can I get your support?"

"Of course. Absolutely." General Latimore stared at Brad for a few uncomfortable seconds, then shook his head as he looked down. "Fuck! Twenty-one American astronaut lives in jeopardy because some rocket scientist didn't think of using a high school combination lock or a simple pin pad to keep no one out! You have my number and my complete support. I will do anything I can."

"You've been busy and have a lot of responsibilities. Thank you, sir." Brad shook the general's hand and walked away, neither feeling any better after the conversation.

———

Chapter 23

Day 4

"Good morning, guys!" Lisa sang out. She was going into the bathroom to take a cold shower, grateful that she still could. Fortunately, even the cold water in South Florida in the summertime was around 70°F, sometimes warmer.

Tiger had come out of hiding to explore his new premises, but as soon as Lisa yelled out her good morning announcement, he made a beeline for the spare bedroom again. Brian watched in amusement. *Well, Tiger may be the best source of amusement for the day,* he thought to himself.

While preparing a breakfast omelet of smoked ham, fresh onions, peppers, mushrooms and cheese served with toast off the grill, Lisa announced that they had better eat up these fresh veggies before they go bad.

"Sounds great! You need any help?" Bob asked. He had turned on the tv while Lisa was busy, and Bob joined him. The newscasters were just finishing up a story on how the Governor had just met with the various power companies and they were planning on disconnecting from each other manually so they could begin to power up each individual power plant on their own, even though it was illegal.

This action had been delayed by some of the larger power companies because their lawyers argued that it was a violation of federal law to disconnect. Most of the smaller companies didn't care what their lawyers said. It was the right thing to do.

Each state had the right and the responsibility to act in the best interest of the people of their state, according to the Governor. But some of the smaller power companies had already taken the initiative themselves and started the process. How long it would be before power started feeding back into the grid was a matter of how many disconnects had to be made and the difficulty or complexity associated with each. Fortunately, most of the power companies had fuel stored on site to service their own vehicles and small backup generators to run the fuel pumps, as long as it lasted. It could vary from very easy to a bit complicated. But once each power plant could verify they were isolated, the start-up could begin.

The Governor scanned the room of reporters and politicians and said, "We all understand this is a situation of dire importance and every possible effort is being made to get power restored. These circumstances are not just dire, in many situations they may be life threatening. The longer we are without power the more lives are put in jeopardy. Some people will not survive this. Please check on your neighbors and assisted living facilities welfare, anywhere help may be needed, and offer to be of assistance wherever you can. This is a neighbor issue, a neighborhood issue, a community issue, a county issue, a state issue and a country issue. This affects all of us. We really need to pull together. The army is patrolling the main streets and highways while police are patrolling the neighborhoods. Thank you." The governor then turned and walked off the stage.

Bob mentioned, "I noticed he didn't take questions again."

Lisa said, "Yeah, probably too many he doesn't know the

answers to or too afraid to address."

"Or probably knows the answers but is too afraid to say it on TV," Bob said sheepishly while looking at Lisa through his eyebrows. Bob was looking at the floor, too afraid to imagine how bad this thing could get.

Brian had been monitoring the tv from the bedroom. He came out in a fire t-shirt and shorts, bare footed as usual saying, "You know that's a fact. There is no way I would want to be in his shoes right now."

The newscasters were bantering about with their usual commentary about the governor's message when they were alerted to something new. They were in the middle of a story of how gasoline was reportedly being stolen from people's cars in different locations around Miami but especially in and around condominiums. Then they started reading a list of health-related issues such as, "If you are a diabetic and cannot keep your insulin cold, you should not use it. The local hospitals are offering it free with ice packs and which dialysis centers were still open and more."

"Oh, no! the pretty blond exclaimed. "Oh, um… we have a couple of things we need to address." The male news anchor came in and took the seat next to her. She acknowledged him by name. "You have something for us James?"

James nodded in affirmation. "Yeah, yes, I do, Gina. Two things were just brought to our attention. The first one is that I have just been informed that we only have maybe 12 hours of generator power left here at the station. We have never had to depend on generator power for this long and it appears that we are running very low. If anyone out there knows how we could gather up some diesel for our generators we would be very appreciative so we can continue bringing you this very important information. Along those same lines, on top of the boil water notice put out by Dade County Water Management yesterday, we are being told that the sewage and all freshwater pumps are now threatened to lose power. People, we could possibly run out of fresh water of any kind and the sewage system may or will stop pumping. What this means is if you are on a municipal sewage system, as most of us are, we cannot flush the toilet, take showers, do laundry or even do the dishes! This is a dire situation! If people continue to flush the toilets the people in the lowest elevations will be flooded with that sewage. This is especially imperative for high rises. If you flush your toilet on an upper floor after the pumps go off-line the people on the first few floors or the streets could be flooded with raw sewage. The health consequences will be intolerable.

The pretty blond newscaster, obviously exasperated, asked, "How does that work?"

"Well, it doesn't, Gina. We have never understood how completely dependent on power and fossil fuels we really are. Not only is our water supply dependent on the pumps running every day but so are the sewage system step pumps which move our sewage along to the water treatment facilities. I was taught to always fill up my tub before a hurricane so we could flush the toilets with a bucket. The municipal water facilities have always had the backup generators running to keep everything moving and the power companies have always gotten power to vital infrastructures before the generator fuel was fully consumed. We also have always had fuel shipped in from out of state to re-fuel the generators if needed after a storm. Now

___

however, we are being told that when the water facilities lose the vital backup generators, the step pumps will stop working as well, and the sewage will simply back up to the nearest lowest point such as houses, streets or in a high-rise scenario, the first or even the second floor will flood with sewage, rendering them completely uninhabitable. That's it, Gina."

Gina was obviously horrified. With a giant frown and a disgusted look on her face she said, "How are we going to get people to stop flushing their toilets? Where are they going to go? You can't just leave it in the toilet? Is the county going to ship porta johns all over the county? This is horrific!"

James replied, "Those are all very good questions Gina. I am sure there are not enough porta johns anywhere in the county to satisfy the demand, if it comes to that. And don't forget Broward, Palm Beach, Orlando, Tampa, Jacksonville and all major metropolitan centers across the country will soon be in the same situation if power is not restored. It is a nationwide disaster unfolding."

Quickly, a piece of paper was handed to him off camera. "Ok, so there you go. Broward County and West Palm Beach County have just issued boil water notifications. So, it is happening."

Bob shook his head, looked at Brian. "You ready?' Brian nodded and replied, "Let me get my shoes on."

Bob and Brian walked up and down the street, first the houses on the North side of the road then the houses on the South side of the road. Brian carried a pad of paper on a clipboard and a pen. They knocked on all the neighbor's doors introducing themselves and first asking if anyone needed anything besides gasoline. They explained that they are retired Firefighters and were thinking of putting together a neighborhood support or emergency response network. They explained that they were going to go to the local police station and see what the police would recommend in case the phone lines went down. Maybe they would suggest a VHF radio system, but where are they going to get the radios? If their neighbors answered the door most of them were not interested in any kind of emergency network. Some of them said something to the effect of, "Smith and Wesson is our emergency network." Others said they didn't know how any kind of an emergency network would work without power. Bob and Brian offered their help, if any was needed. Then they stopped at Mrs. Sandoval's house to say hello. Her front door was open with the screen door closed, as usual. She said that she was fine, just a little hot. Brian asked her if she needed any food or water or anything and she said she was fine again. They told her to stop by anytime and they invited her to dinner that night, but she politely declined saying she had a favorite radio show on at that time and she usually goes to bed right afterwards.

Bob and Brian jumped in Bob's Silverado and headed to Ft. Lauderdale Marina. The boat was tied up to the dock right in front of the Ft. Lauderdale Police Station next to the marina on 15th Street covered in plastic film and wrapped in yellow evidence tape with a big stainless-steel chain through the stern eye bolt. It was securely padlocked to the piling on the seawall.

"Well, at least they trimmed the engines up and used a stainless chain," Brian said.

"Yeah," Bob replied. "I hope that chain doesn't scratch the hell out of the stern and dive platform. Fortunately, there isn't much boating activity with the current crisis – no gas."

Inside Ft. Lauderdale Police Station they had no information about the availability of the boat or even who to call to inquire about its availability, but they took down Brian's landline and said they would call if they heard from the "Feds".

Brian inquired about just siphoning some gas out for their generators and the Sergeant on duty just stared and him and said in a menacing voice, "I wouldn't do that if I were you."

As the two made their way back to the truck Bob moaned. "Well, forget about the gas in the boat for now anyway. I doubt they would do anything about it if we just helped ourselves, but on the other hand I don't want to go to jail for illegally entering a crime scene, not just yet anyway."

"Yeah, I guess we need to make do with what we have. We're going to have to start siphoning gas out of the vehicles tonight to keep the generators running," Brian said as they walked back to his truck.

"Yeah, I actually emptied the last jerry can into the generator this morning before you woke up. You were sleeping like a baby."

"So, we're out of gasoline for the generators?"

"Yeah, we need to siphon at least five gallons to get us at through the night. Since we're driving your truck, and we may need my truck, we could take it out of Lisa's car. If she needs to go anywhere, she can take my truck. I have a spare hose we can use for siphoning."

After siphoning ten gallons of gas from Lisa's car which almost emptied her tank, they topped up the generator which took

<hr>

almost five gallons, leaving them with about six gallons remaining.

"Well, that should last us the night at least."

Bob looked around the fenced backyard which backed up to an undeveloped nature area. After surveying the area Bob said, "Do you have anything like 4x4s or 2x4s or plywood or maybe a tarp?" Brian looked at him quizzically and said, "I think I have a couple of 2x4s but no tarp and no plywood. What are you thinking?"

Bob scratched the back of his neck and said, "Well, we could dig a small but fairly deep hole and cut the bottom out of a five-gallon bucket, put it over the hole and call it an outhouse. The neighbors can't see over the fence and there is only that jungle behind. I was thinking of putting up a tarp or maybe an old sheet for some privacy. Would Lisa be ok with that?"

Brian laughed, "Ha, yeah, she is a trooper. We have some drop cloths we could staple to the two 2x4s. Hell, we don't even need to cut the bottom out of the bucket. Just dump it in the hole when we are done and use that water from the recycle bins to rinse it out. It would be more stable to sit on that way anyway… and more sanitary, I guess. Oh, this is going to be bad."

"Ok, I have a few 2x4s at my house and some paint drop cloths as well, we could make the thing three sided easily enough. Hell, I even have a tarp we could put over the top if we wanted to make it fairly rain proof."

"Or make the thing like a triangle with a narrow opening where you couldn't even see the toilet or bucket from the entrance." Brian suggested.

"Good idea. As soon as they announce the sewage system failure, let's put it together. It should only take maybe an hour or so,"

Bob suggested.

"Kinda like a septic system," Brian replied, laughing.

"And we could use the bucket lid to put over the hole to keep the flies away." Bob added.

"Good idea," Brian agreed.

"I'm starting to feel like we're camping!"

They headed over to Bob's house and picked up the needed supplies and some more food for Tiger. They both figured they might as well get the supplies together just in case.

Chapter 24
The Disconnect

Tim Hodges and Sarah Wilkes had both been with Florida Power for years, most of which they had worked together as a team. Sarah liked to call him "Hodge", and Tim's pet name for Sarah was "Haras" (as in harassment), which is Sarah spelled backwards. Somehow this cemented their strange humorous friendship and rather odd personalities, but it worked.

They finished prepping and cleaning the trucks for today's shift. They had spent the last few days cleaning the warehouse and the equipment, along with their teammates, verifying everything was done and ready to go. Now there was nothing left to do. Having become very good friends over the years, and especially recently, these last few days, they became even closer over numerous games of gin rummy, crazy eights and, when they could get their work comrades to join, they also played euchre. The supervisor, Tyler Cunningham, kept reminding them that as soon as they got the clearance, they would be putting in some crazy work hours, so get ready for the word.

In the meantime, they were to be sure that their trucks were totally fueled up and the handheld radios were completely charged at all times, the required equipment for the upcoming assignments was all loaded in the trucks, the water coolers were full, iced up and all aspects of the trucks were all fully operational. Today was the day! They had been given the green light. Every crew they could muster was heading out with the instructions and plans they had been given over the past few days. All one hundred thirty-five power plants in the State of Florida were sending crews all over the State to begin the isolation process. Florida had fifteen coal powered plants, twenty-seven petroleum, seventy-three gas, three nuclear, two hydro-electric, a couple of biomass units, and an ever-increasing number of solar farms.

Solar, natural gas, petroleum, and hydro would be the fastest to get online. The three nuclear power plants were going to take the longest to fire up after the disconnection was complete. Unfortunately, most of Miami, Dade County and all the Florida Keys were powered by the Turkey Point nuclear power plant, located in Southeast Miami.

Tim and Sarah were based in Broward County. Each disconnect location was mapped out on their previously existing GPS navigation equipment and numbered in the most logical and efficient manner to maximize efficiency and speed. Since GPS was useless, they printed map books from their engineering files to keep them on track. There shouldn't be any risk of shock during the disconnect process, but one never knew if some homeowner may have plugged their generator into the house without shutting off their power main from the grid, inadvertently back feeding and charging the power lines. One never took risks with power, so all safety protocols and personal protection equipment were utilized. With any luck the Broward County crews would have Broward completely isolated by late that afternoon or early evening and the start-up process would begin, at least for Broward. Then they would be sent to Palm Beach County or Okeechobee County or Collier County or Polk County or

God knows where, until every single power plant was isolated from every other power production facility in the state. Who knew where they would end up, but isolating every power plant could not be over emphasized. People's lives were on the line.

Their trucks were equipped with lighting and small generators which would ensure the work could continue way after dark, until fatigue began to present itself as a danger to the crews and rest was required. Supervisors were combing the counties to help or answer unexpected scenarios. Even the peaker power plants used for extremely heavy demand periods were getting ready to go online as well. Peaker plants were used to help stabilize the grid and were hardwired into the power plant they serviced, usually within a mile for convenience and rapid access.

Throughout the day Tim and Sarah were making good progress knocking out four different disconnects until they ran into a rather unusual scenario off Alligator Alley. They had driven a few miles down an abandoned service road which was barely passable, following the powerlines to their next disconnect location. A large nest of hornets had set up home on one of the power poles right on the disconnect. As they approached, Sarah stood on a small mound to get a clearer look over the grass and foliage. As she turned to tell Tim to grab the wasp spray, he could see a black and red glob of something moving up Sarah's khaki trousers glistening, gyrating and slightly reflecting the sun's intense rays. At the exact same moment Sarah yelled, "Ouch! Ow! Ow! Ow! Oh, Shit!"

Tim yelled, "Fire ants!" as he pulled Sarah off the mound back onto the middle of the service road. She started jumping, screaming and using her heavy work gloves to pound, smack and wipe the biting insects off her pants and boots.

She screamed, "Oh, they're biting! They're inside my pants!" as she fell to the ground and began undoing her work belt with its heavy tools, then she began undoing the belt to her jeans.

Tim yelled, "Boots first, boots!" then picked Sarah up while she continued smacking and pulling at her pants, he carried her to the truck, pulling open the tailgate and placing her in the back. He began immediately undoing Sarah's work boots as she screamed and writhed in pain. "Get them off! They're in my boots. My ankles! Oh, my God!" Sarah yelled.

Tim got the left boot off first then the sock and used his bare hands to wipe off the nasty biting creatures. He then set to work on the second boot as Sarah pulled her left leg out of her jeans, still screaming. Sarah had wound the boot laces around the top of the boot several times which made it longer to get them off. Sarah was wiping her left leg and heel off when Tim finally got the right boot and sock off wiping down her ankles and foot. Sarah, still yelling pulled her right leg out of her jeans. Tim tossed it aside. The little red and black ants had somehow made it all the way to her feet and even down to her little toes and in between. Tim inspected each toe and between each toe, wiping the nasty ants away every time he came across another one. He pulled off his shirt, rolling Sarah right to left and left to right, wiping down the tailgate. He then picked all 5'2", 110lbs Sarah up again and inspected the bed of the service truck, wiping it off every time he found another stinging ant. He spun Sarah around a few times while she was standing. placing her in the bed of the truck again. He sat Sarah up and ripped the Velcro strip which covers the zipper, unzipped her jacket and she pulled her shirt up while he inspected her belly and lower back being careful not to miss any of the obnoxious little vermin.

Sarah was still screaming as the toxin began raising little welts all over her legs, ankles and feet. Tim was still inspecting Sarah's arms, neck, and pulling out the straps of her bra around her shoulders and around her back making sure they were free of the biting ants, as Sarah was still wiping her legs off and looking for any more of the bugs herself.

"I think we got them," she said. She then jumped up and turned around and pulled her underwear down. "Look at my butt, just don't enjoy it!" She looked angrily at him. "I will check my front myself," she added as she ran her hands through her pretty blond shoulder-length hair, shaking her head from side to side while bent over. "I just don't want to take any chances."

"Of course not. I agree totally," Tim responded. "I've been bitten enough as well." He snapped her underwear a few times to be sure there were no ants in the stitching. "Ok, just tell me when you're done."

After running her hands up and down her legs, thighs and in between a few seconds more, Sarah announced that she was done, and she was reasonably confident the ants were gone as she pulled her underwear back up.

Tim said, "Ok, just don't move. I am going to check myself out, but I don't want you standing back up on the ground or on your clothes until we are sure we got them. I may actually pull the truck forward maybe ten feet after I check myself. Yep, hang on, don't get down. I have some on my jacket and trousers and my boots. Make sure there aren't any on the back of the truck."

"I'm sure you've been bitten," she said. "I was covered. But I don't see any on the truck bed, not yet anyway."

"You sure were. I kept sweeping them off the truck every time I saw one." Tim responded "Ok, I'm pretty sure they didn't get inside my trousers or jacket. I'm checking out your socks," he said, as he turned them inside out, shaking them, reversing them and checking again.

Every time Tim found one of the mean little critters he would announce it and flick it away. After he returned Sarah's socks to her, he said, "You just stay seated while I pull the truck forward a bit, then I'll get to your pants."

"Ok", she agreed. Then she kind of giggled despite the pain. "That sounded weird." The collective pain of dozens of ant bites was quickly beginning to get real, taking away any sense of humor Sarah had remaining.

Thirty minutes later they had exhausted all of their wasp spray on the fire ant hill. Fortunately, the wasp nest was empty. They disconnected the line and made sure they weren't carrying any more ants on their boots or clothing.

"Did you get bit, Hodge?" she asked him.
"A few times, but nothing like you did. Did you count how many times you were bitten?"

"While you were checking my pants, I counted 33 bites that I could see. I'm sure there are plenty I can't see. I don't think they got above my thighs."

"Well, it could have been worse. How do you feel?"

"A little nauseous, a little freaked out and the bites are really starting to hurt, burning and stinging, but otherwise I think it will pass. I could probably use some Benadryl but I will survive. I need to thank you, Hodge. You performed like a true first responder!"

"Just takin care of my buddy." He flashed her a smile.

"Ok, this stays between you and me," she said flatly, with a dead stare, showing she meant business.

"Just you and me, Sarah. No further," he agreed.

"Ok. I trust you," she said, padding him on the shoulder and running her hands through her hair, slowly exhaling. Sarah was showing no undue side effects other than discomfort and fatigue from the traumatic encounter. The painful red welts would be around for a couple of days.

They reported to their supervisor that they had been delayed for over an hour due to an infestation but their disconnect had been made and they were on their way to the sixth disconnect. The supervisor acknowledged their transmission and added that most of the other crews were close to their original schedule. It looked as if Broward County might be able to begin the spool up procedures tonight around six pm. He then asked if everyone was safe.

Sarah looked at Tim and with a nod of her head and a slightly tired but deviant smile she responded, "Safe and secure." She hung the mic up and had to giggle a little. "Well, that was different." She smiled, kicking her boots up on the dash and closing her eyes while shaking her head. "One to be remembered, just between me and my buddy, Hodgee. I'm not even telling my mother about this one," she laughed. "OMG!"

———

196

Chapter 25
Day 5

"Another scorcher today," the weather guy announced on TV, with a slight Seabreeze coming off the Atlantic. "As far as we can tell, there is no tropical development all the way to the Lesser Antilles. We have a slight possibility of afternoon showers developing over the Everglades. They may push toward the beaches this afternoon, but it is really difficult to predict the weather without satellites. That's it from the weather front."

Gina, the anchor, started with a much perkier smile than usual. "Well, it's good to see all of our viewers are still hanging in there. We're pretty much out of diesel for our generator here at the station. We could go offline any minute. But the good news from Florida Power is that the Port Everglades Natural Gas Power plant is in startup mode and as soon as the systems check out, they can start producing power for Broward County. But only for Broward County. It will be a small roll out at first as all systems are checked, according to their spokesman. The first large facility that will get power will be the Ft. Lauderdale / Hollywood International Airport, then the Dania area, and if all looks good downtown, Ft. Lauderdale and the Greater Las Olas area, then Davie and Hollywood with all of the other cities and towns following. Apparently, the isolation procedures for Dade County are also complete. We're just waiting for the Turkey Point Power plant to complete the startup procedure, which reportedly takes around 24 hours. So, there is hope. Help is coming! On the downside, Dade County Water has announced that the sewage system generators are finally running out of power, as predicted. Sewage is no longer being pumped, so please do not use your toilets or put anything down the drain if you're on city or county sewer. Especially in a high-rise hotel or condominium. As bad as this sounds, we should have water and sewage back online as soon as tomorrow. But please go in the bushes or in a bucket, or if you're lucky enough to have a port a john nearby, use that until we regain power."

Having watched this much of the news with Lisa and Brian, Bob decided to take a quick trip to Golden Akers and check on Marcie's mom again, as well as take Tiger back home where he belongs. "You coming, Brain Damage Boy?"

"Hey! I thought those days were gone." "They are. I'm just kidding."

"Ok, let's go," Brian replied.

As they pulled up Bob's short driveway, the sun was setting over the Everglades, streaming beautiful multi-colored light streamers across the sky. After dropping Tiger off safely inside Bob's house, there was a sudden noise, a grinding and whirring sound. The lights flickered on and the refrigerator suddenly kicked on, then the air conditioner. Bob had power! He yelled to Brian, "Brian, power! We have power!" Brian had to come in from the truck to check it out.

"Maybe we should stay here tonight," Bob suggested.

"Maybe," Brian responded. "I'll ask Lisa what she thinks—unless we have power at my house. I wish you had a landline!"

"Yeah, me, too."

Bob and Brian walked the perimeter of the house and

property looking for any evidence of deviant activity, broken windows, forced doors or anything malicious. The shed doors behind the house were open but it didn't look like anything was missing. Bob may have forgotten to shut them after getting the gas tanks. Otherwise, everything looked good.

As soon as they evaluated Bob's house and made sure Tiger was situated with food, water and a clean litter pan, they headed back over to Brian's house in a hurry.

As soon as Brian stopped his truck, they both ran inside. The generator was off and the lights were on! Lisa shouted, "Power! We have power!" She gave both guys a hug and a smiling kiss.
"Oh, that is so awesome!" Brian bellowed. "So do I!"
"Bob shouted, " Yes! We have air conditioning!" Shaking his fists in the air. "How long ago did it come on?"

Lisa, still smiling from ear to ear happily replied, "About ten minutes after you left. The air conditioner and the fridge were no longer plugged in, but I had forgotten that we left the lights on. When they suddenly flickered on, I plugged in the fridge and it kicked in. So, I then ran to the air conditioner, and it started up as soon as I turned it on. I turned off the generator and unplugged the mini air conditioner. What a relief not to have that constant noise!"

"Oh! That is so awesome. You still want to go to Golden Acres?" Brian asked Bob.

Brian's smile ran away from his face. "Maybe we can just drive by and see if they have power. It would be a load off of my mind just to know that Marcie's mom has air conditioning."

On the way over to Golden Acres, the first stoplight they came to was flashing red indicating a four-way stop, but a few cars were ignoring it and not even slowing down. Bob carefully made his way through the intersection. The next light on University Drive was functioning correctly and it seemed that most of the cars were obeying the rules. As they pulled into the parking lot of Golden Acres, they could see the lights on the front porch and inside the building. Bob laughed out loud, clapped his hands together and smiled.

"Yes!"

"I am very glad we decided to come by," he said. "That's a relief. Thank God they have power. Thank you for coming with me, buddy."

"Not a problem. So glad to see they at least have power. I wonder how close they came to running out of diesel?" Brian said with a sigh of relief.

"I don't know, but let's go ask them."

Before Brian knew it, Bob was bounding out of the truck and up the front steps. He decided it would be the neighborly thing to go along so he jumped out to catch up.

Bob was already engaged in conversation with the young lady at the front door. She was smiling, wearing a pair of hospital scrubs which were blotted with sweat with a towel around her neck. She looked like she had just taken a shower. Brian knew better. Obviously, the air conditioning had just come back to life. But at least the air conditioning was working! Brian listened as Bob offered to be of any assistance, maybe food or something? She seemed a bit disheveled but happy.

"No, thank you, we're fine. Besides, we are not allowed to take food from the public. Some of our residents have special diets

______

so we have to strictly control their diet according to the patient files."

Brian smiled back as he looked around the reception area and ran his hand through his thinning hair. "Whew, that was a close one!" he said. "Can I just say hi to Marcie's mom really quick since I'm here? I'm on the visitors list."

"Sure, if she is awake. We just ate dinner so she may be sleeping. I will check her room. They usually go pretty much straight to bed after dinner. You can come along if you want."

The receptionist walked down the dimly lit hallway for about thirty yards, quietly opened a patient room and peaked in motioning Bob to stay in the hall. She turned around and said, "Yeah, she's sleeping comfortably. You can look in if you want." Bob glanced in to see Marcie's mom on her side snoring loudly under the covers.

On the way back to Brian's house they drove by the closed mall that had the water distribution site set up in the parking lot. The parking lot lights were lit, and the Reservists were still there, but the number of cars waiting to get water or MREs was down to only a couple. The streetlights and businesses lights had suddenly come to life making the neighborhood look much more normal.

"Kind of a weird scene watching all of the lights come back on," Bob noted.

"Yeah, I don't think I've ever seen that before," Brian responded.

"Hopefully, you will never see it again," he said as he stole a glance at Brian.

They could see block by block streetlights and businesses lights turning on all the way down University Drive until the greater

Ft. Lauderdale area appeared "normal", just with very little traffic. If one wasn't picking up MREs or water, where was there to go? And there were still no gas stations open—at least not yet anyway.

After they opened the door to Brian's house, they found Lisa glued to the TV.

She explained that the news station they had been watching earlier was off the air. They were based in Miami and still didn't have power. She switched to a Fort Lauderdale TV station. Most of what they were reporting was the power being restored to most of Broward County, but also the extremely difficult situation in Miami-Dade County.

"Guys, you need to see this!" she yelled as they walked in the door. "Now that the news is getting out that Broward County has power, all northbound roads out of Dade County are jam packed with cars trying to make it into Broward. Probably trying to get into a hotel with running water and a working toilet."

There was helicopter video of a blacked-out Dade County with all northbound traffic lanes completely loaded with cars.

From I-95 to the Turnpike to Red Road, US 1 and even A-1-A were all lit up with cars for as far as the eye could see.

The TV news anchor reported that every hotel they were able to contact in the Greater Ft. Lauderdale area reportedly was sold out.

"So, where are all those people going to go?" Lisa asked.

"Not Dade County. Maybe just a rest area for the night?" Bob responded. "I guess the news helicopter was able to get fuel."

"That makes sense," Brian added. "The airport is right next to the tank farm at Port Everglades."

As if on cue the newscaster reported that Palm Beach County was now almost completely powered back up as well. He then reported that they have not been able to get much in the way of details on the road and living conditions in Dade County other than what they could see from the chopper and some limited landline correspondence. However, sanitation conditions are reportedly headed "downhill" and of course this goes without saying, do not let your children play near or even touch the water on the roads or near any sewage drain, was all he would say, shaking his head. He went on to explain that they still did not have fuel to get around and the road conditions, at least for the moment, were too dangerous. Most of Miami-Dade County and the Florida Keys were not projected to get power until the next morning at the earliest.

And this just in, apparently the Army Reserve is announcing that for Dade County they will be handing out buckets donated by Home Depot for as long as they last. One per household. He concluded with, "It is going to be a rough night."

Chapter 26

Dragon Capsule

Commander Amhurst, Giulia Di Santis, and Henry Wilson were on their fifth day of sitting inside the Dragon capsule. They had spent the bulk of their time sleeping and talking, but the situation was intolerable and possibly life-threatening. Sitting anywhere for an extended time could lead to deep vein thrombosis, also known as DVT's, meaning blood clotting from lack of movement. It could lead to stroke, heart attack, or a blood clot in their lungs. They had been doing exercises while seated, as instructed during training, but that could only go so far. The mental and emotional issues incurred while being locked up in close proximity needed to be considered as well. No matter how much they discussed their safety in the Dragon versus the ISS, it didn't matter; they could no longer stay in the Dragon. They went over every possible option they might face if they went back into the ISS. Nothing changed the fact that they had to get out of the Dragon. The situation was critical. If they stayed much longer, they would die. Simple as that. Henry had been able to get his spacesuit on with much difficulty after they closed the capsule door. It was not like they were in any rush early on. He was able to get it on eventually, with Commander Amhurst's help, and the zero Gs they were once again experiencing.

There were few supplies in the Dragon since it usually reentered the atmosphere and touched down typically within about four hours after undocking, depending on the situation. Six bottles of water and six biscuits (the emergency supplies in case the crew capsule was blown off course) were nearly gone, and they all knew it was only a matter of time before a decision would be forced upon them.

The only information they had was that the banging and smashing they'd initially heard had diminished dramatically. At the last minute, Commander Amhurst had slowly turned the Space Station long-end toward the Earth, which put the Dragon capsule facing directly away from the Earth. He had hoped that most of the debris would be heading their direction from low earth orbit. Turning the Space Station would hopefully put the ISS between the oncoming debris and the Dragon, protecting the capsule from   the bulk of the debris—somewhat like the blade of a snowplow. He knew there were a lot of presumptions in his logic, but they were out of time and information. It's also why he didn't immediately detach and begin a return to Earth. If there was a debris strike, he wanted as much protection between it and them as possible.

Commander Amhurst grudgingly repeated the energy formula in his head; he couldn't stop it. The amount of energy delivered by an impact exponentially increased as the speed increased. Anything to stay in orbit must have a minimum speed of seventeen thousand-five hundred miles per hour or it will re- enter the Earth's atmosphere eventually depending on mass. That speed was fourteen times faster than a bullet exiting the barrel of a gun at twelve hundred miles per hour. A direct hit by that same bullet at orbital velocity would go straight through the Space Station before anyone knew it had been hit. Another key factor in the equation was how much the projectile weighed and whether it was a direct hit. A glancing blow may skip off, and by Commander Amhurst pointing the Space Station toward the Earth, he was able to lower the profile of the Space Station, in relation to the debris storm, thereby increasing the chances of a glancing blow. In recent years, NASA had the astronauts install thin Kevlar padding on the outside of the ISS to help reduce penetration from flying debris or micrometeoroids.

It had been five days, and they had been effectively out of water for over twenty-four hours. After they emptied their first bottles, they rationed the remaining bottles. The batteries were running low on the Dragon, as well. When they considered that the batteries could be too low to launch the parachutes, they agreed they would open the ISS hatch and hope they could formulate some sort of survival on what was left. They needed to act before the dehydration started sapping their bodies of too much energy. There was water and food in the ISS. If worse came to worse, maybe they could dive back into the Dragon and risk the tired batteries for a return to earth.

After much debate they decided Giulia would open the hatch, and when she did, there was only a slight rush of air into the ISS. Giulia turned her spacesuit light on and saw stuff floating around and alarm lights on the navigational panel. Either the evacuation alarm had silenced itself, or the battery running it had died.

She crawled in and floated to the internal atmospheric panel, where it read 16% O2. Not perfect, but good enough for now. The atmospheric pressure gauge indicated 9.6 psi. Not perfect, but survivable. Maybe they could find the hole or holes and patch them. She slowly equalized her spacesuit to the new atmospheric conditions as she exhaled and felt her ears pop and sinuses expand while she yawned and swallowed, trying to get her sinuses to equalize. She felt bubbles forming in the corners of her eyes. She badly needed to hold her nose and blow to open her eustachian tubes, but you can't do that with a helmet on. As she took her helmet off, she rapidly plugged her nose and blew softly. Having equalized to the new atmosphere, she turned around and shouted, "Welcome aboard! According to our current atmospheric pressure we're now at twelve thousand feet above sea level!"

They might feel short of energy, but anything was better than being stuck in that damn Dragon another minute.

Giulia helped the guys get out and smiled at her partners. "I love you, guys." The crew shared a group hug, thrilled they were still alive and in one piece.

The entire Unity Node had to be gone over with a fine- tooth comb to search for leaks, and an inventory of everything needed to be taken. There had been no debris strikes for a while. Giulia tried to remember how long it had been. The strafing seemed to come in groups or bunches at a time. They concluded that it was at least four hours since they had heard the last impact, and the last two didn't seem as bad as the previous five days had dealt them. When the ISS was at its typically prescribed distance of two hundred-fifty miles from the Earth, they would orbit around the Earth every ninety minutes. But now they had no idea what their orbit was, or even how far from the Earth they were.

Commander Amhurst had activated PDAM, which had a predetermined orbit of five hundred miles, but with all the excitement, he wasn't able to verify anything before entering the

Dragon capsule. They decided they had better start looking for leaks and try to get the O2 levels and atmospheric pressure back to more reasonable levels. They silently floated around the Unity node, listening for the quiet, telltale hissing sound that would give away the location of any leaks.

Commander Amhurst decided they wouldn't open the hatches to any other nodes until they had secured the leaks in the Unity node, then they would discuss venturing farther at that time. As they came across the occasional tiny leak, they would patch it up with a special two-part epoxy, then cover that with the universally used heavily reinforced duct tape.

There were three "normal" air bottles of Earth's blended air and two pure O2 bottles in storage. They cracked the valve of one of the air bottles and opened it slightly. After fifteen minutes of listening to the precious air mixture escape from the tank, the pressure slowly started to rise inside the Unity node. They left the tank valve open until they were approximating the altitude of Denver or about five thousand feet in altitude in their artificial atmosphere of the Unity Node.

Commander Amhurst checked the batteries, which appeared to be undamaged. Many of the breakers had blown, or the fuses had tripped in the fuse box. They didn't want to turn on any equipment and start a fire somewhere, so they worked together to jury-rig some lights. Working in the dim light cast by the Dragon Capsule.

They had been in their spacesuits for five days and desperately needed to remove them and clean themselves up. Giulia was the only one who had put the diaper on, and she felt a little guilty that she had no significant cleanup duties. They hadn't eaten or had much to drink, which somewhat limited the cleanup job for the guys. Giulia checked the water stores and filled some drinking pouches, which they all enjoyed.

The next big decision was in front of them. What do they do next? The ISS was filled with cameras so Ground Control could monitor the different experiments and activities. The doctors and physiologists all wanted to "see" them working out or doing various duties and experiments. Many of the ISS astronauts in the past had felt like guinea pigs, constantly under the microscope, with heart rate monitors and respiratory monitors constantly giving the doctors feedback on how their patient was doing day or night, twenty-four hours a day. It was so invasive that an entire crew once turned all the cameras off, disconnected all their bio- monitors, and took them off. NASA decided the doctors had gone a little too far, and the monitoring was toned down significantly after that. But the cameras on the ISS were off now. The radio had no power, either.

While the spacesuits were drying by the hatch, after being cleaned as best they could, they ran a new power line to the radio, and with some ingenuity, they were able to get it to work. They tried to hail CAPCOM but weren't surprised when their hails went unaddressed. The antenna was probably damaged or missing from the top of the Space Station, just as it seemed to be on the Dragon.

As they were about to turn the radio off to preserve the house batteries, they heard, "ISS, this is *Starship X*. Do you copy? Over."

Commander Amhurst stared at the radio like he had heard his long-dead grandfather talking to him. He slowly picked up the mic. "This is the ISS. Copy, four by four, *Starship X*. How do you

———

209

copy? Over."

Commander Amhurst, Henry, and Giulia looked around at each other, not believing what they had just heard. Commander Amhurst checked his watch and scrambled for a pencil to write the time on the wall next to the radio. They looked at the radio, then at each other again, and they all started to laugh at the irony and pure joy of making contact with another living human being, even if that person was on Mars.

"What are the odds?" Commander Amhurst asked. "That was *Starship X* on Mars. They probably want to know what's going on, too." Commander Amhurst had an inquisitive look. "What does that mean? Maybe they heard about the satellite strike? But why are they hailing us?"

"We haven't heard from CAPCOM in five days, but I thought that's because our antenna was missing on the Dragon. It's obviously not missing on the station, or we wouldn't have heard *Starship X.*"

"So, that means that CAPCOM..." Commander Amhurst picked up the mic. "CAPCOM. CAPCOM, this is ISS. How do you copy?" The seconds ticked by, and Commander Amhurst tried again. "CAPCOM, CAPCOM, how do you copy?"

Nothing. No familiar squawk of the mic activating. No friendly voice responding. Finally, he heard, "ISS, this is *Starship X.* We copy you two by two. Good to hear someone's voice out there! Are you in contact with CAPCOM? Over."

Commander Amhurst documented the time. It had been almost twelve minutes. How could *Starship X* hear them? They must be... he was forced to think about the solar system for a minute, thirty-five million miles away?

Commander Amhurst picked up the mic again. "Negative, *Starship X,* we are not, repeat, not in communication with CAPCOM. Due to a satellite strike, we had to execute emergency PDAM. Numerous strikes have knocked out much of our equipment. We were just getting the radio back online. We're surprised but relieved to hear your voice. We have not, repeat, not been in communication with CAPCOM for five days. Over."

Commander Amhurst made a note of the time and wrote it on the wall below the last time stamp. They decided to stay close to the radio and grab something to eat while they waited for the next return radio transmission from *Starship X.* As they sat around sucking down water again. They decided to make some chicken soup rehydrated with cold water. It wasn't good, but compared to what they had been eating, it was wonderful. The soup was supposed to be hydrated and heated by the no longer functioning hot water machine.

Commander Amhurst started making prioritized to-do lists. The number one item was dealing with the offline atmospheric controls before the temperature started getting out of control. The temperature was currently a chilly forty-eight degrees inside the Unity node. Fortunately, they had access to more clothing. Giulia continued wearing the undergarments required for the spacesuit, pants, and a shirt, and one of her NASA sweaters *Thank God these underwear are antibiotic,* she thought.

As they discussed their next move, the radio squawked again. "ISS, this is *Starship X.* We have not been in contact with CAPCOM for five days, as well. We are operating autonomously. Do you have any information as to the loss of comms with CAPCOM, and are you safe? Over."

Commander Amhurst looked at the time stamp he had written on the wall, then checked his watch and made another notation. He was pretty sure he was talking to Steven Henderson, whom he had trained with before Steven was selected for MM1. It was evident Steven was sitting by the radio, waiting for their transmission reply every twelve minutes, just as the ISS crew was. This told Commander Amhurst that they were just as confused as the ISS crew about the break in comms with CAPCOM and anxious to get any information they could.

Commander Amhurst picked up the mic again. "Negative on info relating to CAPCOM. We were sheltering in the Dragon for the past five days due to the satellite strike and subsequent debris field. We know bupkis other than that. We are currently assessing our situation on the ISS. Unity node is our intact domicile. However, power and atmospheric controls are limited. We are still evaluating our situation. Over."

Commander Amhurst purposefully used the term "bupkis" as a code for Steven, which was one of his favorite ways of saying, "We don't know anything." If it was Steven, he would understand it immediately.

To continue assessing the condition of the whole station meant putting their spacesuits back on before opening the hatch to the next node. Each node had been sealed with its airtight hatch and opening a hatch to another node meant risking the air, the atmosphere and the luxury of the space they were now very much enjoying inside the Unity node.

The radio squawked again. "Hey, Commander Amhurst.

You're right. This is Steven. We're in better shape than you at the moment. We all wish you the best of luck, and we will get back to you as soon as we know more. Let's set up a schedule for telemetry every day at twelve noon Zulu. Please confirm. Over."

"Roger that, Steven," Commander Amhurst said. "Twelve noon Zulu. We will do the same. Over."

They discussed the situation and the risks involved with opening the hatch to any of the other nodes. It was possible that some of the other nodes were wide open to space with zero atmosphere and two hundred degrees below zero, Fahrenheit, or worse. They could lose all the atmosphere they were currently enjoying after the five-day nightmare in the Dragon.

On occasion, they would watch the Earth pass by one of the hatch windows, and it now looked tiny compared to its normal size.

As the Earth zoomed by, the fleeting views they caught told them little other than they were still in orbit. The other hatch window would occasionally let the sun come gleaming through at odd, ever-changing angles. But it did seem to be warming the node at times. The hatch windows into the Quest Joint Airlock or the Tranquility node usually stayed black, with occasional darts of streaking sunshine quickly passing through, but no useful visibility. On occasion, they would hear a random scrape or popping of the hull as it would roll into or out of the sunshine, and something occasionally was scraping around outside. But there was little indication of what lay beyond the hatch doors or the condition of the rest of the Space Station.

———

Chapter 27
Mars Sol-5

As soon as Carl was back from his evaluation of *Starship IV*, Commander Carrigan grabbed Carl's attention and motioned him aside. "Can you spare a few minutes of your time?"

"Of course."

They made their way to Commander Carrigan's study. Carl had a pretty good idea of what the conversation was going to be about.

"Thanks for meeting with me, Carl."

"Of course. I was just on my way to the 3D printer to print a tool we need. You want to know how we're going to get the supplies out of the remaining starships, right?"

Commander Carrigan contemplated Carl for a moment, fully appreciating the professional in front of him. "Why, yes, Carl. That, and some other items I'd like to cover with you. I guess you understand our dilemma well enough. Please tell me you've been considering the situation and may have some suggestions."

"I have. And I think I see the dilemma fairly simply. The starships haven't been activated; therefore, the access hatches remain locked, and the cranes won't function. We don't have any kind of remote control to activate them, and we have no way of getting to the access hatches a hundred-fifty feet up. And now, neither CAPCOM nor MMI can activate them because we've lost communication with the Earth, and so have the starships.”

Commander Carrigan smiled and shook his head at the simplicity of their strange precarious predicament and Carl’s short explanation. They both knew that any supply issues this far from Earth could mean anything from slight discomfort to unspeakable pain and suffering—and possibly a death sentence for the entire crew. “In short, yes. As our chief Engineering Specialist, please tell me you have an answer or two for our situation.”

“According to my inventory records, we only have two twenty-four-foot folding ladders, and a hundred-and-fifty-foot drop from one of those hatches to the surface would be deadly.”

“I agree. First things first, though. I ran an inventory and status report this morning which showed our oxygen consumption is above the expected usage rate. Our oxygen tanks are getting somewhat low. Do you know why we may be over-consuming our oxygen supplies?”

“With most items and services, we usually have a twenty percent margin which would be thirty-six days of safety margin built in at normal usage rates. However, we need to set up the MOXIE.” (Mars Oxygen In-Situ Resource Utilization Experiment). “It’s on the schedule for tomorrow’s activities,” the commander injected, rubbing his face with his hands as the stress was becoming evident.

“Right,” Carl answered. “Well, it appears the multiple EVAs we have been forced to conduct due to the fallen *Starship IV* have been consuming more oxygen than expected. At least that’s my original evaluation. Not only have we been conducting more EVAs, but they’ve also been longer and harder and more stressful than expected."

At this point the commander interrupted, "Excuse me. You mean more stressful than being thirty-five million miles from home, separated from friends and family for years? On a planet that has no breathable atmosphere. In spacesuits that, if torn or damaged, could immediately render death? Where we are being pelted with Solar and Cosmic galactic radiation. More stressful than that?"

Carl quickly glanced up at the smiling commander and realized he was joking. It was time to loosen the mood, he guessed. With a smile, he continued, "Well, in a word, yes." They both had a quick laugh. "What that means is that we're out consuming the scheduled usage rate of our breathable air. Today I realized our projections don't include all of these heavily crewed, multiple daily EVAs. Utilizing the equalization room two or three times a day. As you know commander, each EVA pumps five hundred cubic feet of breathable air out of *Staten* onto the atmosphere of Mars. That is a significant amount of air. Now, you have a tired, stinky, sweaty crew breathing off more CO2, using more shower water, and we have to reverse the scrubber bottles they were breathing from while on the surface exerting themselves. So, yes, that twenty days of margin NASA gave us is being consumed at a much faster rate than originally projected."

"I monitor the O2 percentages every day, and they're always around twenty-one percent."

"I also monitor it constantly. That's why we're always near perfect atmospheric conditions on *Staten,*" Carl responded. "I understand and appreciate your attention to detail, Carl.

Given the circumstances, your efforts and dedication help

me feel more comfortable."

"Thank you, commander."

"You're a good man, Carl. I honestly wouldn't know what to do without you," the commander added.

"I've been preparing to set up the MOXIE. I actually just finished my assessment of the numbers late last night, but I didn't understand the results until I was returning from the EVA just now. I could see my numbers weren't matching the consumption rates I was seeing over the last two or three days. That's what the report you ran informed you about. I couldn't figure it out until I was in the equalization room coming back from this EVA."

As the Commander grew silent, Carl knew not to interrupt his train of thought. It was as if he were engaging large gears as he was juggling priorities and considering possibilities.

"So, the extra EVAs is why my report is showing our oxygen tanks are being consumed too rapidly. Okay, Carl. Tomorrow, there is no higher priority than getting that MOXIE unit set up. I will get you all the help you need," the Commander said as he looked at the roster for tomorrow. "What do you need to get that unit up and running as fast as possible? We can't take any chances with our oxygen level."

"Myself and three other people," Carl said. "And we should have it set up and working in about eight hours, maybe less."

Commander Carrigan thought for a few seconds, a concerned expression on his face. "That's two long EVAs. If you think you need more people, I'll give you more personnel. If you need four or five, let's get it done tomorrow. Many hands make light work.

How many people do you want?"

Carl nodded. "I think four is fine. I'll start setting up the gear for tomorrow right now."

Thinking to himself again, Commander Carrigan paused, then asked, "How long will it take the MOXIE unit to return us to twenty days of residual O2 reserves, or more?"

"The specifications show the unit will produce enough pure O2 to start refilling our pressure tanks at a rate of approximately two times our daily usage. Utilizing the specifications for the MOXIE, we should be back to a twenty-day safety margin in ten days, depending."

"Depending on what?" "Usage rate."

"Yes, yes, of course. On another subject, do you know if we have any rope? I mean, I know we do. Do you know where it is and how much we have, just off the top of your head? We may need all of it in the near future. I haven't had time to do an inventory search."

"We have some here on *Staten*. I'll see if I can locate it. Actually, I think I know where it is. For the rest of the rope, I'll have to look it up on the computer. What do you have in mind?"

"Strong enough to lift a person safely, I guess. Two hundred fifty kilograms or so. Life safety line."

"Length?" Carl asked.

"I'm not sure. Maybe five hundred feet. Can you locate how much we have on *Staten*, *Starship IV*, and starships I and II? I am not sure what I'm thinking of at the moment. What are your thoughts around getting the hatches open on the other starships?"

"I've been thinking about that. The nylon netting used to secure the inventories and supplies are all secured to the aluminum framing attached to the inside structure of the starships, correct?"

"That's correct."

Commander Carrigan had an idea. "If we disconnect all of the nylon cargo netting and remove all of the inventory in *Starship IV*, can we remove the aluminum framing and weld it together in the shape of a hundred-fifty-foot ladder or scaffold, and maybe use the cargo netting to help reinforce the scaffold or secure it to the starship to act as a safety net or guard? You know…wrap it around the scaffold or something?"

"Hmm…you know, I think we could. Let me think about that and come up with some ideas. It would take a few days, but I think we can. I have electric grinders with cutting blades, aluminum welders, torches and some other equipment on *Staten* that we will need. We could use the Mars car to haul it over to *Starship IV*, and I could do the work on the surface outside. I would just need power."

"Yes, well, we haven't off-loaded the Kilowatt nuclear generator yet. We've just been too busy. We'll need it for the MOXIE tomorrow anyway. Please draw up any ideas you may have for the ladder or scaffold, and we'll prioritize that as soon as *Starship IV* is emptied, and we take a day off."

"Wait! Take a day off?" Carl asked. His face clouded over in confusion.

"Yes, after the MOXIE is up and running along with the generator, we're going to take a day off. We will have been working hard for nine days straight by then. It's time for a crew day off. Off-loading all the equipment on *Starship IV* then assembling the scaffolding is going to be a lot of hard work on the Martian surface, making for more heavily crewed EVAs. After that, water lines are going to be a major priority. I only see three thousand feet on *Staten*'s inventories, and we are getting low on water as well.

"Yeah," Carl said, maybe a little concerned. We're low on oxygen and water. Wow!"

"Okay, I'm going to assemble the crew for an update. Yesterday, the drinking water tank was noticeably low, but O2 is our priority, and there's nothing we can do about water until we get to some of our supplies and the water lines. It looks to me that we can continue for a little while. I'll have to start putting restrictions on water usage soon. No more showers after day nine, until we get to those water lines. Do you agree with my assessment there?"

Carl thought about it for a few moments. "Well, the fuel cells are working at a reduced rate, but they're still working. The drinking water levels are definitely getting low. We always knew we had to deal with them. They are on the work order manifest, of course, which includes service on the hydrogen fuel cells, but I won't be able to get to that for a while. Unless I do it on the day you have us scheduled off."

"No, thank you Carl. You need a day off, too. I know servicing the hydrogen fuel cells is a big job. And you're going to be very busy on these next multiple EVAs. Let's set up the MOXIE and the scaffold as we discussed. I need to call Team *Staten* together for a quick update. I'm sure they're wondering what we're going to do."

As the announcement went over *Staten*'s all stations PA, Commander Carrigan felt a little relaxed for the first time in a while. I don't know why I'm feeling relaxed, he thought to himself. We're still in a rather precarious position. Prior to the meeting, he made his way to the helm-turned Comm room and pulled Steven to the side to bring him up on the next EVAs and the plan to use the aluminum framework inside *Starship IV*.

Steven listened intently. "Commander, I've just been in contact with the ISS."

Chapter 28
Joint Chiefs

General Eugene Taylor looked around the beautifully polished mahogany table at the meeting of the Joint Chiefs. It was beyond comprehension that they had little more information than they had four days prior. The people at this table were not familiar with being caught off guard by an attacker who played upon their weaknesses, men who depended upon information, technology and training to stay one step ahead of any foe who might challenge the supremacy of the United States of America. It appeared in this case they not only were caught off guard, but the attacker was able to disappear without a trace.

They reviewed the satellite feed that had been downloaded at the time of the rocket launches. The view was from four different geostationary satellites over the Southern Atlantic Ocean and the Gulf of Mexico. They could see from the images a deep blue sea suddenly erupting in a brilliant white foam, which was the launch location of each of the rockets. Unfortunately, the focus of three of the satellite cameras wasn't anywhere near the launch point of each of the rockets, and only one satellite had the target somewhat in focus. But even it was of little help. All it showed was a calm, beautiful sea exploding in white, and some cigar-shaped cylinder belching yellow with black and white smoke and steam following it.

The camera only had four seconds of the digital image before the target flew off camera. No amount of digital enhancement produced any further details, and nothing specific could be identified. It could've been made by anyone— no markings of any kind. The shape was unremarkable and generic in nature. The only reference point as to the size of the rocket was the state of the seas reflecting the wind-driven wave pattern at the time of launch. The hydrology and ocean specialists reported the timing from initial blast to exiting of the water suggested the missiles may be approximately 60 feet in length.

Secretary of Defense Robert Thornton and the President were going crazy. No one had any leads as to who the guilty party might be. There was no sign of a launch platform or vessel or extended wake or prop trail following any kind of launch craft, other than a small fishing boat from Fort Lauderdale with two retired firefighters aboard.

The firefighters' stories checked out, and just prior to the launch, one of them reported seeing a "black thing" bobbing in the water around a half-mile off the port bow. The Coast Guard and Navy conducted a hundred-mile radius physical search. The Bahamian Government supported a search of Grand Bahama Island, Bimini, all The Berry Islands, Andros, and the busy island of New Providence, with no further findings of interest. In the Gulf of Mexico, approximating the launch point was a bit more difficult but only a few sailboats, six cargo vessels, a few oil tankers, along with a handful of fishing boats were located and boarded. No helpful results could be substantiated, and they were all hampered by the lack of usual satellite communications.

Admiral Roberta Cohen, Commandant of the Coast Guard and operating through the massive red tape of Homeland Security, launched an investigation of every float plan of every vessel that could have even the slightest possibility of being in the vicinity of either launch which might offer more insight or a first-person account of the launches. She also announced a top priority order for investigators to visit every boatyard up and down the East Coast of the U.S. and the Gulf of Mexico while checking every electronically filed float plan. However, there were thousands of boatyards and thousands of float plans that went through the target areas.

It was as though everyone forgot how to do anything without satellites. The satellites watching Cuba 24/7 had been downloading pictures and video as usual, which resulted in nothing. No unusual activity for the previous twenty-four hours to the launch. Then the satellites were blown up, and all satellite signals were lost and probably would never yield anything more since they were programmed to download all their images within twenty-four hours. The technicians said they would be overwriting their memories by now if they had survived the debris storm, which they probably hadn't, from the sound of it.

Never had it been considered that all the satellites would lose contact with the ground-receiving stations for more than a minor blip, or the short time it would take to come over the horizon to communicate with another dish or antenna array. In our modern, technology-dependent world, no one had stopped to ask the question, "What should we do if we lose the satellites?" The Joint Chiefs were asking that exact question now, and no one had any answers.

The United States was blind, as were all countries overly dependent on satellite resources. The United States was in a de facto state of war, but with whom? They didn't know. All nations around the globe were now dependent on WWII technology to protect their boundaries. The whole world was back on an even playing ground, which drove each of the Joint Chiefs from the Navy and the Marines crazy. No one was getting any sleep. They were all coming up with different ideas and were busy chasing down false leads to no avail. Each of the military branches gave a brief report on what they were doing in the aftermath. The Navy had sent out every aspect of its multiple fleets to monitor the perimeter of the continental United States where needed. Every possible aspect of the seas and skies were now under constant monitoring with penetrating radar. The powerful sixth fleet had been recalled from the Mediterranean, much to the chagrin of the Saudis and Israelis. The United States Navy was reduced to using ham radio to communicate with its fleets in some of the more remote areas. Even the tallest antennae were only good for around five hundred miles offshore. This attack sent all military branches into a tizzy, the likes of which would probably never be seen again.

All aspects of the armed forces were on high alert, but everything was silent, as if they had been blindfolded and sucker-punched, and now they were deaf and blind. The Joint Chiefs from each division of the armed forces speculated as to who or what country or players could be responsible for the attack, but no one could come up with any evidence, fingerprint, trail or any reason for this act of aggression.

In an unprecedented action since WWII, each military branch was coordinating to back up each other's positions. The National Guard and all the reserves were overwhelmed with demand, coordinating and helping food and supply shipments get through, stopping the looting, and monitoring the curfew at night. FEMA was working with them, trying to keep the peace at home and distribute food and water in the inner cities. Chaos reigned supreme. Shots could be heard in most major cities at night and even during the day at times. The gangs were having a hay-day over the lack of cell network. However, the good news was the power companies were reporting that if they completed disconnecting the interlinked power grid, they could start producing power as soon as they ran systems checks.

The Air Force was working with the Civil Air Patrol, which rallied to the call, having been denigrated in the past to no more than a club of people licensed to teach kids and each other how to fly, and taking occasional weekend excursions. Now they were running border observation missions, reporting anything that could be of interest to the Air Force. And the Air Force was actually listening to them and recording their sightings. Rocket scientists brought in from NASA and every leading independent rocket corporation in the United States responded with their knowledge and expertise when questioned about the type of missile that may have been used, and how.

How could anyone launch in what appeared to be the middle of the Gulf Stream, 20 miles off the coast of Fort Lauderdale with no launch pad, platform, or barge? Could it have been a submarine launch? The Navy responded to this saying they had every submarine, domestic and foreign, accounted for, and there weren't any in the area of concern. When questioned as to how they knew that, they just smiled smugly and said, "Trust us. We know." This didn't help tempers any.

What they learned from the rocket scientists shocked them all. It turned out the ocean offered a stable and anonymous platform for a rocket launch. It was much easier than any of them thought possible. Almost all rockets are densest at the base, with watertight and airtight fuel tanks, combustion chambers, and plenty of trapped air pockets leading toward the nose cone. If the nose cone were lighter than the base, as most rockets were, it would float upright, and if it were painted black, it would look to anyone passing by that a channel marker or a piling had broken loose in a previous hurricane.

According to the Navy and Coast Guard, there were always things like that floating around the ocean. Anyone could study the ocean currents, drop off their airtight/waterproof rocket, and get out of Dodge. Twenty-four to thirty-six hours later, the drop off vessel could be five hundred miles or more away, and they could launch with a high degree of certainty of hitting the target if the programming for navigation and the timing was done correctly.

Today, the technology, save for the programming and coordination timing, was not all that difficult. Many countries had the technology. Ironically, the launch code could've been sent from a satellite phone—and it probably was. So, the initial search pattern of a hundred miles was five times smaller than what it should've been, and even that may have been too small.

It was becoming apparent they would find no evidence trail leading to the guilty party. After days of interviews and exasperating arguments, David Burdick, the secretary of defense, suggested the Joint Chiefs were never going to find the evidence they needed. He suggested the Joint Chiefs start considering the facts from the perspective of who would benefit from such an attack—someone, or some country, that could benefit from the results of the attack, which effectively leveled the playing field.

What country would benefit from every nation being reduced to World War II technology all over again? This angle brought up some interesting conversations. Russia, or the Soviet Union, and all the developed world was immediately removed from suspicion since they had also become victims due to their dependence on satellites. As usual with the government, a joint task force was convened to evaluate the situation.

From the shifting of eyes and the telling of a few faces, a new quiet awareness was creeping into perspective. A few generals started scribbling furiously on notepads as a flurry of aids quickly entered and left with hurried memos. They had sneaking suspicions, and they weren't feeling good about them.

Chapter 29
Mars-Sol 6

Commander Carrigan had been in his study cubicle, thinking and planning. It was 11:00 Zulu. Soon they were going to have to adopt their own clock for Mars time since a day on Mars was forty minutes longer than a day on Earth. For telemetry purposes, all communication equipment would always use Zulu. However, soon the two clocks would be incompatible. It will be tomorrow on Earth, while it was still the day before on Mars.

Over an hour before the sun was due to rise on Mars, Carl and his team were already on the EVA setting up the MOXIE oxygen-generating equipment. The temperature this early in the day, even during the Martian summer, was -40°F. Strangely enough, this was also -40 degrees C. The tiny atmosphere on Mars didn't retain much heating of the sun from the day before, and before noon, it would be above freezing again and probably approaching 50 degrees or more.

Fortunately, the weather had been friendly to them. They would have to set up the Kilo power portable nuclear generator for power production for the MOXIE and for the welding equipment when they welded the scaffolding together. Hopefully this would give them access to the other starships where two more power units were stored. As winter approached, *Staten* would soon need the power units to keep her batteries charged, as she would be demanding more power to keep her and her crew warm.

The commander wanted to be out there helping and overseeing the set-up of the MOXIE, but he needed to think. He knew Carl could handle this important work on his own.

Steven Henderson had just arrived in Commander Carrigan's office. He wanted to discuss the comms from the night before with the ISS and their implications. Steven had given him a short breakdown of what the communication over the radio had been the previous night, and they wanted to digest it a bit.

The commander had just announced the all-crew meeting was about to start when Steven pulled him aside and informed him of his conversation with the ISS. During the meeting, *Staten*'s crew was surprised at the oxygen issues, just as he had been, but they were also relieved they had an answer to the problem that would be implemented the next day. The crew was interested in the news that they had been in communication with the ISS and the ISS crew was safe, for now. Of course, they wanted to know why *Staten* could talk to the ISS but couldn't talk to CAPCOM. It was the question of the week, and one to which no one had an answer.

Commander Carrigan would much rather tell the crew he didn't know the answer to a question than have an uninformed crew suspicious of rumors they had heard. After all, it would be easy for a crew member to overhear the radio communication with the ISS then wonder why it wasn't mentioned in the crew meeting, bringing them up to speed.

The crew was also looking forward to getting their first day off since landing and seemed interested in the theory of how to access the other starships. The commander hoped they would somehow be able to get them to come online manually. Otherwise, they would have a lot of heavy lifting and unloading to do, and many more EVAs scheduled, putting them further behind the original schedule of discovery, research and science on their new home for the next eleven months and twenty-four days or so. Every EVA held potential exposure and risk to crew members and equipment.

Commander Carrigan was sitting at his desk, thinking about these things and what the future may be for them when Steven, who didn't look like he had gotten much sleep, walked in and took a seat. Commander Carrigan looked at Steven for a moment and immediately wondered why he looked more stressed than yesterday. "Hello, Steven. My takeaway from your telemetry with the ISS is they don't know why they're not in communication with CAPCOM, either."

"Good morning, Commander. Yeah, that's my take on the situation as well," Steven said.

"There's something you're not telling me."

"They had to engage PDAM and were hit with what sounds like a lot of debris. That's why they thought they couldn't talk to CAPCOM. They thought they had lost the antenna."

"Oh, my, God," Commander Carrigan said, grimacing.

"They're lucky to be alive."

"Yeah, they are. The conversation got me thinking and I've been going over it all night. I have an idea I'd like to go over with you."

"I'm listening."

Steven sighed. "I'm concerned that the Kessler Effect may

have been triggered."

Commander Carrigan frowned. "You think there may have been enough debris to initiate a chain reaction creating more debris and further satellite damage?"

"Yeah, that's pretty much it," Steven said. "Even though we only communicated with the ISS for a few minutes, they explained to me that they had to engage PDAM. They evacuated to the Dragon capsule and rode it out for five days after enduring what sounded like some serious impacts. For example, they were surprised to hear us because they thought the radio antenna was missing from the Space Station. That's why they thought they hadn't heard from CAPCOM. Now they are camped out in the Unity node with no atmospheric controls. They are trying to manually maintain a livable atmosphere. The ISS crew haven't even tried to enter any other portions of the ISS yet. Fortunately, it sounds like it's holding pressure so far. Imagine five days stuck in that tiny capsule!"

Commander Carrigan's eyebrows raised, wrinkling the skin on his forehead. He sat back in his chair looking at the ceiling and paused visualizing the scenario. "My God, it must have been torture, five days strapped in that Dragon? I don't think I can imagine five days continuously in my spacesuit. What kind of hell must they have had to endure? That is truly incredible. What is the state of the ISS?"

"We really don't know." Steven said. "They reported they are only utilizing the Unity node. They lost communication with CAPCOM at approximately the same time we did, after a satellite strike. Did that satellite strike cause enough debris to finally cross the threshold and create the Kessler Syndrome?"

"Hmm…Okay," the commander said. "Let's say for the

____

sake of conversation that the Kessler Syndrome threshold was finally crossed. That would prohibit any rocket or spaceship of any kind from entering or leaving Earth safely. What does that have to do with communicating with CAPCOM or NASA?"

Steven rubbed his forehead. "That's what has been eating at me all night. The only thing I could think is that maybe the Kessler Effect is somehow charging the atmosphere, absorbing the radio signals."

Commander Carrigan squinted as he considered his response. "So, you're saying the debris is somehow creating an electric or a static charge, absorbing any radio transmissions so no radio signal can get in or out?"

"That's all I can imagine could be happening," Steven said. "I've been thinking about it all night. It's similar to the ion layer associated with solar flares. Ham radio and CB radio operators learned to use the energy 'dome' to bounce signals from the underside of the electron dome to 'skip' signals over the horizon, sometimes to the other side of the earth. Now that we know the ISS isn't receiving radio transmissions with CAPCOM, either, but they can hear us, that definitely tells us the problem is with Earth. We suspected that all along, but now we might know the reason."

"Ok, this is ludicrous. But, Steven, if this is the case, can anyone do anything about it? I mean, I'm sure that given the right amount of time, gravity will prevail. Can NASA or any other agency do something…anything?"

"Yes, of course. Given the right amount of time—an unknown variable—gravity will, as you said, prevail. Otherwise, unless you know something I don't, your guess is as good as mine."

"So, any launch or landing to or from Earth may be jeopardized or impossible for an unknown period of time?"

"Unless someone is specifically trained in atmospheric sciences and all of the specificities related to this issue, it's anyone's guess. But, Commander, that is a possibility. One that I've been going over all night."

Commander Carrigan had to think about what Steven just put on the table—that it could take time to clean up. How much time? If the Kessler Effect had, in fact, taken place, could this even be a possibility? Could this situation make it impossible for them and the ISS astronauts to return home? If *Staten* misses its return window next summer, they couldn't attempt to return to Earth for another two years due to the huge variations in the orbits of Earth and Mars. The distances were just too great. The seriousness of the situation began to bear down on him. Commander Carrigan began to realize this might not be just a communication issue. Could this communication breakdown and possible Kessler Effect prolong their scheduled one-year stay on Mars? How long could it last? Could they survive on this planet for three years or more? They did have more than one year's supply of food, but only as a redundant precaution. About a total of eighteen months of food was packed into the starships, with another six months left on *Starship X*. Giving them a residual of about two years total. They did not have a three-year supply. They did have seeds and pressurized greenhouses, but for scientific research purposes only, not for living on Mars.

No one knew how long it would take for something like the Kessler Effect to dissipate and make launches and re-entry to and from the Earth safe for travel again. *Staten* had the most highly trained crew in the history of space travel, yet they didn't have anyone specifically trained in this type of atmospheric science. He needed to do further research on the Kessler Effect and consult with Barbara Black before discussing this with the crew—when it was the right time.

Commander Carrigan was obviously shaken by the conversation. "Steven, how much have you looked into this possible scenario?"

"You know, I am by no means a specialist in atmospheric sciences. But after talking with the ISS crew yesterday, I started researching it. I was up all night trying to sort through the data and scenarios and found a good bit of data on *Staten*'s computer. If the Kessler Effect has taken place, as far as I can tell, we may be here longer than we anticipated. That's why I wanted to meet with you this morning. I'm still following up, but we may want to reconsider our in-situ resources and the length of our stay."

"You have spent time on this," the commander said. "I'll start researching it as well. If we determine that it has happened, everything changes. If the full Kessler Effect has taken place, then we immediately move from a scientific exploration mission to a survival mission. So far, all we know is we lost communication with CAPCOM at approximately the same time the ISS was engaging PDAM due to a satellite strike. Then they lost communication with CAPCOM as well. But why? I'm afraid that little detail may be ominous. Can there be any other reason for the simultaneous loss of comms? Let's follow up with this disturbing conversation when we have more facts or evidence.”

“Commander?” Steven asked almost silently, knowing they already knew.

“I know what you’re going to tell me!” Carrigan growled, frustration rising in his voice. “You’re going to tell me we already know. The only reason the ISS could communicate with us and not to CAPCOM would be that the Kessler Effect has indeed taken place. We now know a satellite has been hit, and the debris caused significant damage to the ISS. It’s the Kessler Effect, isn’t it?”

“I’m pretty sure it has taken place, Commander Carrigan, yeah. Not positive, but I’m pretty sure,” Steven said quietly.

“Yeah, I’m afraid there can’t be any other reason. I had no idea.”

“Nobody did. That’s why I’ve been up all night researching this Kessler theory.”

“Okay, Steven. Let’s wait until we’re as close to one hundred percent as we can get before any of these details are discussed outside of this room. Man, I hope this isn’t the case, but I’m afraid you may be right. Let me know as soon as you have anything further. By the way, have you found out anything about booting up the other starships?”

Steven shook his head. “I’ve been trying to find anything I can about activating the other starships. I just don’t see anything.”

“Yeah, Carl White has been looking into it as well. So far to no avail. Once we gain access, we can try to fire up the computers from inside,” the commander said. “If they don’t fire up, we’re back in the same position we’re in now—manually unloading all the supplies. We’re back in the 1800s manually humping supplies on

Mars," he said as looked down at his desk with depression sinking into his voice.

"I'm going to get back to monitor the EVA," Steven said. "Unless you have something else?"

"No, I was going to go out with them this morning, but we needed to have this conversation."

"Yeah, we've been here for six days, we've done like ten EVAs, and I think only one of them was actually on the first week's official schedule. Crew safety is our primary concern, and every EVA so far has been an attempt to access our required equipment or install the appropriate equipment to keep *Staten* functioning."

"Well," Commander Carrigan said, "no one expected *Starship IV* to fall over. And no one expected the starships would not be autonomously up and running by now. I'd like to evaluate *Starship IV*'s stringers that we're going to remove for the scaffolding, as well as get a look at how Carl's coming along with the MOXIE installation. We will need a back-up crew of at least two. Why don't you come along, Steven? Have you been out on an EVA yet?"

"I have to talk to the ISS at twelve noon Zulu," Steven said as he looked at his watch, "which is almost right now."

"Go ahead and make the radio call with the ISS. We can go as soon as you're finished. I have a few things to finish up here anyway."

"Okay," Steven said. "I'll coordinate with Mary. She's monitoring the EVA."

"Sounds like fun. I need the distraction. By the way, it's not an issue if I discuss the Kessler syndrome with the ISS, is it? They may be considering it by now anyway."

Commander Carrigan paused solemnly and looked into Stevens eyes, "The more they know, the better their chances of survival."

"Yeah, that's what I was thinking. They're in pretty rough shape. I wonder if the Russians survived reentry. They didn't mention them at all—just that they spent five days in the Dragon crew capsule. I just assumed that the Russians made a run for it. Imagine spending five straight days in your spacesuit."

The commander shook his head. "It sounds worse than Apollo 13."

"I think it probably was. May God be with them."

"   Okay, make your transmission, then let's suit up. We have an EVA to go on!"

Steven thought Commander Carrigan actually sounded happy.

———

Chapter 30

Johnson Space Center-Day 6

Brad Brown was back in his chair, now wearing a Johnson Space Center jumpsuit with nothing underneath. After six days, his MMI team shirt and the khakis he was wearing were a mess. He badly needed a change of clothes, though he realized that if that was the worst of his problems, he was in good shape.

Brad and his team had just finished going over the MM1 computer protocols on *Starship X*. These were the protocols the crew for *Starship X* had available to them on their shipboard computers. There was no mention anywhere in their protocols on how to start up the other starships if MM1 didn't send the command. No one saw this situation occurring. This was a huge oversight, and one that would not be repeated.

Brad had been working with the computer programming engineers, design engineers, electrical engineers, and anyone else who might have some insight into the engineering and design. If CAPCOM or Ground Control happened to regain comms for a few minutes, or even a few seconds, Brad wanted to be ready.

They were transmitting the initiation orders every five minutes just in case one of the transmissions was able to get through. The engineers had been working on this problem for the past five days, and they concluded that there was a manual boot- up option to start the computers on the starships. It turned out that if they simply grounded the computer frame directly to the ship's ground, the system would boot itself up. Simple, but Brad doubted anyone would think of that.

It seemed like a technique from the 1960s—not modern-day sensitive computer stuff. Apparently, it would throw a switch that wasn't part of the computers, but the switch would initiate the power to the computers as if they had experienced a power glitch or temporary interruption. It was explained to him that it's like a manual reboot. Just unplug it and restart it.

Brad asked the programmers if there was any way the *Starship X* crew could figure this out on their own? They explained that the super important switch in this situation was only added at the last minute by a team of very sharp engineers at the launchpad after they decided they could very easily remove it if the higher ups vetoed the idea. They responsibly forwarded the newly implemented change to the MM1 engineering committee which apparently missed getting it into the operating manuals after deciding it was a great idea. As a result, this action wasn't part of the regular flight training, or available on any other resource for the crew, but that it should have been. And they pretty much doubted that anyone on MM1 would know of the newly implemented switch or try it.

Brad's phone rang. It was his wife letting him know they had power and that she was thrilled they were going to have air conditioning that night.

"It is so good to hear your voice," he told her. "So much has gone on over the past few days."

She knew she probably couldn't be informed about his activities at work, so she didn't ask. She reported as much as she could on the few days since they had spoken. After Hurricane

Harvey, her father had some solar panels installed on the roof with a Tesla Powerwall, which was enough to run some fans, keep the refrigerator and freezer working, and keep the TV on using some old wire from the garage. But there wasn't enough battery back- up to run the air conditioning, also. They hadn't gotten much sleep due to the heat, but at least the Powerwall was being fully charged each hot sunny day, and that kept the fans running all night.

She said the TV news was reporting that the power stations were starting to come back on, though many people had died because of the heat alone. The retirement homes and hospitals had banned the press based on medical privacy issues, but there were rumors of many heat related deaths, especially amongst the elderly. Many of the retirement homes and communities had too little or no generator power. Most of the hospital power generators in the Houston area had run out of diesel two days earlier. The hospitals were operating on skeleton crews and taking only life-threatening cases, of which it seemed there was no shortage.

The hospitals were out of a variety of supplies, and the National Guard was operating helicopters to resupply the hospitals. Many water plants all around the US had run out of back-up generator fuel as well, so some cities and towns weren't getting running water. In some cases, they were getting water, but they were on boil water orders from the water department, if they were able to get the message.

Fortunately, Brad had suggested she take all the food they had in their house to her father's, which helped tremendously. Unfortunately, her father had an electric stove that drew too much power, so they ate mostly cold food and cereal until the milk was gone.

Her father had started a campfire outside, which they used to heat water for coffee and pots of soup. Fortunately, he was on well water. He had added a small old timey hand pump to a disused well a few years back to save power for things other than pumping water after a hurricane. The bread and milk were now gone, and some of their meals had been cold beans and fruit from a can, but they were doing fine otherwise. Her father had loaded his twelve gauge and kept his German Shepherd tied up by the front door. The heat was devastating. It was 105 degrees yesterday. The news also reported that some major metropolitan cities across the U.S. which had run out of power were now starting up power generation plants, and in some cases, distributing power. She complained that her cell phone still wasn't working. Brad explained that it wasn't going to work for a long time because the satellites were down. She was thankful he suggested going to her dad's place. It had been the right move to get away from Houston, and the kids enjoyed being with their grandfather.

"A sort of holiday for the boys," she laughed.

Then Brad heard the back-up generator at the Johnson Space Center turn off. Finally, it was quiet again. It was good to hear her laugh. It took a load off Brad's conscience.

She said, "Thank you, I love you," and was gone.

Brad was very thankful for the few minutes they shared on the phone. It was extremely relieving to know they were safe.

Brad suddenly realized that it had already been almost an entire week since they'd lost communication with the crew on *Starship X* and the ISS. What kind of special hell the ISS was going through, he couldn't imagine. MM1 had assets and supplies designed for an extended mission if required. At least their spaceship wasn't in the firing line of objects heading towards them at twenty times the speed of sound. Brad caught himself wondering if they could see Mars from the ISS. Of course, they could see...then Brad remembered General Latimore mentioning the rescue capsule being built with extra thick, specially hardened steel. It gave him an idea.

Was it possible . . .?

Chapter 31
The ISS-Day 6

Day six, Giulia thought as she looked at Commander Amhurst.

"Day six," Commander Amhurst said, as though he were reading her mind. "Giulia, Henry, let's have a chat. As I'm sure you're aware, tomorrow will be one week since we had to scramble into the Dragon. I've been thinking about our situation as have many, I'm sure. CAPCOM and NASA and various agencies are scrambling to try to do something to ameliorate our situation. What that something is, I have no idea. Have you guys given it any thought?"

"Henry and I talked a little about it last night while you were sleeping," Giulia said. "We were wondering if there really is anything they can do."

Commander Amhurst said, "Yeah, I've been thinking about it, of course. The answer is we just don't know. What we do know is we had better be ready for anything. The good news is the impacts from the debris seem to have subsided. We need to start considering our options. We have discussed going into the other nodes, which may destroy the wonderful atmosphere we're enjoying, so that's not a good idea. What I want to hear are your thoughts or ideas on anything else we can or should be doing."

Giulia looked at the others. "Go fish," she said. Commander Amhurst looked at each of them. "What?"

"We have our spacesuits by the Dragon hatch, ready to put on in case of an emergency. This morning we took a full inventory and status of everything here in the Unity node. Thank God the oxygen tanks and water tanks have full integrity! The atmosphere is satisfactory for the moment. There isn't much we can do but play cards and bide our time. This may be the most difficult time of our journey, sitting on our hands, and trying to decide the right time to act. The debris could be missing us by a few inches or a few hundred or thousands of miles for all we know. I'm sure NASA and the other agencies are working on a solution. So, we turn the radio on at twelve Zulu, talk with *Starship X,* and see if we can involve them in our decision-making process—or at least get some input from them. The more ideas we have to work with, the better. Plus, if anything should happen to us at least someone else will know what we chose to do."

"When the time comes to decide, we will make it together. Every day we sit here, Earth's gravity is cleaning up the debris a little more than the day before. If we should need to take the Dragon home, we'll have a little better chance of surviving our trip the longer we wait."

Commander Amhurst and Henry nodded in agreement, Henry smiling back and nodding.

"It looks like we're going to spend some time here," Giulia said.

"Unfortunately, the longer we're here, the better our chances are of making it home in one piece. We don't have any playing cards. Do you have any other ideas?"

"Let's play two lies and one truth," Henry said.

Giulia and Commander Amhurst both replied, "What?"

"You've never heard of two lies and one truth?" He could tell from the confused faces that they hadn't. "I used to play this with

---

my parents all the time on road trips. I'll start off, so you can see how to play. I'll tell two lies and one truth. You each get one guess as to which one is the truth. If you're right, you get to go next. If you're both wrong, I get to go again, but I have to tell you about the truthful statement and the story behind it."

Commander Amhurst and Giulia were surprised to see the typically quiet Henry perk up with his game idea.

Again, they replied, "Okay."

Henry began. "Statement number one, I had a pet rabbit growing up in Wisconsin. Statement number two, I took a flight that never existed on a commercial airline. Statement number three, on my eighth birthday, I was given the same gift by three different people. Okay, Giulia, you go first. Tell me which one is the truth."

"If I had to guess, I would say growing up in Wisconsin with a rabbit as a pet would not be unusual, but then again, getting the same gift from three people on your birthday is pretty unusual, but not hard to believe. Taking a commercial airline flight that didn't exist sounds really intriguing but hard to believe. I have to guess which one is the truth, right?"

"Yes, you have to guess which one is the true statement." "I think that having a pet rabbit is the true statement."

Henry and Giulia both looked at Commander Amhurst, "I have to agree with Giulia that the pet rabbit is pretty realistic sounding, but the point of the game is to confuse the guessers, so I guess I'd have to say that taking a flight that didn't exist on a real commercial airline sounds pretty outlandish, so that has to be the truth."

"Your final answers?" Henry said.

They nodded.

"I can't believe you got it that easily, commander. I guess I need to be more subtle next time."

"How did you take a flight that didn't exist on a commercial airline? Whatever that means. You need to explain that one."

"Well, I was dating a flight attendant who worked for one of the smaller airlines. She had gotten me a 'space available ticket', which means if they have a seat, you can go. We had arrived quite early for the flight because she was working on it. She went on the plane with her other flight attendant co-workers, then came out of the boarding ramp all smiles and informed me that the flight was canceled since the airline didn't sell enough seats. There was another flight, and the few paying passengers had been transferred to that one. She said they still had to ferry the plane to the original destination and the captain said I could have a seat on board while they transported the empty plane. So, I took a flight that didn't exist."

"So, I got lucky, and I'm going to get lucky again because it's time to turn the radio on. Game delay until further notice."

"Okay, but you won, Commander, so you start the next game."

Commander Amhurst agreed as he switched on the radio. "We don't want to miss our friends on *Starship X.*"

As the three shared some water and reconstituted apple juice, they heard the radio crackle to life. "ISS, ISS, this is Starship X. How do you read?"

Commander Amhurst picked up the mic. "Copy you, five

by five, *Starship X.* How do you copy? Over."

After twelve minutes, the radio sparked to life again. "ISS, this *is Starship X,* copy you two by two. Over."

Commander Amhurst said, "Good to hear your voice again, Steven. Over."

Twelve minutes later, they heard from Steven. "Yeah, good to hear your voice again, too, Charlie. We were wondering how bad the situation is there and if there's anything we can do for you from thirty-five million miles away."

"Good question, Steven. That's one we've been pondering here as well, and we decided as a group that you can.

We could use your opinion and insight. We don't have a lot of options here. We do have a good atmosphere in the Unity node, and it looks like she's holding pressure. We only turn the radio on fifteen to twenty minutes prior to our expected conversations to preserve the batteries. The Dragon seems to have good integrity as well, but we may have depleted a good portion of the batteries sitting in it for five days with the radio and life support running. With the batteries being somewhat discharged we are a little concerned as to their ability to fire up the parachutes on reentry. If we want to do a spacewalk and inspect the rest of the station from the outside, we will export a decent amount of our usable atmosphere. We are afraid to open any of the hatches into the other nodes and lose the atmosphere that way as well. We don't seem to have a lot of options here other than standing by for changes or information." Commander Amhurst looked at his crew for any input. "Do you guys have any other questions for *Starship X?*" They just shook their heads, so

———

248

Commander Amhurst finished the transmission. "Over."

Another twelve minutes later, they heard Steven on the radio again. "ISS, this is *Starship X*. I have made detailed notes of your situation. We've had numerous conversations about the loss of communication with CAPCOM, and we were wondering if it could be the Kessler Effect. I assume you're familiar with it. We have a theory that all of the space debris could be creating a static charge, blocking, or absorbing any radio signal. We were curious as to your thoughts. Over."

Commander Amhurst looked at his crew, and Giulia and Henry shrugged. Commander Amhurst responded, "*Starship X*, this ISS. Until now, we haven't thought about the communication loss being related to the satellite strike, but it makes sense. Over." "ISS, this is *Starship X*. I will discuss your situation here with the crew and get back to you at twelve Zulu tomorrow. By the way, do you know if your solar panels are producing? It sounds like you took some pretty hard hits, but I wonder if you have any power coming into your breaker box. It could be helpful. Talk to you tomorrow. Over."

Commander Amhurst picked up the mic again. "I doubt if we have any solar panels left at all but will check it out. Roger next communication at twelve Zulu tomorrow. Over." Commander Amhurst looked at Giulia and Henry. "So, that's that for today."

They didn't know what to say, neither did he. Commander Amhurst was more aware than ever of the importance of these daily "chats" with *Starship X*. He wanted to come up with some words of encouragement for his crew or some cheerful takeaway. He really liked both Henry and Giulia and could see on their faces that another twenty-four hours before they got feedback was a long time. He loved his crew and was concerned for their future.

Commander Amhurst smiled. "Any thoughts about the Kessler Effect and the satellite strike related to radio communication with CAPCOM?"

"Well, I guess it gives us something to think about," Henry said. "What do you think, Giulia?"

"I suppose it is possible. I hadn't really given it much consideration."

Commander Amhurst nodded. "Yeah, I was thinking about it. It never occurred to me that it could be what Steven said—a static charge built up from all of the bits and pieces floating around. I guess we better find out if we have any solar cell production as Stephen suggested. Anyone know how to figure that one out?"

Henry rubbed his six-day beard while Giulia scowled in consideration of their options.

"Who's the best electrical engineer here? You guys jury-rigged the radio together."

Giulia glanced at Commander Amhurst, then at Henry.

"I guess that's me," Henry said. "Okay, let me check the breakers and see if I can find any power."

"I'll give you a hand." Commander Amhurst put the mic back and turned off the radio.

Within an hour, they found out they had enough voltage going into the breaker box, from some unknown source, to power up a jury-rigged 120v LED light. All they did know is that the power source was not the Unity node's batteries. Maybe things were looking up. With a source of power available, they began searching the storage locker for a battery charger and an ammeter... or something that might help.

Commander Amhurst thought, Well, if you play your cards right, you might just get to play another day.

———

251

Chapter 32

I Will Love You All the Way to Mars and Back

Commander Carrigan was thrilled with Carl and his team's work. He wasn't going to let those efforts go unrewarded. Not only did Carl and his crew set up the MOXIE, but they set up the power generator, started it up, and plugged it into *Staten*. Oxygen was being pumped into *Staten*'s O2 tanks at a rate faster than it was being consumed, at least for the moment.

It was SOL 7, or the seventh day on Mars. The crew had been working their normal shifts during the six-month journey to the red planet. Every ten days they were required to schedule a day off or else it would automatically appear on the roster during the long trip. Most of the crew didn't want days off during the trip but were required to take them for mental health, focus and concentration. However, most of the crew had this day off. It was a rather unusual event to have most of the crew off at the same time. A skeleton crew, not assigned to any diligent work other than the normal monitoring of telemetry, life safety related operations and general systems operations, was operating the ship.

Steven Henderson had another radio conversation with the ISS crew. The rest of the crew could be found in their quarters reading, in the game room, or in the galley relaxing and talking. Ping-Pong in the game room at ⅓ Earth gravity was popular with the crew and helped with hand-eye coordination, balance, and crew morale. Haratu Suzuki, being Japanese, was the clear choice for tournament champion, but he always found a way to make the score close.

Commander Carrigan was in his office thinking and planning the next two weeks of EVAs, with the next three days entered into the scheduling system. The next big job for his crew was to go into *Starship IV* and remove all the supplies, some of which could be put to use right away—like the solar panels. Most of it needed to be stocked and protected from the Martian dust. He estimated it would take the better part of two days to unload, and he would need Carl for the removal of the stringers, or the aluminum frame used to secure the cargo and it added to the ship's integrity. Carl was becoming worth his weight in gold. Of course, all the crew members were extremely valuable in different aspects. Commander Carrigan made a point to check on Carl and make sure he was taking it easy. He needed to be rested and refreshed for the upcoming EVAs. They had a crew meeting the night before, and *Staten*'s crew received the news about the situation aboard the ISS. They asked that their thoughts and prayers be sent to the ISS and Russian crews. Some of the crew were visibly upset knowing the options for the ISS were extremely limited.

Again, the crew asked why *Staten* could talk to the ISS and not to CAPCOM or NASA. Commander Carrigan asked Steven if he could field the question, and he thought he handled it well. Steven explained that the ISS was informed of a satellite strike at approximately the same time *Staten* had lost comms with CAPCOM. He discussed that it may be possible that a static charge buildup from the debris may be absorbing any electronic signal, causing a comms blackout. But no one knew anything for sure, this was just a theory. The crew also had a few questions that simply couldn't be answered, like when did they think it would be possible for them to be able to communicate with CAPCOM or NASA or their families and how would this loss of communication change the mission? Stephen simply shook his head and said, "We just don't know at the moment."

Commander Carrigan decided he needed to step up adding, "We're still evaluating the situation, and as soon as we feel confident a change of direction is needed, we will involve all of team Staten. We absolutely appreciate any feedback, suggestions, ideas or insights, in group or in private. We're all professionals with unique training and yet a singleness of purpose. Unless there are any more questions. Mars Mission 1 team is dismissed."

Commander Carrigan was satisfied with his decision to remove the stringers from the stricken *Starship IV*. He was sure they could be manufactured into an excellent frame for the scaffold, and Carl's curious eyes agreed as they opened wide with imagination. Commander Carrigan could already see the wheels and gears kicking in and turning over as he went off into his own internal world of design. It was going to be a lot of work cutting all the welding points, careful not to damage the stringers when they cut them out. Some were undoubtedly bent and broken from the starship falling over. Carl could do it—he had no doubt. That was becoming a commonly repeated phrase: "Carl could do it." There was also some aluminum framing, not a part of the stringer system, that he could use to reinforce the scaffold. Carl had gotten back to him on his request about the rope and the amounts stored on board *Staten* and *Starship*

IV. There was plenty to do the job.

Carl's design for the scaffolding was impressive and detailed. It included bolting it together at different lengths, so it could be dismantled and moved to the next starship. Later, Commander Carrigan reviewed the design, taking in all its details and specifics. A portable scaffolding, huh, great idea!

Andrea was doing pull-ups while Pedro was lifting weights in the exercise room. Pull-ups were crazy easy on Mars, so instead of the normal twenty she would do on Earth, she wanted to do sixty. Every kilogram taken to Mars costs a ridiculous amount of money, so the weight machines were adjustable hydraulic resistance machines secured to strong points on the walls. Andrea was on her twenty-second pull-up. "I'm trying to get this situation with the radio and communication with CAPCOM through my head. Even though we can talk to ISS, we can't talk to CAPCOM because of some static charge? I'm having a hard time understanding that one."

Pedro enjoyed the fact that he could curl fifty kilograms on Mars. "Do you remember the old HAM radios they used years ago? The ones they used to hand-tune?"

Andrea was on pull-up thirty-four and still going strong. "I've seen pictures of them and other old radios on display in museums."

"Well," Pedro said, "those units required the HAM operator to tune in to the correct frequency, and even when they were on the right frequency they would often have to hand- modulate or keep tuning it in to get the best reception. Even when they were perfectly tuned-in, the atmosphere could change, and they would start losing reception and have to tune it in again or fine-tune it. If they didn't, they would lose the person they were talking to, and all they would get was static. These days, all of our radios are auto-tuning. They know when they're losing the reception, so they automatically follow the signal. Even on good days, the atmosphere can change the signal frequency. Some days the atmosphere would allow you to 'bounce' your signal off it like throwing a ball against a wall, or better yet, the ceiling, and you could pick up people thousands of miles away."

"So, what does that have to do with us not being able to contact CAPCOM while we can talk to the ISS?"

Pedro was into his third and final set, huffing and puffing. "Wow, I can tell I haven't worked out lately. It's kinda the same thing. All of the debris circling Earth is generating all kinds of static at different frequencies and interfering with both CAPCOM's signal and our signals as well. It's like trying to talk to a wall with people on the other side. They need to open a window or something, so they can hear you."

"So, it's like they're blocked from hearing us?"
"Yeah, pretty much. As far as CAPCOM and the Deep Space Network are concerned, I think their signal is being absorbed like a towel absorbing water. Our signal is so weak, it probably just gets lost." Pedro finished with his last set and started jumping around to loosen up. He had to be careful not to jump too high and hit his head on the ceiling. "Hey, I wonder how high we could jump on a trampoline here."

Andrea was on pull-up number forty-seven and slowing down quickly. "I think sixty is a good goal for me eventually, but too much for today. Like you said, I can tell we haven't kept up our routine as much as normal. I'll be lucky to do fifty-five," she blurted out as she counted off pull-up fifty-two. "Three more, ugh. Fifty-five. Sixty tomorrow. I'm done for today. I would think you could jump about three times as high on a trampoline as you could on Earth," she said while trying to catch her breath.

Pedro turned around to watch her. Andrea was in excellent shape, as all of the astronauts were. She had great legs, but those eyes. When she focused on him, Pedro could feel her gaze touch him with a deep warmth that remained even after she had gone. "Yeah, but you weigh less here, too, so when you come back down, you don't get as much spring to go back up. I guess we'll never know until someone brings a trampoline."

A poster of the first Falcon Heavy launch when Elon Musk launched his Tesla Roadster into space caught Pedro's eye. When he turned around, Andrea was right behind him. His gaze met hers for a second too long. Instead of moving, they stared into each other's eyes as the sweat ran down her face.

"What are you looking at?" she asked.

They were both covered in sweat, and he could feel her breath on his face. "I was looking into your beautiful eyes, but now I'm looking at your lips."

"Me, too."

He kissed her mouth. It was soft, warm, receiving and welcoming as she kissed him back. He'd wanted to do that for a long time. The many years of working together, of learning how to interact without judgment or competition and still feeling wonderfully anxious about the next time they could simply be together sharing stories of growing up, and the early days of training, when they hardly knew each other. Emotions and feelings created a connection they both knew was there. It was now sealed with a kiss.

As they withdrew, Andrea said, "Come with me."

In the shower, Pedro followed her movements, wiping down her toned, supple body with a damp towel. She returned the favor smiling softly and enjoying his physic.

"I'm in bunk 39A," she said. "Meet me there in two minutes."

Soon after, Andrea opened the door to her bunk, and Pedro walked in. She was already naked again. "Now," she said. "Where were we?" She giggled a little and grabbed both sides of his head, planting another kiss on him as she heard the door shut.

Pedro looked her up and down. "My God, you are beautiful."

She just giggled again and slowly laid her body next to his. As they stared into each other's eyes, Andrea kissed him. "You know, if we do this, it cannot change our relationship outside of this room. If I'm in charge of an operation, you must carry yourself as you have so far on this journey, and if you're in charge of an operation, I must act as I have to this point. I don't want to announce that we're in a relationship to everyone on the ship, and I'm pretty sure you don't, either. I don't think we want the whole crew to start treating us differently."

"I don't see why it should change any. I like you a lot, Andrea. I've liked you for a while and I know you enjoy being
with me, too. I am sure the crew has seen it already. I'm ok with that. I also admire and respect your judgment. None of that will change. We're simply enjoying each other's company at the moment. We're extremely fortunate to be here in the first place, and being together

right now, here with you, is only icing on the cake. I'm not going to allow this moment to affect our relationship when we're working together."

"I was hoping you'd feel the same way. We're still professionals. We're just enjoying the afternoon together. We deserve to be human, too, don't we? We deserve to protect and enjoy our humanity."

With that, Pedro kissed her, and she felt her body melt into his. A deep, stirring warmth rose even more as she felt his strong quads and abdomen.

He was as aroused as she was, and it had been a long time for both.

She mounted him and felt her legs go weak, feeling nothing but the wonderful pressure of first penetration. Andrea felt a flood of moisture and had an immediate orgasm as she felt him go deeper. She had never felt such arousal, and neither had Pedro. It felt right. And being that they were on Mars and most assuredly the first humans to ever make love on Mars made it even more erotic, sensual and important to each other.

They kissed deeply as their passion drove them to the inevitable finish. Pedro realized that he may have liked her a lot more than she liked him, but that was okay.

Andrea wished the moment would last forever as they came together in a final thrust of exhilaration and collapsed into each other's arms. "Can we do this forever?" she whispered. They had never had so much private time to be together and they both fully enjoyed the opportunity. Who knows when they could be together like this again?

They fought to catch their breath, and before they knew it, they had fallen asleep cuddling naked in the cool air- conditioning of the tiny cabin.

Chapter 33
Mars Sol-8

"Today is the day!" Commander Carrigan announced over the PA. "Full-crew pre-EVA meeting."

As everyone assembled and took their seats, the commander referred to the notes on his tablet. "I hope everyone who had the day off yesterday enjoyed it and is well rested. We have a large A shift and partial B shift EVA about to commence. C shift and the remainder of B shift, you're on ready standby. I need to go over what we're going to be doing."

As the short briefing progressed, Commander Carrigan outlined the objectives of the EVA everyone had already received in their inbox the previous night. "Good. We have one six-hour EVA today. Currently, the temperature is minus forty degrees—a typical Mars summer morning. The EVA will take place from twelve Zulu to sixteen hundred Zulu. We have a planned break from fourteen hundred Zulu until fourteen thirty Zulu. This complicated EVA will require two commands. As a result, we will be using frequencies one alpha and two alpha, and both frequencies, of course, will be monitored by *Staten* Command. Carl White is deemed '*Starship IV* Command' and is responsible for all activities inside *Starship IV* and will not activate until inside *Starship IV*. Outside *Staten* and *Starship IV* is 'Surface Command', just to keep everything simple. Surface Command will be Pedro Lopez. We will need both Mars cars and the trailer. According to the inventory lists, there should be another Mars car trailer on *Starship IV*. Let's put it to use as soon as we get it unburied. Any water hose should be staged to move to starships I and II. Let's put some tape over the ends of the water hose to keep Mars out of our water supply. Any rope that we unbury should be set aside in staging for ease of access as well. We will stage all inventory and mark it with the location from where it was removed from *Starship IV*, so we can find it using the inventory lists I have set up on your pads." Commander Carrigan quickly scanned the room with his steel-blue eyes. "Any questions so far?" The crew was attentive. A few shook their heads, so he continued. "I scanned the inventory listing and the location numbers. Two crew will position the supplies for staging on the surface. Surface Command and Starship Command, you will receive any coordinating information required from *Staten* Command. Today *Starship IV* Command will primarily be emptying *Starship IV*. Tomorrow, they will be removing the frame used to secure the load and hopefully start building a scaffold out of it following removal. This scaffold will allow us to gain entry into the other starships. Does everyone understand what we're doing? Carl? Pedro?"

"Yes, sir," they quickly replied.

Commander Carrigan surveyed the crew, looking for any signs of confusion. "Okay, this is going to be a tough couple of days. Let's be safe out there."

As they were suiting up, Pedro whispered in Andrea's direction, "Hundred fifty feet on a handmade scaffold."

Andrea nodded with a concerned look as she secured her helmet in place.

Commander Carrigan went to the helm and sat with Steven

and Mary, knowing this was going to be a confusing evolution. Carl filled the Mars car trailer with most of the tools they were going to be using over the next two days, which he had carefully staged at the end of the last EVA.

They had to drive quite a bit slower to keep the tools from bouncing out, but soon enough, they arrived and began off-loading the inventory of supplies from *Starship IV*. They then sent the Mars car back to *Staten* to pick up the rest of the crew. The first thing Carl did was locate the rope he had seen on the inventory list. Most of the supplies had been shrink-wrapped on lightweight plastic pallets to help hold them together during the trip yet keep the load as light as possible. Webbing had been used to secure the shrink-wrapped pallets in place, much like how airlines secure cargo to keep it from shifting during flight. After removing the webbing, Carl wrapped the rope he had previously unburied around the pallet and pulled it to the open hatch. They then picked the pallet up and slid it down the ladder using the rope. As it arrived at the bottom of the ladder, Pedro and Andrea loaded it into the Mars car trailer and dropped it off for the Surface Command crew, who then placed it in the correct staging position appropriately labeling it on their pads. Surface Command had drawn a giant starship in the sand and were using that as a design aid to help organize all of the supplies.

Even with the reduced gravity on Mars, it was a lot of heavy lifting. Steven was running *Staten* Command while Mary monitored and took notes for quick reference. Carl, acting as *Starship IV* Command, would tell *Staten* Command every time they pulled supplies from the next storage position. Mary would make a note of it, and Steven would raise Pedro, acting as Surface Command, and let him know when to change to a new location position number. Pedro was able to put the location position numbers inside the first wrap of the shrink-wrap to hold it in place. It worked better than the duct tape they had brought with them.

He joked, "At least we don't have to worry about rain," as they were staging the supplies.

The *Starship IV* crew consisted of mission specialists Haratu Suzuki, Adnan Ashari, and James Galway. The Surface Command crew, with Pedro in command, consisted of astrobiologist Barbara Black, Andrea Tripp, and Wayne Peters.

Two hours had gone by, and they were about a third into the load. It was going better than they had expected, and it looked like they might possibly empty it all out that day.

As Carl helped James pull a particularly heavy load of double shrink-wrapped hardware, he said, "This load must have been around five hundred pounds on Earth. It feels like it is almost two hundred pounds here on Mars."

They put the rope through the gaps in the pallet underneath, then ran them over the top and tied them off. Every pallet had to be turned over because they were all on their sides, as was the ship. They were hauling it over to the ladder sliding it across the "floor" to the ladder. Carl said, "Just hold it there on the ladder. I'll give you a hand lowering it down."

They just finished placing it on the edge of the ladder, pallet-side down, when some of the shrink-wrap caught on the upper legs of the ladder. While James was trying to loosen the plastic wrap and hold the pallet in place at the same time, the intense weight suddenly broke the plastic wrap off the ladder leg, and it started heading down the ladder in an uncontrolled fall. James knew Andrea and Pedro were standing at the base of the ladder, and he was still holding the line wrapped around the bundle.

As he tightened his grip on the load to keep it from falling, it jerked him forward over the ladder, pulling him out of balance. At the last second, James pushed off with his feet, so he wouldn't get tangled up in the ladder. Carl grabbed for the rope as it whipped around between his legs and jerked away from him. Both James and the heavily loaded pallet careened straight down toward Pedro.

James was in a head-first dive over the top of the falling pallet. The loose end of the rope wound its way around the leg of the ladder and jerked it, pulling the ladder over sideways. With a loud crash, the ladder hit the open hatch door of the starship.

Andrea shouted, "Look out!" which sounded more like a scream, along with a lot of commotion and banging. It sounded like a major catastrophe over the radio.

She jumped clear of the falling James and equipment, but Pedro kept his ground trying to break James's fall—which he did. The issue with James's fall wasn't really the speed of his fall, but the momentum. Unfortunately, the top of James's helmet plowed into Pedro's face shield and helmet, and both James and the two- hundred-pound bundle, pallet and all landed on Pedro, then broke apart. It ripped open, strewing its heavy metal tools and equipment all over the ground and half burying Pedro. Immediately compressed air rushed out of Pedro's suit as his regulator went into full free flow. James tried to untangle himself and stand up.

Over her helmet mic, Andrea shouted, "Pedro is down, Pedro is down!"

Knowing Pedro must be badly hurt, Mary paged Commander Carrigan on the ship-wide PA.

Commander Carrigan, in the dayroom right below the helm, had heard the commotion and informed the crew on ready standby to suit up and deploy immediately. Then he hailed Tammy Spencer, the flight surgeon, to get medical sector ready for a possible trauma incident.

Chapter 34

Johnson Space Center-Day 8

Brad Brown was on the landline with General Latimore's secretary again. Twice before, she had taken his message that he needed to speak with General Latimore as soon as possible, and each time she promised to relay the message.

This time she said she had spoken to him directly and knew he had it on his agenda to return Brad's call. She asked as to what it pertained so the general could be prepared for the call. Brad explained that it was in reference to the rescue capsule being assembled for the ISS. She understood and promised to pass the information along to the general.

Wow, Brad thought, red tape was difficult enough to get through when the satellites were working.

He had gone home the previous night to get some sleep. Now that the power was on around most of the country, the aftermath of the satellite loss was being broadcast nationwide on affiliates that still had the old-fashioned antenna transmitters. The economies of the United States, Canada, and all of Europe were a disaster. He didn't know about any other countries. It was difficult to find a station showing anything besides food trucks, helicopters, and the National Guard distributing water and patrolling the curfew. Some personalities were arguing their theories on who destroyed the satellites, but they really had no idea and no facts to back up their assertions. The armed forces all gave the same response, "This is an on-going international investigation led by the commander-in-chief.

We take our lead from him." The President's office was not taking calls.

Obtaining food was still a major issue because no one had access to cash. Even if they did, the grocery stores were still mostly empty, and the frozen and refrigerated food warehouses had to throw all their food out after losing power for a significant number of days. They could last a day or two on the back-up generators, but most of them had run out of diesel.

People were taking spoiled food from overflowing dumpsters home to eat. The army reserves were convoying food deliveries from warehouses to major metropolitan centers. Some people were going mad, attacking the trucks which were trying to get supplies to the grocery stores. If it wasn't accompanied by the gun-toting National Guard, it was in danger of not making it to its final destination.

Brad thought, are most people normally insane, or does it just take a little stress?

The National Guard passed out MREs (Meals Ready to Eat), which had been produced in the millions for the armed forces. The television told people to eat nothing but canned foods and to throw out all perishable frozen foods. Diabetics were being told not to use their insulin if they hadn't been able to keep it cold. It was still a mess all over the United States, but the situation was slowly getting better.

The President made national appearances on a daily basis, trying to explain what the government was doing to help the situation. He reiterated that martial law was still in effect, and the curfew was now at sunset since most clocks were no longer correct after the loss of the satellites and power.

The plight of the Mars Mission I crew, and the ISS was quickly becoming one of the prime-time news stories, and news trucks were starting to stack up at the entrance to the Johnson Space Center. It had become obvious that there was nothing more the MM1 Engineering Team in Houston could do other than stay diligent on the communications equipment.

The communication attempts were still ongoing every hour, on the hour, on the same frequencies and on the back up frequencies, with no response—as usual. The ISS Ground Control was having the same issues trying to communicate with the ISS, though at least they had different ground telescopes watching it. Not that there was much any telescope could tell them, other than that it was still there, damaged but holding together and so was the single Dragon capsule.

It had been eight days since *Starship X* landed on Mars. The MM1 Engineering Team had gone over all of the figures, and they estimated that *Starship X* would soon need water and oxygen. Fortunately, they had a MOXIE and the portable Kilowatt power unit on board *Starship X*, which would help provide power and oxygen. Who knew if the crew on *Starship X* would be able to access the fallen *Starship IV* or any of its supplies?

Brad was sure they wouldn't be able to access any more of the badly needed supplies from the other starships because the access hatch was a hundred-fifty feet off the ground. The MM1 engineers had been working nonstop on the situational possibilities of what the *Starship X* crew may be experiencing and how they may be using their in-situ resources. The engineers decided the crew had probably started the MOXIE and the power unit by now. This would give them oxygen before the water crisis would arise. The crew on Mars would have no way of refilling their water tank without the supplies on the other starships.

Brad's phone line rang, and he answered. "Brad Brown."

"Brad, this is General Latimore. You called?"

"Yes, General. How are things with you?" Brad cringed at his own question.

"Starting to get some things back together. I badly wish we had cell phones. I can't travel and stay in touch with my secretary. We've opted for handheld radios, and some vehicles are being refitted with mobile radio units. The old radio infrastructure and antennas are all but gone now, so our range is dramatically reduced. The messages build up, and when I get back to my office, it takes me a whole day to answer all of the questions and coordinate with everybody. How can I help you, Brad?"

"I was wondering how the rescue mission for the ISS is going. I need to somehow get a message on the capsule for the ISS astronauts before they board it to come back."

"A message for the astronauts before they return to Earth?"

"We have a theory that the ISS crew may be able to talk with the MM1 crew on Mars. If the ISS crew are in communication via their radio with *Starship X*, we have an extremely important message that could be of lifesaving importance which needs to be communicated to them before they return on the rescue capsule. That is assuming you're still planning on the rescue mission."

"So, Brad, you think the ISS may be able to communicate

———

with the MM1 crew via their radio?"

"We're not sure of anything, but we think it's entirely possible. They could be far enough outside of the static barrier circling the Earth that is blocking our transmission attempts."

"I see. Okay, we have been working on what is, in effect, a giant, three-layer shield covering the top three-quarters of the Crew module specially designed in a well-coordinated effort between Space Force, NASA and a few other space agencies. It's made out of a specially designed, three-inch-thick hardened steel attached to the existing capsule that can take some serious impacts and will be the base layer of the shield. Then we will be placing two layers of a Kevlar-like reinforced material with dead-air space between—you're probably familiar with it. It is called a Whipple shield designed for hypervelocity impacts. It is also called a trans-hab on occasion. I have been informed that a variation on the theme has been used on the ISS in different places."

"Yes, I'm familiar," Brad said. "That three-inch-thick steel cover has got to be crazy heavy. It's a good thing we have an extra Starship booster available which was already prepped in ready backup. It can handle that kind of weight. When do you foresee a launch date?"

"Fortunately, we had an available crew capsule as a backup as well and we're fitting the last of the protective Kevlar jacket on it now. Kennedy Space Center has a tentative launch date scheduled in about ten days. I am satisfied that we're moving as fast as possible. This is an extremely rushed launch time by anyone's parameters. I have to reiterate that this is not being advertised or released to the press, or anyone, including the families of the astronauts, because we don't know if they're even alive. Not to mention what kinds of conditions they might be experiencing. So, we felt it would be best not to have it covered by the press. Kennedy Space Center is closed to the public right now under a national security lockdown. This is a national security operation."

"Of course. This conversation is on a need-to-know basis only. If it launches in ten days, that will mean the astronauts aboard the ISS will have been up there in who knows what kinds of conditions for eighteen days since the attack."

"Exactly. Do you know how you're going to get your message to the astronauts on the ISS?"

Brad had been thinking about that exact question.

General Latimore continued, "The whole operation is going to be automated. We will program the radio on the crew capsule to automatically hail the Space Station minutes prior to its arrival. Once they board and lock the crew capsule hatch closed, it will autonomously return, requiring no input. The best thing would be something that they simply could not miss. We could program a message into the control computer that they must acknowledge prior to departure."

"Yeah, that would be perfect. And if we attach an envelope with the detailed message to each of the seat belts in a way that they couldn't be removed, fall, or float away without the seat belts being undone, they will definitely see it before leaving and they could literally read it over the radio to the crew on Mars after they remove them from the seats. If we print 'Do Not Disembark Without Reading' in large print on the envelopes, they will get the message. We could also pre-program the computer to transmit the same message, just in case. That sounds like a good plan."

General Latimore paused for a moment then asked inquisitively, "What exactly is the message for *Starship X*?"

"Remember, when we were in conference room G, I told you the crew on Mars can't get to their supplies because we're unable to send the authorization codes to the other starships that will activate them? Well, we found a way for them to start up the computers, which will give them access to their supplies. They still have to access the one hundred and fifty-foot-high hatch, but it will significantly shorten the time and effort it will take to offload their supplies. This may mean the difference between twenty-one astronauts dying and a successful first mission to the red planet."

"Okay, you put your envelopes together, Brad, and we'll be sure to get them to the ISS crew. I'll make sure they confirm that they transmitted the message to MM1 prior to departure. Let's just hope you're right and they're in communication with the crew on Mars."

"Yeah," Brad said. "Let's just hope the heavily reinforced capsule can survive the round-trip journey, and the astronauts on the ISS are still alive. Thank you for your help, General."

"You're welcome, Brad. We want to do everything we can to help those guys and get them back home safely! The world could use a little good news right now."

Brad hung up the telephone. He began to think, Well, at least we've done something for the crew on Mars. Just how the hell are they going to gain access to those hatches one hundred and fifty feet high? With an aching heart he picked up the telephone again.

Chapter 35

ISS-Day 9

Commander Amhurst was doing his daily rounds of checking the atmospheric gauges. The O2 levels had dropped a bit again, now at seventeen percent. It was time to add more oxygen to their atmosphere.

They must have had some small leaks behind all the equipment mounted on the walls of the node. He didn't know how long the air and oxygen bottles would last. No one did. Their atmosphere would probably be the deciding factor as to when they had to leave. There were no pressure gauges on the bottles—too easy to bang or knock off. They were just used until they were empty, and things like pressure gauges tended to get bumped and broken off while in transport. The last thing they needed was an out-of-control oxygen bottle flying around inside the station or in the resupply ship.

NASA had engineers and automated programs that signaled when they would need new air tanks. Manually opening the tanks would wake up the heartiest of sleepers, so he went through the food inventory. Even though it was still cold in the Unity node, they should be coming out of the shadow of the Earth soon and the sun will warm the place. They were extremely lucky to have access to the food stores. He decided to rehydrate and eat a few strawberries that came in a plastic pack. They were still remarkably tasty.

Giulia and Henry started to awaken and float out of their sleeping bags.

———

"Good morning, sleeping beauties," Commander Amhurst quipped.

"Morning," was the mutual response.

"You guys want some nice cold coffee?" Commander Amhurst joked.

Giulia responded with a smile and a stretch. "Sounds great!"

Commander Amhurst could always count on Giulia to lighten the mood and he considered them very fortunate to have her with them as a member of the team. You simply cannot teach personality, he contemplated.

"Sure," Henry responded as he began to brush his teeth. "Love some."

"I'm rehydrating some strawberries right now," Commander Amhurst said as he pushed cold water into the packet. "We also have peaches we can rehydrate, one fresh apple—well, it used to be fresh—and some cold scrambled eggs for breakfast. And of course, granola bars. By my estimate, we have a nice variety of foods to last at least another thirty days. After that, it'll be granola bars, nuts, coffee, and water." As he made his way to the dry food stores, he took out three packets of instant coffee and began filling them with water. "I was waiting for you guys to wake up before adding some oxygen to the atmosphere from the O2 tanks. It's around seventeen and a half."

"No wonder I feel so lethargic," Henry muttered as he swallowed his toothpaste and floated over to get some water.

"Yeah, get some coffee. I have the fruit hydrating now. Whoever wants the apple can have it. I'm going to open the oxygen bottles." When Commander Amhurst opened the oxygen tanks, he could tell they were a little lower pressure than they had been before when the air blasted out. After ten seconds, he closed them and made his way back to the atmospheric gauges. They were reading nineteen percent at thirteen psi, so he decided to let the air mix and check it again in a little while. Then he thought about the power they'd found at the fuse box. "Hey, Henry! Do you think we could run that power from the fuse box into the air handler with the CO2 scrubbers?"

"Let me check the air handler and see what kind of power it's designed to handle." Checking the small data plate on the unit he confirmed, "Yeah, they're one hundred twenty-volt, ten amps. If that power coming into the box has much amperage, it should work. It should move some air, anyway. It's just a fan, right?"

"Yeah, I think so. Let's get some wire after breakfast and see what we can put together."

During breakfast, the usual conversation came up. Possible projections as to when would they be able to head back to Earth? When will it be safe enough to try? What about the batteries in the Dragon? Could they be charged with the equipment on board? They considered different theories on how long it would take for the debris to clear up. Commander Amhurst didn't want to explain to his crew that the debris problem could, most likely, take years. Each day they stayed in what was left of the ISS was another day they stayed alive.

The crew was all too aware that they were consuming tangible, irreplaceable resources. Once the oxygen started to fade, their time would be limited. They had to discuss these issues before they were out of time.

With breakfast finished, Commander Amhurst helped

himself to another packet of coffee. He decided it was time to review the decision-making diagram. "Okay, team. I've decided that we should review some things. Since we probably can't depend on NASA to save our butts here, this is what will come to pass in the next unknown number of days. I'd like to discuss and consider our options so we're all on the same page and prepared when we take the actions that could easily make the difference between life and death for us. From my perspective, oxygen is our most critical issue. Starting the air handler with the carbon dioxide scrubbers gives us some critical breathing room. Sorry for the pun."
Giulia and Henry smiled.

"I believe the oxygen will be our limiting factor, so we need to consider our options before it gets to critical levels and our concentration is affected. I've been thinking about the rest of the Space Station for quite a bit. As I see it, we have two possible choices. First, if I go out for a spacewalk to evaluate the rest of the Space Station and the solar arrays from the outside, we may be able to reclaim some of the arrays and evaluate the rest of the nodes. It will allow a larger perspective of the condition of the entire station, including the solar arrays. It may be possible to reclaim, for example, the Russian Zvezda node, where we can manufacture oxygen from the solid fuel oxygen generator, assuming we can figure out how to power it.

"What we're talking about here is taking some risks. Assuming that one day soon we're down to the last of the oxygen and can't find any other sources, we'll have to make one of a couple choices. And please chime in if I'm wrong or you see another alternative. As I said, we have to make these decisions before the oxygen levels get so low that we can't think clearly. I should be the one on the space walk, just because I'm in command, and for no other reason. We are all qualified. As we've discussed in the past, that's one of our options. A second option is all of us suit up and go into the Zarya node, then shut the hatch as fast as possible to try to preserve what is left of our atmosphere in here, which won't be much. Then we'll conduct a thorough evaluation of both the Zarya and the Zvezda nodes from the inside. That will give us a more comprehensive picture of the two nodes to see if they're salvageable. We can start the salvage operation, and maybe even get the solid fuel oxygen generator running, then start to repressurize the other two nodes. Of course, this action risks the atmosphere in here, so we probably shouldn't pursue that until our atmosphere is pretty much spent. The problem with that is if we can't reclaim the two nodes and start the solid oxygen generator, then we're stuck in our spacesuits. Period. I guess at that point, we'll climb back into the Dragon, head for home, and hope for the best."

"That sounds pretty scary," Giulia said. "It's like putting all of our cards on the table at the last minute."

"Once we go into the Zarya node, there's no returning. We are committed. Either we make it work, or we leave and take our chances in the Dragon."

"Okay, I don't think I care about waiting for the last minute. If we do the space-walk option, we only lose the atmosphere during the equalization, not the whole Unity node."

"Yeah, I'm guessing we might lose maybe one day of breathable air when I do the space walk, but I should be able to tell from the outside if either node is damaged beyond repair."

Giulia sipped on her coffee, holding the straw by her teeth to free her hands. As she began moving her hands all about, the guys knew she wanted to say something, but she still had the straw in her mouth. "If it looks intact from the outside, we can determine if the Zarya and Zvezda nodes may be intact enough to reclaim. Then we can take our chances on the other two nodes if it looks like they may be intact. If not, we still have another couple of days of good air in here—hopefully. We could regroup and consider our options then?" Commander Amhurst and Henry both agreed.

"Yes, I wouldn't even get out of my spacesuit if it looked intact. We could wait until we're down to the last two or three days of breathable air, then I could go out and do an inspection outside. If it's damaged beyond recovering, we'll know not to try making an entry into the Zarya node, and that might leave us at least a couple days of air."

Giulia put on a sly grin. "See? You smart guys still need the occasional direction from the Italian sector." She threw her head back in laughter.

It was the first time in a long time anyone had truly laughed on the Space Station, and when they were making life and death decisions, a little laughter went a long way.

"So, it's settled then," Commander Amhurst said with an appreciative smile and nod. "We will wait until we think we're on the last few days of breathable air, then I'm going to take a walk. Unless, of course, we discover some new information in the meantime."

"Sounds like that makes the most sense at the moment,"

Henry agreed. "Now, let's take a look at that air handler."

Chapter 36
Mars-Sol 9

As soon as Andrea got back on her feet, she helped the stunned James Galway get up as well. They hurriedly unburied Pedro. His helmet lights were blinking on and off, and his regulator was making a shrill screaming sound. The sound of the free-flowing regulator was loud enough for everyone to hear above the depressurization alarms.

Finding the hole in Pedro's suit was priority number one. Andrea pulled out her roll of duct tape and started looking for penetrations, as she instructed Wayne and Barbara over the radio to bring the Mars car and backboard, which was staged at all work sites. She found a couple of small tears and penetrations around Pedro's quads and knees. James straightened Pedro's suit over each hole then Andrea covered each of the holes with the strong tape, wrapping the holes with three or four pieces of duct tape. Pedro's regulator slowly started returning to a normal volume as his suit returned to a more humane atmospheric pressure and the low-pressure alarms quieted down as well, going quiet one at a time.

Wayne and Barbara Black brought the Mars car over with the backboard. Wayne picked up the ladder and replaced it on *Starship IV*, so Carl could get down. They put Pedro across the back seats and sped off to *Staten*. On the way, Andrea informed Steven via her helmet comm what had happened as Pedro mumbled incoherently. She tried to keep her voice calm, while inside she was filled with deep fear. Despite their agreement she found she cared more about Pedro than she realized. She was able to keep the tears to a minimum as she swung her head from side to side to clear her vision, but it dotted her visor with tiny tears. She still stayed in command, keeping Steven abreast of any changes.

Upon arrival at *Staten*, Pedro was immediately loaded onto the deck of the crane as Andrea blew him off with the high- pressure hose. He was brought into the equalization room on the backboard, where Commander Carrigan and the ready standby crew had just equalized to the Martian atmosphere.

Before long, Pedro was out of his Mars suit and in medical, being evaluated by flight surgeon Tammy Spencer. Her immediate head-to-toe trauma assessment revealed that Pedro had a hyperextended right knee, a small contusion to his forehead, and a possible concussion, along with some smaller bruises and contusions. Neurologically, he was aware and responsive, but he couldn't remember what happened. Vital signs were taken, and he was given a local anesthetic for his painful knee, which was already red and swollen. With a little manipulation, Tammy was able to get his knee back in the correct position after the local anesthetic was administered, and he was left to rest in medical.

After thirty minutes, all vitals were within normal limits, and his pain was dissipating. There didn't appear to be any rapid decompression illness or barotrauma, lung sounds were clear and equal, and his oxygen saturation was normal on room air. Tammy placed him on oxygen as a precaution. She said she wanted to keep him for at least twenty-four hours for observation.

She left medical to get Andrea's full story about what happened, then told Commander Carrigan she felt Pedro was extremely lucky. She said he'd be walking, albeit gingerly, with a leg brace and crutches in a few days, assuming there were no tendon tears or ligament damage. Her verbal medical report and recovery recommendations to the commander consisted of rest for the next forty-eight hours and maybe thirty days of rehab. Assuming there were no medical complications, he could probably return to light duty in thirty days upon conclusion of the rehab and a reassessment at that time. She hoped there would be no long-term tendon or ligament damage that might require surgery.

Once Carl's crew from *Starship IV* arrived back at *Staten*, Commander Carrigan organized the entire crew. James did most of the talking at first, describing what happened. Then Carl explained how he saw the accident unfold. As a crew, they went through a whole post-accident briefing and evaluated every aspect. Andrea was privately grateful Commander Carrigan did not ask for her input. She was unsure if she could keep a calm voice without revealing her inner emotions.

The common conclusion was that they were performing a difficult operation without the necessary equipment, which was simply not available. The second point of consideration was whether they needed to off-load the heavy load as one piece or could they have broken it down. The group decided they could've taken the load apart. It would've taken significantly more time, but James would not have been pulled over the ladder and dropped the load if it had been broken down into smaller and lighter pieces. Carl added, "It seemed perfectly manageable based on the previous loads they had handled. But in hindsight it obviously was too much. Perhaps a block and tackle could have been fashioned somehow to further reduce the static load of the pallets?

The critical assessment was that they had been performing above the expected rate and wanted to finish the job quickly. So, the time frame for the performance took precedence over safety. The whole crew agreed, and it was decided that from now on a safety command officer would be added to every EVA. The safety officer's job was to stand back as an impartial observer and watch for any operational activity that could go bad and would intervene as soon as it seemed necessary. All activity within the command would cease the second anyone on the surface announced "stop".

After the review, Commander Carrigan sent James to Medical for a quick assessment after he discovered that James had fallen twenty feet onto Pedro. Forty-five minutes later, Flight Surgeon Tammy Spencer, after doing a complete head to toe assessment involving repeated evaluations of his c-spine and back, cleared him for light-duty work after twenty-four hours of rest. James had no significant complaints and said he was fine, thanks to Pedro blocking his fall. Pedro's and James' helmets were taken out of service and replaced with new ones out of Starship X's inventory.

Commander Carrigan put C shift in charge for the remainder of the shift and went to his office to fill out the electronic accident report forms. He was grateful that neither Pedro nor James was more badly injured. After filling out the report, he went to the helm and asked Steven to join him for an EVA back to *Starship IV*. He asked Mary to do the comms. He wanted to take a look at the scene in person.

Upon arrival, the scene was exactly as everyone had reported. Commander Carrigan and Steven looked at the ladder set-up and couldn't see any way to secure the ladder without causing a tripping hazard or significantly complicating the off- loading operation. It just wasn't tall enough to do the job. They considered placing rocks around the foot of the ladder to help secure it in place since they didn't have any other way to secure it. They decided that the crew could probably make some sandbags out of some of the supplies or extra shrink-wrap which could secure the feet of the ladder. But there was no safe way to secure it at the top.

They discussed the set-up and if there was anything that could've been done differently. This wasn't a "normal" operation, but then again, *Starship IV* wasn't expected to fall over and have to be manually off-loaded either. In the end, they concluded that unloading *Starship IV* is not a scheduled or practiced event and caution should be the utmost concern. They were using equipment not designed for the task, increasing the risk of an undesired outcome.

Considering the crew was ahead of schedule, it could hardly be that they felt pressure to speed up. They weren't rushing due to time constraints. Still, if Commander Carrigan had been on the scene prior to the accident, he may have been able to recognize the danger. *Starship IV*'s command, crew, and even the Surface Command and crew should've been able to recognize the precarious instability of the ladder. Still, it wasn't the ladder falling over which caused the accident. It was the over-sized, heavy load. Commander Carrigan was disappointed with himself for not being there observing or maybe acting as a Safety Officer himself.

It was hard to find fault with Pedro, who may have been holding the ladder or standing on the bottom rung to stabilize it. After all, he broke James's fall. It looked to Commander Carrigan that

James may have suffered a broken neck if the pallet landed on him while he was upside down at the base of the ladder. If Pedro hadn't held his ground and blocked James's fall, who knows what the outcome might've been.

Commander Carrigan shook his head as he turned to Steven. "It looks like it's time to award Pedro the medal for Valiant Performance."

"Yeah, I guess, though I've never heard of astronauts getting medals before."

"Well, if it weren't for Pedro, it might've been much worse."

"I agree."

Chapter 37

Mars Sol 10

The next day, in a full-crew meeting, Pedro was awarded the "Valiant Performance" citation printed off *Starship X*'s computer, which was as close to a medal as Commander Carrigan could find. Pedro was also rewarded with a standing ovation from the rest of the crew as they all tried to crowd into the tiny medical facility, much to his embarrassment.

The crew suited up for another EVA to get as much of the job done as the added caution would allow. Commander Carrigan suited up as well and acted as a safety officer on the scene. There was nothing he could recommend differently, so after a few hours, when the work was winding down, he declared himself off the work scene and walked the mile back to *Staten* by himself—really alone for the first time in months. He had forgotten how nice it was to be alone, and the walk picked up his spirits, also realizing how truly grateful he was that no one was permanently hurt.

Surprisingly quickly, they finished emptying *Starship IV* with no further incidents. Some nylon bags had been found and filled with Mars soil to stabilize the ladder. The speed of the accomplishment astonished Commander Carrigan. He didn't know if he should praise them for their efforts or chastise them for being too efficient and effective. When they saw his confusion, they reported to him that most of the remaining inventory on *Starship IV* was lightweight, which included the Mars car trailer, and they had already attached it to the second Mars car (called MC2) and put it to good use.

James Galway didn't seem to have any significant injury and spent time with Pedro. Pedro was confused about the attention since he couldn't remember the accident or his part in saving James. All he could remember were incredibly beautiful hazel eyes, which brought a warm, comfortable feeling with them. This he kept to himself until Andrea swung by.

Andrea's heart swelled with pride as she recalled Pedro's heroism. She stopped in to see him a few times a day as her schedule allowed. He was appreciative of her attention, but it was different in medical: they could be easily observed. Their privacy pact was going to be difficult to keep. Both realized the accident stirred deeper feelings. Feelings of love, deep caring, emotional support and a newer, deeper stronger and more powerful, almost overwhelming feeling of potential personal loss. Andrea's empathy for Pedro was profound. It was difficult to put into words and even harder to keep it all inside. But they had to, it was part of the deal. Few crew noticed the frequent visits to sick bay, but then again most of the crew stopped in on occasion to see how Pedro was doing. Andrea struggled with maintaining her professionalism, but she had come too far, worked too hard. A steely determined resolve kept her emotions in check. At least for the moment.

Chapter 38
Mars-Sol 11

It was time to remove the framing from *Starship IV*, then begin to weld the scaffolding together. Commander Carrigan was having second, third, and fourth thoughts about a one hundred- fifty-foot scaffolding. A crew member just fell twenty feet down a ladder. He had engaged Carl in conversation on more than one occasion to find another way to open the hatches on the other starships. They just didn't know of any other way, and the supplies on all the starships had to be off-loaded sooner rather than later. They needed the water lines to refill *Staten*'s water tanks as soon as possible. This was not a convenience; this was a requirement. A requirement for life.

"Ah, Carl… just the man I wanted to see," Commander Carrigan said. "Take a seat, sir. I'm nervous about the scaffolding since the accident with the ladder on *Starship IV*. We really don't want a repeat performance, and this time we're talking about one hundred-fifty feet up—not twenty."

Carl sat and pulled a file out of his chart case, rubbing his chin as he examined a drawing. "I'm sure I can put together a stable scaffolding using the rope to secure it to the Starship every twenty or thirty feet. It will use up most of the rope we took off *Staten* and *Starship IV*."

"I want to personally inspect it before we implement it. Not that I don't trust you, Carl. It's my responsibility." Commander Carrigan was still feeling a good bit of remorse about the accident with Pedro; after all, he accused himself most of the blame for not being there. Not only did it happen on his shift, but he designed and issued the command.

"Of course, Commander. You've seen the design, but that's not the same as seeing the finished work. It is going to take two or three days, no longer."

"Carl, I know you're loaded down with all of these responsibilities. Is there anything I can help you with or give you more support for?"

"The crew of four you assigned are fine for the job. I don't need any more people to assemble the scaffolding. I don't want them using the cutter though. I'll do the cutting. At least until I get them trained. It's very important to keep the framing intact. Any slips with the cutting head could damage the whole stringer. The other three can be off-loading and staging the stringers and framing as I remove them. It won't take long to remove them, then we start to weld. One, maybe two people can hold it in place while I weld and teach them to weld. We'll trade off positions, so we can rotate around and take breaks without interrupting the work. It's not a difficult job once the torch and power units are in place. The fourth person will retrieve another length of frame from the staging pile. It's pretty simple at that point."

"Ok, I am going to assign Chief Pilot Mary Pfeiffer as safety. She hasn't had an opportunity to be on an EVA yet. There's just one more item that I need to cover, Carl. I need to get an update on *Staten*'s vitals from your perspective."

"I knew you'd want my take on our water and oxygen levels.

The bottom line is, we're going to need water in the next two days."

"Yeah, I know. We're cutting it close. Do you know how much water line we got off *Starship IV*?"

"There was one thousand feet on *Starship IV*," Carl said, "and we have three thousand feet on *Staten*."

"Yeah, that's what is on the inventory lists. I figure we need almost six thousand feet to make it from Starship II to *Staten*."

"I estimated that much, as well, a little over a mile. The inventory shows three thousand feet on Starship V, another three thousand feet on Starship VI, and three thousand feet on *Starship VII*.

"Which is the best one to start off-loading first? Assuming we can gain access."

"We're going to gain access, Commander. Don't you worry about that. I suggest *Starship VII*. It has the third Mars car and trailer, which we could use. It also has a better variety of different foods which we don't have on *Staten*," he added with a sheepish grin. "The water line has priority. Let me get to it. If you want to rotate the crews out there with me, that's fine."

"So, you're telling me we have about two days of water at the current usage, and it'll probably take two days to get to the needed water line? Oh, man, that is cutting it close! Get to it. Don't let me hold you up anymore. I'll tell Mary she is the safety officer. Ugh!"

"Ok. At the current usage rate, yes, that's right." With that, Carl headed off with his crew to *Starship* IV.

Pedro's injury and James Galway's fall was a grave reminder to Commander Carrigan that MM1 was functioning way outside of its designed parameters. It also gave the commander reason to pause. He knew they were lucky no one was killed in this incident. If someone fell from a hundred fifty feet, they would die. If they didn't get the supplies they needed off the starships, the whole crew would die from lack of water. It would only take about three days after the water ran out.

They needed water. *Staten* was designed for recycling as much of the water as it possibly could. Even urine was recycled. Humidity was taken out of the air they breathed, and after sanitizing and putting it through the reverse osmosis system, it was added to the water tanks.

Every EVA took roughly seven hundred cubic feet of compressed breathable air with it through the equalization chamber. Commander Carrigan took Communications Specialist Steven Henderson and Astro-Biologist Barbara Black out to inspect the work Carl and his crew were doing, as well as to inspect Starships I and II. He also had a small deviation in mind, which he thought might be interesting.

Before leaving, Commander Carrigan took Andrea to the side and intimated he was going to "tour" a bit of the humongous Valles Marineras with Steven and Barbara, also asking her to monitor the comms and to please keep this little trip he had planned to herself, unless they needed help, of course.

Explaining that he wasn't sure what their trip may yield, probably nothing, "But then again, you never know," he said with a knowledgeable smile.

Andrea just nodded and added a quick, "Yes, sir." Not knowing what to think of this strange request of the commander. Secrets are not normal, she thought to herself. A little confused, but willing to support her commander, she took the comms desk, checking her frequencies.

Carl was acting Command at *Starship IV*, utilizing frequency 1 alpha. Commander Carrigan told Andrea he would be Mars Command on frequency 2 alpha so as to not confuse the crew working on *Starship IV*. He then asked Barbara Black if she had evaluated the soil samples they took on the first day of the EVAs. She said she had and determined they did indeed contain perchlorates, reinforcing the need to decontaminate prior to re- entry.

Human beings were walking biological petri dishes, taking thousands of different types of bacteria, yeast, mold, fungus, viruses, and even parasites along for the ride. Most of them are symbiotic and, in reality, a requirement for life…mostly. Barbara was constantly swabbing every nook and cranny and taking her swabs back to the lab for ongoing analysis of contamination and microbiological activity of any kind. She normally would find the run of the mill staph and yeast varieties. She took a sampling kit with her everywhere she went. She could be found crouched in the odd corner or swabbing areas of the galley, showers, bathrooms, and around the equalization hatch. If she discovered anything of significance, she would report it to the commander immediately and a full clean-up crew would be assigned. She usually had one of the crew along as an assistant trying to teach them as much as she could. The entire crew had been trained in microbiology and could run a few simple tests, but Barbara tried to keep their distant past training current with constant reminders and small quizzes as they migrated around the huge ship from room to room, inspecting high use surfaces as well as virtually unknown spaces, air ventilation systems, and the water system. Toxic fungi love wet plastics.

They arrived at *Starship IV* in MC2. Carl and his crew were moving along much quicker than Commander Carrigan had expected. They already had all the framing and almost all of the stringers removed from *Starship IV*, which was probably more than would be needed. *Starship IV* had eight sets of aluminum, L- shaped framing that ran the entire length, from top to bottom, for attaching the cargo netting and securing it in place. Carl had removed the Kilowatt power unit from Staten, which provided the power to run his welding equipment.

Commander Carrigan decided to leave Carl and his crew alone and head over to Starships I and II, taking with them the four thousand feet of water line in the trailer that had just been off- loaded from *Starship IV*. Unfortunately, there was too much line to move all at once, and the trailer couldn't take the weight, so they had to make four trips to get it all moved over to *Starship II*.

Commander Carrigan asked Steven to drive so he could take in the Martian scenery. At fifty-four degrees Fahrenheit with a beautiful cloudless sky, it was a gorgeous day on Mars. The red Martian soil and rocks bore a stark contrast to their white Mars car. Starships I and II gleamed brightly in the sun.

They off-loaded the water line, staging it approximately every thousand feet, starting at Starship II. A quick inspection of starships I and II revealed that all of the autonomously running equipment was working as previously verified. The water tank was full, hydrogen was being manufactured, oxygen was being made, as was methane. They almost had enough methane to completely refill *Staten*'s fuel tanks. In less than a month, enough fuel would've been made for the trip back home when Earth and Mars's orbits had moved close enough together again.

Satisfied that Starships I and II were functioning as expected and having finished the four trips with the water line, they were done with the difficult and heavy objectives of the day's EVA, as far as Commander Carrigan knew. He suggested they look at one of the cliff outcrops that had a dark spot located on the canyon wall around some large rocks. This outcrop had been visualized by the Mars Reconnaissance Orbiter and had been deemed a location of primary interest before the mission plans were finalized. Commander Carrigan was not sure what the dark spot was, but it had to be interesting.

The charge on the Mars car was three-quarters full, and the outcrop looked to be about three miles away, or maybe a thirty-minute ride according to the *Starship X* navigational system. Commander Carrigan estimated they could see over twenty miles in the thin Martian atmosphere. They tried to drive as much as they could in a straight line, avoiding a boulder field and the larger meteor craters.

Commander Carrigan explained to Andrea where they were going and why. She could see their beacon on *Staten*'s locator map and most probably with the naked eye. He didn't want her to get concerned and he had no idea what to expect from this short venture. Twenty-five minutes later, they stood looking up at the dark spot on the canyon wall, partially obscured by some large boulders. They crawled thirty feet up the steep angle of the canyon, losing forward momentum in the soft sand parts of the cliff and slid halfway down again. They finally were able to get to the same level as the dark spot by switchback navigating at severe angles to stay away from the softest sand. They came around a large boulder which was partially blocking their view of the black spot they could see from the valley floor.

No autonomous rover had ever seen a cave or climbed up the side of a soft-soil cliff with this type of severe angle or degree of inclination. This was virgin exploration in many ways. But a possible cave opening, or whatever it is, had never been inspected. Steven was the first one to see it. He looked back at Commander Carrigan shouting, "You're gonna want to see this!"

Commander Carrigan stood next to Steven as they surveyed the entrance.

Barbara walked around the two of them and gasped, "Oh, my, God! A cave!" she pretty much screamed into her helmet mic. Andrea's ears nearly burst. She was about to lower the volume on her headset, but she didn't want to miss any of this!

Commander Carrigan let out a hoot as he looked inside what was definitely a cave. The opening was maybe five feet wide, just under six feet high, and somewhat round. It was taller than it was wide. They could see about fifteen feet inside. It looked to them that the floor turned darker in color deeper into the cave, but there was also less light. They told Andrea on comms that they were going into what appeared to be a cave three miles northeast of Starships I and II, and they asked her to give them a time stamp and expect possible loss of communications with the group.

"I have you on the locator map. Timestamp is zero-six-twenty-one Zulu. Be careful." She suddenly realized that saying "be careful" was probably not protocol, but she was concerned. She made a quick note at the communications desk.

"Zero-six-twenty-one Zulu. We will stay in contact as long as we can."

The group checked their wrist computers and confirmed the time. Commander Carrigan set a stopwatch and walked three feet into the opening, looking up and down with every hesitant step. "Barbara, you'll want to sample some of this soil."

`Barbara walked in next to Commander Carrigan and started putting samples in a little glass bottle from her case. She then told Andrea which numbered bottles she was using for the different samples, so she could review it back in the lab and have a documented record without having to write everything down. Andrea started making a log which Barbara could refer to when they came back.

The crew turned their helmet lights on as they progressed fifty feet into the cave. They began seeing small reflections on the ceiling, growing larger the farther they went down into the cave. They were crystals.

After another hundred feet, Barbara said, "Make sure not to touch any of these crystals. We don't know what they are yet."

The crystals seemed to grow out of cracks between the rocks, along the ceiling, and on some of the walls of the cave. Some of them had grown to be up to two feet long. The deeper they went the larger and more magnificent and colorful they were. Another hundred feet down and the narrow ten-foot-wide cave opened up to a larger, more spacious tunnel thirty feet wide or so. As they progressed, it curved around to the right as it descended. The floor continued to angle downward as they scuffled through the dark sand

———

that appeared darker and more compacted the further they went. Occasionally it would flatten out for a few feet and then start to angle down again. They couldn't see very far ahead so every step and every corner was a mystery.

Commander Carrigan said, "The ceiling and floor seem to be stable so far. Make sure to watch your footing. We don't want anyone falling into a cavern or something."

"How deep do you think we are, Barbara?" Commander Carrigan asked as they continued on a slow, gradual descent and rounded another corner.

"Maybe two-hundred feet below the valley floor where we left the Mars car. We only climbed up the canyon wall maybe like fifty feet, it was just very steep. We have been on a decline since we entered the cave. I would estimate we have come a pretty decent distance already."

As they walked a little further along, Steven said, "I'm going back to the Mars car to get the atmosphere meter and the flashlight."

As they waited for Steven, they examined the beautiful ceiling. It shimmered in multiple colors and reflected their helmet lights. There were rocks and boulders strewn around the cave floor, some with jagged edges from falling off the cave ceiling.

Barbara was busy swabbing some of the clear crystals and stashing her samples in her swabbing kits. "They look like quartz, or maybe salt crystals, some of them on the ceiling are huge!" she said in amazement. She then broke a small piece off the side of the cave using swabbing to handle it. She hailed Andrea but received no response. "Try to remember that we lost comms at zero-six-fifty-eight. We've been in here for almost forty minutes already."

Steven was back with the atmosphere meter and taking a reading. "I wish I had brought this the first time, breathing heavily. The temperature seems to have risen a bit. It's eighty degrees, and the humidity readings are ninety-five percent. That is crazy warm! I'm picking up readings of five percent oxygen and about two percent methane, eighty one percent carbon dioxide, trace readings of nitrogen and sulfur dioxide and some inert gases including helium. That's the highest oxygen, methane, humidity, and temperature readings I've ever heard of on Mars!"

"Methane could be expected from geological sources, but oxygen? Oxygen wouldn't normally be expected, at least not from a geological source," Barbara whispered.

Commander Carrigan was silent with astonishment. They continued their walk into the cave, continuing down another fifty feet, when the floor took a deep dive into what appeared to be a large open cavern.

"Careful here, guys!" Commander Carrigan didn't want any more accidents.

At the bottom of a fifty-foot drop, something dark and shiny was moving. Steven's light reflected off the bottom of the cavern like a distorted mirror onto the opposing side of the cave. They could see the cave continuing beyond the moving surface. It looked like a black pool slowly boiling up from the bottom. They couldn't hear any noise or sound.

"The atmosphere in here is getting thick and it's foggy with ninety-eight percent humidity. Ninety-eight percent! This is like a tropical rainforest!" Steven said.

"Ha!" Commander Carrigan laughed. "Can we get down there?"

Barbara looked around in amazement at the beautiful and unexpected find. "I think we can get down over there."

Steven shone the light in the direction of a more gradual slope that led around the slowly bubbling pool as they made their way around the inside of the large cavern. "How far across would you estimate this cavern to be?"

"I think it's maybe one hundred feet in diameter, maybe more. It's hard to tell because of the fog," Commander Carrigan replied.

They made their way to the bottom of the cavern next to the pool. As Steven continued monitoring the atmosphere. "I'm reading one hundred percent humidity at eighty-nine degrees," he said. "Not only that, but I'm reading that we have an atmospheric pressure of two psi." Something dropped onto his meter and splattered. "Hold on! Barbara, come take a sample of this!"

Barbara followed Steven's gaze and his flashlight to the ceiling a hundred feet above them. It was glistening with shiny stalactites and a spongy material, like something on the beach after a storm, or seaweed hanging down in short strings. She took out a swab and sampled the drop.

Commander Carrigan was looking at the pool. "I . . . I think that's water! It certainly looks like it!"

Barbara immediately took out another glass jar and carefully removed a sterile spoon, sampling the liquid. "Oh, I wish I had a thermometer to get the temperature of this liquid.

Andrea…. Andrea…. *Staten*, do you copy?"

Again, no response.

They walked around the pool carefully watching their footing and looked farther down into the cave, where it exited the large cavern then continued on down deeper.

Steven shined his light where the cave continued around another corner.

"What type of formation do you think this is, Barbara?"

"Off the top of my head, I'm guessing this is a lava tube and I am guessing that is a hot spring," she answered as she gestured to the pool. "I wanna see where that leads." She pointed to the tunnel that continued down.

"Okay, we've been out of radio range for almost thirty minutes. I suggest we head back before we make Andrea too nervous. I'm showing we've been here for almost an hour already. Next time we get a little more organized. Spelunking can be dangerous. We need safety lines, more lights, and equipment. The crew isn't going to believe this. Barbara, do you want to take any more samples of that liquid before we leave?"

"Yeah, I think it may be water, like you said. It certainly looks like it." After she took another two samples, she closed up her sample case and they slowly made their way back up the steep embankment.

Before leaving, they all turned around and had one more look.

"How deep do you think we are in here?" Barbara asked.

"Deep enough to give us just a little more than double the atmosphere on the surface and an increase of fifteen degrees as well as a completely different mixture of atmospheric elements," Steven responded in awe.

"I think we're pretty deep. I would guess we've descended over four-hundred feet. That cavern ceiling is probably fifty feet above the pool itself. I can't wait to get a look at my samples."

Commander Carrigan was looking at the ceiling again following Steven's light. "Next time we come back, Barbara, bring a thermometer. I'd like to get the temperature of that pool." "Yeah, that would make this a much more comfortable microclimate than outside. And it doesn't receive all of the radiation the surface does.

"Does anyone want to guess if it's like this year-round?" Barbara posed.

"That's a very good question," Commander Carrigan replied.

They were all in complete amazement of the cave. With that, they slowly walked out single file, being careful not to touch any of the crystals. After reestablishing comms with Andrea, they informed her that they had exited the cave and were making their way back to *Staten*.

Immediately upon their return, Barbara made a beeline to the lab and began carefully analyzing the liquid samples. Within a matter of minutes, she had a basic analysis of the liquid and had inspected it under the microscope. She immediately went to Commander Carrigan's office, where he was writing up notes from the excursion.

"I've got something to tell you! Water!" she said, with an expression that said she was going to cry.

"What?" Commander Carrigan said. "You got to be kidding me. Really?"

"Water!" she repeated with a giant smile. "It's water with small amounts of electrolytes and salts such as sodium chloride, magnesium chloride, potassium chloride, and some other salts . . . and no perchlorates! But there is something else." She began to cry and then laugh. She bit her index finger with excitement. The usually scientific, demure, and serious Barbara was having a breakdown.

Commander Carrigan could not believe what he was witnessing. Barbara was a complete basket case.

"Water... and something in it?" he almost yelled. "What is it? What is it?"

"I don't know," she said, trying to get a hold of herself. "It's going to take time to identify whatever it is." As she regained her composure, she took a deep breath, she cleared her throat and said purposefully, "It looks like a diatom...maybe."

Commander Carrigan's face lit up. "You discovered water in liquid form, and possibly life at the same time?"

"You could drink it, I think," she added, giggling. "I haven't done a full analysis, but the pH is seven-point-nine, just slightly basic, which means it probably tastes good, too. It's definitely water. Water with electrolytes. It might actually be good for you. I wanted to give you the news as soon as I had it confirmed. I'm going back to the lab to take another look at this diatom thing, or whatever it is, and incubate some of that water in some different medium petri dishes and see if anything grows. I'm also curious about the soil and crystal samples I took. I...I can't believe it!" She turned to leave, still shaking, and wiping tears from her eyes. She turned back to the commander and shook her fists in joy, slightly crouching as though she were cheering on her favorite football team. Then she stood tall, threw her head back and headed back to her lab.

"Congratulations!" Commander Carrigan yelled after her as she scampered away. He broke into a deep convulsive laugh which he couldn't contain. How crazy!

Two minutes later Commander Carrigan couldn't focus on anything else. He had to go to the lab and see this thing Barbara had found.

At the same time, Steven was making his usual radio shout out to the ISS. There was nothing new for either to report. He didn't think they needed to hear about the falling incident and the injury to Pedro. The ISS crew had nothing they could do but wait it out until their atmosphere was almost gone, then they were going to attempt what Steven thought of as a hail Mary toss to the end zone. If it worked, they could stay for an indefinite amount of time, or at least until their water ran out. He wished them good luck, patience, Godspeed, and signed off.

What kind of hell must it be knowing that sooner or later they're going to have to climb into that Dragon again with low batteries, hoping they can survive reentry, and trust that the parachutes open, if they aren't smashed into pieces on the way. I never thought I would question space travel. But I am very concerned about their odds of surviving this ordeal. May God watch over them.

———

304

Stephen was close to tears wrought with emotion.

Soon enough, Carl and the crew working on the scaffolding returned to *Staten*. Commander Carrigan announced a full-crew meeting in thirty minutes over *Staten*'s all stations, PA. He had popped into *Staten*'s laboratory to see Barbara Black previous to the meeting. She opened the lab door, which usually remained locked while she was working.

He greeted her with a big smile and surprised himself when he said, "What's up?" knowing that wasn't like him.

Barbara looked at Commander Carrigan. "Mask. Gloves."

Back to her scientific self, he thought as he followed her into the lab. "Of course, we don't want to contaminate these samples, that's for sure. We're having a crew meeting in about fifteen minutes. We need to tell the crew what we know, and probably a fair amount of what we suspect. Where is the diatom thing?"

"Diatoms," she corrected him. "They're in the incubator. Since we didn't get a temperature of the water sample I took, I'm trying to keep them at thirty-two degrees C, the same temperature as the room we found them in. If they are diatoms like on Earth, they won't live long. Most diatoms have short lives. Maybe a few days."

"What do you think they may have been utilizing as a food source?" he couldn't help asking, even though he knew better.

"That's why I'm trying to analyze the water for nutrients and anything else. I also need to go back and get more samples of the water, the edges, the bottom of that pool, and the ceiling of that cave. Most diatoms in the oceans and fresh-water sources on Earth live off of photosynthesis. But some live off carbon sources for energy— especially the ones found in caves. I also want to leave a digital recording thermometer near that pool, so we can get the temperature changes over time."

"I need to talk to Steven before the meeting. We have to tell the crew what's going on and what it is we've discovered. So, I'll describe our little journey today, and I'll take us as far as approaching and entering the cave. Then I'll turn it over to you to explain since you're the specialist in these things. Are you comfortable declaring that we found water?"

"Sure. I feel comfortable saying we've discovered water and a living organism that so far looks very much like a diatom. They'll have questions all night if I don't tell them everything we know and everything we don't know. And even then, they'll understandably be full of questions. I'll handle it. Let me put some things away," she said as she started busily cleaning up the small lab.

"See you at the meeting in ten."

"Okay, see you there," she replied with a smile. "I'm so happy to be able to put my skills to work."

"I'm sure you are. There's no one better for the job."

Commander Carrigan went to the helm where he found Steven finishing up the communications log. "So, what do you think of our discovery today?"

Steven looked up from the log screen and smiled. "I can't believe it."

"We probably discovered the first liquid water on Mars." "It was water?" Steven said.

"Looks like it! I just wanted to give you the basics. Barbara verified that it is water, but that's not all..." Commander Carrigan said with a wide smile. "That's not all!"

At the beginning of the meeting, Commander Carrigan made the announcement that *Staten* was under strict water restrictions until the water line was completed, meaning no more showers until the water line was intact in a couple days. He asked Carl to give everyone a quick update on the construction of the scaffolding, which was moving along at a rapid pace.

The team was working like a smoothly oiled machine. They were about to start adding the cross-support structures to the first two levels already. He explained that they were bolting the structure together every twenty-five feet, so it could be dismantled and easily moved from starship to starship. Even then, that meant six different pieces of the scaffolding had to be moved each time they moved to the next starship. The base would be the worst piece to move because it was so wide and bulky. Like a pyramid, the upper structures were smaller and narrower. Fortunately, the approximately one third weight on Mars helped a lot. He had devised a way of using the Mars car and the trailer as a type of dolly with two astronauts walking alongside to keep it stable as the Mars car in front pulled it along.

Commander Carrigan asked Carl how he planned on getting the supplies down once he made entry. Commander Carrigan was a little concerned about asking this question because he himself didn't know the answer to that question. Carl was right on top of it, though, and said he would disconnect the computer- controlled crane and rewire the contacts from the on-board batteries through the manual controls system, which is like a very large wired remote, then to the crane's motor.

"No big deal," Carl smiled back.

"Good to hear." Commander Carrigan felt encouraged. Chalk another one up for Carl! he thought to himself. Man, am I glad he's on the crew!

Commander Carrigan explained the rest of the trip to Starship I and II, stating that they had delivered four-thousand feet of water line and staged it for rapid assembly as soon as they had enough line to connect to *Staten*. He went on to explain that there happened to be one of the formations identified by the MM1 task force for exploration, an "area of interest" not far from the Starships I and II. He outlined their trip up to the point of discovering the cave, then he handed off the rest of the explanation to Barbara, who explained the whole exploration event from the minute they arrived at the cave to the discovery of the liquid pool, which she had since been able to identify as water.

The crew clapped and gasped with amazement.

Tammy Spencer asked a pertinent question. "How can water in a liquid state remain liquid and not immediately sublimate and disappear?"

Barbara had been thinking about that ever since they left the cave, as had Commander Carrigan and Steven as well. "Steven was giving us atmospheric changes from the atmospheric and environmental meter. From the moment we entered the cave, the atmosphere began to display changes. As we approached the lowest point of the cave, the atmosphere was definitely changing. The lower we went, the warmer it became, and slowly, the atmosphere began to increase in pressure until we arrived at the edge of the pool of water, where the temperature had risen about twenty degrees. And the atmospheric pressure was more than double that of the surface pressure. I believe he reported that it was at two psi." She looked at Steven, who nodded in confirmation. "We also noted the humidity was approaching one hundred percent, and it appeared to be producing—or at least we witnessed—what appeared to be a fog or a humidity high enough to perhaps condense on the walls and the ceiling. I'm guessing the added atmospheric pressure was keeping the water in a liquid state, or so it appeared, it was slowly boiling instead of sublimating directly into the atmosphere. If I didn't know better, I would've guessed that we were in a hot spring in an Icelandic lava tube in Mars suits. We obviously need to evaluate it further."

The next question was from Mary Pfeiffer. "How big is the cave?"

Commander Carrigan explained that the size was somewhat difficult to explain since it started about fifty feet up the cliff face, where it was only five feet or so in diameter, and slowly opened up to over one hundred feet wide after they had descended to somewhere around four hundred feet below the valley floor.

"What were the crystals, and what could cause them and the stalactites?" Ashanti Sumbika asked.

"All I can imagine is that the processes that operate in caves on Earth are doing the same thing on Mars—with the lower gravity of Mars." Barbara stopped for a moment to think, then added, "As you know, since we've been here, the temperature in Valles Marineras has been way above freezing during the day. It's also understood that at least during the summer, Mars expresses humidity, which we are using to convert to water. I'm just guessing, but as the ground warms up, the ice in the ground melts, and it slowly percolates down through the rock and accumulates below, such as in the cave pool. Another thought, which is total conjecture on my part and not backed up with any scientific fact, is just like on Earth there may be groundwater heated by geothermal activity or volcanic activity just like in Iceland. We are not all that far from Olympus Mons—the largest known volcano in the solar system, and the other volcanoes surrounding Olympus Mons. I am of the opinion that what we were in was not a cave but a lava tube. Apparently, it's low enough to create its own microclimate. We will be studying this phenomenon for some time." She glanced at Commander Carrigan, who smiled and nodded again.

"Of course, this cave or lava tube is fascinating and definitely requires further organized investigation," added the commander.

Wayne Peters had his hand up. "If we put an airtight seal on the entrance with a small equalization room. Do you think it would pressurize? Maybe, closer to an Earth type atmosphere?

The commander looked surprised and glanced back at Barbara, who fielded the question.

"I don't think anyone knows the answer to that question. But it certainly gives us something to think about. What you're shooting at is; could we have an underground habitat with an Earth type atmosphere? Would it pressurize? It is definitely something to consider. It may be a possibility. That is an interesting consideration. It certainly would protect us from radiation in the event of a solar storm."

"The cave or lava tube continues on from where we stopped.

There is obviously more to investigate. It appears to go deeper. Who knows what secrets it has to reveal. The final aspect
of today's little journey is, when I arrived back here at *Staten*, to say I was interested in evaluating our samples would be understating it just a bit." Barbara added with a smile from ear to ear.

A few giggles, whispers and some laughter could be heard as she paused. They knew something big was about to be revealed. "The liquid, as you know, turned out to be water. As any biologist would, I evaluated it under the microscope while my other tests were being run. And guess what?" No one said a word. "I found tiny algae; I think. It looks like diatoms, but it is definitely life! We found life and water on Mars—all at the same time!"

There was no organization to the spaceship called *Staten* for a good twenty minutes after Barbara uttered those words. There was shouting, screaming, handshakes, high fives all around, and many, many colorful curse words uttered in a rainbow of emotions and jubilation. After all, they were not only the first crew to land, walk, and live on Mars, but now they also, as a crew, discovered water and apparently the first life forms on another planet!

Commander Carrigan stood back and took it all in.

Every member of MM1 realized the significance of this moment. Man had been looking for extra-terrestrial life for years. The now historic Mars Mission One crew had just added two more firsts to the quickly building first-in-history list.

Commander Carrigan loved every minute of watching his crew enjoy the benefits of their hard work and dedication. As he watched them, he considered what each of them had done, all the risks they had taken to get here and to assist with the success of the mission. They deserved it, and it was gratifying for him to see them celebrating this success—this milestone of the journey. Despite all the issues with the mission, the loss of communications with the Earth, *Starship IV* falling over, Pedro being hurt and who knows what this Kessler Effect situation may mean for them, these crew members, these people of *Starship X* and MM1 worked their asses off to get here. They were good people who made it all worthwhile and they deserved every second to celebrate the success of today's discovery. Commander Carrigan sat back watching by himself as tears came to his eyes, the dedication, the common goal, the imagination, the risks they all took in the name of discovery and here it is right in front of him. Beautiful. No man could be more appreciative of this moment. He loved his crew. He loved their dedication, and he loved their heart.

Chapter 39

Johnson Space Center-Day 12

Weather or Not?

The engineers at Cape Canaveral installed the message of acknowledgement on the crew capsule's navigational computers and programmed it to not respond until an acknowledgement had been entered. They also seat-belted the prompt in three separate envelopes. The capsule would not return without the crew answering the question, "Did you send the message to *Starship X*?" There was no way they could miss it.

The capsule would be placed on the booster the following day. Fueling would begin the day after that, assuming everything went smoothly. They were hoping for launch in three days.

The hurricane season started on June 1st in the Caribbean, so Brad went to the internal NASA launch control website to check on the tropical outlook. So far, so good. There was a tropical depression off Puerto Rico, but that was over a thousand miles away. Currently they were calling for a good weather window.

Brad made a quick call to Meryl, an old friend at ISS's Ground Control. "Hey, Meryl, it's Brad over at CAPCOM, MM1. How are you guys holding up?"

"We keep doing our damnedest. How about you guys?" "Same, I guess. I stuck a message on the capsule going to the ISS asking the crew to contact MM1 if they had indeed been in communication with them as CAPCOM had theorized."

———

"Yeah, I heard," Meryl said. "Who knows? All we can do is hope for the best and stay tuned."

"I suppose. We all kinda feel like hamsters running furiously on that circular treadmill. Running like mad, but just not going anywhere."

"That's just how we feel, ol' buddy."

"You guys looking good for the launch on Thursday?" Brad asked.

"Yeah, if the weather holds. I wish we could move the launch up another day. According to Launch Control, there's a tropical depression off Puerto Rico and it looks in favor of development."

"Yeah, I was wondering about that. A tropical storm can develop into a hurricane in twenty-four hours or less. How can they tell what the hell the weather is doing without any satellites?"

"Mostly radar, I guess. Of course, the NOAA weather planes fly if they think we need their hurricane hunters with all of their super-sensitive equipment. The US Coast Guard has a base in Puerto Rico, too. Fortunately, they have landlines back to the mainland. Hurricane Maria took out most of the power grid in Puerto Rico, as well as their radar back in 2017. So, they have a fancy new, state-of-the-art, super-powerful Doppler radar system. I heard they went to solar power all over the island in a big way after the storm and the earthquakes of 2020. Maybe that kept them online. I really don't know. Anyway, we're off generators now, so that's a big relief. I can actually go home at night as long as I have a landline. I also carry a radio with me everywhere I go."

"Yeah, Meryl, I have one that goes home with me as well.

When I do go home. We don't have a landline or food at my house. Thank God they feed us here!"

"You got that right, buddy."

"Okay," Brad said. "I just wanted to check with you on my message for MM1 and the weather outlook for the launch. Let me know if the weather is going to throw a wrench into our plans. Good talking to you, say hi to Brenda for me."

"Ok, I will, and say hi to Susanne and the kids for me as well."

"You got it, bud. Let's hope the weather stays at bay for a clean launch on Thursday." Brad hung up the telephone and stared at it as he thought about the conversation. There's that word "hope" again. We're getting that a lot lately.

Chapter 40
ISS-Day 13

Giulia opened her eyes to a blurry, distorted image. She couldn't see anything, and she wiped her eyes with her sticky shirt sleeve. She was in her sleeping bag on the ISS. Something was wrong. She was covered in sweat, and she could hear the guys stirring, so she crawled out of her sleeping bag and grabbed a towel. She opened the privacy door and looked around.

"Good morning, sunshine," Henry said. "Breakfast will be ready in a minute."

"Morning. What's the temperature in here?"

"You're on the hot side at the moment. I think the thermal insulation may be damaged on your side of the station, which is facing the sun right now."

"Oh, my, God. It must be a hundred and twenty degrees in there."

"Yeah, we're about to enter Earth's shadow. It'll cool off soon enough."

Commander Amhurst piped in. "Yeah, we're not in a 'normal' controlled orbit. The station is slowly rolling around as it's orbiting. We have no control of yaw, roll, or pitch, so you're getting the sunny side right now. Welcome to day thirteen!"

"Ugh, I have to change my clothes. I am soaked."

After toweling off and changing into some dry clothes Giulia pulled up to the traditional breakfast nook to join the guys and have some rehydrated fruit and cold coffee.

"Okay," Commander Amhurst began, " are you guys up for our morning briefing?"

He looked expectantly at his astronaut partners.

"I think we should go over a couple of things. First thing this morning I did my normal rounds. The O2 is back down to nineteen percent. We will open up the O2 tanks right after breakfast. How that goes will pretty much determine if there's anything else we need to do. You guys have been great at minimizing water usage from the way it smells in here."

They all had a good chuckle from the commander's unusual joke.

"Have you noticed anything or need to bring any mission-related issues to the table?"

"Not me," Henry said. "You, Giulia?"

"Yeah, I need the air conditioning turned on in my sleeping quarters," she said, smiling sleepily.

After breakfast, Commander Amhurst made his way to the O2 bottles and opened them one at a time. The bottles were noticeably quieter and losing pressure. He shut them down after a few minutes. The commander then watched the atmospheric monitors for a good minute, tapping them on the monitor screen, as though that would make any difference, then turned to look at his fellow astronauts. "Well, it's up to twenty percent now. It may climb a little more."

He didn't have to say anymore. They all knew they were getting close to having to make some difficult decisions. The air bottles weren't lasting so long as they had hoped. The CO2 scrubbers never worked, either. They were from the early 2000s and had been sitting unused in storage for years. When the power was hooked up to them, they blew air okay, but no one could tell if they were working or not, and after a while, they quit blowing air altogether.

Commander Amhurst looked at his crew and exhaled. "I think we have three or four days, tops. Next time it goes down to nineteen percent will probably be the end of the bottles."

"I'm going to take that CO2 scrubber apart," Henry said. "Wanna help, Giulia?"

"I will. What the heck."

Upon further analysis, they discovered that the carbon dioxide absorption canisters had been wrapped in a plastic film, which should've been removed prior to being inserted into the blowers. The plastic had wound around the fan and burned out the fan motor. They probably would have worked if the film had been removed.

Henry and Giulia looked at each other with downtrodden faces. They knew the scrubbers would've helped a lot. Henry thought to himself, this is the kind of thing that saved Apollo 13.

Henry disconnected the power and slowly unwound the plastic film that was wrapped around the fan. Then he reconnected the power and tried to coax the fan motor back to life, but it wasn't going to happen.

"Well, I guess that's that."

Giulia agreed and went over to the atmospheric gauges.

They still read twenty percent O2. She looked at Henry. "Go fish?"

Henry's sad eyes said, *What do you do when there's nothing you can do?*

Giulia understood, wordlessly.

Chapter 41
Mars-Sol 13

As Barbara Black continued researching her findings from the cave, Commander Carrigan was suiting up for another EVA.

Carl had already finished the scaffolding frame and was out adding strengthening crossmembers to add, as he put it, "rigidity" to the final construction. Commander Carrigan checked the fresh-water tank in the hold first thing that morning. It was almost empty. He estimated they had one or two more days before they were completely out.

Water restrictions had been in effect for two days. He guessed that they were down to less than one hundred gallons and the sensor meter or float showed nothing. This may sound like a lot of water, but twenty-one people use approximately twenty-one gallons per day on a normal day just for drinking. Almost all of their food required water to be rehydrated. Without water they really could not eat. The days on *Staten* were anything but normal. His crews worked hard, especially when on an EVA. Commander Carrigan sent out an email to all crew members detailing the water restrictions, and he also placed it on the bulletin board as if to bolster his announcement in the crew meeting two days earlier.

Commander Carrigan hated making any announcements over the all-stations PA because inevitably, depending on their shifts, some crew members were sleeping in their private quarters. But running out of water was no joke. The crew was starting to smell a bit ripe; their olfactory systems would have to endure the insult until they had their water tanks refilled.

Carl had used stainless steel bolts and nuts to hold the scaffolding together every thirty feet, which allowed disassembly for moving it to the different starships. To make the project easier to manage, he welded the base structure at *Starship IV* and then moved the welding equipment and all the supplies to *Starship VII*, where he finished welding and manufacturing the rest of the scaffolding. Fortunately, *Starship VII* wasn't far from *Starship IV*. Commander Carrigan asked Mary and Andrea to accompany him, and he asked Steven, who was running *Staten* Command, to raise Carl on the radio and get him to bring one of the two Mars cars over to pick them up.

When they arrived at the bottom of the crane, Haratu Suzuki was already waiting for them with a giant smile, which could be seen even through his tinted faceplate, and a welcoming wave. Haratu ran them over to *Starship VII*, and as they approached, it was evident Carl had done his magic with the scaffolding. He could see Mission Specialist Wayne Peters was the acting safety officer. The commander walked around the huge structure and was amazed. Carl had found some flat square aluminum plating to use as feet. He had somehow wound the rope around the starship, tying it off to the scaffolding to make it secure. Then, instead of cutting the rope, he ran it farther up the scaffolding, secured it again, and ran it around the ship until he ran out of rope. Commander Carrigan thought it smart, then wondered how the hell Carl got the rope around the starship, up fifty meters to the top, and at each level where it was tied off. He didn't see Carl anywhere, he assumed he must be up top.

After hailing Carl on his helmet mic, Carl confirmed that he was at the top of the scaffold. Commander Carrigan started climbing the stairs made of some slatted aluminum material, probably more of the stringers. Wow, what a lot of cutting and welding! Even with the reduced gravity of Mars, Commander Carrigan weighed around one hundred-fifty pounds with his gear on, and after sixty feet, he started huffing and puffing. At ninety feet, he had to take a break. At one hundred twenty feet, he took another short break with only thirty feet to go. Man, am I glad I've been working out, he thought to himself. He could see Carl was just finishing tying off another length of rope which had been wrapped around the giant starship.

Commander Carrigan stopped to take in the view. Carl and his team of four astronauts had done the whole thing. Don't ask me how, Carl thought.

Commander Carrigan was still trying to catch his breath. "How did you do this, Carl?"

"One piece at a time." Smiling, and obviously proud of his work, Carl made a big performance out of it, explaining some of the different steps required as if he were revealing the scaffolding on "The Price Is Right".

Once Commander Carrigan pulled himself up the last three steps and landed on the platform, he was amazed. Carl had put the ladder at a comfortable angle, and every thirty feet where he tied off the scaffold, he had created a rough deck, which he wrapped the cargo netting around to act as a type of handrail or safety netting. But it was apparent to the commander that the cargo netting was also adding tension to the structure, helping to stabilize it.

"Wow, you must have used almost all of the rope."

"Pretty much. What's left will be used as the guide rope for the crane."

"Did you make any safety belts or tie-ins for you and your team up here?"

Carl turned around and showed Commander Carrigan the tie-in with a stainless-steel snap link attached to his Mars suit. "Yeah, we have them. They're not to go up or down without tying in, and they swap them out with the guys below if they're going to change positions. I made them out of some of the luggage straps and snap links from *Starship IV*."

"Excellent. You've done an incredible job, Carl." Commander Carrigan looked around. "A hundred fifty feet in the air on Mars. Who would've thought we'd have to do this! I don't know how you did it, Carl, but it's amazing. And very sturdy. It's hardly moving."

"Yeah, well, it weighs a lot. I used two of the stringers on top of each other to give it double thickness for extra strength on the first two levels, and of course I reinforced the frame with those crosspieces that look like giant Xs. That adds to the strength and rigidity. Plus, tying it off every thirty feet to the starship adds a lot of stability also."

"Well, once we get the water flowing, we'll throw a party in your honor."

"Don't do it for me. All I did was a bunch of welding. Do it for my team. After we got started, they watched me diligently and understood everything we needed with very little follow up required on my part. I hardly had to tell them anything. After only about an hour, they were doing it all on their own. I just watched and supervised."

"As you should. Good job! Have you tried the hatch yet?" "Was just about to do that, but I wanted to wait for you." "Very considerate of you, Carl."

With that, Carl inserted a crowbar-like tool with two large teeth into the access and popped out the manual-release mechanism. In the manual release were two large holes, in which he inserted the crowbar apparatus and began to turn counterclockwise. After six turns, a hissing sound could be heard as the hatch seam popped. They waited for the giant starship to equalize to the Martian atmosphere and then they swung it open as the lights inside *Starship VII* turned on.

Carl held the door for the commander, and they stepped into the artificially lit interior. It didn't have the equalization room just inside the door as *Staten* did. They were met with a flat deck large enough to hold five or six people. Just below them were aluminum shipping containers with heavy shackles welded in the middle on a reinforced plate sticking out for the crane to attach to for autonomous removal, and now manual removal. There was a narrow walkway to the helm with a low railing. The helm had two very flimsy chairs attached to the floor where the computer programmers would sit while installing and testing the multiple controls, navigational, and monitoring computers.

Commander Carrigan examined the set-up as Carl crawled under the computer and turned on some lights underneath the helm. Commander Carrigan took a mental note of the layout and walked back to the platform to assess the crane. He found a remote control inside a manual control box—just where it belonged. He punched the power button. Nothing. He tried it again. Still nothing. Carl's sudden voice made him jump.

"Yeah, it's not going to work without booting up the computer system. Just as I thought."

Commander Carrigan nodded. "Yup, that does appear to be the case. No manual boot-up instructions hidden away or under the console either, I'd guess."

"Haven't seen any yet, but I'll look around before tearing into that crane. I'm hoping I can run some wires to the motor with that remote control inline. That would almost be as good as firing up the computers." Carl paused. "Okay, well maybe not that good. This is still going to be a lot of work. But impossible without the crane."

"Do you think it'll let you do that, Carl? I mean, do you think you can activate the crane?"

"I don't see why not. The computer system is designed to follow the programming they showed us in training. It's just a dumb computer. It doesn't know how to think outside the box, so to say. It doesn't have anything like self-defense mode or sentry mode or an automated lockdown. It's already locked down as far as it's concerned."

"That's great news, Carl. Do you know where the water hose is located?"

"I'll get the bin and location number from Steven. Let's hope they're not at the bottom. It could easily take two days or more to off-load this bad boy. If I can somehow get to them quicker, I will. I'm hoping to have the crane operating before the day is out today. I just have to get my tools up here." He looked down the fifty-meter scaffolding.

Commander Carrigan gazed down at the height of the scaffolding. "Well, whatever you do, be careful. Do you have any rope left?"

"I'll have to check. There's supposedly some more on this load, along with the third Mars car, and, of course, the waterline."

"Do you need any more help?"

Carl looked back at the helm and the dark screen of the computer monitor, deep in thought. "If I can't find another two hundred feet of rope, I might."

"Let me know via the radio. We'll head over to Starship II and start stretching the waterline out. That way when you get to the waterline, it'll be a simple job of just connecting in the last one thousand feet. Let me know personally as soon as you're able to pull it out, please."

"Yeah, no problem. If I need more hands, I'll tell you as soon as I have it figured out."

"Actually, Carl, I can get you four more personnel suited up immediately. If you don't need them, you can cancel."

"Ok. Sounds good."

Commander Carrigan raised Steven on his helmet mic and gave the order for four of the five crew members of C shift to mobilize. They were to report to Carl as soon as they arrived at *Starship VII*.

He took Mary and Andrea to Starship II to start unbuttoning the waterlines they dropped off two days ago. While doing this he sent the Mars car they had to autonomously return to *Staten* to transport the new four C shift crew to help Carl and programmed it to return to Starship II to help finish stretching out the waterlines for more than a mile to *Staten*. They had all the bundles free, and the first thousand feet were already hooked up to the water tank on Starship II, when he heard C shift arrive at *Starship VII*. The next thousand feet had been laid out for rapid deployment in a huge zigzag shape, slowly running toward *Staten*. When the mars car returned, they began stretching out the precious waterlines, being careful not to let them kink or snag. They would stop every couple hundred feet or so and make a pyramid out of the largest rocks they could move to mark the water hose line. This was about twenty-five stops, very time-consuming but important. Commander Carrigan decided to dredge some small ditches in which to put the waterline. Somewhere in one of the starships were five aluminum ramps designed to put over the waterline but who knew when they would see them. Ugh! After we get water running, I'm going to ask Carl if he could make some flag poles or markers or something, so we don't accidentally drive over the waterline and put a hole in it. He was imagining one of the Mars cars running the waterline over and the expansion ratio of the water hitting the one percent atmosphere. It would probably create a geyser a hundred feet high as it turned into a cloud of humidity. No, that we could do without.

They made it most of the way back to *Staten* with the hose, running short only about one-thousand feet away. One thousand feet is like two city blocks! Frustrating. After making sure the bitter end was taped up, Commander Carrigan, Mary, and Andrea drove back to *Staten*, as the sun was about to set. They then sent the Mars car back to *Starship VII* to return with the crews. Commander Carrigan confirmed this with Carl.

For the time being, *Staten* had a policy of no one out after dark. The temperature dropped rapidly. They didn't need anyone getting disabled, injured, or lost, even though *Staten* was the tallest lighted object on the planet (not to mention the only lighted object). Still, if they could help it, Commander Carrigan didn't want anyone out in the dark. What if their helmet light went out? Crew members are not allowed to do any EVAs in groups of less than three. A single astronaut or crew member cannot carry another crew member by themselves. The bulky suits and awkwardness made it impossible. The only reason to be out after dark was to take in the incredible night sky. He agreed they all needed to do that in the near future, but only in designated areas for the time being. It really was out of this world. And they could see the Earth most nights and sometimes even during the day. What a feeling of vastness that created.

After equalizing, Commander Carrigan quickly made his way to the tiny lab Barbara Black jokingly called her home.

"How's it going?" Commander Carrigan said with a smile.

"Almost all of the diatoms are dead. Oh, well, it was to be expected, but I found DNA. They're using DNA, just like us! And I found a few different forms of carbon and other organics in the water. I know there's more to find in that cave. When can we go back? I have so much more to do and see, like the water source and the ceiling. When are we going?" Her childlike exuberance for discovery was heartwarming.

"Woah! Hold on a minute." Commander Carrigan couldn't believe her energy. She was like a little kid in a toy store for the first time. "We went quite a way in without much of a plan and no safety equipment. The next spelunking expedition will need to be planned out with safety backups," Commander Carrigan said. "You know we shouldn't have gone as far as we did without at least a safety line."

"I know, I know. We can do all of that on the next trip. So, when do we go?" She looked at Commander Carrigan with pleading puppy eyes as she clasped her hands together in a quiet applause.

"Soon," was all he could come up with. He wondered if Carl would find more rope in *Starship VII*. "We'll have to organize it, but first, we have to get water. If you didn't know, we're almost out of water now. I'm thrilled you found DNA. Have you been able to type match it to any earthborn DNA?"

"No, I haven't had the time to match it yet. At least the computer hasn't found any matches that I am aware of yet. I just started the search about ten minutes ago. It's kinda complicated," she said, peering into her microscope.

"Further exploration of the cave is, of course, a priority. But water is THE top priority at the moment. If you locate and organize the equipment, including about one thousand feet of safety line, I'll let you know when we can put it on the schedule. Probably in a few days—as soon as we get water."

She smiled ear to ear, then went back to her microscope.

Commander Carrigan left the little lab feeling like he had just had a conversation with a five-year-old. He couldn't help but chuckle.

On his way to the cargo hold to check the fresh-water levels again, he heard Carl and his crew arriving back at *Staten*. Making his way toward the water tanks, Commander Carrigan entered the dungeon-like cargo hold. The lights automatically came on, exposing the giant tank. The fresh-water tank was registering "empty". Well, that will be the last time I check it until we get water coming back on board, he thought. He wondered if they could last one more day, maybe if they reduce consumption to eight ounces per day? It was impossible to tell since the water level was now below the gauge. It was anybody's guess. "Boy, I sure hope Carl finds the waterlines soon," he said out loud to himself.

Commander Carrigan sat on the steps of the cargo hold and imagined crews having to carry water containers out to the water line to fill them up, then realized that the water would evaporate and boil off, even before they could get the caps back on the containers. He sat for a moment, trying to think of something else they could do to get water.

The water would have to go into a self-bleeding pressurized container, straight from the five-thousand-gallon tank at Starship II, or it could go into a low-pressure container that became pressurized as the water was added. Still, it was the same problem. They didn't have any containers like that, which would need to be specially manufactured for the job. The container would have to have an airtight seal between Starship II's tank and the container, and the container had to be rigid, because of the low atmospheric pressure on Mars, it would blow up like an overfilled balloon. It might even explode.

Commander Carrigan now understood why the waterline was braided stainless steel with heavy-duty connections. That's also why it weighs so much, he thought.

"I have to talk to Carl!" he said out loud to no one.

It was now dark outside, and some of the crew members were preparing dinner with what could be their last meal until they got water. The cook and kitchen positions were designated on the roster, but some of the crew members enjoyed making dinner, and they volunteered to do it.

Commander Carrigan found Carl exiting the depressurization chamber. The commander didn't have to ask him anything.

"We got the crane powered up, and we pulled the first container out," Carl said. "After getting it to the surface, we opened it up. No water lines in this first one. Not too surprising. Steven said the waterlines were about halfway into the load. There are give or take fifty containers to each starship, and they're tightly stacked on top of each other. There's no way to get to the middle of the stack without taking the containers off the top. Thank God *Starship IV* wasn't loaded using containers like these. It would've been a real mess."

"Do you think you'll be halfway into the load tomorrow?" "Barring anything unforeseen, that's exactly what I'm hoping to achieve by the end of the day tomorrow." "Ok, sounds good, Carl. Thank you.

Commander Carrigan announced a full-crew meeting, realizing these full-crew meetings were becoming entirely too frequent, but he really had no choice. The developments were life-threatening, and his crew deserved to be prepared.

"I'll keep this as short as possible," he said as soon as

everyone has a seat, including Pedro, who sat into a chair and placed his crutches carefully out of the way.

Pedro's knee was in a brace, locked into position. He was still sleeping in the medical bed because it was easier to get in and out of compared to his bunk. But he seemed to be in good spirits.

"How's the knee, Pedro?"

"Pretty good. It still hurts if I move it, but I can tell its healing. Give me a couple of weeks, and I'll be back out there."

"Good to hear," Commander Carrigan said with a smile, then he glanced toward Tammy, who just smiled with a slight shake of her head. "The reason I've called us all together is rather serious. To get right to it, we're at the end of our fresh-water tank. We've been surviving on the stores we brought from home and the fresh water that the hydrogen fuel cells were producing, as well as the ship's recycling systems. The hydrogen fuel cells need to be refreshed, but they don't produce enough water to be a significant source. Carl and many of you have been valiantly working on gaining access to the last bit of waterline we need to finish the run from Starship II to *Staten*. Mary and Andrea and I have run five thousand feet to within maybe one thousand feet of *Staten*. I've been meaning to ask Carl if one of you guys can weld some markers or flags for the waterline, so we don't accidently run over it."

Two hands immediately shot up.

Commander Carrigan looked at Carl, who nodded in approval. "Great. Can I get you guys to take care of that in the morning?"

The two volunteers readily agreed.

"Thank you. I will put it on the EVA roster for the morning.

The waterline is listed in the manifest and inventory as halfway down the containers, inside *Starship VII*. So far, we have one container out. By my calculations, we have twenty-four more, give or take, before we should have the one container with the badly needed waterline. Carl, how long would you estimate it takes to hook up to the container you removed today, safely off- load it on the surface, then recall the crane back on board?"

Carl looked a little hesitant and thought for a few seconds as he stared at the ceiling. "Twenty to twenty-five minutes."

"Would you say that's a good rate to safely maintain?"

"Yeah, I think we could probably average twenty-five to thirty minutes per container. It takes a good ten minutes to pick one up and get it ready to guide it the hundred fifty feet down, then another five minutes or less to recall the hook. So, yeah, no faster than twenty minutes, and some may take thirty."

"Okay, Carl says about two per hour. Whatever rate we maintain, I want to be sure we are staying safe in our work practices. We're told by the computer inventory spreadsheet that we must get to container number twenty-five. If our rate is two per hour, that means that we have a long, ten-hour day of solid work. We may get twenty more containers off-loaded, which means we'll be short four containers of getting to that waterline, or about two more hours of work. If we stick to it for two more hours, we may get to container twenty-five, but we'll be out of daylight, and we'll still have to find the hose and hook it up, attach it to *Staten*, and turn it on at Starship II without running over the waterline with the Mars car or steering into a crater or a ditch in the black of night. I just want everyone to see the picture here. We can start the day just prior to sunrise and continue to rotate crews every four hours. It looks like we will be out of water sometime between now and by the time you wake up. We're really at the bottom of the barrel. I'm further reducing our water consumption to eight ounces of water per day, per person, though I don't think it's going to make any difference. Out means out. All of our food must be rehydrated. Anything we drink must be rehydrated. Because sugar and caffeine both cause dehydration, they're both banned until we have water—and you know how much I love my coffee. I suggest we go with fruit rehydrated in our mouths for breakfast—if we have any water. I have to make some difficult decisions about tomorrow's workday, and I'm open to your suggestions."

Silence followed, then Wayne raised his hand. "Commander, how many people does Carl need to keep the unloading going at the rate of two containers per hour?"

"Carl?" the commander questioned.

"Including myself, seven. Two up top and four on the ground. With me acting as safety officer."

"And how difficult would you say it is to learn each position?" Wayne asked. "How long would it take any one of us to learn the different jobs?"

Carl answered immediately. "The work isn't hard to learn. The positions up top have to push the container around to get it out the door. The person on the guideline has to be sure the container clears the scaffolding without getting tangled up, and the other three on the ground have to coordinate with the guy on the guideline, pick up the container, and move it to staging. I estimate each person will have to manually pick up about one hundred pounds, depending on the supplies in the container. Two aluminum bars from *Starship IV* go underneath the container to act as handles. It should take maybe thirty minutes to learn each position just by watching. The guys on the surface are there only to pick the container up and move it to staging, but they cannot move it until the guy on the guideline allows me to get the hook back inside."

Wayne said, "Sunrise is at what time, Commander? About fifteen hundred Zulu?"

"Yes."

"So, if the first six of us start at fourteen hundred Zulu, we should be at *Starship VII* by fourteen thirty. As the sun is starting to rise, we can work until, let's say, eighteen hundred, when six more come to relieve us. Let's say we give them thirty minutes to learn the drill and we come back in at eighteen thirty. They can work until twenty-two hundred when another six come to swap them out, and they get the thirty minutes of training. So, they're working from twenty-two hundred to O-two hundred Zulu, or whatever it takes to finish the job. Four straight hours per shift with no breaks. That leaves us with two extras in case breaks need to be taken or someone has to be swapped out. With twelve hours of uninterrupted work, we should be bringing down the twenty-fifth container by the end of the day and you already have one on the ground." Wayne looked around, proud to have whipped that off the top of his head.

That's what Commander Carrigan was hoping to hear. Before the room broke into conversation, Commander Carrigan spoke. "I think that just might get us water by the end of the day tomorrow. If the last crew takes Mars car one to Starship II to turn on the water once the water line is connected by the other crew in

Mars car two, they may even make it back to *Staten* before sundown."

It was all in the math and shift rotation. Pedro announced that he would run *Staten* Command, which would free up one more person.

Barbara Black was heading to the galley, she was at the sink when she yelled out, "It's gone! It's gone! No more water!"

The room went silent.

"Okay, people," the commander said. "I suggest each one of us go to the ice maker and get one piece of ice. That will be our water for the night. Ashanti, can I get you for night watch, please? And we can all enjoy one piece of ice in the morning, and one piece after our four-hour shift if it lasts. With any luck, we should have plenty of water tomorrow night."

Chapter 42

Johnson Space Center-Day 14

In Brad's mind, the news couldn't have been much worse. The tropical storm off Puerto Rico had turned into a full-blown hurricane and was rounding the northern tip of Andros Island.

The name of the hurricane was "Brad", and it was looking to be a category two by the following day, with winds in excess of one hundred miles per hour. Currently about one hundred miles wide, it was causing havoc from Cuba to Miami to Andros, and soon Bimini, with a forward speed of sixteen miles per hour. It was projected to head due north, up the east coast of Florida, with Ft. Lauderdale in its sights. If the forward speed of progression continued, it would be in Cape Canaveral the following day.

Brad picked up the phone. "Hey, Meryl. It's Brad. I guess you know why I'm calling."

"I could take a wild-ass guess," Meryl said with his usual sense of humor.

"You'd probably be right," Brad said. "You ever heard of a hurricane called 'Brad' before?"

"Can't say that I have, buddy. But then again, they always retire the ones that do any damage. You may be interested to know that due to the hurricane, they've decided to move the launch up to today. It was fueled up yesterday and early this morning. We have the launch scheduled in T-minus three hours and counting, scheduled for fifteen hundred Zulu. That means the crew could be back on Earth by 6:00 p.m. eastern. Your wish may be coming true, my friend. With any luck, it will go today. It has to go today, or it probably won't go for a week. Cape Canaveral locks everything up tight for hurricanes. I'm actually surprised they're a go for the launch. Have you spoken with our boss lately?"

"Only to keep him apprised of the situation, as usual. I have spoken with General Latimore a few times, but only to coordinate the message for MM1 and to get his consent, this being an armed forces mission and all."

"Okay, I was curious," Meryl said. "I guess they're far enough along to get it off today. I hope those guys are still on the station."

"Well, their Dragon capsule is reportedly still there. So, we are hoping they are as well. Have you heard anything about the Russians? I heard they left in their Soyuz capsule."

"Yeah. No comment from our Russian friends. With all of the chaos in the world, I'm sure they're hoping that it'll be missed in the thirty-minute attention span of today's news cycle. There is plenty to report on these days."

"Wow, no comment, and three cosmonauts dead. What a country! What must their families think? These guys should be heroes trying to push their country forward in the exploration of space, not swept under a rug like an embarrassment."

"Yeah, I know. I wonder if they'll even get a funeral."
"Okay, Meryl, thanks for the update. Let's give our guys a chance."

"You got that right, bud. They deserve whatever help we can give them."

Brad stared at the handset as he set the phone down. He thought to himself, *What must it do to the morale of the armed forces and cosmonauts to know that their comrades died, and that Mother Russia swept it under the rug? The next thing they know, they'll be saying the cosmonauts didn't have permission to leave the ISS and were told to stay, so their deaths are by their own hands.*

Brad turned to his computer and pulled up the NASA in-house net, then scrolled to the launch window. T-minus two hours and thirty-eight minutes. It looked like a beautiful day in Cape Canaveral. Brad decided to grab a sandwich and soda and watch the last hour of the launch as he went over his notes.

Had it really been two weeks since he spoke with the MM1 crew? Brad had commissioned himself and all MM1 staff to start imagining what the *Starship X* crew was going through and what he and his staff would do if they were in the same predicament. "I want any imaginative stuff you guys can come up with, I don't care how far-fetched and crazy it may seem. If it 'could' work, if it has the smallest possibility of working, I want to see it. Make drawings or designs on your CAD/CAM or drawing software or by hand. I don't care. How are they going to access the one hundred-fifty-foot hatches on their supply ships? That is what we need to know so we can help them. So far, they had projected that the crew on Mars would've probably off-loaded *Starship IV* by hand using *Starship X's* 20-foot ladder. That would've given them one thousand feet more of water line, but not enough. They should be running out of water any day now so that gives them three days to get the water from *Starship II* back to *Starship X*."

They had no idea what *Starship X* would do for water, except maybe refurbish the hydrogen fuel cells, which would deliver some water, but only the bare minimum—not enough to keep twenty-one crew members alive for long. Brad's team had considered using the ropes and lines from Starships X and IV to somehow lasso the huge starships, maybe using the hydrogen in a large plastic bag as a balloon to float a line over the top. But that seemed impossible to control. They considered stacking the Martian rocks alongside the starships using the Mars cars and trailers, but the sheer number of rocks was confounding.

His team estimated they'd need around six thousand rocks to reach the hundred-fifty-foot-high hatch, which they figured would take six months to assemble. At this point, he and his team decided that the twenty-one astronauts on *Starship X* were living on the edge of dehydration. Man cannot survive for more than three days without water. If they were dehydrated, they certainly couldn't carry a bunch of rocks. Just the simple act of breathing would dehydrate them, and almost all the food on *Starship X* was dehydrated, which would dehydrate them even faster—if they ate.

They considered the possibility of tipping a starship over to gain access, using a jack or lever of some kind. It didn't seem possible. They considered that the crew might use shovels to dig under the huge platform like landing pads or feet of the rockets, thereby tipping them over by undermining them. Many of the starships had containers inside them, stacked like poker chips. If the rocket was knocked over, the containers would smash together and be almost impossible to remove. Not only could it be impossible to unload but they would undoubtedly damage some of the cargo. This action would jeopardize many aspects of the mission, but would it give them access to the precious waterlines? What if the starship should roll over onto the access doors? Too risky. Ugh!

So, this avenue was now thought to be the highest probable action. All planning revolved around what seemed to be the most logical idea. Trying to figure out which starship the astronauts would try to knock over was a toss of the dice. There were three different starships to consider. They decided to draw up different outcomes for undermining each of the three starships that had waterlines. The outcomes were all pretty much the same in the end: some damaged equipment, but would it give them access to the waterlines? The answer that kept coming up: "It depends."

Different strategies were drawn up on how to move forward with the mission depending on what equipment or supplies were damaged. This gave Brad the chills. They may damage one of the nuclear Kilowatt power units, and they were sure to damage one of the three Mars cars. There had to be a better way. Brad hoped they would find a better way into those starships, but he was confounded as to how they'd do it. The situation looked pretty grim from Houston.

At T-minus twenty seconds, the countdown stopped. After about twenty seconds the clock began to count down once more. Brad could breathe again. Finally, the gigantic ship, with its super-reinforced payload, launched, belching flames as it slowly gained altitude. God Bless, and Godspeed, Brad thought.

The flames lit up the inside of a foretelling cloud and disappeared downrange, rolling to its correct azimuth for orbit around the Earth and hopefully eventually docking with the ISS.

Chapter 43
ISS-Day 14

The inner hatch was closed and locked behind Commander Amhurst. Giulia and Henry heard the slow hissing of their precious air as it was equalizing in the airlock to the vacuum of space.

"There he goes," Henry said to Giulia, who was looking a little strained.

Who could blame her? Five days in a spacesuit, locked in a capsule the size of a Volkswagen Beetle with two other guys. Then almost ten days in a cylinder with the same two guys, never knowing when the air was going to run out or when the next round of debris would kill her.

Henry had to give it to her for being such a trooper. "If I weren't already married, I would be tempted to ask you to marry me. What the hell, I think we're way beyond our precious policy and procedures and protocols by now."

Giulia smiled inwardly and outwardly. They had become more than co-workers. They were very good friends. She truly loved these guys, and she knew they loved her and would give their lives to save hers. She would've done the same. As difficult as it may sound, it was true. Living that close together, they might as well be married—just no sex. At least they weren't having sex. There were rumors about some previous astronauts. Living so close together, each person knew the physiological intimacies of the others around them. In zero G, the stresses on their bodies were terrible. They knew if someone had diarrhea or gas. They knew if they were hungry. Everyone had body odor—some just smelled worse than others. The hair was totally unmanageable, bloating was common. All the blood was pushed from the extremities to the central core, making circulation very difficult. Most astronauts' hands and feet were always cold, digestion was affected because the food didn't always stay down and so on. It was not for the lighthearted.

She laughed. "Can I marry both of you?"

They floated over to the windows and turned up the radio to listen to Commander Amhurst, who was just exiting the outer hatch.

He was giving the play-by-play, so they could hear what he was seeing. "Exiting the hatch now and going up top to get a better view. On top of Unity now, looking at the damage to her. I'm surprised we have any pressure inside. Unity is pretty banged up. A lot of the impact protection jacket is floating around in loose patches here and there. Oh, my, God. I don't know where we're getting power from because the solar arrays are all blown apart. Yeah, so are the heat radiators. That is amazing. The only solar arrays still here are free-floating and attached only by the power cables. That's probably the occasional scraping sound we're hearing. I can see the Harmony node now. Yeah, numerous obvious strikes. It's not looking good, guys. Okay, I'm making my way over to the Zarya and the Zvezda nodes now. Coming over the top of Unity. The Russian Soyuz is gone, but we already knew that. Oh, I can see both the Zvezda and the Zarya. I can see the Zvezda—or what used to be the Zvezda— best from here. I'm afraid there's not much left of it. It's completely open to space on one side. I guess there's no reason to go any farther. Oh, I can see the Zarya a little better now, too. It looks somewhat intact from this side, but I don't need to go any farther after seeing the Zvezda. I guess I'm coming back. No reason to waste more oxygen. I guess we have our answer. I'm back on top of Unity, heading to the hatch. Opening the hatch now. Heading back inside now. Closing the hatch. Okay, I'm in. Equalizing now."

Giulia and Henry could hear the hissing of the air as the airlock slowly re-pressurized from the onboard tanks. Henry floated over to the atmospheric gauges. No wonder he was feeling a little foggy today; the O2 percentage was down to fifteen percent. They were waiting until after the spacewalk was finished to add whatever oxygen remained in the tanks to their atmosphere. He had seen Commander Amhurst check the levels before suiting up, but he didn't say anything. Now Henry knew why. Humans need a minimum of nineteen percent oxygen for normal activities and 16 percent, minimum, to stay alive. Below sixteen percent, the human brain and the cells of the body begin to go into hypoxia. Confusion begins, followed by rapid heart rate and rapid breathing as the body burns oxygen in a vain attempt to gain more oxygen and reduce the carbon dioxide build up. The lips and mucous membranes turn blue, as do the nail beds.

"How are you feeling, Giulia?"

"Besides smelling like I haven't taken a shower in two weeks, I'm okay," she said with a slight giggle.

"No, I mean mentally," Henry said.

"Maybe just a little foggier than normal."

Just then, the hissing noise stopped, and they opened the hatch to let Commander Amhurst back in. The first thing he did after they helped him remove his helmet was look at the atmospheric gauges. He was shocked to see the O2 level at fourteen percent. Commander Amhurst immediately went to the air tanks and opened them up. For about ten seconds, the sound of the O2 could be heard as a slight hissing noise, then . . . nothing.

He floated over to the gauges again. "Sixteen percent O2," he said through labored breath. "Well, that's the last of the oxygen. I suggest we hydrate. We have to move pretty soon. How's everyone feeling?"

"Maybe a little more foggy than usual," Henry said.

As Commander Amhurst began to remove his spacesuit, Giulia floated over to give him a hand.

"As soon as the O2 falls below sixteen percent again, that's it. No one can survive for any length of time at that level. We will have to suit up and load up into the Dragon. I'm almost wondering if I should even bother to remove my suit. It may be only a matter of minutes. Boy, you guys should see the attitude of the Space Station. We're all over, end over end with a small roll to port. Fortunately, the motion is slow, but we will need to push away quickly in the Dragon, so the station doesn't hit us in the butt as we leave." The commander began removing his suit anyway.

Henry checked the atmospheric gauges again. "Yeah, it's flickering between sixteen and fifteen percent right now."

Commander Amhurst sat using the bulkhead to hold him upright, obviously out of breath. "Okay. I guess that's it. We might as well suit up and get ready to leave. I'm going to radio *Starship X* to let them know our situation before we go." He was growing agitated and was huffing and puffing more than usual.

Henry tuned the radio to the right frequency to reach

Starship X.

"Go ahead and raise them," Commander Amhurst said. "I'm going to sit here for a few minutes to catch my breath."

Commander Amhurst was looking pale. Giulia took his hand and pinched his fingernail between her forefinger and thumb. "I'm fine," he said.

She inspected his face and pulled his lower lip out, noticing its dark purple color. "You're cyanotic," she said. "All of the strenuous activity outside combined with suiting up and equalizing. You need oxygen."

"I'll be fine. Just let me catch my breath." He puffed as he wedged himself into a corner, still in his spacesuit trousers. "You may not be able to catch your breath in this atmosphere."

"Just give me ten minutes. If I can't catch my breath, I'll put my suit back on."

Henry picked up the radio mic and tried to raise *Starship X.* "*Starship X, Starship X,* this is ISS. How do you copy?" He grabbed a pencil and wrote down 10:05 Zulu, knowing they should hear back in about twelve minutes, assuming they were still within range of the ISS's weak radio transmissions.

They floated around, keeping an eye on Commander Amhurst. Nothing had to be said. They knew they were in a dire situation, but they didn't know the extent to Commander Amhurst's hypoxia. Giulia kept checking his nail beds, but nothing was changing.

He laid down, trying to relax as best he could. At 10:17 Zulu, the radio burst to life. "ISS, ISS, this is *Starship X.* We copy you two by two. Good to hear from you guys. How are you holding out? This is Pedro Lopez, flight engineer. I know you guys usually talk to Steven. He's out on maneuvers. I'm monitoring comms today. Over."

"Hello, Pedro, this is Henry Wilson on the ISS. We are about to evacuate. We will be attempting re-entry in the Dragon and want someone to know what we're doing. The oxygen stores are completely exhausted. Commander Amhurst did a spacewalk today to evaluate the remainder of the ISS. We've concluded that the station is no longer habitable, and we intend to board the Dragon for an attempt at re-entry. Copy?"

Once again, Henry wrote down the time. It was 10:20.

Commander Amhurst was still losing color, slowly turning pail.

"Giulia, is it okay to sleep in hypoxia?" Henry asked.

"I am not sleeping," said a lethargic Commander Amhurst. "I'm just resting. You're doing a great job with the telemetry, Henry. Giulia, why don't you suit up? Henry can, too, when his transmission is finalized."

Giulia went over to the atmospheric sensors again. "Reading O2 level at fourteen percent. And the atmospheric psi is at twelve. Is the hatch sealed correctly? It can't be, unless . . ." She floated to the hatch and put her ear next to it, then she began moving to the repairs they'd done the first day they reentered the Unity node. One of them was making a small hissing noise. She looked more closely and saw that the edges of the duct tape they'd put over the repair job looked a little loose. She checked the edge of one of the repair jobs, and the duct tape pulled right off. The adhesive used on the tape wasn't

———

holding. It was oxidizing and losing its stickiness, it also looked wet.

She immediately put more tape over the repair job, but it wouldn't stick well. As she was checking the other repair sights, she found two more were leaking, so she taped them over again. "I see," she said. "Our breath is causing condensation to form on the walls of the station now that the insulation has been damaged on the outside of the station. It's underneath the tape and causing it to lose grip. I'm not sure why I'm fixing these repairs if we're going to leave."

The radio chirped at 10:36. "ISS, ISS. This is *Starship X*. We copy you on your intention to evacuate the ISS in the Dragon. We will enter this communication into our ship's log, as usual. Do you have a specific time of departure? I have relayed this information to Steven, who is out on the Martian surface. He asked me to relay a personal message, but first a message from *Starship X*. We cannot possibly know what you've been through and what you may face. We wish you the best of luck and Godspeed. Steven's message is 'Aut viam inveniam aut faciam'. He said you would know what it means. Take care. You are in our prayers. *Starship X*, over."

Henry picked up the mic. "*Starship X, Starship X*. ISS, we copy you. Our intention is to depart immediately upon conclusion of this transmission. Best of luck with your mission as well, and we thank you. ISS, over." With the radio transmission concluded, Henry hung the mic back in its clip and turned to check on the commander. "We need to get him in his spacesuit and in some better oxygen."

Commander Amhurst could barely stand while Henry and Giulia got him into the rest of his suit. After putting his helmet on and making sure he had air flowing, they opened the hatch and helped him climb into his seat in the Dragon. As they climbed into their

———

348

spacesuits, they noticed the commander's health improving, and he was beginning the startup sequences for the Dragon capsule. When they were ready to board, Giulia floated back over to the atmospheric gauges. The O2 was at thirteen percent, and the atmospheric pressure was at eleven psi.

"Still losing oxygen and air pressure," she said as she put her helmet on and locked it into place.

Henry looked into the Dragon and asked Commander Amhurst if he wanted the middle seat as usual.

"Hell, yeah," the commander said, surprising them. "I wouldn't miss this for the world." He slowly crawled back out, allowing Henry to take his usual port side window seat."

Henry nudged Giulia. "I guess he's feeling better."

She snickered, "I guess so."

Henry crawled in, with Commander Amhurst and Giulia filing in behind. Will the batteries have enough charge to launch the parachutes? They didn't know, and it had not escaped their thoughts. What could they do about it? Nothing. So, it wasn't discussed. They had to go before the CO2 scrubbers on their spacesuits were saturated, and they had to be close to that by now. They were out of ideas and the only options remaining were not good ones.

Giulia shut the hatch on the ISS and was about to shut the Dragon as well and lock it down. "Aut viam inveniam aut faciam!" Commander Amhurst said aloud as he prepared for the release.

"What was that?' Giulia asked.

"It means—"

"No, not that! I heard something on the radio in the station.

Henry, did you turn the radio in the station off?"

"No, I guess I didn't think it mattered much." "Maybe it did matter."

Hang on a minute." The Dragon went silent as they heard a computerized voice.

"I heard it again!" she shouted.

The men were now silent. Ten seconds clicked by, then, "ISS, ISS, this is the unmanned Crew Rescue Capsule Thirty- Two. Prepare for automated docking and subsequent evacuation." It was a computer-generated voice. That wasn't *Starship X*, so what was it?

Henry peered out his window at every possible angle.

Commander Amhurst commanded, "Open the hatch, Giulia!"

She was already doing just that. Giulia threw the hatch open and pulled herself out, then immediately went to every window as the guys were pulling themselves out. "I don't see anything!" she yelled.

They heard a quiet hissing, followed immediately by what seemed to be almost a popping noise, in rapid sequence.

"Those are cold gas thrusters!" Henry yelled.

The entire station moved slightly, and immediately after, they heard and felt something bump into the starboard hatch. They floated over to the hatch as it became dark, then black.

The radio chirped. "Crew Rescue Capsule Thirty-Two, good docking. Hatch secure."

Commander Amhurst opened the hatch to the seal of a beat-up but secure hatch on an obviously heavily reinforced crew capsule. It was the most beautiful capsule he had ever seen.

Giulia yelled, "I can't believe it! I can't believe it! I can't believe it!"

Henry laughed out loud, and Commander Amhurst joined in, saying, "I think I just died and went to Heaven."

It was so brightly lit. Their eyes had been in the artificial light they'd jury-rigged on the Space Station for just over a week, with just the strange angles of the sun occasionally coming through the windows. In the seats were three envelopes with instructions. He passed them back to Henry and Giulia as he opened one. They were instructions to be relayed to *Starship X*.

"They must be important!" Commander Amhurst yelled from inside the new crew capsule.

"How did this thing make it up here?" asked Giulia.

Commander Amhurst said, "If it made it here, odds are it'll make it back. Yes!" He was grinning ear to ear and shaking his fists looking up.

Henry was back on the radio before Commander Amhurst and Giulia were out of the new crew capsule. "*Starship X, Starship X*, this is ISS. *Starship X, Starship X*, this is the ISS. Stand by for instructions from CAPCOM." Henry then read the instructions into the mic. When he finished, he repeated the instructions once again, then said, "Please confirm instructions."

Giulia and Commander Amhurst came back out of the new crew capsule as Henry declared, "Now we wait." The pencil was tiny in his bulky spacesuit glove as he tried to write 11:19, the time of transmission, on a clear area of the ISS wall. He circled it to make it stand out.

Commander Amhurst let out a big breath. "I would have to say that our odds of making it home in one piece have just improved

---

significantly. I want to get a better look at that capsule from the outside."

There was only one window from which it could be seen, it didn't provide a very good view. Still, the view they had gave them a glimpse of the same kind of blanket the ISS was wrapped in, though in some areas it looked different. The crew capsules were usually white, and this one appeared to be black underneath the Kevlar covering blanket. It also looked bulked up. They could barely see the cold gas thrusters under all of the padding.

At 11:31, the radio squawked back to life. Henry grabbed his instructions, so he could follow them as an excited Pedro read them back to him from 35 million miles away.

"ISS, ISS, this is *Starship X*," Pedro said. "Repeat, ISS, ISS, this is *Starship X*. The instructions you transmitted previously; we copy as follows." He then read them word for word back to the crew on the ISS. When he was done, he added, I don't know if this is going to work, but if it does, it'll totally change our current condition. We are out of water only because we cannot get the starships to activate. If this works, it'll be like a miracle. I don't know how you came by this information, but it means that somehow, you've been in communication with CAPCOM or MM1. Please return form of communication. We are still in a radio blackout and can only communicate with you. Thank you. This is *Starship X*, over. Copy?"

"Commander, do you want to follow up?" Henry said.

"Hell, no. You're doing a great job. Carry on, young man. I think I'll have me a seat," he said as he went back into the crew capsule and sat in the commander's chair.

Giulia thought, I wonder if his CO2 scrubbers are working correctly.

Henry picked up the mic. "*Starship X, Starship X*, this is the ISS. Your instruction copy is correct to the word. This information arrived at our location from CAPCOM MM1 via a heavily reinforced crew capsule. It appears to have taken some hits, but it is intact, and it will be our new ride home. Again, radio communication with ISS CAPCOM or Ground Control is still not intact. Again, this information came to us in written form on a heavily reinforced automated crew capsule. It's obvious to us they went to great lengths to get this information to us, so we could transmit it to you. It is our privilege to provide this information to you. Aut viam inveniam aut faciam! We will be evacuating the ISS upon completion of this transmission. May God be with you. Over. This is the ISS, signing off." Henry let go of the mic. "Let's get out of here."

Commander Amhurst laughed. "Damn good idea!"

"I couldn't have said it better myself!" Giulia said.

Inside the crew capsule, it felt to Henry and Giulia like they were about to take a ride in a luxury sedan.

The automated computer had a question they had to answer before they could do anything. It said, "Did you transmit instructions to *Starship X*?"

They pushed the pressure-sensitive screen where it said "Yes" and felt the capsule release from the ISS. But something was wrong. Something was beeping at them.

Then Giulia noticed something on the control monitor.

"Put on your seat belt, Commander Amhurst!"

After Commander Amhurst put on his belts, the beeping stopped.

Giulia sighed. "Okay, I'll marry both of you, and don't give me that shit that you're already married."

As the crew capsule began re-entry into Earth's atmosphere, they heard different bangs, booms, scrapings, pops, and other mysterious noises. Some sounded as though they might destroy the capsule due to the severity of the hit. The crew capsule shook, vibrated, and even flipped end over end. For a while, they didn't know if it was going to recover.

Can it get the heat shield side down with all of this interference? Commander Amhurst thought. *Will the heat shield survive this?*

Eventually, the noises died down and they felt the heating of re-entry. The sound of air or wind building up and screaming by sounded worse than a hurricane. They didn't know where they would land on Earth, but they didn't much care. They all felt they had a high probability of making it through the debris now, and when they felt the heating of the atmosphere, their hopes began to swell. When the enormous parachutes deployed and swung them back and forth, they could not stop screaming with joy. They had made it when only minutes ago they were sure they would not. The rescue capsule splashed down in a beautiful blue calm Pacific as an extremely oversized inflatable float popped out of the heat shield and righted the capsule.

Aut viam inveniam aut faciam.

Chapter 44

Johnson Space Center-Day 14

Brad's phone rang and caused him to jump. It hadn't rung in such a long time; he'd almost forgotten about it.

It was Meryl. "We have radar confirmation! The crew capsule is making re-entry. Get on the radar website!" Then he hung up.

Brad didn't have to pull it up. Someone at MM1 Ground Control had put it on one of the seventy-inch screens overhead. There was no audio. The capsule looked beautiful streaking through the sky. The first drogue chute opened, leading to the opening of the oversized parachutes, then the capsule slowly drifted down and splashed into a calm Pacific Ocean.

After the inflatable boats launched, a helicopter circled overhead as the crew capsule auto-inflated an oversized collar to keep the heavy capsule afloat. A ragged crew, still in their full spacesuits, emerged and fell into the waiting inflatable boats, where they were whisked off to the aircraft carrier.

Were they able to transmit the data to *Starship X*? Brad guessed that the low-quality images he was watching were probably being transmitted via the aircraft carrier to an AWACS plane overhead. The AWACS plane was probably retransmitting via line of sight to Hawaii, then converted to a secure telephone line running twenty-five hundred miles to the West Coast of the US, then converted to secure internal web feed.

It's no surprise that it's a little fuzzy, Brad thought. We had

———

no idea how dependent we had become on satellites before this.

The carrier appeared to be a huge catamaran vessel; one he had never seen before. The inflatables ran between the two enormous hulls, the crew was helped onto a large ramp, then onto a dry ship deck. For a few minutes, the screen only showed reruns of the splashdown. It then cut to a presentation ceremony where an exhausted crew was seated in brand new NASA flight suits. Splash down to stage presentation in less than an hour.

There was no press to welcome them home. They waved to the applauding crew of the carrier, however, due to the extended zero-gravity exposure, the entire ISS crew could barely stand on their own and were seated immediately once they were helped to the stage. It was obvious they were thrilled to be back on Earth's surface.

Brad was glad to see the crew and knew how lucky they were to even dock with the reinforced crew capsule, not to mention to return in one piece. But did they send the instructions? He was pretty sure they would have since there was no way to board the capsule without seeing the all-important message. The pre-programmed undocking sequence would not have started unless they acknowledged receiving the message. But were they in contact with the crew of *Starship X* on Mars? No one asked the question. Of course, they didn't. No one knew about the mission to rescue the crew from the ISS or any message to the crew on *Starship X*.

Brad immediately picked up the phone and dialed General Latimore. His secretary said she would take his message and relay it to the general as soon as he was available. There was no way Brad could make a phone call to the carrier, and he was sure that his boss Gerald Adams was also watching this transmission and would also want this question answered. So would General Latimore, wherever he was.

I wonder if he's on that aircraft carrier, Brad thought.

Brad changed the screen on his computer to the coverage of the landing, so he could get a closer look at the cheering crowd of Navy personnel. There was no audio—only video feed. He knew he would hear sooner or later, but the anxiety was going to kill him. As the crew began shaking hands with the different officers, he spotted General Latimore in the congratulatory line. The general leaned forward while he was shaking Commander Amhurst's hand and said something to him. Commander Amhurst nodded his head and pointed at Henry Wilson. When Henry shook General Latimore's hand, he nodded vigorously, and the general slapped him on the shoulder in a congratulatory gesture. They were both smiling. Was that the confirmation?

Brad was pretty sure what he had just seen was good news. At least they weren't shaking their heads and looking down or upset. Brad considered how long it would take the general to fly back to the States. Probably eight hours or so. It was 22:05 Zulu, which meant 16:05 in Houston. The general wouldn't be back until almost midnight central time, if he didn't stay too long for the ceremonies, which probably wouldn't last long anyway; the crew needed rest. He knew they would be going straight to sick bay for a health eval and a shower.

Maybe the general will get his messages before going home for the night, which means I may not hear until tomorrow. Brad thought. Well, looks like I'm not going home or going to get any sleep tonight.

Chapter 45

Mars-Sol 14

As soon as Pedro finished with the transmission to the ISS, he waited the twelve minutes for the confirmation return. Sure enough, at 11:45 Zulu, *Staten*'s radio came back to life.

He was thankful for the new computerized radios that prevented him from missing incoming transmissions. The radio was on and tuned to the right frequency, but Pedro was paying attention to the activities on the EVA. Fortunately, the new radio lights blinked on and off as each new transmission came in, so Pedro didn't miss anything.

"*Starship X, Starship X,* this is the ISS. Your instruction copy is correct to the word!" Pedro had the fully automated recorder running, and he was writing down every word as well. As soon as he received confirmation back from the ISS, he was in touch with Commander Carrigan via radio. "*Starship X* Command to Commander Carrigan."

"*Starship X* Command, this is Commander Carrigan."
"Commander Carrigan, switch to Bravo frequency."

"Commander Carrigan switching to Bravo frequency.

What's up, Pedro?"

"Commander, you are not going to believe this, but the ISS just sent us the instructions from Mars Mission I CAPCOM via written communication on how to activate the Starships."

Commander Carrigan was so surprised to hear this

information, he forgot all communication protocols. "I'll be right there!"

Ten minutes later, Commander Carrigan was leaving the equalization room, heading straight for the helm, where Pedro was working at the telemetry station and monitoring *Starship VII* Command.

"You said something about the instructions to activate the other starships," the commander said.

"Yes, sir, they're right here if you can read my writing. They are also recorded, of course."

Commander Carrigan read the instructions. "You have to be kidding me. Is it that easy?"

"Sounds pretty simple to me," Pedro had to admit.

Commander Carrigan rubbed his forehead in thought.

"We're about two hours ahead of schedule, which is better than we could've possibly hoped. I'm not sure what would happen if we awakened *Starship VII* while we're in the middle of unloading it. Besides, Carl has disabled the crane from the automated computer system. I think we should continue manually off- loading the rest of *Starship VII*. But to get the other starships to autonomously off-load as they were intended is welcome news indeed. Is there any ice left?"

"No, we're completely out of water and ice now."

"And the crew is out there working hard, too. Well, if all goes well, we should have the tanks filling before the sun sets," said the commander.

Commander Carrigan went back to suit up again. He needed to talk to Carl. After equalizing to the pressure of Mars, Commander Carrigan made a mental note to recheck the O2 levels in *Staten*. They have been stealing away the kilowatt power unit to weld the scaffold. On his drive over to *Starship VII*, Commander Carrigan was concerned that with all the equalizing for the multiple crews and EVAs and water-focused activities taking place on the Martian surface, it must have taken a toll on *Staten's* O2 levels. If it weren't for the MOXIE working so well, they would've been racing to attach the O2 lines to one of the back-up storage tanks on Starship II as well.

What's more important, water or oxygen? *Boy, we're still hanging by a precarious thread,* Commander Carrigan thought. *If any one thing stops functioning correctly, or if we don't get the water lines out today, we will be hurting . . . or worse.* Just one day without water can sap a crew's strength and morale. Two days any meaningful work is almost impossible and on the third day you're dying.

Upon arrival, Commander Carrigan looked around for Carl, who was, of course, all the way up top. He waited until the crane off-loaded another container, then headed up the scaffolding. He did better this time, only having to stop once on the climb up. *I need to keep doing this,* he thought. This will keep me in shape.

Commander Carrigan ducked inside as they were hooking up another container and getting ready to push it out the hatch. Wayne was operating the crane, and Adnan Ashari was manhandling the big snap hook set in place of the automated clenching teeth. Carl had explained earlier that it was faster doing it this way. It took more personnel to operate it, but it was about two minutes faster per container.

Carl was up at the helm, well out of the way of the work he

was monitoring.

"How's it going?" Commander Carrigan asked.

"Couldn't do it any better if I was doing it myself. Looks like we have somewhere between one and two hours before we get to the container that has the water hose. We're averaging three containers per hour. Maybe one hour left, assuming the packing list is correct."

"That's great, Carl. We have more people out here than we need. Why don't we have a few of them open the containers and verify their contents against the packing list? That way, if it is accurate, we'll have more confidence in locating the water lines."

"Sounds good," Carl responded.

"I would like to talk to you on the surface anyway. I have a surprise for you," announced the commander.

When Commander Carrigan was safely on the surface, he hailed Pedro on Alpha frequency. "Starship Command, show Carl and I switching to Bravo frequency for a few minutes."

Pedro repeated, "Roger, Commander Carrigan and ES White switching to Bravo."

Once they both changed frequencies, they dutifully signed in. "Commander Carrigan on Bravo." "Carl White on Bravo."

Pedro responded, "Engineering Specialist Carl White and Commander Carrigan on Bravo."

As they walked toward the two Mars cars parked near *Starship VII,* Commander Carrigan said, "Carl, suppose we knew how to activate the starships to go into autonomous mode. Which one do you think we'd want to start up first?"

Carl's eyes lit up. "Excuse me? You wouldn't be asking me

this unless you knew something."

"You're too smart for me, Carl, and you're absolutely right."

Carl's eyes were the size of dinner plates. "You're kidding me, right?" He smiled.

"This afternoon, we received a call from the ISS. Apparently, they had a reinforced rescue capsule arrive at the ISS which had a written message for us. The crew on the ISS relayed the message just prior to their departure. The message explained that if we connect the computer frame to ground, it should reboot itself. Can you believe that? All of this work, and all we needed was some jumper cables."

"You got to be kidding me! I almost did that the first day you and I were on *Starship VII* together, but I didn't because I thought… well, I thought I shouldn't because I didn't know what I was doing. All of this sensitive computer shit. Oh, my, God. So, why are we here? We should've tried it on *Starship VII* while we were there."

"I thought of that, but we're almost halfway done unloading it, and the scaffolding is in the way of where the crane will be unloading the supplies. Not to mention that you disabled the crane," Commander Carrigan said.

"Hmmm, yeah, you're right. Besides, who knows what it would do now?"

"Exactly," said Commander Carrigan as he sat in one of the Mars car seats. "Oh, this feels good. As I see it, we need to offload the rest of the containers on *Starship VII* manually, as we are. Once we obtain the rest of the water line we need, we can perhaps slow the rate of the work. We don't want to stress the crew out any more than they are. And I have to tell you, Carl, you and your crews are doing a phenomenal job out here. Once we refill *Staten*'s tanks, we'll have some breathing room. But that's not why we're having this little chat," Commander Carrigan paused.

Carl's face clouded over as thoughts and ideas raced through his brain. "You're wondering what the autonomous unloading system will 'think' when it 'sees' the scaffolding outside or in its way? After all, it was designed to start unloading on its own—not with someone rebooting it from inside."

"Well, that was one thought that crossed my mind," answered Commander Carrigan.

"That should not be a big deal. It'll just start to boot up, which will take a few minutes, but it should 'see' the scaffolding and avoid it or pause the off-loading process until the unloading zone is clear. This wasn't part of our training, but I was talking with some of the engineers while we were in training. I was curious about the off-loading system and they had explained it in casual conversation."

"I was wondering if we could simplify the scaffold to be more like a giant ladder once we have *Starship VII* off-loaded. After all, we only need to go up once and reboot the remaining starships. I mean, you did an absolutely incredible job with this wonderful scaffolding structure. But you understood during the construction that we were going to go up and down many times. Once we finish with *Starship VII*, all we need to do is go up once and get out of the way, probably relatively quickly. It's probably not important."

"Oh, sure, I can do that," Carl said. "All I have to do is cut away some of the beefier sections of the scaffolding and reinforce the ladder portion. No problem. It'll make the transport of the ladder a lot easier, too, since it'll weigh a lot less. I could put some legs on it that will be supported by the starship itself instead of having to use all this rope. One person goes up, boots up the computer, and we take it down." Carl was still thinking about the job at hand. "I bet I could reassemble the ladder idea in as little as a few hours."

"Do you have any other ideas?"

"I have a lot to do with all of this construction on the surface, yet we need service on the hydrogen power cells as backup to the solar and the water systems. I'm being pulled away from my normal maintenance routine, and I could use some help with *Staten*'s day-to-day operations."

"Of course," the commander said. "What do you need?"

"Frankly, I need two of me." He shook his head, making his helmet bob from side to side. "We have an incredible and competent crew who continue to amaze me with what they're capable and willing to do. But I'm afraid if anyone else touches any of these sensitive systems on *Staten* and screws them up, we could all be in for a world of hurt. We either get water, or we get the starships up and running, or we run out of O2 . . ."

Commander Carrigan suddenly realized how hard he was pushing Carl. None of this work on the Martian surface, plus keeping up with the maintenance regimen on *Staten* was in the protocol or plan or Carl's job description.

"Carl, you've been doing all of this work with four or five of the same crew, right?"

"Yeah, well up until today," Carl said as he sat beside the commander.

"Well, they know how to weld and use the cutting torch by now, don't they?"

"Yeah."

"Well, let them do what you taught them. I've been listening to you on the radio. You're great at teaching and instructing. Let them do the work on the surface so you can get on top of the demands of *Staten*. Tell them what to do, check in with them from time to time to see if they need anything, and inspect their work on occasion. I'm sure they can do it. I am going to schedule different crew members to go with you while you do your daily maintenance starting tomorrow, so we can all stay up to date. Things change. We have been cross trained but anyone out of practice loses familiarity and forgets details."

"You're right," Carl said. "They can do the work while I get caught up on *Staten*. I want James and Wayne for sure. I know they're on different shifts, but I trust them, and they're comfortable with the torches and welding equipment."

"You got it, Carl. Put them in command while you're doing other tasks, and they can train more crew members. Which starship should we attempt this first reboot procedure on?"

Carl considered his options. "I think we're okay on O2. We'll be okay on water once we get the water line in place and after I attend to the hydrogen power cells. This is kinda like Christmas," he said with a smile. "I think we need another Mars car. I'm so tired of swapping personnel with limited transportation. So, whatever starship has the third Mars car loaded inside, that's the one I suggest."

"I think that's a great suggestion and you're absolutely correct, the third Mars car will make us more efficient as well. So that's our next goal. Now, let's see how far they've gotten to getting us water. I don't know about you, but I'm getting pretty thirsty."

As Commander Carrigan and Carl returned to *Starship VII*, they saw the crew jumping up and down. They had both forgotten to switch back to Alpha frequency. They hailed Pedro and instructed him to recognize that they were changing frequencies.

Pedro said, "Commander Carrigan and Carl back on 1 Alpha."

Commander Carrigan *and* Carl switched over to 1 Alpha frequency to hear, "Yes!"

"Well, bring it down!"

"Give us a second to get it out." "Do you really have it?"

"Yeah, I think so."

"Commander Carrigan on Alpha. Sorry, guys. I was having a conversation. What do you have?"

"Commander Carrigan, this is Haratu. We're bringing it down now. We have the water line." His normal quiet and thoughtful demeanor was replaced by a contagious excitement.

As Commander Carrigan was about to instruct them to attach it to the crane, Haratu started climbing down the scaffolding ladder with some of the water line over his shoulder.

"No, put it on the hook!" shouted the commander. "Don't try to manually bring it down!"

Haratu was swinging his foot over the ladder and tried to stop in mid stride, the heavy hose shifted its weight on his shoulder.

The momentum pulled his arm and shoulder away from his clutch point on the ladder, and the heavy hose won the battle of momentum as it swung across his back, leaving him with one hand on the ladder. His left foot slipped off, and he flipped end over end with the water hose entangling him on the trip to the surface. He landed upside down with his entangled arm outstretched, his head somewhere between his legs, and his feet slamming down on top of him. His body bounced off Mars's surface at least twice.

Everyone froze. It was obvious that Haratu was most probably dead. Right in the middle of success and happiness was death, failure due to lack of consideration of the possible. The exhilaration of the moment was suddenly destroyed by catastrophe.

Commander Carrigan immediately hailed Pedro to activate flight surgeon Spencer and to have her ready for a trauma alert.

Why didn't he tie in with his safety belt? Commander Carrigan thought, damn it!

Per protocol, the whole team scrounged for the backboard. They applied C-spine stabilization using the duct tape, followed by rapidly loading Haratu onto the nearest Mars car. He was not conscious, and he wasn't breathing. His body no longer took on a natural shape.

On Mars there was no way to monitor a trauma patient in a Mars suit. Blood loss could not be stopped other than wrapping the location with duct tape. CPR was performed for the duration of the ride back, but CPR was not effective while wearing the bulky Mars suit. None of that would have mattered for Haratu Suzuki. His internal and spinal injuries were beyond paramedic or emergency surgical intervention.

Haratu was taken aboard *Staten* where Tammy Spencer met them upon equalization to *Staten*'s climate. She checked for life signs. It had been twelve minutes since the fall. She confirmed he was dead. No heartbeat, no respirations, and blown pupils confirmed brain death. The crew, to a person, was stunned by the loss of their friend, confidant, and fellow team member.

Every space faring nation and more have signed on to many different space, interplanetary travel and satellite treaties, pacts and accords. One of the major primary agreements was that any astronauts or equipment on another planet, moon or body was to not contaminate that body with earth born organisms. As soon as Pedro's Mars suit was penetrated in the accident at *Starship IV* this accord was violated for the first time and in Huratu's accident it was violated for a second time. As per protocol, his body was removed from *Starship X* and taken to a hillside on the side of the canyon overlooking *Starship X*. His body was placed next to a marker, which would be substantially personalized and detailed over time with handmade engravings, memorabilia and more and left in state. He was still in his white mars suit which was already gaining a light red dusty cover. The pressurized suit was punctured and severely damaged in the fall. His body would slowly dehydrate, and his remains would be packed in *Staten* prior to their departure.

Still with a job to do, Commander Carrigan instructed those still on the surface to connect the last of the water line to *Staten* and to turn on the pressurized water tank from Starship II. He then asked two members of the crew to walk the line from Starship II to *Staten*

———

and confirm the integrity of the line.

Despite the fall, the water line was intact, and soon they heard water filling the tank. What should have been a momentous occasion was met with a depressing acceptance. Commander Carrigan gave the crew some time to deal with the loss, get hydrated and everyone took a hand towel shower. After some time to depressurize he announced to no one's surprise a full staff meeting. Rather unusually, Commander Carrigan went into the cargo bay and found 21 drinking glasses that survived the trip. He filled them with water and personally placed them at each dining position.

"We are here tonight to mourn and give thanks. Haratu Suzuki died today in service to our cause. Every one of us knows the risks we all took every day just to get here and the risks we continue to take on a daily basis. Being on the surface of this planet without air, without any significant atmospheric pressure, without water is a high-risk assignment. Haratu was a wonderful person to work with. He was always full of positive energy and enthusiasm, which may have been his untimely demise. He was so excited to have located the water line that he misjudged its weight on his shoulder, and this excitement led to his last act. He was a true astronaut, a trooper amongst troopers. He was my friend, as are all of you." With a whimper, the commander showed his humanness and added, "I will miss him. I will miss his smile and his willingness to participate. It didn't matter the type of task or job; he was always there willing to help. I want to dedicate this water line to Haratu Suzuki. He helped save our butts. Until the day we leave, this will be the HS water line, dedicated to an astronaut's astronaut. If Haratu were here, he would say, 'Never give up, never stop trying. Imagination leads to discovery; imagination leads to us being here on Mars.' You people are here because of imagination. You people are here because you're just like me. You people are of the same substance as he was and as he is through you! We all share the same energy, the same focus. We know the pressures and tensions of getting through the relentless interview process, yet we all made it. Let us spend the rest of this evening talking about Haratu, his focus, his dream, and the times we spent together. We all dream the same dream— exploration and discovery—which is driven by imagination and courage. Nothing will be changed by Haratu's death. Nothing! It was a terrible accident. Haratu died, but he would want us to celebrate his love for all of us, to prove that we can survive on Mars. Not just survive but thrive! And we will! And we are! So, I say thank you, Haratu, for your service to our cause, for your attitude, for your companionship, for your love of our future, for your imagination, and I say thank you, Haratu, for your courage to help make it a reality. Today, tonight, we start to live on Mars. Because of you, Haratu. Because of your energy, your compassion and love for all of us, we are here today. Please enjoy this water Haratu made possible. I love you all, goodnight."

There was a quiet clinking of glasses as toasts to Huratu were raised amongst many wet eyes and flowing tears. In the silence, Haratu's love and energy was felt and missed throughout *Starship X.*

Chapter 46

Johnson Space Center-Day15

Brad Brown spent the rest of the evening going back over his plan if his messages were to get through to Starship X. Just knowing they had a way to access the other starships made him feel a little better, even though he knew they only had two 20-foot ladders, which would not get them close to the hatches on any of the starships.

Brad tried to imagine the conditions on board *Starship X*. If they were able to start up the MOXIE for oxygen and the Kilowatt power unit, they might still be alive. If they didn't, they were probably all dead by now. Just how would they get to the hatches? He kept going over the inventory on *Starship X* to see if they had anything they could use. Maybe the rope? They had a lot of rope. Could they lasso the top of one of the starships? No. No matter what he thought of, he couldn't imagine any way to get to the hatches. Except what his crew came up with, knocking the starships over, he couldn't see any other way. What a mess that would be if they had to do that. He was getting depressed.

His team continued in their attempts to initiate the starships by boosting the signals and sending them from different antennas and reflecting the signal off deep space satellites. They had no way of knowing if any of their transmissions were getting through, but they certainly weren't getting anything back.

Brad listened to the 11:00 news while he had a bite to eat. The President announced the reopening of the New York Stock Exchange as a test the next morning with emergency stops ready to be imposed. Anything that started to move excessively would be frozen. Even so, due to no electronic trading being available, volume was projected to be extremely low. The local TV reporters were commenting on the old-fashioned cable system installation from the 1980s, with modern conductivity and recent technological upgrades. The reporter, who specialized in communications, was asked why couldn't traders or phone companies utilize the millions of miles of fiber optic cable for communications or trading? The answer was difficult to explain. It turns out there are a few different kinds of fiber optic systems. The largest and most profitable companies were able to utilize their in-house or direct wire systems. Most of those companies were on Wall Street and international trading boards. But most fiber optic systems somewhere along the line still utilized the internet or direct satellite communications due to the sheer distances involved from say, Los Angeles to Rome, or New York to Tokyo. Food had been slowly returning to grocery store shelves with forced government guarantees of payment in place and armed escort of the trucks. People were using checks or cash, and the old credit card impression machines were back again. The banks were forced to return to paper documentation. It was working—just slowly. According to the news, anyone and everyone who held digital currency was just plain out of luck. Without the internet their investment or savings was simply frozen. The civil unrest of the previous two weeks was beginning to simmer down. Everyone wanted to know who blew up the satellites and destroyed the convenience of life to which they had become accustomed.

The news was following a presidential, congressional and international investigation into the matter. Congress was having hearings every day without getting anywhere. Many countries had been thrown into the exact same situation; everyone was looking for the guilty party. All the security agencies around the world were pooling their energies as well as running simultaneous investigations on their own. There were terrorist-plot theories, Russian theories, Cuban theories, and even conspiracy theories that the United States did it to gain a new economic high ground. The press seemed to be as perplexed as everyone else, coming up with inexplicable theories upon theories. All of it was conjecture with no factual evidence.

Unbelievable what BS the press can come up with, Brad thought.

People were beginning to return to work, but everything was harder and slower. Most gas stations were still closed. It was as if the entire country had a bad hangover, was still suffering from a headache and didn't want to do anything. The cultural shock of not being able to text, call or email friends, family or anyone was devastating. Brad felt the same way. He just couldn't see a happy ending in sight.

It was almost two o'clock in the morning, so he decided to go home and get some sleep. He guessed that the general must have gone home before getting his messages, he had nothing good to report or maybe he still wasn't back in the states.

Right then Brad's phone rang, piercing the silence. Brad jumped and checked the number. It was blank. It rang again. "Hello? Er . . . um, Brad Brown," he said, trying to get a handle on his emotions.

"Brad! It's General Latimore."

"Hello, General! You're keeping some late hours," Brad said, not knowing where the general was at the moment.

"Hello, Brad. I just landed at Edwards. My personal assistant leaves my messages on a voicemail system I can access when I'm on one of our bases. Anyway, I bet you'd like some feedback on your message."

"Yes, yes, sir."

"It turns out your theory was correct. The crew from the ISS was in communication with *Starship X*, and they were in communication with them for some time. I'm not sure how long, but it sounded as though they'd been in daily contact for maybe a week. They did get the message you provided, and they relayed that they felt the information was important for them. *Starship X* crew reported to the ISS that they had run out of water, but the information was of significance and could improve the situation. So, maybe the information you supplied helped. I'm not sure, but it sounded like they had just recently run out of water. At least they didn't carry on about it in distress. Apparently, they were working on the issue and had a plan in place. The person they usually spoke with on the radio was on the surface of Mars, addressing the situation. My details are a little sketchy because I didn't have much time with the crew. They were tired and stressed. I'm sure you'll get more time with them at a later date. Suffice it to say, your message was sent and received, and they seemed to think it was important and welcome news. Brad? Hello?"

"Yes, sir. I'm just trying to put this together in my head.

Thank God they were able to get the message. Thank God they're still alive! It's going to take me a bit to digest this. We didn't even know if they were still alive, General. Very good news, sir," Brad said with some relief. "Do you have any more information or—"

"I'm afraid that's all I have, Brad. I would like to congratulate you on a job well done. You made a difference today. You probably saved some lives. I have to tell you that none of us thought that message would get through or that the ISS crew was actually in contact with the crew on Mars. Good job."

"Thank you, sir. I do appreciate it. Hopefully, it will help."

"You're welcome, Brad. I'm sure you'll be able to get in touch with the ISS crew once they return stateside and get a better debrief. But you can rest assured that they did get the information. Once again, congratulations on a job well done. We will talk later. Good night, get some rest. Oh, and Brad, the crew was pretty tired and groggy, but one of them repeated something a couple of times. He said, 'Aut viam inveniam aut faciam.' I don't remember much of my Latin anymore, but I thought I would pass it along."

Brad repeated, "Aut viam inveniam aut faciam. Got it as he scribbled it down. And thanks again. I am so glad to hear the MMI crew is still at it and the ISS crew is home safe and sound!"

"Me as well. Goodnight."

With that, the general was gone. Brad sat back, half-mesmerized by the conversation. They were out of water. That probably means they hadn't refurbished the hydrogen fuel cells. They can't survive on the hydrogen fuel cell's byproduct of water alone, but it would help. Brad's mind was no longer working effectively. It was time to get some sleep.

Brad stared blankly at a wall across the room. *I wonder what they're up to. They must be trying to get the remaining water line for the run from Starship II. How much water line was on board* Starship X?

He quickly pulled up the packing manifest for each starship. *Hmm, yeah, three thousand feet. Why didn't we put enough water line on* Starship X *for the run from Starship II to the landing zone for* Starship X? *Because the starships were supposed to be completely off-loaded on the first day as soon as they landed. That's why. No one expected the starships not to autonomously off-load. What else is going to happen that we didn't expect? What did the general say? Aut viam inveniam aut faciam,* he checked his scribbled note. Brad looked it up on his computer. Nothing. In his office upstairs, he had a handbook of Latin sayings. He ran to the room and pulled out the book.

Aut viam inveniam aut faciam.

"I will either find a way or make one."

Chapter 47
Mars Sol-15

Before the night shift was off and before the day shift started, as everyone expected, Commander Carrigan called a full- crew meeting for the post-accident review.

The results of the description of the accident were simple. Haratu Suzuki made a poor decision because he was excited to have found the water hose. His emotions overwhelmed his decision-making process, and it led to an unintended and unexpected outcome. Commander Carrigan reiterated that the dangers of the job were magnified by the fact that they were way outside the original operating parameters of their designed constraints. No one expected to have to climb a tall scaffold on a daily basis. Yet they still had to continue to climb the scaffold until all of the starships had off-loaded their supplies.

The situation was more stable now that they had water and their O2 was holding. Commander Carrigan reiterated the first accident injuring Pedro was caused by rushing to get the job done.

Overzealousness and understandable excitement caused both accidents.

"Let's be careful out there, people. Let's not let our emotions control our actions. Does anyone have anything they want to add or contribute?"

No one said a word.

"I'm sure you've heard by now that the ISS gave us the

instructions on how to boot up the autonomous systems on the other starships. We will still have to climb the precarious scaffolding to engage the system since it cannot be done from the ground. Also, that was the last message from the ISS. They evacuated the Space Station just as it was becoming uninhabitable. Apparently, our instructions were sent to them on a heavily reinforced Crew escape capsule. MM1 or CAPCOM was guessing or hoping that we were in communication with the ISS. Pretty good thinking back at CAPCOM. Those of you who were on A shift can get some sleep. B shift will be working on off-loading *Starship VII* for four hours. Does anyone need Carl working with them for instructional purposes? He's been out there relentlessly for days on end, working way too much."

Again, no one responded.

"Please be careful, people. It is twenty hundred Zulu. B shift, get something to eat, and suit up. That is everyone except MS Adnan Ashari. Adnan, you're working with Carl today, he will fill you in. At twenty-two hundred C shift will replace B until oh six hundred. Take as long as you need to do your job safely. If anyone feels tired or not up to the job, let me know. I don't care if it takes three days to finish unloading *Starship VII*. I want all of you safe. For *Staten's* use only, I will be adopting a Martian Time Zone since Zulu will be moving a whole day ahead of us soon. The new Mars time zone will come with an "M" after it in place of the Zulu. An example would be 08:00 M. The new Mars time zone is for Mars use only. Any extraplanetary communications will remain on Zulu. You can always refer to the computer if there is any confusion. All documented reports will remain on Zulu time as well. Just refer to the computer for Zulu time. Otherwise,

Staten's time zone will be the official time on Mars from now on. If anyone needs to talk to me or needs personal time, I will be in my office or assisting Carl. Let's be safe out there." Commander Carrigan grabbed a cup of coffee. "Carl, can I see you in my office, please?"

Commander Carrigan intended to check on the O2 levels, but he wanted to talk to Carl first, and he knew Carl knew what he was interested in finding out. "Once again, I'd like to get an update on *Staten*'s vital signs. Did you get a chance to check on the water tanks and the O2 levels this morning?"

"Yes, sir. Those are the first two items I do every morning."

"I know. I know, you're a good man Carl, you're usually one step ahead of me," the commander responded with a smile.
Carl looked up and smiled back "I appreciate that commander. The water tank is full, and our O2 has been stressed out due to all of the activities and EVAs over the past few weeks. We're holding steady at a ten-day level of oxygen reserve, but the MOXIE has been working since we returned the Kilowatt power unit and I expect our reserves to rebuild slowly."

"That's what I figured as well. How are your energy levels? You've been so busy lately."

"I'm okay. I'm just glad we have water now and the O2 levels are no longer at emergency levels. I am feeling a lot more relaxed, as is the whole crew and you as well, I'm sure. I am impressed the batteries worked as well as they did, considering how little the hydrogen fuel cells and the solar panels were producing before we set up the power unit."

"I agree. What do you have on your schedule for today now

that you don't have to help with the off-loading?"

"Well, I have to get to those hydrogen fuel cells that need servicing. They're a good backup if the Kilowatt power unit goes down. The carbon dioxide scrubbers need cartridge replacements and so forth. You know, I need to get caught up on my normal maintenance routine, which I've been getting way behind on."

"I asked MS Adnan Ashari to trail you today. I appreciate you sharing your information and routine with him. As we agreed. Is there anything else I can help you with?"

"Hmm...yeah," Carl said. "I would love a hot tub to soak in."

"Hah! Wouldn't we all! Could you imagine what the press would say if they found out we had a hot tub on board?"

They both shared a laugh at the unexpected humor.

"Is there anything else that needs to be brought to my attention that I may have overlooked? We've been so busy. We don't want any rude surprises related to crew safety, security, or quality of life."

"No, I think we're secure at the moment, and I don't see any cause for concern on any life safety systems, atmospheric systems, or internal environmental conditions. I do need to go over my extensive service logs to review every aspect. I don't see anything surprising us at the moment."

"That's really good news, Carl. Thank you for the update. I'll be here if I can help you."

After Carl left, Commander Carrigan had some time to depressurize and think about all the situations that had occurred over the past weeks—and what their future may hold. He was in command of the first mission to ever have humans walk on Mars. The low oxygen situation that threatened the entire crew, and the possibility of running completely out of water. James Galway, getting knocked off the ladder as they were unloading *Starship IV* and the pallet of supplies that fell on both him and badly injuring Pedro. Haratu Suzuki falling to his death. Discovering water and life on Mars in the cave on the same day, only about four miles from *Staten*. Loss of communication with CAPCOM. Eleven months left to finalize their planned mission on Mars. What else could the cave be concealing for future discovery? How much farther down does the cave or lava tube go? Could they use it for protection in the case of a significant solar flare? Will they even know now with loss of comms if a large solar flare is released from the sun? Is the space weather monitoring satellite system even working? He doubted it. Even if it was, it could no longer communicate with the Earth. There must be more caves or lava tubes like that one around. Do they have life living in them as well, and if so, what kind? How common was life in these caves? Can Barbara and *Staten*'s crew get food to grow in the soil from the cave? He knew the protocol outline to study the seeds they had on board was to rinse the perchlorates out of the Martian soil and study plant growth and development, but their lives may now depend on those seeds if they were to have an extended stay. Is the water in the cave fit for human consumption? Barbara said, "You could probably drink it." Is it a replenishable resource? Will they be able to return to Mother Earth after eleven months? How will they know when it is safe to return if they cannot communicate with NASA or Capcom? It appears the Kessler Effect has taken place. How will I tell the crew what that means? Will the Kessler Effect ever get cleaned up enough

———

383

for them to return? How will the crew react if we can't return home? Apparently, the crew from the ISS was rescued. Can they do that same thing for the MM1 crew of now twenty? How long can we last? How long will the MOXIE last?

These were just some of the issues Commander Carrigan needed to consider and research for the future of Staten and the first humans on Mars—Mars Mission I. He had accepted the enormity of the responsibility several years ago, but it was difficult to actually live alone in that role day after day. He remained close with Steven and had ultimate confidence in him on a professional level as well as he could be counted on for confidential advice and sound situational considerations. Mary was more than capable of running the mission and getting them home, and Carl, well… Carl seemed to be able to accomplish miracles with his engineering skills. He was blessed to have such an amazing crew who could make dreams come true, even when the odds were against them.

The commander was shaken from his thoughts by a sudden yelling from somewhere up by the helm then a sudden pounding on his door.

"Commander! Commander!" Steven rushed in without an invitation. "They're doing it!

"Who is doing what?"

"The starships just started up on their own. They're off-loading their supplies on their own! They're working!"

Chapter 48
Shocking Reality

Everything appeared to be in order at home. The air-conditioning cooled the house off again after the power outage. The water utilities were pumping fresh, potable water again. Things were slowly getting to be a little more normal. The cell phones still didn't work and neither did the cable. The news was reporting that the cell companies were going to have to change all of their computer systems and transmission towers to technology last used in the 1990's and early 2000's. Bob heard a car outside. It was Brian. It had only been a few hours.

"Hey, Bud, how is everything here? Did you miss me?"

"Hah! Give me at least a day."

"Let's run over to Station 8 and see how they are getting along."

"Yeah, and we need to run by the police station again and check on our boat status."

Station 8 looked just like it always had in the past. They were in luck. Battalion Chief Delaney was in his office. A big man, probably six five and pushing two hundred-fifty pounds. They had run plenty of different calls together.

"Hey, guys, good to see the two famous fishermen," the chief chirped.

Brian was surprised as he eased into one of the chairs in the tiny office, glad that he wasn't the size of the chief. "How did you know that was us?"

The Chief gave him a two second stare and responded,

"What other two retired firefighters out twenty miles off Ft. Lauderdale fishing on a Worldcat catamaran boat could it possibly be? We all know you two are always out there. Hell, the whole department knew it was you two as soon as it hit the news. I want to hear all about it."

"Well, Bob is going to have to fill you in. I don't remember anything about it. I hit my head pretty good, I guess after it started up. I don't remember anything."

"Are you ok?" the chief questioned. "Yeah, just a bump on the head."

After Bob related everything, he could about the unexpected missile launch, they were curious as to how bad it had gotten on shift.

"Well, you guys know the drill from all of the hurricanes we've been through. But this was much worse. All shifts were called in and not allowed to go home until this morning. So, we've been overwhelmed with crew sleeping everywhere, in the chairs in the day room, on the floor, in the back of the rescues without air-conditioning, in the engine bays and in the workout room. Spare vehicles were brought up from every non-essential service and their staff were pressed into service. We were spelling each other when one or the other of us had to go home to address any number of personal emergencies that may have popped up during the crises. I guess three hours or so after the power went down, we started to get the calls and they just kept coming. How much do you wanna know?"

"Well, we were curious how bad it got here," Brian said.

Chief Delaney started, "We just had power restored

yesterday, which immediately reduced the call volume, so we started sending the extra crews back home. We just today started regular shift rotations. All of the assisted living facilities constantly were calling. The few in our territory that didn't have enough fuel for their generators kept having patients with hyperthermia, dehydration, and a good share of cardiac arrests. We were keeping half of the rescue units and the back of the engines stocked with frozen ice packs and frozen saline bags, just to keep people cool, at least as much as the sixty-quart coolers could handle. The coolers were always in the way for the rescue guys, especially if they had to work a patient. It was a pretty sad scene. The hospitals were so overwhelmed with hyperthermia patience that they instructed us to deal with it on seen and not to bring them to the ER period. There were so many DOA's. The county coroner was totally overwhelmed. The coroner was so busy that they could no longer pick up the dead bodies. So, we ended up transporting a lot of dead bodies to the hospital where they were put straight into a refrigerated truck. As you know, once death is pronounced on scene it is normally considered a crime scene and we don't touch them after that. Transporting a dead body is a violation of our policy and procedures but it was just something that has to be done. I guess the coroner will be backed up for months dealing with all of the volume. I don't know how it didn't make it in the news. Thank God it didn't. The family members were already distraught enough with everything else going on. We were looking at having to draft water from some of the canals to keep the tankers full after every fire. The county told us we couldn't use the hydrants until further notice. There was virtually no water pressure anyway. For the first two days car accidents were all over the county at every intersection with numerous high-speed accidents on the turnpike and I-95, even on US 1 and A-1-A! People were driving like idiots. Paper reports were required since the tablets were worthless without internet, and most of the stations didn't even have the antique paper reports from the early 2000's, so there was a huge scramble to get those out to all of the stations. However, the county did not have enough to go around, so many reports were never filed. Dispatch was the only way we knew how many calls we ran. We couldn't get food from the grocery stores, so the county worked out a deal with a couple of those huge frozen warehouses that usually only sell to the wholesale food service companies. It's been crazy! We were being delivered frozen beef quarters and frozen eggs in 5 gallon buckets! Not only that but the National Guard is chauffeuring the food trucks around to each of our stations, arriving just ahead of them, and standing guard until they offloaded a week's worth of food for us. They are guarding them like Fort Knox. Sad."

Changing the subject, "So, what is happening with the crew on Mars?"

Bob and Brian both looked from the Chief to each other. They both were silent with shock. It took a few seconds for one of them to respond.

Bob cleared his throat. "That's a very good question, the Mars thing, that is. No one knows," he said, looking at Brian.

"It's really hard to keep up on developments without the internet. The last word we heard is that they are pretty much on their own. But no one seems to know anything since the satellites were destroyed and we lost all cell phone service and internet access."

Then the Chief added, "Yeah, I hope we never have to see

_____

this situation again. We are pretty much out of diesel for the rescue, the engine, and the station, too. If we lose power all of our food that's not in cans will spoil. They keep telling us that there is diesel on the way, which I'm sure there is, but when you're out, you're out. and we are pretty much out. What are we supposed to do? Bring in horses?"

Chapter 49
The Oval Office-Day 16

"Mr. President, we believe we know who was behind the attack," reported Secretary of Defense Robert Thornton.

President Gerald Gary Griffin preferred his friends to call him Gary, and was referred to by some as "The Triple G." He was not a man to be taken lightly, as was witnessed by his aggressive presidential campaign and subsequent time in office. He had been on the phone with prime ministers and presidents from Russia, the UK, Canada, Japan, France, Germany, and more. They all had ideas, but no one had facts. Now, here was his own secretary of defense telling him they believed they knew who it was that did this terrible deed. President Griffin was a facts man, and a statement starting with 'we believe' belonged in a church, not in his office. "What do you mean, you 'believe'?"

"Sir, we have a high level of confidence in our information," said Secretary Thornton. "The odds of finding the offending party in any crime are reduced with time. Due to the loss of our satellites, we cannot say with one hundred percent certainty. We have not shared this information with any other government, nor have they shared it with us. But simple deductive reasoning of what would motivate a government to do something like this consistently returns us to one country, which has only recently developed the technical skill to pull off this type of action, and one of the few countries with anything to gain from the consequences."

President Griffin was listening. This was the first time anyone had come up with a theory. He hated theories, but it couldn't hurt to listen. "Go on."

"This is obviously a rare situation. Every developed country, and many undeveloped countries, is a victim in this case. If you ask yourself what country could possibly stand to benefit from this, you look at countries that don't like satellite flyovers. Your first thought is Russia, but when you realize that all of their satellites were knocked out of commission as well, then you have to ask yourself: 'Would Russia shoot themselves in the foot to gain virtually nothing?' One could easily see that Russia is worse off after the attack, just as we are, so it wouldn't make any sense for them to initiate it. Their economy was hit as bad as anyone's. If you look at it purely from an economic standpoint, you might say that only third-world countries weren't affected, but that isn't true either. We have years of history of trading with countries such as Vietnam, Cambodia, and Bangladesh, and even China. After the incident, all GPS satellites were lost, as were all banking transactions. And all trading with these countries has stopped— not slowed— stopped. The money flow has stopped. If their ships loaded full of goods for the United States could sail, they would have to navigate by the stars. And they couldn't off-load their supplies until they are paid in cash. Who is going to meet them at the dock to pay millions in cash, so they can off-load their goods? They have literally been isolated from the money supply. We keep talking about how bad it is here, but Mr. President, some of these countries are looking at serious famine and possibly revolution. No one has stopped to look at how interdependent we all are in this modern day of trading and banking. Backing up just a bit, you might say 'yeah', but none of these countries possess the kind of technology to initiate this attack and not be significantly injured from the effects. And that is the key. When you go down the list, there's only one country that doesn't rely on their own satellites or at least very little. There is only one country that does not trade with many other countries. There is only one country that was predominantly untouched by the implications of this attack, yet has the technology to carry it out, therefore, leveling the playing field. We know who it is. And if we know, it is only a matter of time before the other big-time players know. So, you need to decide how you want to play it."

Chapter 50
Ryongsong Residence, North Korea

Having just arrived from another children's dance-and-drum presentation at Pyongyang, Kim Jong-Un smiled as he relived the presentations, reminding himself to authorize an extra food allocation for the children's families. They worked so hard to please their Great Leader.

On his desk were the notes from his personal assistant. He had received an official message from the Norwegian Embassy, which wasn't surprising, but it was strange that the diplomatic courier hadn't stayed to personally deliver it. The envelope itself had gone through the normal security checks, so it was a bit odd it had three different seals on it, demonstrating an unusual amount of security for normal communication with Embassy personnel.

Still taking every precaution, the Great Leader had his personal assistant open the envelope, which contained another sealed envelope. She opened the second one as he impatiently looked on. There was a third sealed envelope inside.

The Great Leader rudely tore the envelope from his assistant and ripped it open. In the middle of a single piece of folded paper was a typed message in French: NOUS SAVONS. "We know."

His personal assistant watched his eyes to read his

———

emotional response to this rather strange note.

"The Russians showed up unexpectedly and are in reception," she said quietly, still watching him for a reaction.

The paper slipped from his hands to the cold marble floor…

THE END

ABOUT THE AUTHOR CHRISTOPHER LEE JONES

After growing up in Southern Michigan, Christopher has spent much of his working careers traveling around the United States and some years in Europe, finally settling in South Florida working as a Firefighter and Paramedic for Miami-Dade Fire Rescue.

He is an avid scuba diver and has been able to dive all over Florida, the Florida Keys, Central America, the Caribbean and in the Mediterranean. He is also a boat captain, retired fire fighter, Paramedic and obvious space enthusiast.

When not out on his boat, he is constantly traveling to further his education researching Mars, the Kessler Effect, the different efforts at trying to clean up the space debris mess we have created, and anything space related.

Investing serious efforts into extensive research. He prides himself on accuracy and the factual basis of virtually all the tools, equipment, facts and details he presents in his books, which he jokingly refers to as "factual fiction".

This book is the second edition to his first book of the same title.

He is currently writing the thrilling conclusion to Mars Mission I: Surviving the Kessler Effect.